JAMIE'S GOT A GUN

To Kassandra, nice to see you again! Gail Sidonie Sobat

Spyder Yardley

JAMIE'S GOT A GUN

A GRAPHIC NOVEL

BY GAIL SIDONIE SOBAT

WITH ILLUSTRATIONS BY
SPYDER YARDLEY-JONES

GREAT PLAINS
TEEN FICTION

Great Plains Teen Fiction
(An imprint of Great Plains Publications)
233 Garfield Street S
Winnipeg, MB R3G 2M1
www.greatplains.mb.ca

Great Plains Publications gratefully acknowledges the financial support provided for its publishing program by the Government of Canada through the Canada Book Fund; the Canada Council for the Arts; the Province of Manitoba through the Book Publishing Tax Credit and the Book Publisher Marketing Assistance Program; and the Manitoba Arts Council.

The author gratefully acknowledges the support of the Alberta Foundation for the Arts.

Design & Typography by Relish New Brand Experience
Printed in Canada by Friesens

LIBRARY AND ARCHIVES CANADA CATALOGUING IN PUBLICATION

Sobat, Gail Sidonie, author
        Jamie's got a gun : a graphic novel / Gail Sidonie Sobat;
illustrated by Spyder Yardley-Jones.

ISBN 978-1-926531-88-5 (pbk.)

        1. Graphic novels. I. Yardley-Jones, Spyder, illustrator
II. Title.

PN6733.S615J34 2014   J741.5'971   C2013-908737-0

ENVIRONMENTAL BENEFITS STATEMENT

Great Plains Publications saved the following resources by printing the pages of this book on chlorine free paper made with 100% post-consumer waste.

TREES	WATER	ENERGY	SOLID WASTE	GREENHOUSE GASES
11	5,138	5	344	947
FULLY GROWN	GALLONS	MILLION BTUs	POUNDS	POUNDS

FSC
www.fsc.org
MIXTE
Papier issu
de sources
responsables
FSC® C016245

Environmental impact estimates were made using the Environmental Paper Network Paper Calculator 3.2. For more information visit www.papercalculator.org.

For Duane Stewart
Thank you for the...
Answer.
That you are here—that life exists and identity,
That the powerful play goes on, and you may contribute a verse.
—GAIL SIDONIE SOBAT

This book is dedicated to my father John Yardley-Jones and my (late) mother Mary Yardley-Jones who both gave me the best gift ever, my artistic talent.
—SPYDER YARDLEY-JONES

This is my f$%*ing!! book. So get your hands off it! Keep out.

If you find this book, return it to Jamie Kidding at Apt 20, 4689 Walker Road NE.

I'm not asking. I'm telling.

If you don't, I'll find you and hunt you down and kill you.

Despite my last name, I'm not f$%*ing kidding.

You don't know me. Even if you know me. You don't.

My name is Jamie.

And Jamie's got a gun...

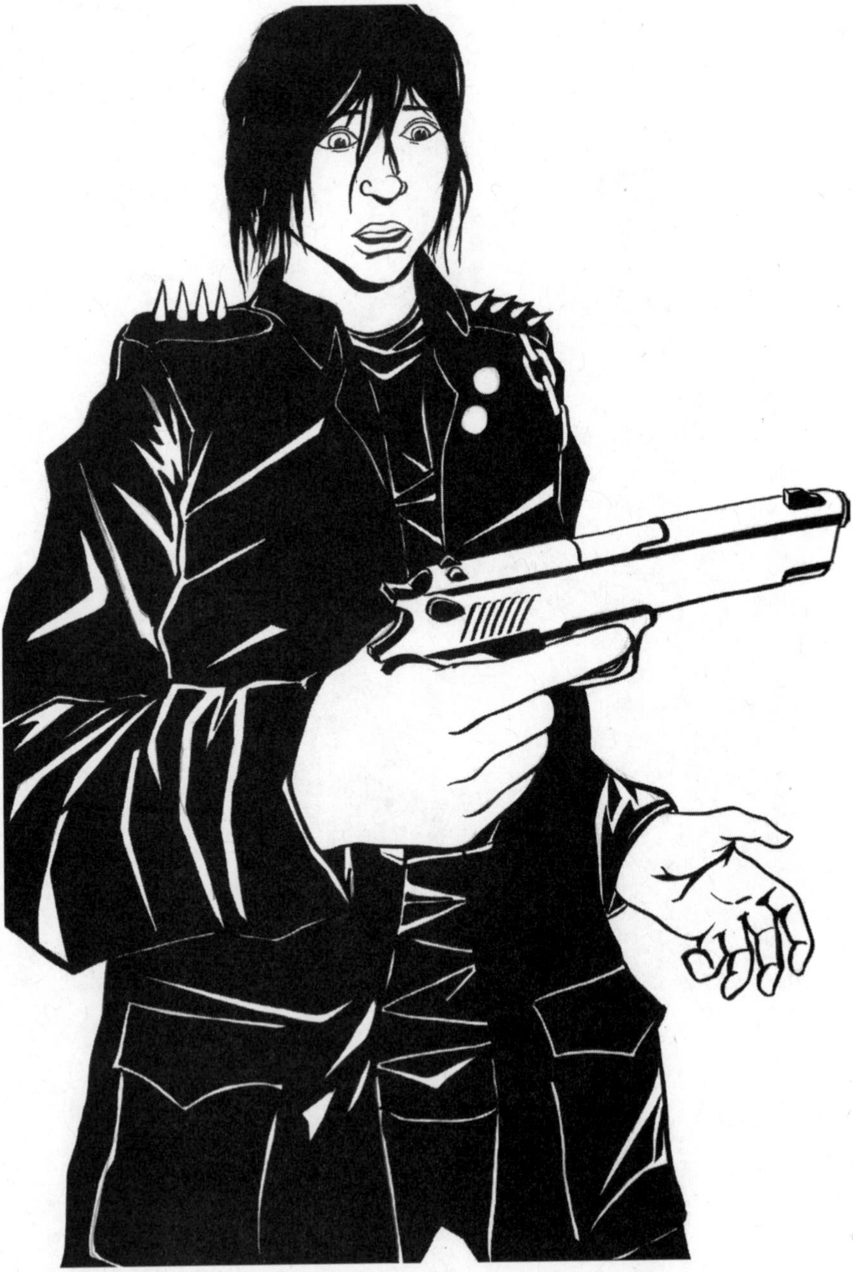

Ok. Just so I'm clear. I'm not one of those Littleton-Columbine-Taber sicko shooters.

I'm no copycat.

Let's say, I'm sympathetic. I get it. Why those guys did what they did.

I come from the wrong side of town. The northeast. Where all the dealers and meth-heads and crack-heads and whores have ended up because they've been pushed outta the inner city. They headed to our neighbourhood. Because it's poor and unimportant. Cops don't like to come out this way.

Especially for the domestic violence calls.

Anyways, the northeast is the place where guys like me live. Below the poverty line. Even though. Even though my mom works two jobs. It's still not enough.

While my stepdad works none.

We live in a cheap walk-up apartment. But the rent keeps going up in this boomtown, so maybe we'll have to move. Only where? How much cheaper can you get?

But I guess if my stepdad has his way, I'll get thrown out soon and that'll be one less miserable mouth to feed, as he puts it.

He and mom always fight about me getting off my miserable ass and getting a McJob. But she is real stubborn about me staying in school and working on my art. I can hear them screaming now about that very thing. Jamie this. Jamie that. Soon our neighbour, Mrs. McDover, will be banging on the wall to shut them up. The walls are pretty thin in this clapboard place.

Might be an idea for my stepdad to get off his fat pratt and get a job. But no. That'll never happen. He collects Workers' Compensation for some stupid minor injury he suffered three years ago. They keep threatening to cut him off and someday maybe they will. Even I can see that he's milking the system. It's not much dough anyhow. If and when they cut him off, Mom assures me he'll find work.

Right. And angels of mercy will come flying out of my butthole.

I try to help Mom out when I can. I draw posters for this metal band, GraveRype. Personally, I think they're Metallica wannabes, but they pay me $100 per poster design. Even if I think their music is shite. That they've sold out for a modicum of small-time success. But maybe that's sour grapes.

Wouldn't I sell out, too, for a syndicated shot at some national newspaper? Jamie the cartoonist hypocrite.

And then sometimes my little sister and me go out dumpster diving and bottle bobbing. It's amazing what gets thrown out, even in poor neighbourhoods. Bottles alone helped pay for her dance lessons last year and this year, too!

All this means that there's not a lot extra for stuff like a computer or Wii or Xbox. I've only ever dreamed of those things and rarely touched them except the school and library computers. And at my cousins' house. Victor and Richard Prichard, the twins. AKA Vic and Dick Prick, who have every bloody electronic device known to man, the spoiled little cretins.

Hell, our television is almost as old as I am. Which is seventeen.

And getting art supplies is a drag. Sometimes I think some multinational CEO guy dreams up ways to make art supplies completely out of the price range of artists like me who have nothing. And I guess most artists have nothing. Or so my stepdad likes to remind me until I want to puke.

But I have my ways of getting art supplies. My art teacher whose name hardy har har is Art Letterman sometimes gives me leftover paints and paper. And when I'm desperate, I've been known to be quite handy at getting my hands on other materials I just can't afford in certain snooty art supply shops.

But I'll never tell Candy that. Candice. My little sister. 13 going on 30, sometimes. The main reason I'm still living at home. I'm her hero. And she's sorta mine. Heroine, I mean. So I try not to let her know the nasty stuff about her big brother.

She has no idea about the gun. And never will. Unless. Unless I have to use it...

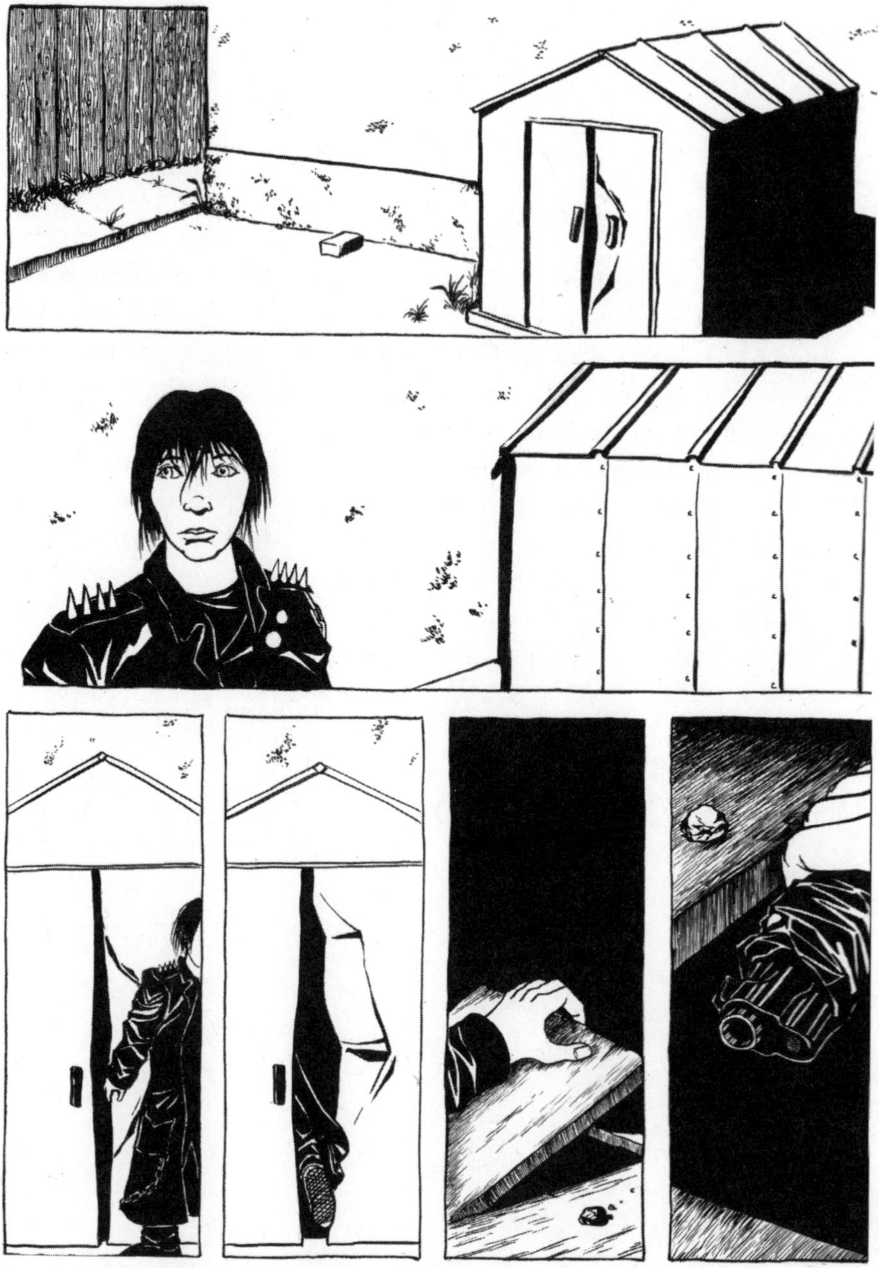

So. This is where I write my crappy thoughts down. But it's also where I draw. Obviously, I'm better at drawing than writing. It's because I'm dyslexic. Which is why I don't have especially great marks. I mean I'm passing everything. Some things barely. But I AM trying. On account of my mom and my sister.

My stepdad says I should take the auto mechanics course at the school. Get my ticket. Get a trade. Get a job. Get the hell out.

Auto mechanics. That'd be good for me. Most I can manage is to keep my bike under repair. Motors baffle me. And wouldn't auto mechanics be good for my hands?

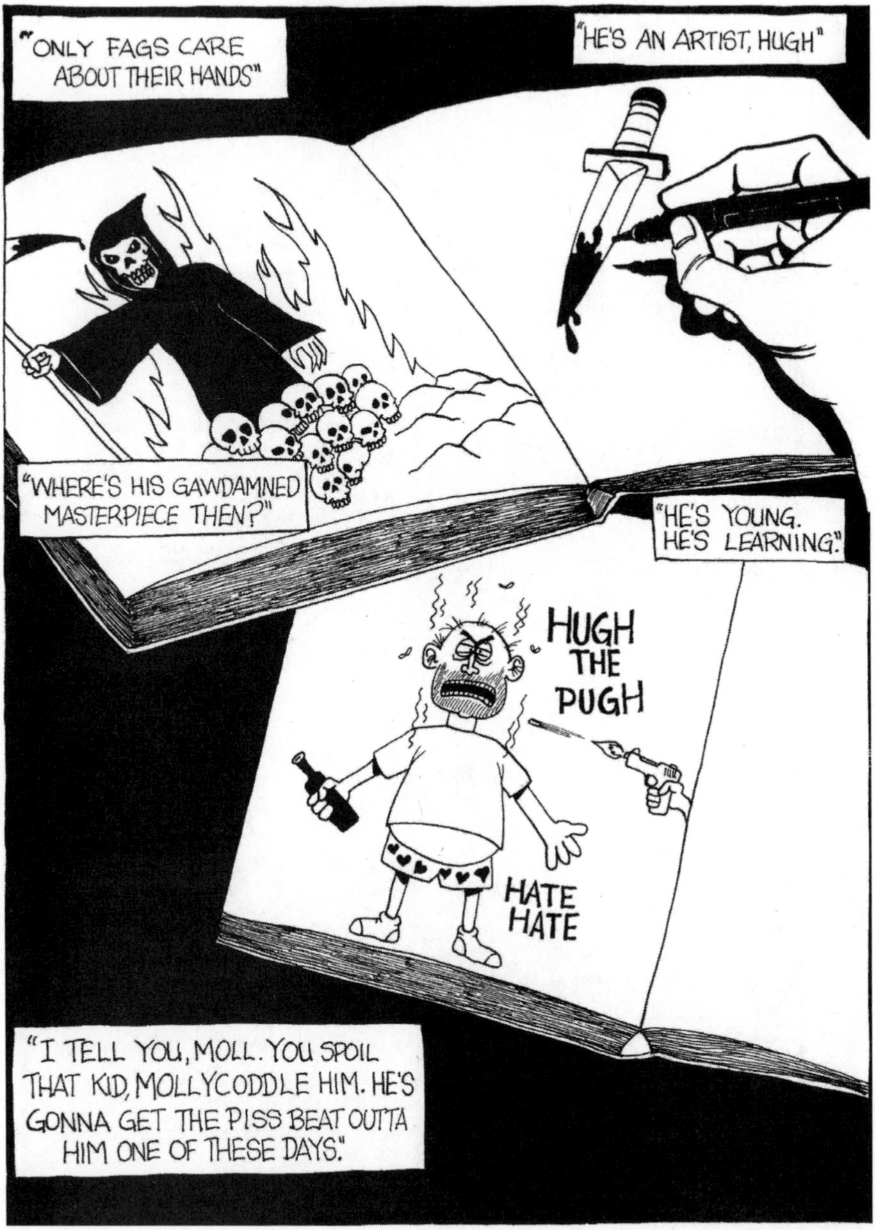
"ONLY FAGS CARE ABOUT THEIR HANDS"
"HE'S AN ARTIST, HUGH"
"WHERE'S HIS GAWDAMNED MASTERPIECE THEN?"
"HE'S YOUNG. HE'S LEARNING."
HUGH THE PUGH
HATE HATE
"I TELL YOU, MOLL. YOU SPOIL THAT KID, MOLLYCODDLE HIM. HE'S GONNA GET THE PISS BEAT OUTTA HIM ONE OF THESE DAYS."

That's Hugh. My stepdad. Hugh the Pugh, Candy calls him. 'Cause he used to be known as The Pugilist. Hugh was a boxer. Used to be. A has been who still is.

Hugh thinks my dyslexia is all in my head. A ploy to cover up my laziness. My lousy marks. My loser life.

This is how I see the print on a page:

GENERAL
LABELLED LAZY, DUMB, CARLESS, IMMATURE
FEELS DUMB, HAS POOR SELF-ESTEEM, EASILY FRUSTRATED AND EMOTIONAL ABOUT SCHOOL READING OR TESTING
SEEMS "HYPER" OR "DAY DREAMER".
HEARING AND SPEECH
CONFUSED BY LETTERS, NUMBERS, WORDS SEQUENCES OR VERBAL EXPLANATIONS.
READS AND RE-READS WITH LITTLE COMPREHENSION
SPELLS PHONETICALLY AND INCONSISTENTLY
Dyslexic and Proub
BEHAVIOR, HEALTH, AND PERSONALITY
EMOTIONALLY SENSITIVE, STRIVE FOR PERFECTION. EXTREMELY DISORDERLY OR COMPULSIVELY ORDERLY. CAN BE CLASS CLOWN, TROUBLE MAKER, TOO QUIET. STRONG SENSE OF JUSTICE
MEMORY AND COGNITION
EXCELLENT LONG TERM MEMORY FOR EXPERIENCES, LOCATIONS AND FACES. POOR MEMORY FOR SEQUENCES FACTS AND INFORMATION THAT HAS NOT BEEN EXPERIENCED
WRITING AND MOTOR SKILLS
DIFFICULTY PUTTING THOUGHTS INTO WORDS. CAN BE AMBIDEXTROUS, AND OFTEN CONFUSES LEFT/RIGHT AND OVER/UNDER.
MATH AND TIME MANAGEMENT
CAN COUNT, BUT DIFFICULTY COUNTING OBJECTS AND DEALING WITH MONEY. DIFFICULTY AT TELLING TIME.

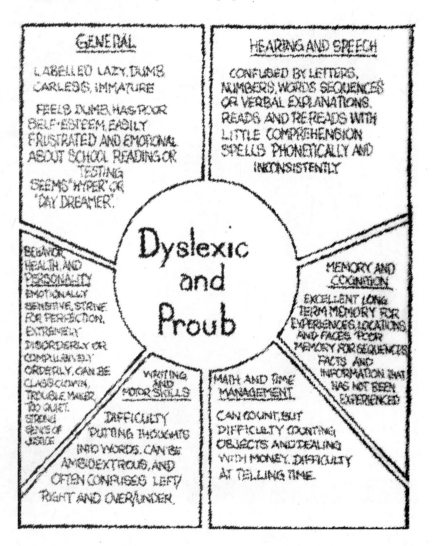

I've been tested and there are expensive computer programs out there for me to use with my home computer. (Enter laugh track here.) But at least this year, my grade-eleven year, my teachers are letting me use the school laptops for some assignments and written tests. And the librarian has loaned me some audio books to help with my reading. That's because of Ms. Gable. The counsellor. She's taken some kinda interest in me. For some reason. She's been talking to the teachers on my behalf. I'm her current person of interest.

And I'm also Blade Attaman's.

I know for a fact it was him who slashed my bike tires two weeks ago. I'd be completely without wheels if Uncle Mac—father of Vic and Dick Prick—hadn't given me some birthday cash so that I could replace the tires.

Uncle Mac is my mom's big brother. He's mostly on the edge of our lives. Sometimes looking in, if only to shake his head at the mess he thinks my mom has made of her life. Uncle Mac sells cars for a living. Yup, a car salesman. Think stereotype. So I don't know what it is he thinks he's done that's so hot in his own life. But I guess when you're solidly middle class you can look down your nose at those who aren't. Pass judgement. Offer advice. Especially if they're family.

He drives a black Ford Escape SUV with the license plate NEMO, after his favourite Disney movie. Fancies himself a little fish in a big pond. Or maybe thinks he's Captain Nemo, like in the Jules Verne Classics Comic, 20,000 *Leagues Under the Sea*. But Uncle Mac doesn't really know Jack shit. *Nemo* means "nobody" in Latin. I looked it up. So he's driving around proclaiming that he's really a great big nothing. And that's about what he gives us.

I never notice him offering my mom much of a hand.

But he did give me birthday bucks.

After Blade cut my tires.

How do I know it was Blade? Besides his stupid nickname? Because he cornered me in the school can and told me next time it would be my face.

Why didn't I fight back? Tell someone? Besides because of his stupid nickname and rep?

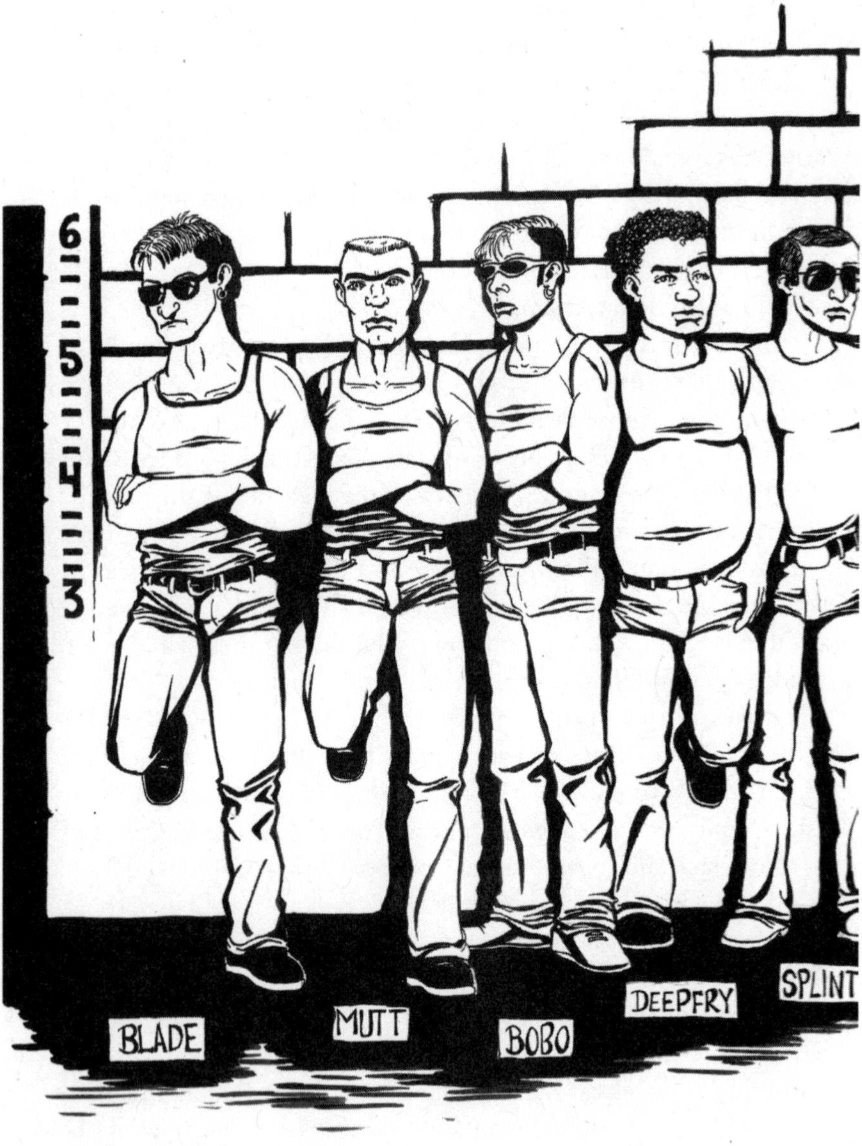
6
5
4
3
BLADE
MUTT
BOBO
DEEPFRY
SPLINT

Because of the posse of badass knuckle crackers that Blade always has tailing him. Mutt and Bobo and Deepfry and Splint. Who make up in brawn what they lack in brains. These four guys are the bench-pressing, iron-pumping steroid kings of our stinking school. And everyone knows it. They deal in the parking lot. Pretty much have their pick of the girls, especially the vacuous and racked types. Bootleg for profit off the underagers. They've always got Blade's back.

And for some reason, Blade's always looking to jump mine.

I don't say much to him.

I don't say much to anyone.

It's probably the way I dress. He and his buddies wear wife beaters, even in winter to show off their bursting biceps and pumped-up pecs. They have buzz cuts with stupid designs razored, like logos for running shoes, just for originality.

But me. I like the black. I found a long midnight trench coat with chains all over it at Sanctuary. I waited for a bloody year to pay for it on layaway. Twenty bucks here. Ten there. My sister gave me five. That sort of glacial payment system.

But finally, last fall, I got to take it home. And man. I almost cut a figure when I wear it, which is everyday.

It's like my uniform. When I put it on, I just *feel* better, somehow. Like I'm armed against the world. And believe me, I've learned that I need to wear armour if I'm going to survive.

My old man—my biological father—left when I was four and Candy was only a few months old. He up and moved to Chicago. Started a new family. Like his other one never existed. My mom pursued him for years for child support, but he's a classic deadbeat dad. Every once in a while he sends a cheque in the mail. But he never calls. Once he sent me a birthday card when I was nine. Haven't heard from him since.

I remember him, though. As much as my four-year-old memories can muster. He used to come through the door at the end of the day—we lived somewhere else in this city, somewhere nicer in the West end—and swing me up on his shoulders. He was tall, like me. But it was effortless

for him. And he'd always laugh and say, "Hey Jamie! How was your day, Jamie boy?"

I remember that. And some other stuff, too. But I try not to think about it much. Because I always end up wondering what it was about me that made him leave. Because it couldn't have been Candy who was a gorgeous baby. Or my mom, who was and still is pretty beautiful, even with the circles under her eyes. And the occasional bruise.

So it had to be me, didn't it?

I try not to go there. But sometimes it's hard not to. It's the only explanation.

I find it better to cover up. When I was little, I used my blankets. Nowadays there's drawing. And my midnight special coat. And oh yeah, the gun that no one knows about.

And I think it's the coat that gives Attaman the most trouble with me. He calls me "vamp-boy" or "black drag fag" or "Emo-loser" and lately "skinny blood-f***sucker" and so on.

Incidentally, I'm not afraid of the f-word. In fact, I use it too much for my mom's liking or my sister's. Candy is the reason. Not that she reads this. But she dared me not to use the word for a whole year. Bet me $50 I couldn't do it. Six weeks and the word has not appeared in my cartoons, in my scrawl, in my tags, in this book. Nor has it left my mouth.

I guess I want to prove something to her. And my mom.

And even though there is not a better word for Blade Attaman than f***wad, it has been entertaining to look up and discover colourful synonyms. Even the shortened version "fwad" is not bad. "Smegma" is better. I've tagged his locker with both words at different times. Nothing too artistic, so he wouldn't suspect it was me. Man, was Attaman pissed! Despite the fact he didn't know what the second word meant.

So euphemisms are my new hobby. Who knew a dyslexic loser would ever be interested in wordplay? Maybe I'm a distant relative of Shakespeare. (Guffaws of disbelief.) Looking up insults is how I spend my time in the library when I'm bored or broke or need to get out of this cramped apartment. Which is pretty often and pretty much feels like right about now...

I t's pissing rain out.
That kind of rain that shows no sign of letting up. Cold, hard rain.
Dark puddles turning to minor lakes in the streets. Sad skies gloomy as
this freaking apartment with Hugh yowling on and on about the fight
on TSN.

Candy's at dance class. Mom's at her waitressing job. I'm trying to
do homework.

But I only feel like drawing...

Drawing's the only thing I'm good at. Believe me. I know.

Sometimes I wish the rain could come and wash away my
pathetic life.

I have no friends. No one at school gets me.

I'm a loner.

Girls? That's just funny. I've never had a girlfriend. Probably
never will. I don't know even where to look when I try talking to a
girl. Like even during group work in social studies or something. I
have trouble meeting her eyes. So I look down. Only then I feel like
a pervert staring at her chest when I don't mean to. So I look down
further. It just gets worse. Now I'm ogling her or something. So I'm
reduced to just staring at her feet. Which makes me seem anti-social.
Which I guess I am.

Dufus. Should be my middle name. Jamie Dufus Kidding. Ha. Maybe
that'll be my new artist nickname. I'll sign all my pieces Dufus.

Shit, I hate the rain.

There's really only one girl I really would like to talk to anyways.
Yeah. The girl in my social class. The one I can't look at. Except her
shoes. I know them very well.

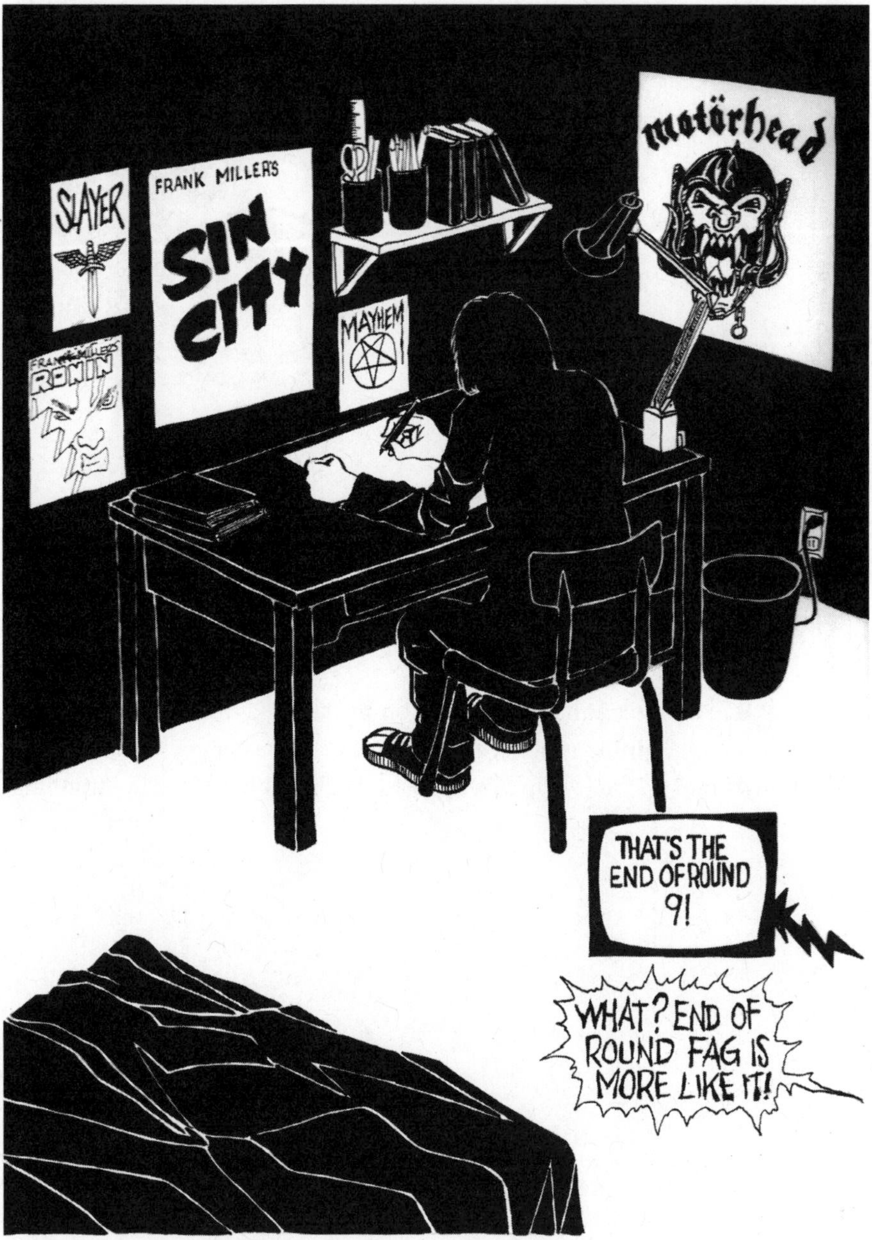
SLAYER
FRANK MILLER'S
SIN CITY
FRANK MILLER'S RONIN
MAYHEM
motörhead
THAT'S THE END OF ROUND 9!
WHAT? END OF ROUND FAG IS MORE LIKE IT!

Ok. So I look at her sometimes on the sly. Ok, often. When she isn't looking. Ok. I look at her whenever I can. I'm not some creepy stalker or anything. I- I can't help myself, is all. She's so bloody well… stunning.

The one I can't look at. Except her shoes. I know them very well.

SHE'S SO BEAUTIFUL I CAN'T DRAW HER.

I just can't do her justice. I dunno why. I just can't.

Her name is…

I'm almost scared to write it. Just in case I jinx my chances of ever… you know.

Who am I kidding? That's right. Jamie Kidding.

Screw it. Her name is perfect. Just like her. Tatiana Oleshenko. Tatiana. Wow. Must be Russian or something. Ukrainian. I'd ask her if I had any balls.

Which I don't.

Crap. Hugh's pounding like a madman at my door. I'll bet he's been into the booze. I have to put this away…

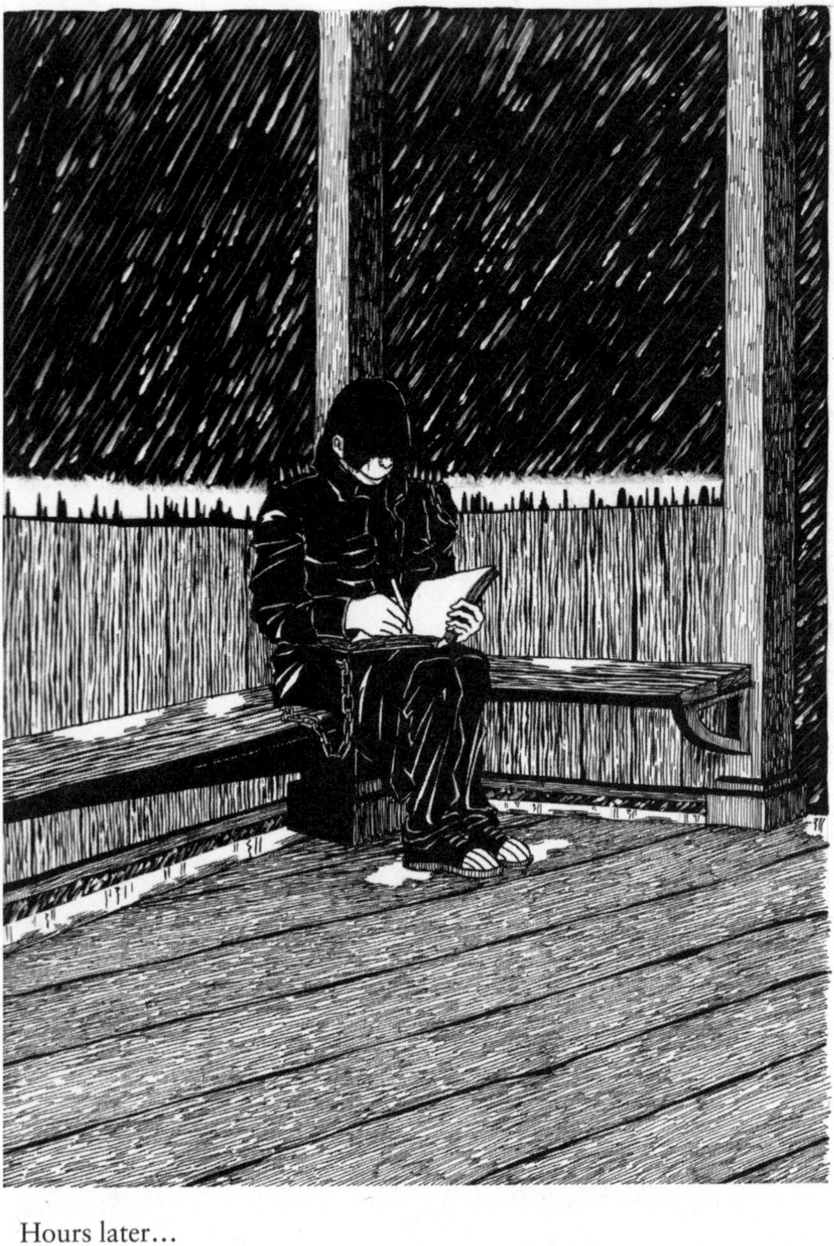

Hours later…

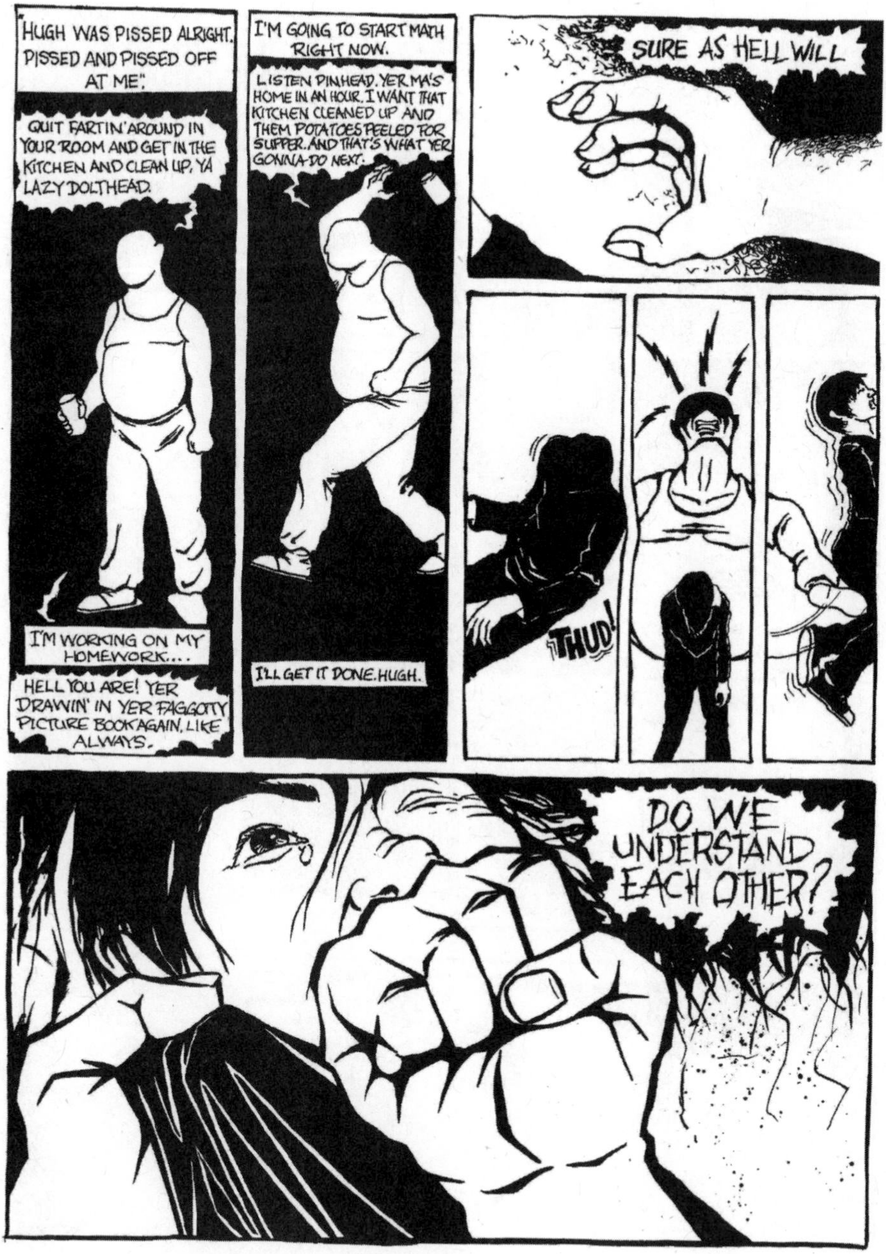
"HUGH WAS PISSED ALRIGHT. PISSED AND PISSED OFF AT ME".
QUIT FARTIN' AROUND IN YOUR ROOM AND GET IN THE KITCHEN AND CLEAN UP, YA LAZY DOLTHEAD.
I'M WORKING ON MY HOMEWORK...
HELL YOU ARE! YER DRAWIN' IN YER FAGGOTTY PICTURE BOOK AGAIN, LIKE ALWAYS.
I'M GOING TO START MATH RIGHT NOW.
LISTEN PINHEAD. YER MA'S HOME IN AN HOUR. I WANT THAT KITCHEN CLEANED UP AND THEM POTATOES PEELED FOR SUPPER. AND THAT'S WHAT YER GONNA DO NEXT.
I'LL GET IT DONE. HUGH.
SURE AS HELL WILL
THUD!
DO WE UNDERSTAND EACH OTHER?

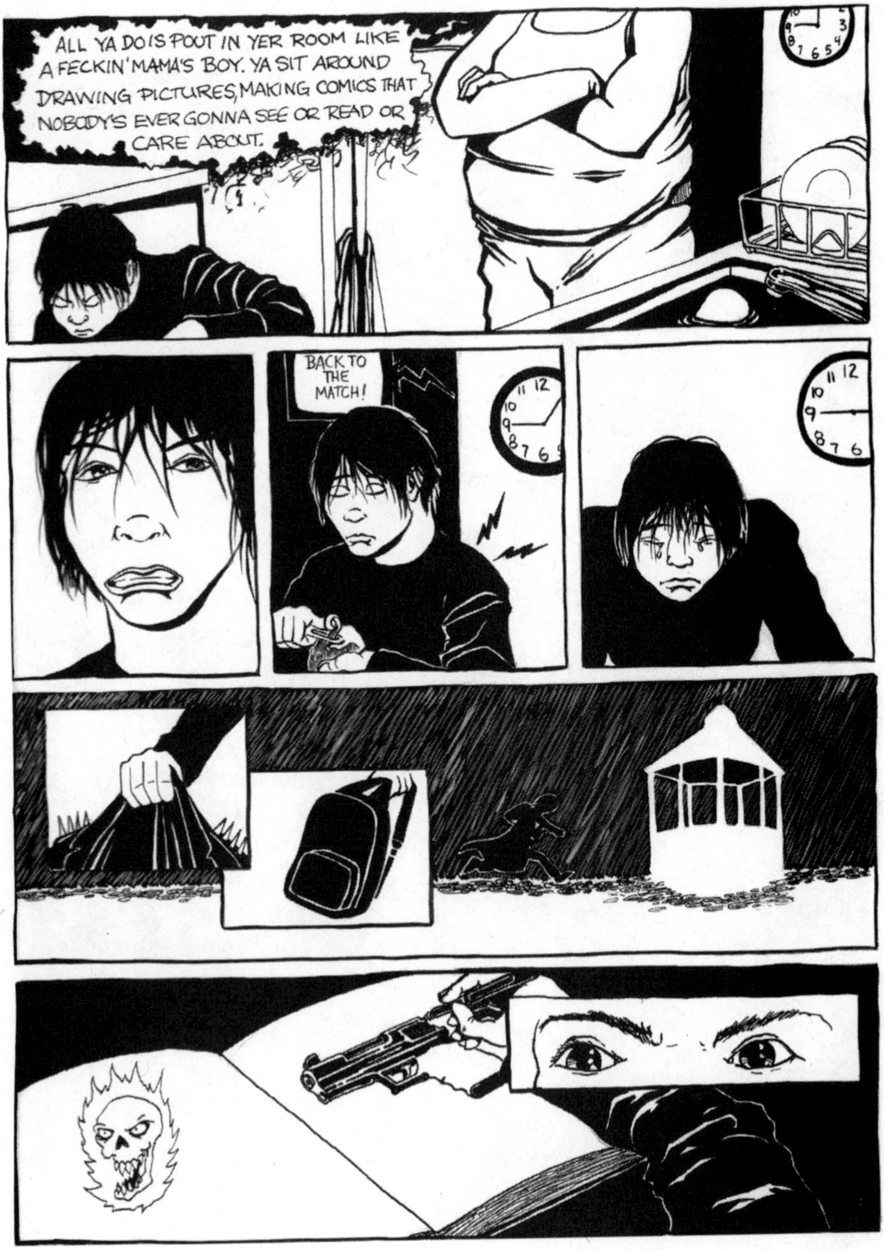
ALL YA DO IS POUT IN YER ROOM LIKE A FECKIN' MAMA'S BOY. YA SIT AROUND DRAWING PICTURES, MAKING COMICS THAT NOBODY'S EVER GONNA SEE OR READ OR CARE ABOUT.
BACK TO THE MATCH!

Tomato soup cures all ills. Well, that's what my mom says, anyways. It's not really true. But it's kinda true, too.

I got home after midnight. Hours after Hugh nearly destroyed my shoulder. Threatened to beat my face into a pulp. Said those words.

Mom was waiting up for me, smoking a cigarette. Which she only does when she's upset. The soup was waiting on the stove. The saltine crackers were on the table. Our little kitchen looked warm and inviting. My mom painted it. Yellow with red accents. She's real good with colour. Wishes she could have been an interior designer. But she would need another lifetime for that, she always says.

One without kids. At least without this one, I'm pretty sure.

She tried to hug me. I just stood there. Shivering like crazy. I didn't hug back. She pulled off my wet coat and draped it over a kitchen chair. Turned on the oven and opened the oven door to try to help speed up the drying. Mom knows how much I love that coat. How much I paid for it.

She handed me a towel. "Sit down, Jamie."

So I did. Dried my hair while she ladled soup into a bowl. And I devoured the tomato-y goodness with crackers mulched in. And another bowl.

"Hugh's sorry."

I said nothing. Yeah, right. Hugh's sorry. And I'm the flipping Tsar of Russia. Truth is, Mom's the one who's sorry that Hugh lost his head. I'm sure Hugh told her nothing about throwing me into the wall or threatening to do worse. Or anything of what he said to me.

Hugh the Pugh probably didn't even remember most of what happened. And he cared even less. He was snoring the drink off in their bed, Seagram bottles dancing in his dreams.

I kept spooning soup and crackers into my mouth. Saying nothing.

My mom looked real sad.

Well, I was real sad, too. (Still am.)

But the warmth in my stomach and in the kitchen was helping. Her sitting with me—even if we weren't talking—was good. I finally stopped shivering.

"Where's Candy?"

"Where do you think? She's asleep. Went to bed in tears worrying about you."

"Geez."

And I felt all bad about that. Because I hate to desert my little sister, ever. But I had to get out. I wasn't sure I was ever coming back. But where exactly would I have gone? No money. No food. No plan. If I ever do leave, I need to think it all through. Including what to do about Candy.

And I'd love to leave, believe me.

Because Mom will never throw that punchy paunchy boozer out. I don't understand the attraction, I really don't. Maybe in his heydey he was something. He was somebody. But as soon as she met him, almost, he moved in and, uninvited, took up the role of daddy when neither me or Candy wanted one. Especially one like him.

And then his drinking grew steady. And worse. And then he rolled up his sleeves and starting punching.

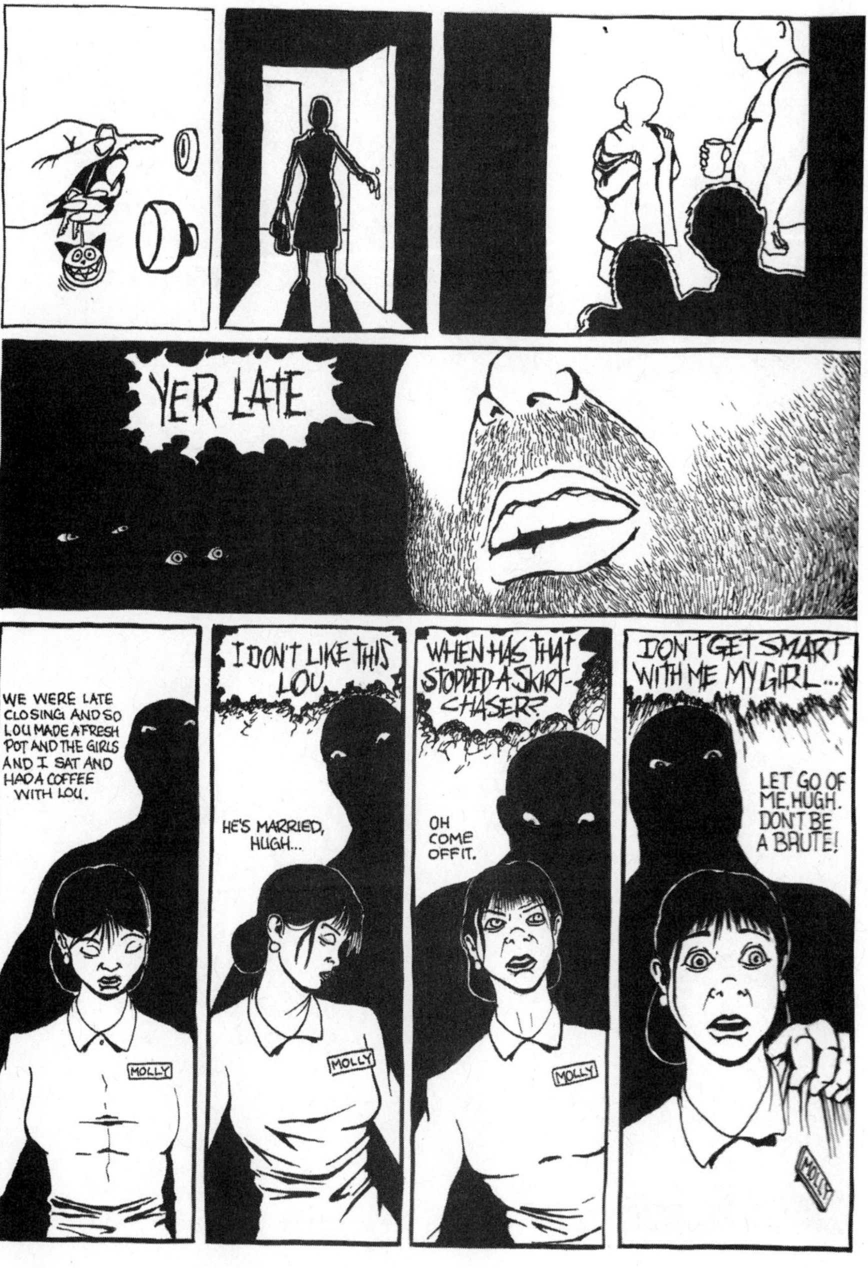
YER LATE
WE WERE LATE CLOSING AND SO LOU MADE A FRESH POT AND THE GIRLS AND I SAT AND HAD A COFFEE WITH LOU.
MOLLY
I DON'T LIKE THIS LOU.
HE'S MARRIED, HUGH...
MOLLY
WHEN HAS THAT STOPPED A SKIRT-CHASER?
OH COME OFF IT.
MOLLY
DON'T GET SMART WITH ME MY GIRL...
LET GO OF ME, HUGH. DON'T BE A BRUTE!
MOLLY

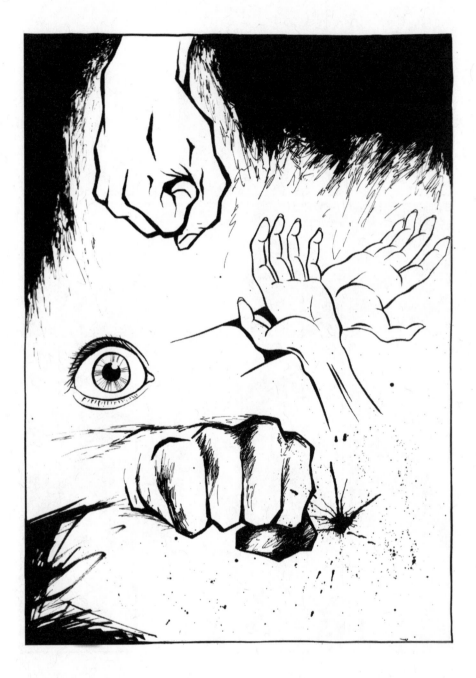

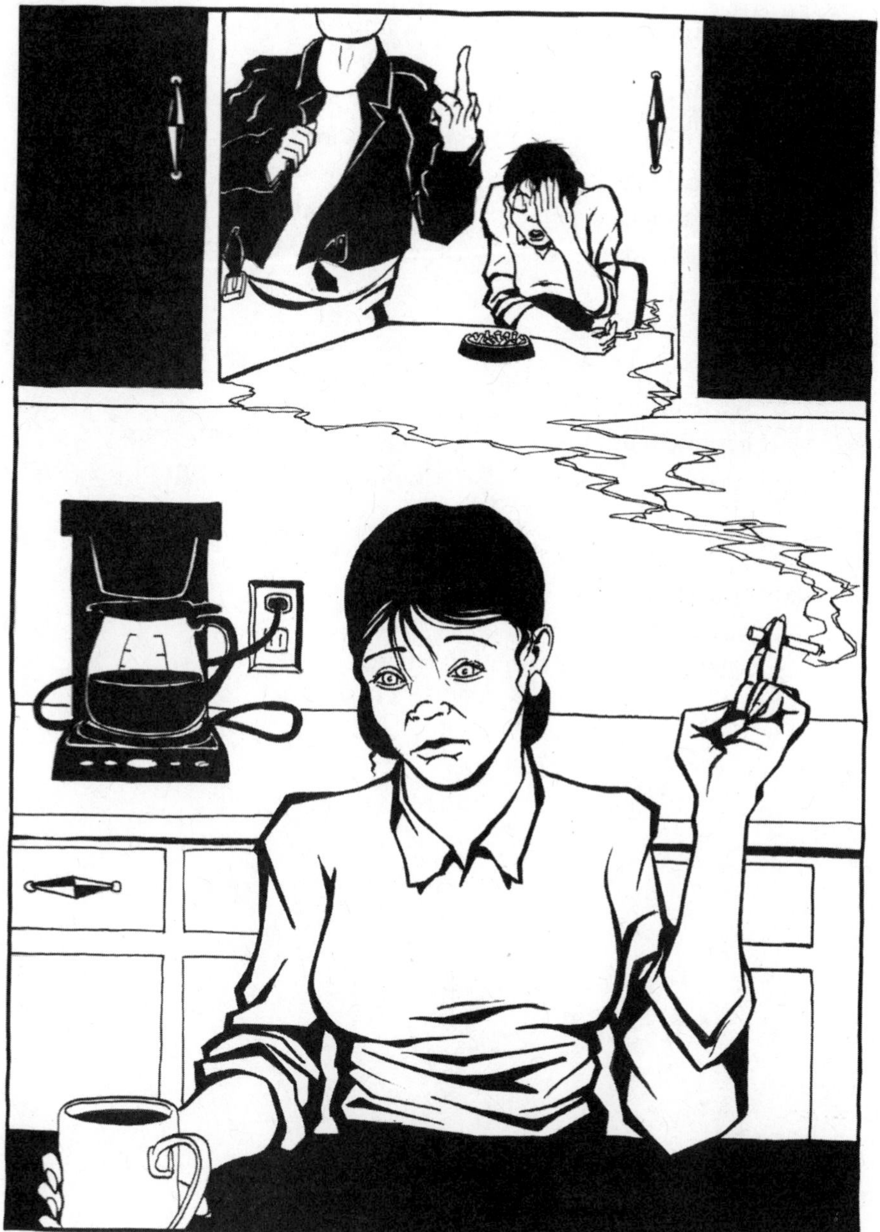

What on earth does she see in him? Why did she... why does she stay?

But as I watched Mom she seemed so vulnerable and lost. She took another drag on her smoke and turned to look at me.

"Those things'll kill you, Molly."

"If my teenaged son doesn't first." She half-smiled.

I grinned. And her smile went whole. My Mom has a terrific smile. Candy inherited it.

"You're ok?"

"Yeah, Mom. Ok."

"We're ok?"

I hesitated. But I told her what she wanted to hear. "Sure."

She stamped out her cigarette butt. Kissed the top of my head. Turned off the oven.

I washed up my dishes while she went off to bed. I hoped Hugh might die in the night.

But he didn't.

It just kept pissing rain until dawn.

The view from my window is a scene from *Sin City*.

Ok. Not every night. But some nights. My broom closet of a bedroom faces the alley. And there's always action in the alley.

Usually, there's some old guy poking around for bottles. We've got a lot of bottle bobbers, for sure. I learned most of my techniques from the old hat experts. There's this one old codger who has rigged a contraption that is part bike, part wagon, part supermarket cart. It can hold a ton of bottles, especially when he adds the airbags. Which aren't really airbags, but extra containers for the empties.

The old bugger's name is Willie. Sometimes he says hi and other times he looks as though he wants to kill me. Especially when we're competing for bottles in the alley.

It's a dog-eat-dog world out there.

Anyway, last night there was old Willie ambling down the alley. Minding his own business. I was hanging out my window watching the sights, long after everyone else had gone to bed.

Opposite of Willie, I see another figure approaching. His gait is off, as though he's loaded. And he's wild-eyed, weird-seeming. The two meet just at the dumpster to the right of my window.

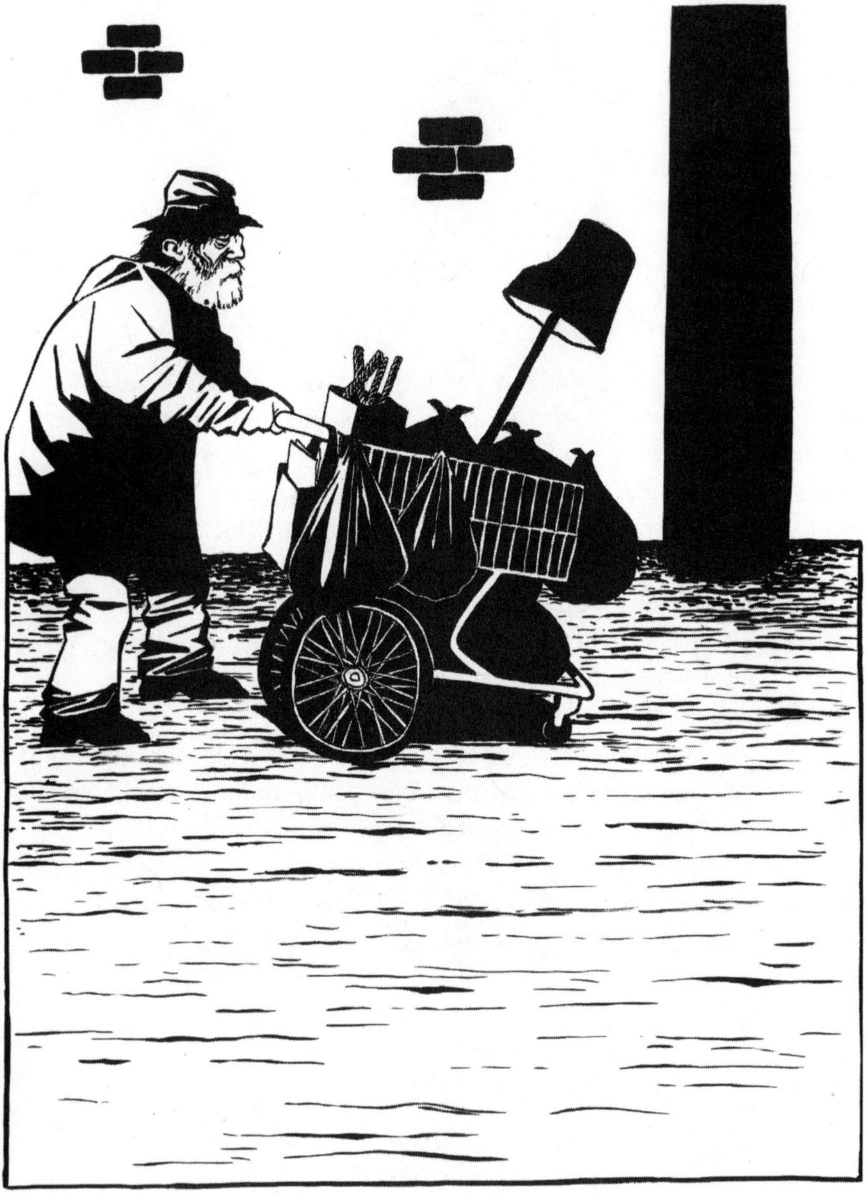

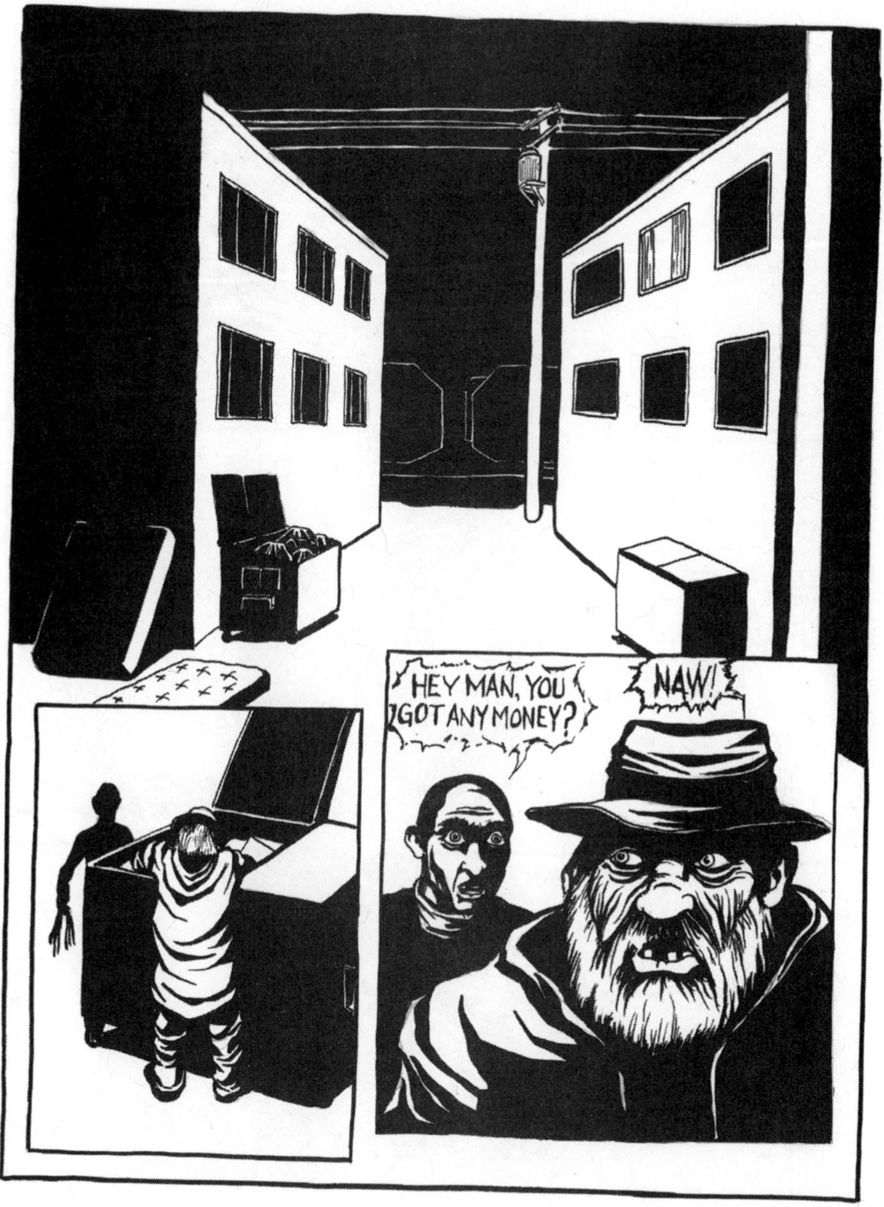
HEY MAN, YOU GOT ANY MONEY?
NAW!

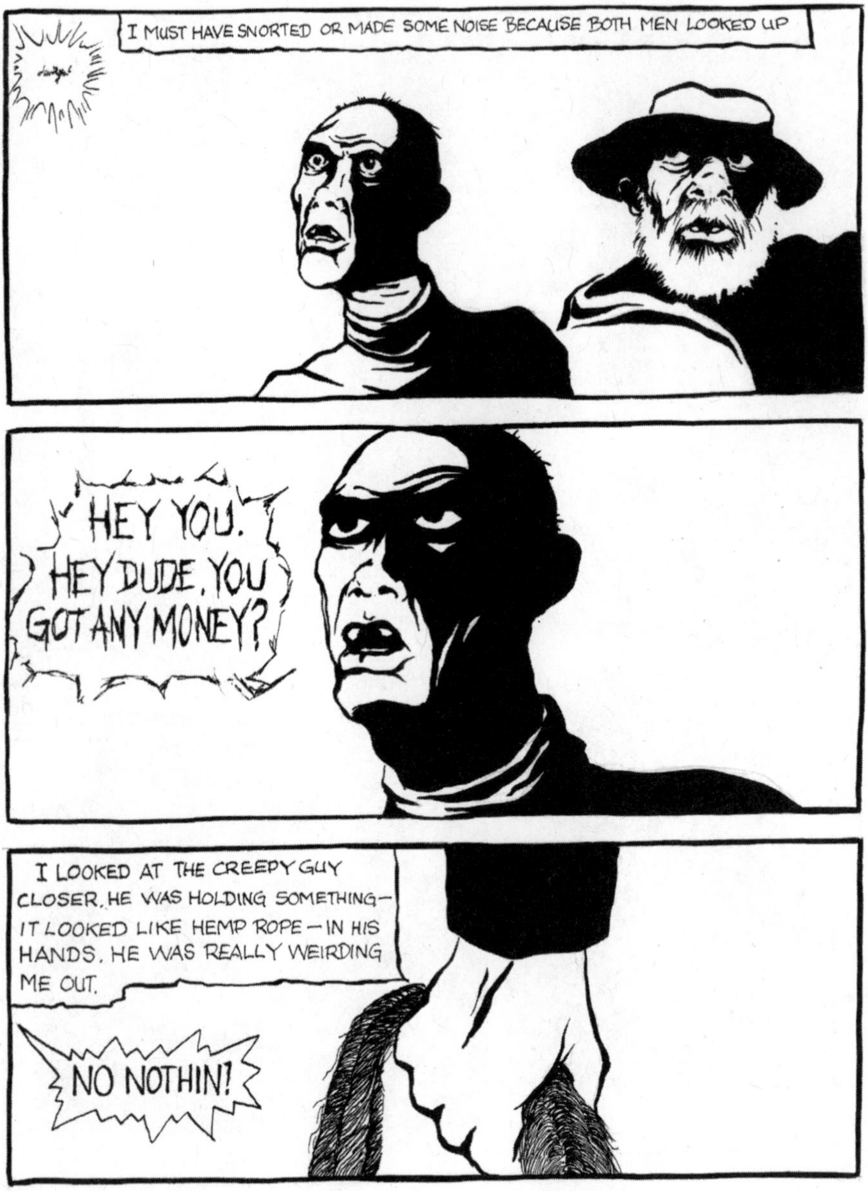
I MUST HAVE SNORTED OR MADE SOME NOISE BECAUSE BOTH MEN LOOKED UP
HEY YOU. HEY DUDE, YOU GOT ANY MONEY?
I LOOKED AT THE CREEPY GUY CLOSER. HE WAS HOLDING SOMETHING— IT LOOKED LIKE HEMP ROPE — IN HIS HANDS. HE WAS REALLY WEIRDING ME OUT.
NO NOTHIN!

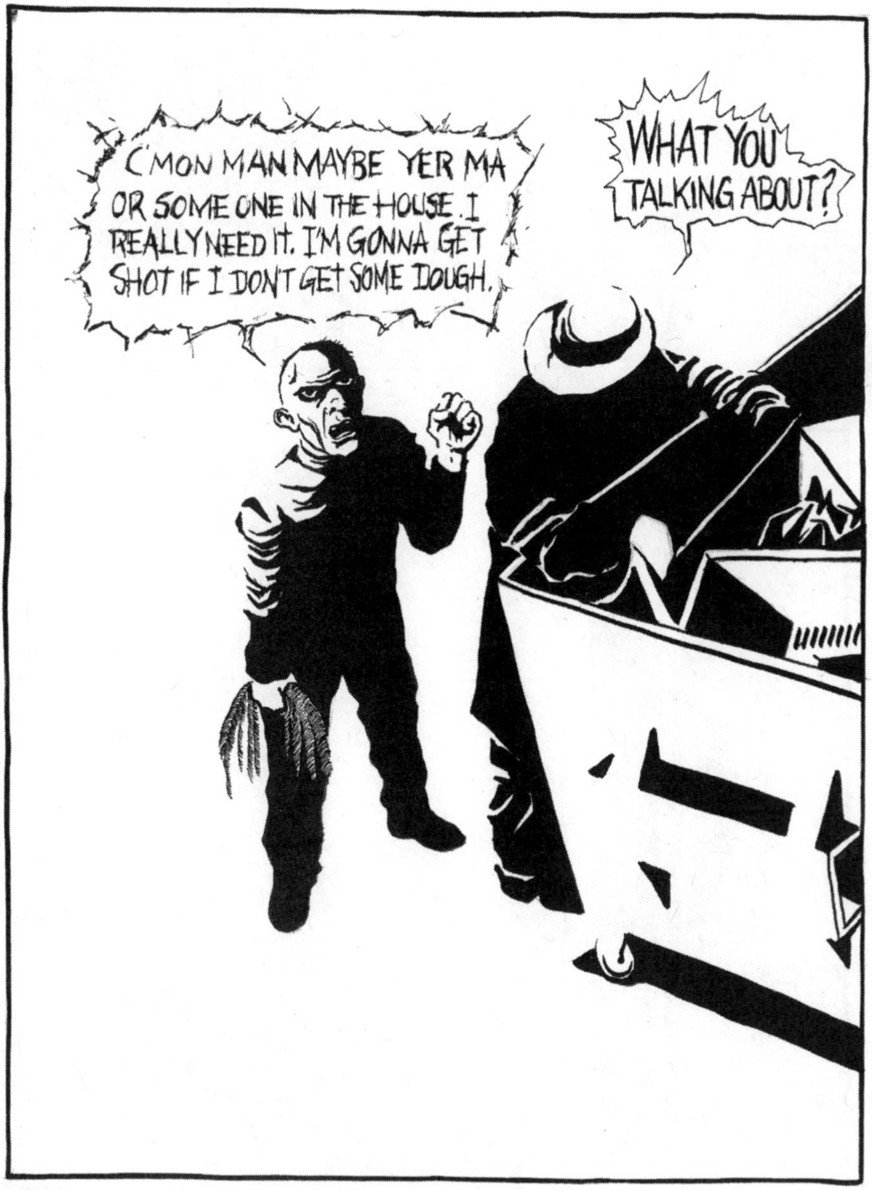
C'MON MAN MAYBE YER MA OR SOME ONE IN THE HOUSE. I REALLY NEED IT. I'M GONNA GET SHOT IF I DON'T GET SOME DOUGH.
WHAT YOU TALKING ABOUT?

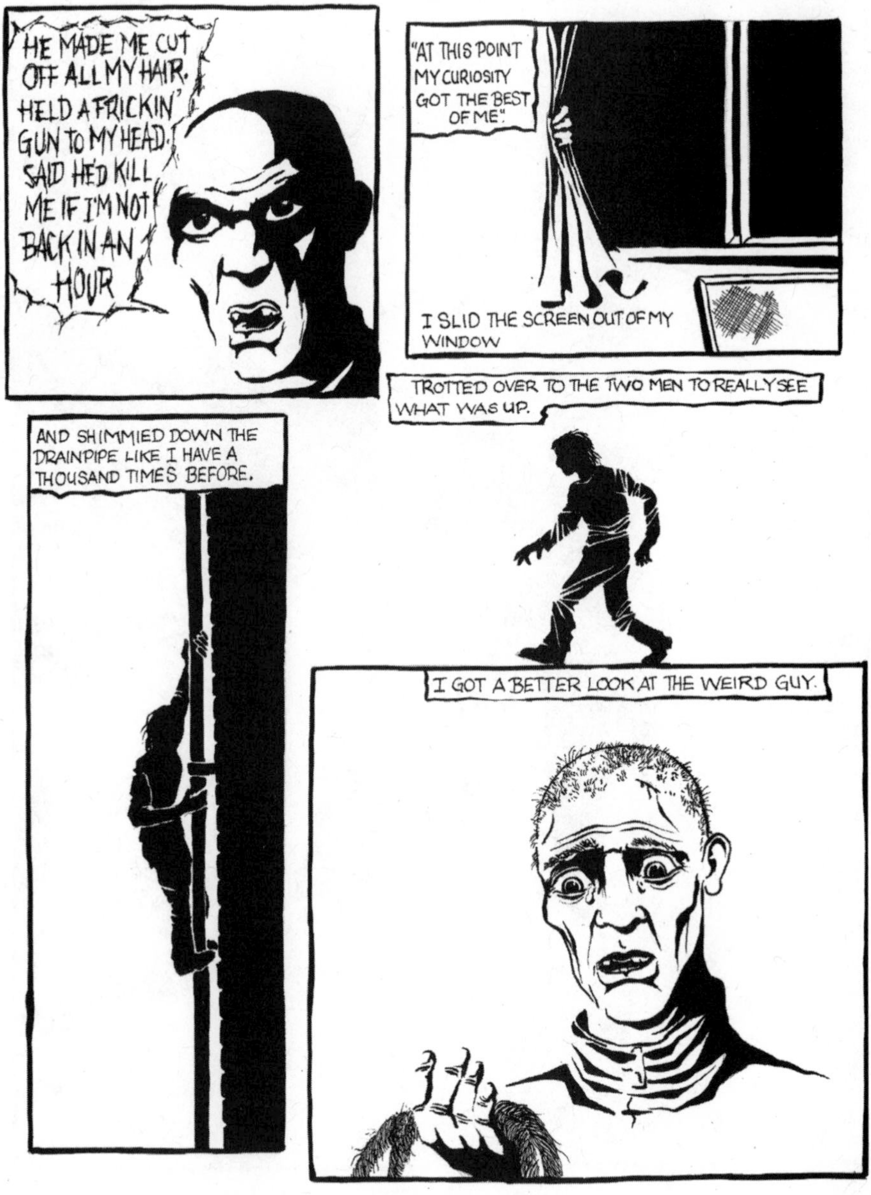
HE MADE ME CUT OFF ALL MY HAIR. HELD A FRICKIN' GUN TO MY HEAD. SAID HE'D KILL ME IF I'M NOT BACK IN AN HOUR
"AT THIS POINT MY CURIOSITY GOT THE BEST OF ME."
I SLID THE SCREEN OUT OF MY WINDOW
AND SHIMMIED DOWN THE DRAINPIPE LIKE I HAVE A THOUSAND TIMES BEFORE.
TROTTED OVER TO THE TWO MEN TO REALLY SEE WHAT WAS UP.
I GOT A BETTER LOOK AT THE WEIRD GUY.

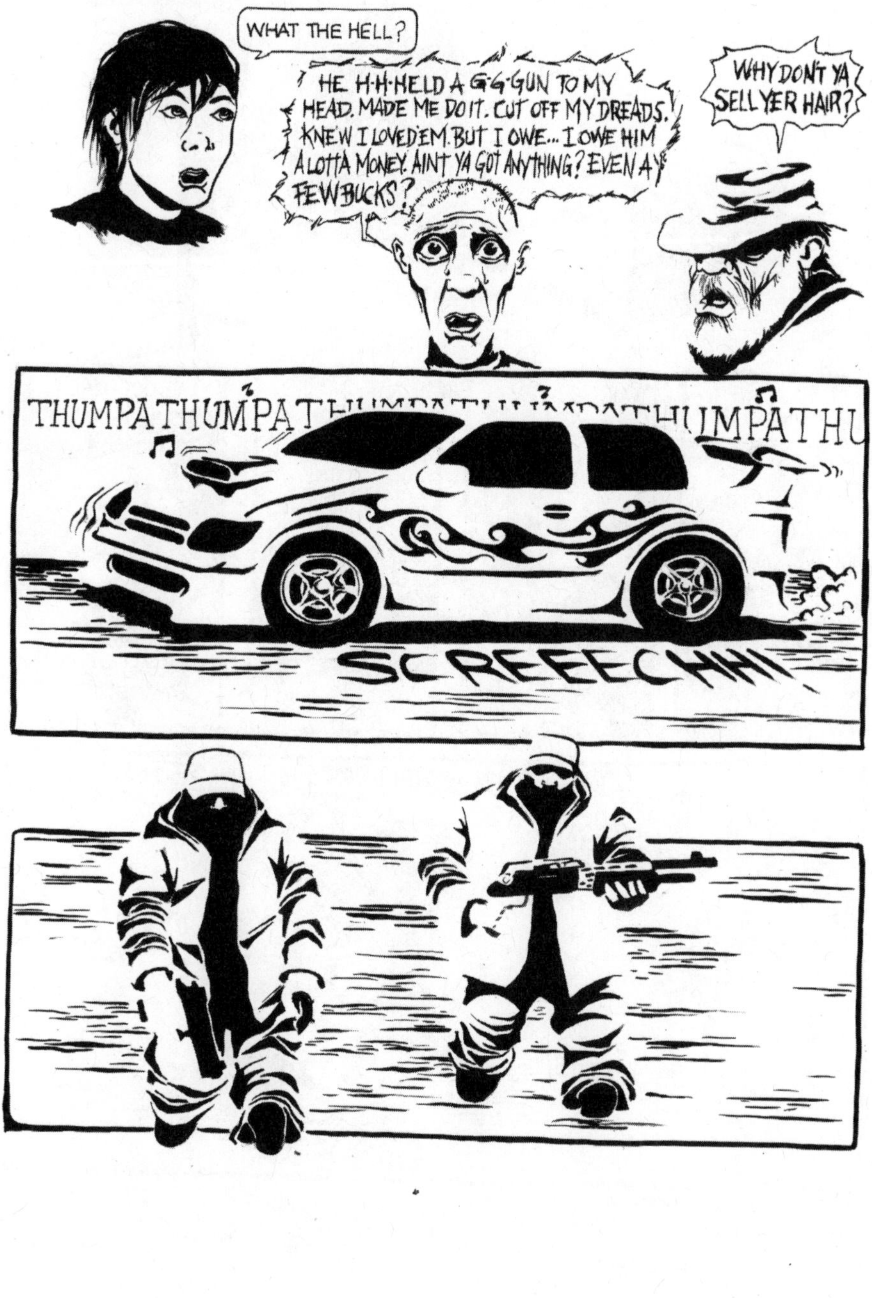
WHAT THE HELL?
HE H-H-HELD A G-G-GUN TO MY HEAD. MADE ME DO IT. CUT OFF MY DREADS. KNEW I LOVED 'EM. BUT I OWE... I OWE HIM A LOTTA MONEY. AIN'T YA GOT ANYTHING? EVEN A FEW BUCKS?
WHY DON'T YA SELL YER HAIR?
THUMPATHUMPATHUMPATHUMPATHUMPATHU
SCREEECHH!

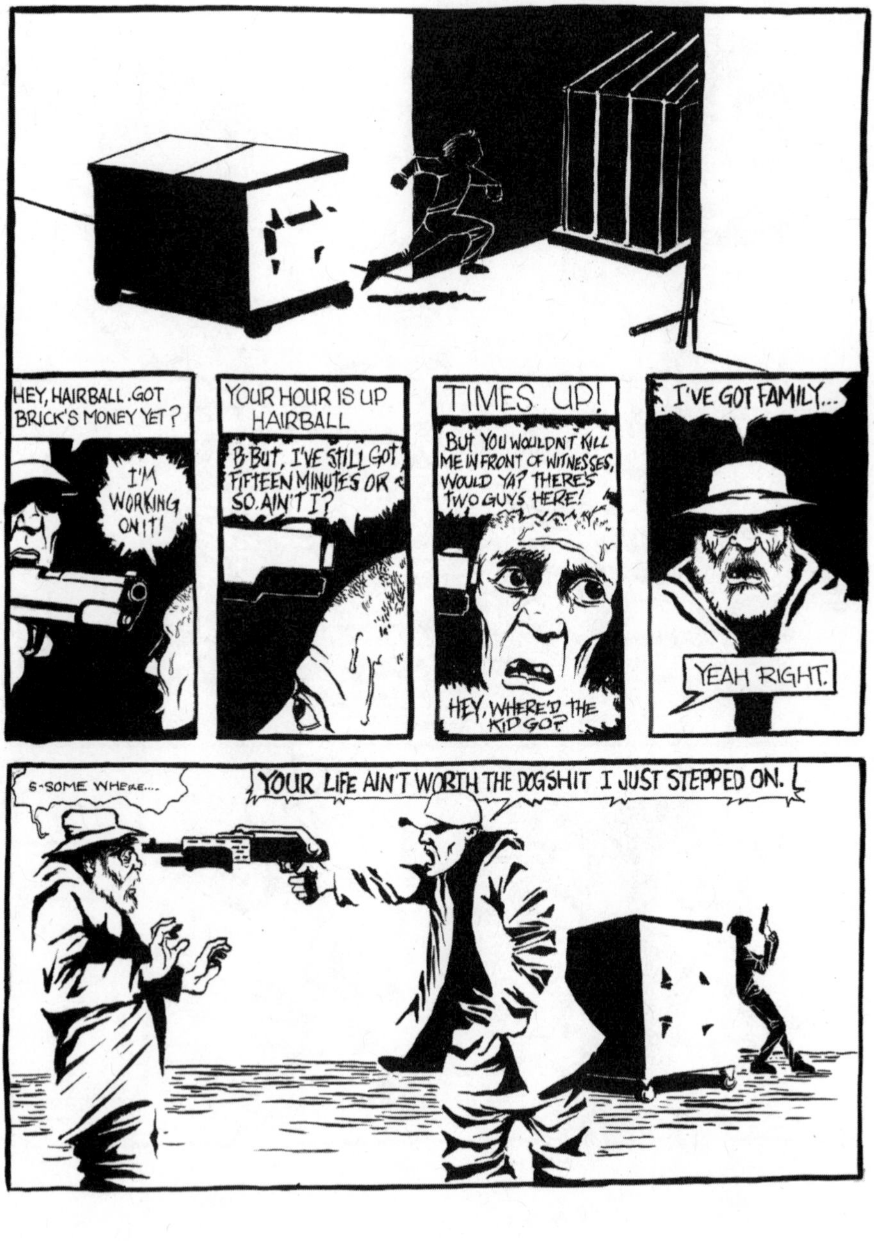
HEY, HAIRBALL .GOT BRICK'S MONEY YET?
I'M WORKING ON IT!
YOUR HOUR IS UP HAIRBALL
B-BUT, I'VE STILL GOT FIFTEEN MINUTES OR SO. AIN'T I?
TIMES UP!
BUT YOU WOULDN'T KILL ME IN FRONT OF WITNESSES, WOULD YA? THERE'S TWO GUYS HERE!
HEY, WHERE'D THE KID GO?
I'VE GOT FAMILY...
YEAH RIGHT.
S-SOME WHERE....
YOUR LIFE AIN'T WORTH THE DOGSHIT I JUST STEPPED ON.

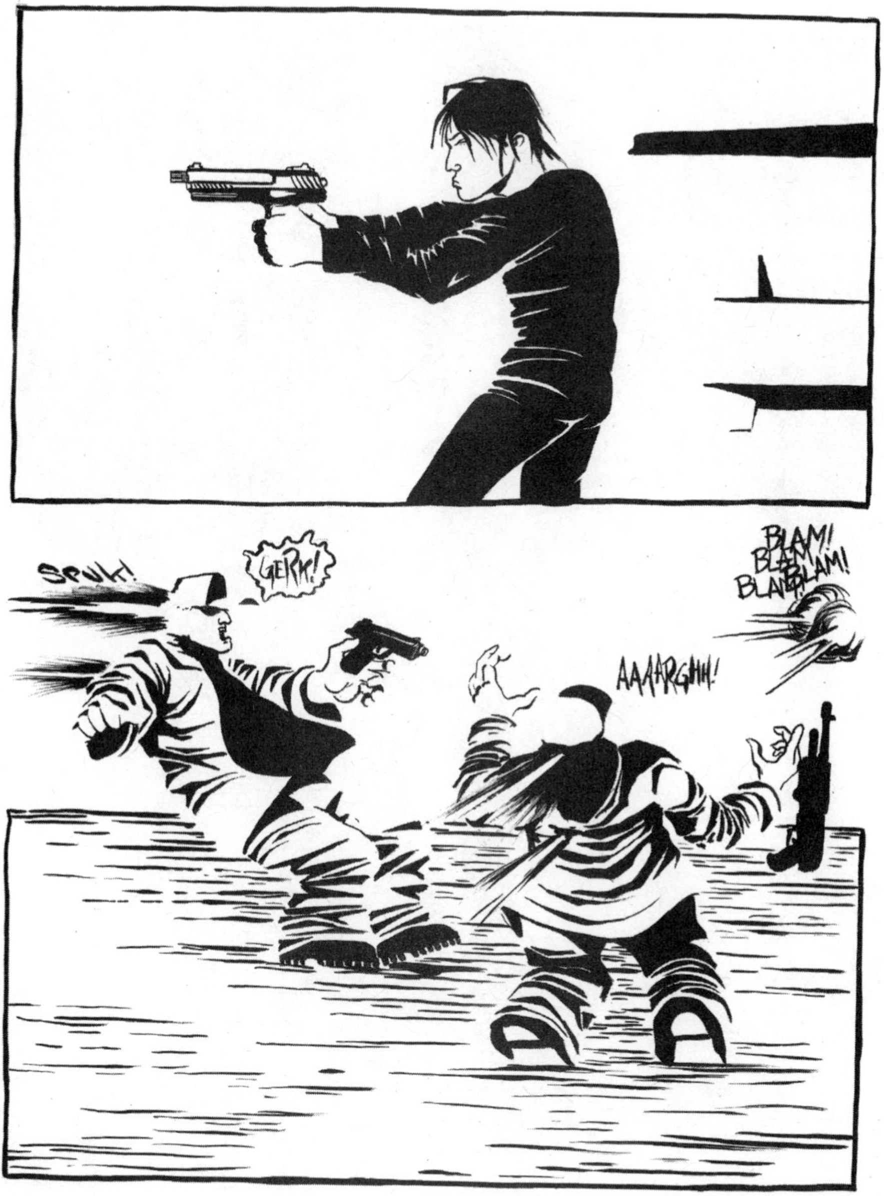
SPUK!
GERK!
BLAM!
BLAM!
BLAM!
BLAM!
AAAARGHH!

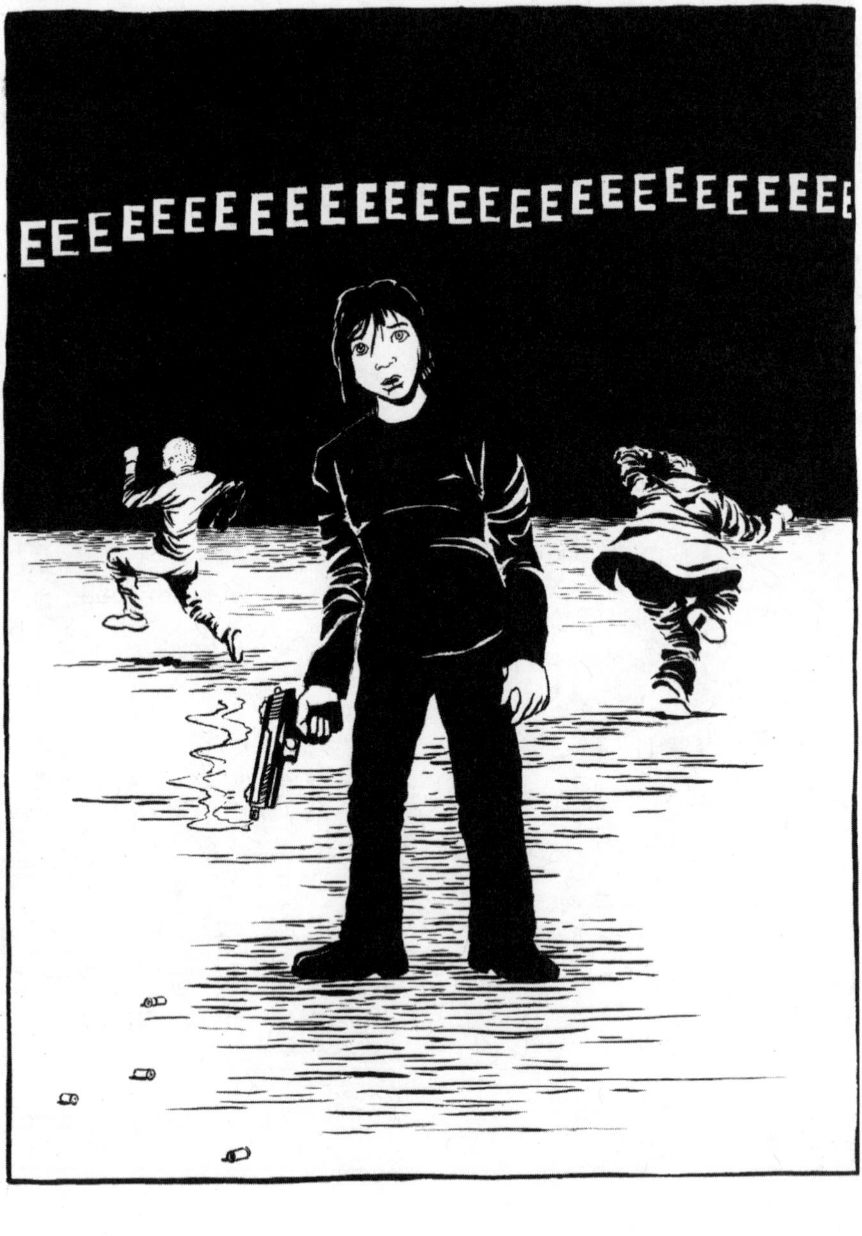
EEEEEEEEEEEEEEEEEEEEEEEEEEE

Ok. So maybe it didn't happen exactly like that. Maybe I'm exaggerating just a little.

But Willie did wheel by.

And some druggie with a handful of dreadlocks also stumbled along about 2 am.

The rest. Well, Jamie's kidding.

But it could have happened.

Guess it's obvious that I've been reading Frank Miller lately. Hugh got me one of the issues I'm missing. On Friday. His way of apologizing.

But. The apology's not accepted. I'm not very good at forgiving. Or forgetting. Especially since my shoulder's still sore. My right shoulder, attached to my right arm. Attached to my right hand. My drawing hand. And Hugh can't take back those words he said. And meant. Even if he was polluted at the time. Not that he'd ever take back anything he ever said. Pigheaded bastard.

But I took the comic. Why the hell not?

And I've already read it five times. I know the whole series. And I've seen the movie about eight times.

Frank Miller is one of my idols. His *Batman the Dark Knight Returns* will go down in history. And then there's Daredevil, one of my faves! Not to mention Elektra. X-Men. The list goes on and on. And no one does setting like Miller. Dark and downright creepilicious! I try to copy the masters, but I'm a poor fake at best.

'Course, I have so many masters that I study and admire. Stan Lee as writer and superhero creator, for one. There's a guy who cares about a good story. I read once that he even expanded the vocab in his comics at Marvel because he thought that it was a good thing for readers to sometimes have to look up words. Even a dyslexic like me needs new words for his text. Like tintinnabulation: the ringing (in the ears) that happens when a villain's head is clobbered by the Incredible Hulk's fist!

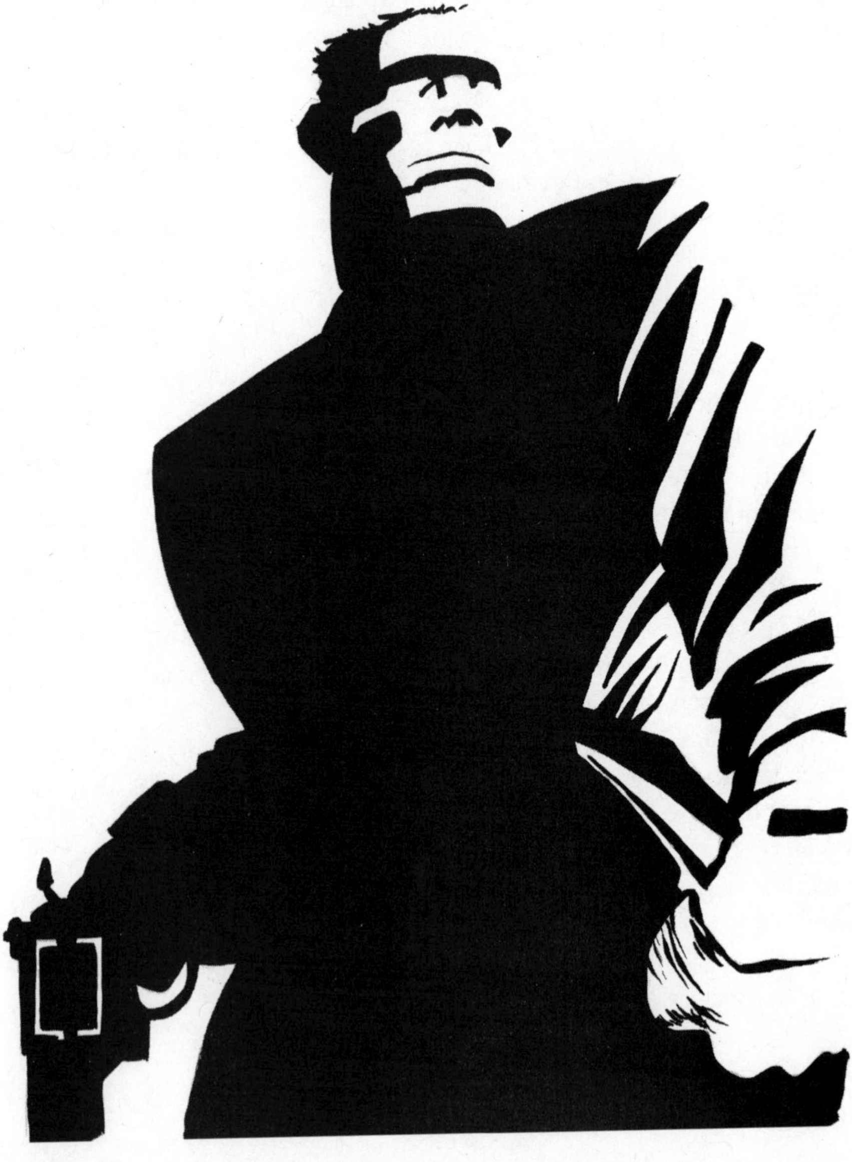

And speaking of the Hulk, there's my man Jack Kirby. King Kirby. Master of movement and energy. Nobody mixed body language and cinema and fight scenes like ol' Jack. Not to mention those Kirby dots, the Kirby Krackle!

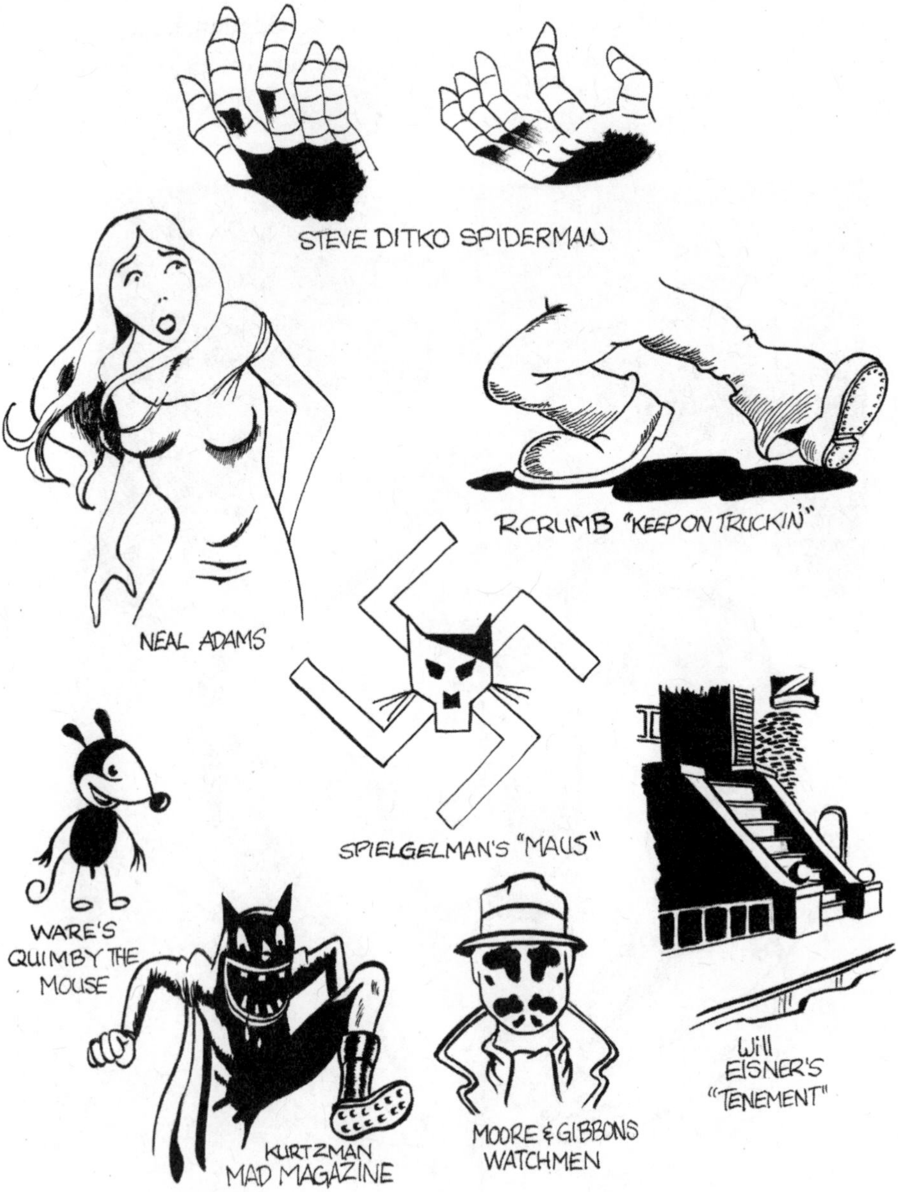
STEVE DITKO SPIDERMAN
R.CRUMB "KEEP ON TRUCKIN'"
NEAL ADAMS
SPIELGELMAN'S "MAUS"
WARE'S QUIMBY THE MOUSE
KURTZMAN MAD MAGAZINE
MOORE & GIBBONS WATCHMEN
Will EISNER'S "TENEMENT"

Then there's reclusive Steve Ditko. Creator of Spiderman. But also artist of the underground horror series *Uncle Creepy* and *Cousin Eerie*. Ditko. Genius of ink wash. Mastermind of detail. Especially hands. So expressive. I love Ditko's drawings of hands!

Maestro Neal Adams also did issues of *Creepy*. And who can forget his Green Lantern or Green Arrow? Superheroes who were human first, super second. What Neal Adams brought to cartooning changed the industry. He and his writer partner, Denny O'Neil, tackled racism and drug abuse, even during the worst of the stupid Comics Code years. And man, can Adams draw a dame!

Then there are my underground comix gurus: Robert Crumb, Art Spiegelman, Chris Ware, Harvey Kurtzman, Will Eisner, the legendary creator of the graphic novel, and the amazing *Watchmen* team Allan Moore and Dave Gibbons.

What a legacy for a kid like me from the badass side of town. No wonder I never have any money – between art supplies, Candy's dance classes, and my obsession with comix. No wonder Jay, the owner of Happy Harbor Comics, is pretty much sick of my ugly face. No wonder my imagination gets a little carried away from me sometimes.

My latest secret: I've been working on a strip of my own for the bi-weekly school newspaper. It's appeared twice, so far. Even have a decent title: *The Adventures of the Incredible Disappearing Boy*. Obviously semi-autobiographical. But I sure as hell don't sign my name. Only my art teacher, Mr. Letterman, and the newspaper teacher supervisor, Mr. Dropko, know I'm the artist. I can't go too far, of course. That would be breaking the rules. And we don't want that. School's all about rules.

But I get my digs in. This week's strip features a rather ingenious poke at the pump-you-up boys, Attaman and his thickskulled thugs.

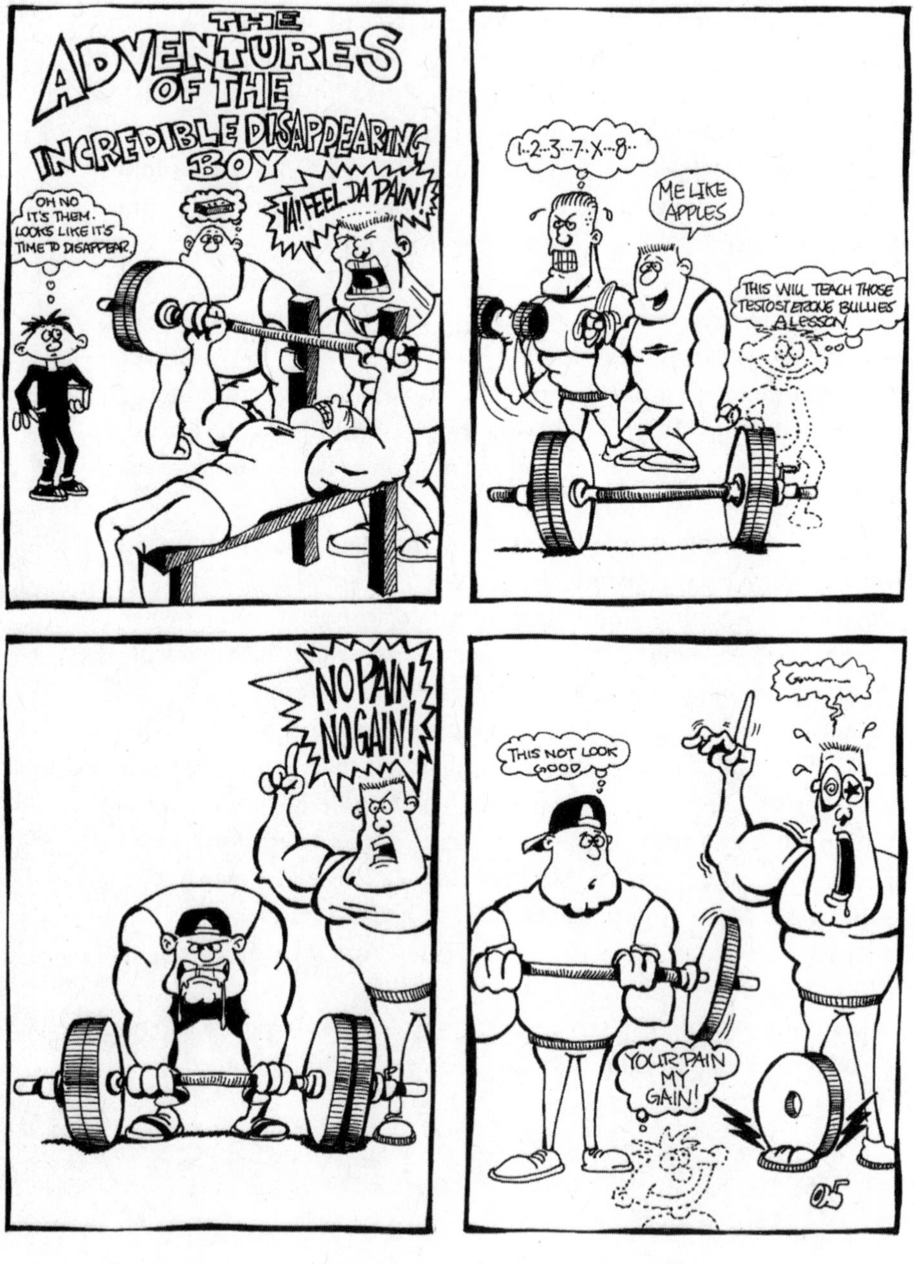
THE ADVENTURES OF THE INCREDIBLE DISAPPEARING BOY
OH NO IT'S THEM. LOOKS LIKE IT'S TIME TO DISAPPEAR.
YA! FEEL DA PAIN!
1..2..3..7..X..8..
ME LIKE APPLES
THIS WILL TEACH THOSE TESTOSTERONE BULLIES A LESSON.
NO PAIN NO GAIN!
THIS NOT LOOK GOOD
YOUR PAIN MY GAIN!

'Course, it could all backfire on me. After all, Attaman knows I'm an artist. But the ratzass can't read. So I should be safe.

And if not, I'll just engage my incredible disappearing powers.

Yeah, right.

And tomorrow I'll win the Pulitzer for graphic novel.

Posthumously.

Once they retrieve my scattered, bloody limbs from all over the schoolyard.

Diving into dumpsters can be perilous to a guy's health. Not to mention downright stinko disgusting.

After all, in the quest to find the jackpot, sometimes there are rotting things, dead (or live) rodents, dogshat (not to mention human), broken glass, sharp-edged cans. All manner of rot and putrescence (new rad word—love it!). And most serious of all—until recently, that is—junkies' needles.

Yup. That's all I'd need to end my short and perfect life. A prick from some prick's AIDS- or Hep-C-infested needle. Just to make sure I die before ever getting laid.

Or before my first international exhibition. Whichever comes first. (Hey, a guy's gotta have some dreams, right?)

So I suit up. Like the superhero I am. The Incredible Disappearing Boy!

THE INCREDIBLE DISAPPEARING BOY

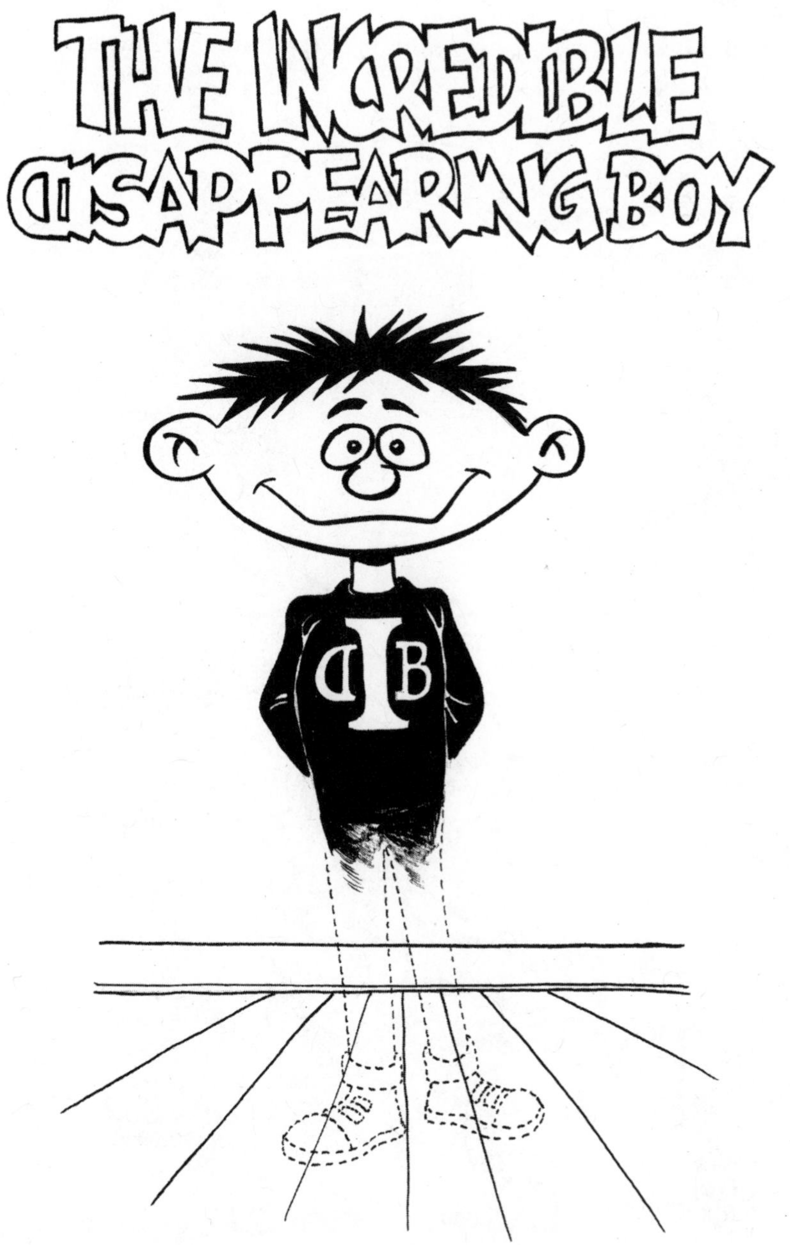

Ok. Not so much.

But I do wear protective clothing, even if it makes me look like a fricking geek.

JAMIE'S DUMPSTER DIVING GEAR

GOGGLES

SECONDHAND COVERALLS

WORKGLOVES. DUCT TAPE REINFORCEMENT

FLASHLIGHT

PLASTIC BAGS

MILKCRATE FOR COLLECTING

POKING AROUND STICK

HUGH'S OLD WORKBOOTS

PINESOL TO CLEAN BOOTS

Ok. So I get a little stinky. Every few weeks I take my diving clothes to the neighbourhood coin laundry to clean away the gunk and $#it.

And I do have an amazing superheroine sidekick: Caped Crusader Candy!

She loves when I draw her like this. Well, let's face it. The kid loves to be drawn. And photographed. And watched. No wonder she's in dance. Candy is a born little show-off. Destined for the spotlight. Attention-seeking little brat.

Gawd, I love that kid!

Anyway, as my trusty sidekick while we're shopping at D-Mart, it's Candy's job to watch out for winos, the law, shopkeepers, and other dumpster treasure seekers. We have an excellent system of signals: a low whistle means "unknown approaching"; a two-hander means "cop sighting"; a loud whoop means "impending danger from angry, broom-wielding supermarket manager." It's great! We've had some narrow escapes involving squealing bike tires and screaming little sister. But we haven't been caught yet. An unbroken record when we work together.

But I do sometimes work alone. Long after Candy's in bed and dreaming of her Broadway debut. At night and in the dark with a flashlight, my torch, as Hugh calls it. And I've had encounters on a few occasions. By a competitor who was cranked up and crazy, who swung at my leg with a two-by-four. Lucky he didn't break my kneecap. I got away on my bike, but man was I bruised and sore. Another time by a couple who'd decided that the shadows cast by the dumpster were perfect for their um... paid liaison. I had to wait in the disgusting dive-bomb while they did it. It only took minutes, but it stank like hours. Thought I'd puke before they split. And once I was chased by a cop on foot patrol. It could've been exciting except the cop was donut-round and slow as hell. Escape was easy. I was on my bike. He was puffing behind me. I seized my opportunity. Ducked between buildings and gave him the slip.

Usually, when I go diving alone, I'm looking for stuff to resell. Or I'm out tagging with my spray paint can and stencil. Or both, I'll admit. Sometimes I find contraband...

Stuff I've/we've found and resold:

- old record albums
- discarded CDs
- a bicycle
- a tricycle
- a baby crib
- toys
- men's magazines (I swear I only read them for the articles and then resold the things)

- porn dvds: *Babes at a Boston Tea Party* and *Ride 'Im Cowgirl* and my fave, *Go Down on Me, Moses* (our player was broken, so I just took these classics to the pawn shop, sight unseen, sadly)
- an old desk lamp that still worked
- hubcaps

Stuff I've/we've found and kept for ourselves:

- Princess Barbie (ok, guess who kept that)
- comics
- day-old donuts, still in the box
- a scarf we washed and gave to mom as a gift
- someone's discarded bouquet of still-fresh flowers we also gave to mom
- a vase, ditto
- a magazine holder (now in our bathroom)
- and of course, bottles and food that were almost at expiration but not quite
- oh yeah, and a gun

I know people would frown on me. But dumpster diving is an honoured practice that dates back to the Middle Ages. Ok. So there weren't dumpsters in medieval times. But there was garbage. Lots of it. And the poor have always been the garbage pickers. The first recyclers were rag and bone men and gypsies who sorted through the refuse of the rich and middle classes and took what they could to stay alive, eat and even make a living. I learned that in social.

So me and Candy are merely carrying on that honourable tradition.

And there *is* a code of honour for dumpster divers internationally. Basically:

1. Don't take what you can't use, stupid. Somebody else may need it more than you.
2. Don't take more than you can use. Ditto.
3. Don't take personal documents (to use the info illegally).

4. Get the hell out if you're discovered or asked to leave.

5. If you make a mess while digging around, clean up afterwards and put the trash back in the dumpster.

6. If you take something and find you can't reuse or resell it, recycle it or take it to the Ecostation – don't just throw it away in the trash again, like some lazy dumbass.

And over time, I've learned some pretty good tips about the sport of urban foraging:

- Monday nights are best for bargains behind the supermarkets. It's when they dump most of their food to make shelf room for the new week.

- University and college dorm dumpsters are treasure troves at the end of term.

- Cardboard boxes are your friends: a) they carry stuff; b) when flattened they're great sorting pads; c) they act as decoy if you're caught – "Oh, I'm moving and was just looking for boxes…"

- Sometimes just asking nicely will get you what you need. I know a certain supermarket manager who just hands me produce when I come to the back of the store.

- Cats and rodents will scatter if you bang first before diving.

- Never dive in head first. That's just a stupid and extreme prep-boy trick.

- Rich people throw out some incredible stuff. Like my CD Discman and headphones that are in perfectly good working order. I can't afford an MP3 player or the computer to download tunes or anything like that, so my portable player has done me well. Especially when Santa (aka Candy and mom) gives me CDs.

So I've become something of an old hand at the game of alley surfing. The neighbourhood pawn shop owners know me by name. Mom thinks I get the extra food from money from my art (which is sometimes true, but not always). Hugh the Pugh-pig never complains when there's extra eats around. Candy and me spend quality time together, get some fresh air and exercise on our bikes. No injuries to date. Though I did get a tetanus shot at the Medicentre, just in case.

Sometimes it's not so fun. Like when I was attacked. When I put my hand in a pile of excrement. When I bruised my ribs leaning too far over the edge.

Sometimes it's scary.

Sometimes you don't find anything but spend long hours getting filthy and retching from the stench.

And sometimes you find a gun.

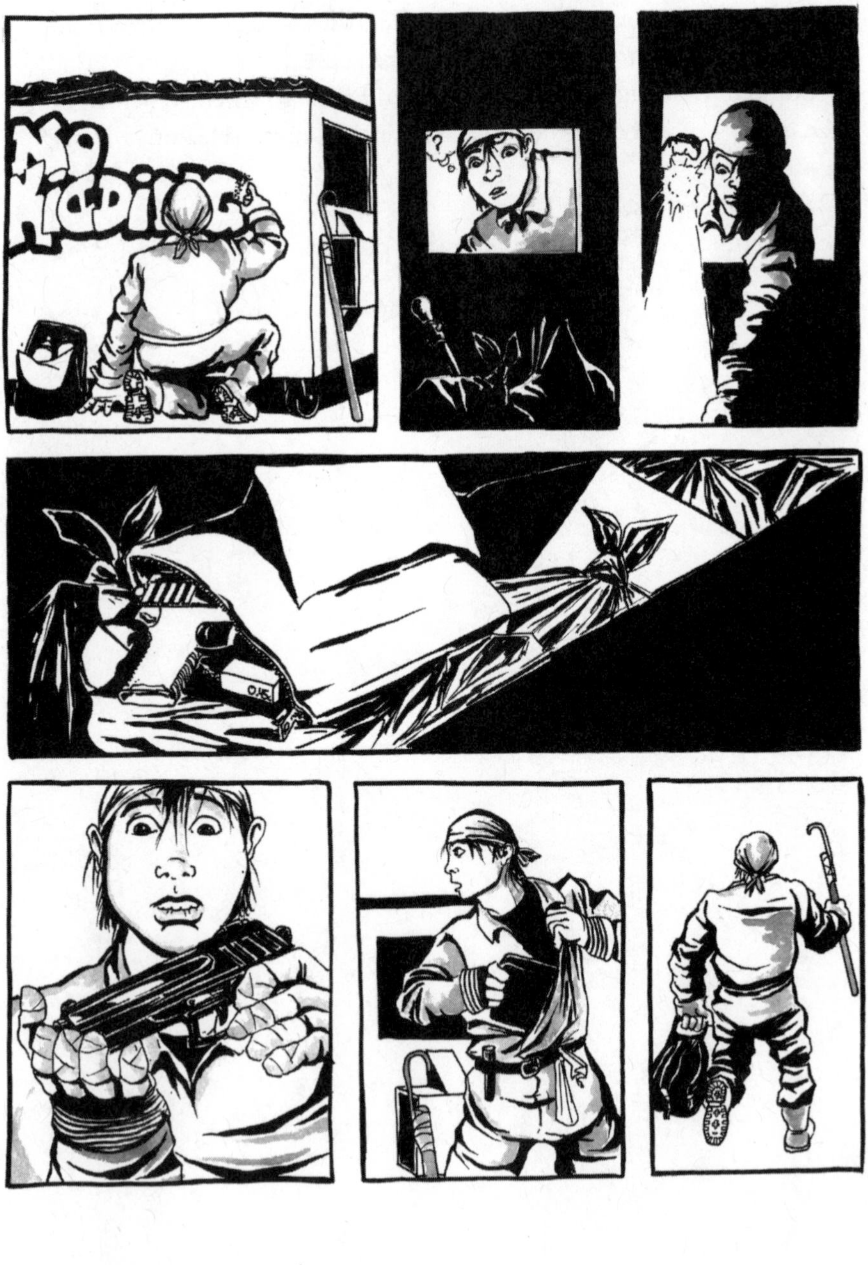

I dunno who would throw something that valuable out. Maybe he was gonna come back to fetch it. It's worth a lot of dough. That much I'm sure of.

And another thing I'm sure of. No one throws out a legally registered weapon.

So I'm now illegally in possession of an illegal weapon.

One more thing I'm sure of. A guy like me can use a gun like this. I've got my reasons. I've got my enemies. I may be invisible. Pretty much silent. An art geek. A feckin' loser stepson. But a gun has a loud voice. I'd finally be seen and heard with a gun. People would take Jamie Kidding seriously. At last.

So what am I not sure of?

When I'll use it.

But I'm sure I will.

D ipstick.
 Dweeb.
 Dirtbag.
 Dorkface.
 Dolt.
 Dunderhead.
 Dud.
 Dope.
 Dunce.
 Dummy.
 Dimwit.
 Dungbeetle.
 And that's only the d's. I could go through the whole alphabet after yesterday.
 She will never ever talk to me again.
 I am such a blockhead. (Insert Charlie Brown face here.)
 I blame the Kidding plumbing system. It's always been faulty and prone to plugging. Genetically, we're geared for constipation. And then when something moves us... well, be forewarned. It's a purgative experience. A potentially international fecal incident.
 And I blame Molly's baked beans. Her Sunday night special this week.
 My mom has a wicked recipe that apparently she inherited from my granny. It involves brown sugar and molasses and a bit of bourbon. (When there's any in the house that Hugh hasn't gulped down his gullet.) And, of course, beans. Lots of them. And whenever she makes these beans, well, I can't help myself. I have to have seconds. Sometimes

thirds. And well. My gluttony just causes problems further on down the line. The sewage line. Mine, that is.

So yesterday-Monday, after another lunchtime helping of the beans extravaganza—I was helping the drama teacher move the flats from storage upstairs to the drama room for painting. That's what I do. My extra-curricular contribution. Mr. Letterman told the drama teacher, Miss Sokolotosky, that I'm a good painter and she got the idea that I could be very helpful. So now I help with scenery and flat painting. Basically, whenever she tells me to. Like now. Because the drama class is putting on a play. Obviously. Some stupid musical.

I hate musicals.

Anyways. I was doing her bidding, moving about 800 flats from upstairs via the service elevator downstairs. It can only handle one or two at a time because I have to angle the flats.

Unexpectedly, who should be helping me, but her. The girl. Tatiana from social class. Tatiana Oleshenko.

The one I can't draw.

The one I can't stop thinking about.

Turns out she's the costume designer for the production. She was moving costume racks from storage, and then Miss S. roped her into helping me move the flats.

Now flats aren't heavy. They're made of canvas stretched over light wood frames. But they're awkward because they're about 8 or 9 feet high. So it was good to have the help.

Ok. It was great. To have her help. To have her near.

Because good gawd she smells great. Like vanilla. I'm not kidding. Just like it! And I know this because the scent of her just filled up the entire service elevator as we moved flats up and down. Up and down. While she talked and I mumbled lame-ass responses.

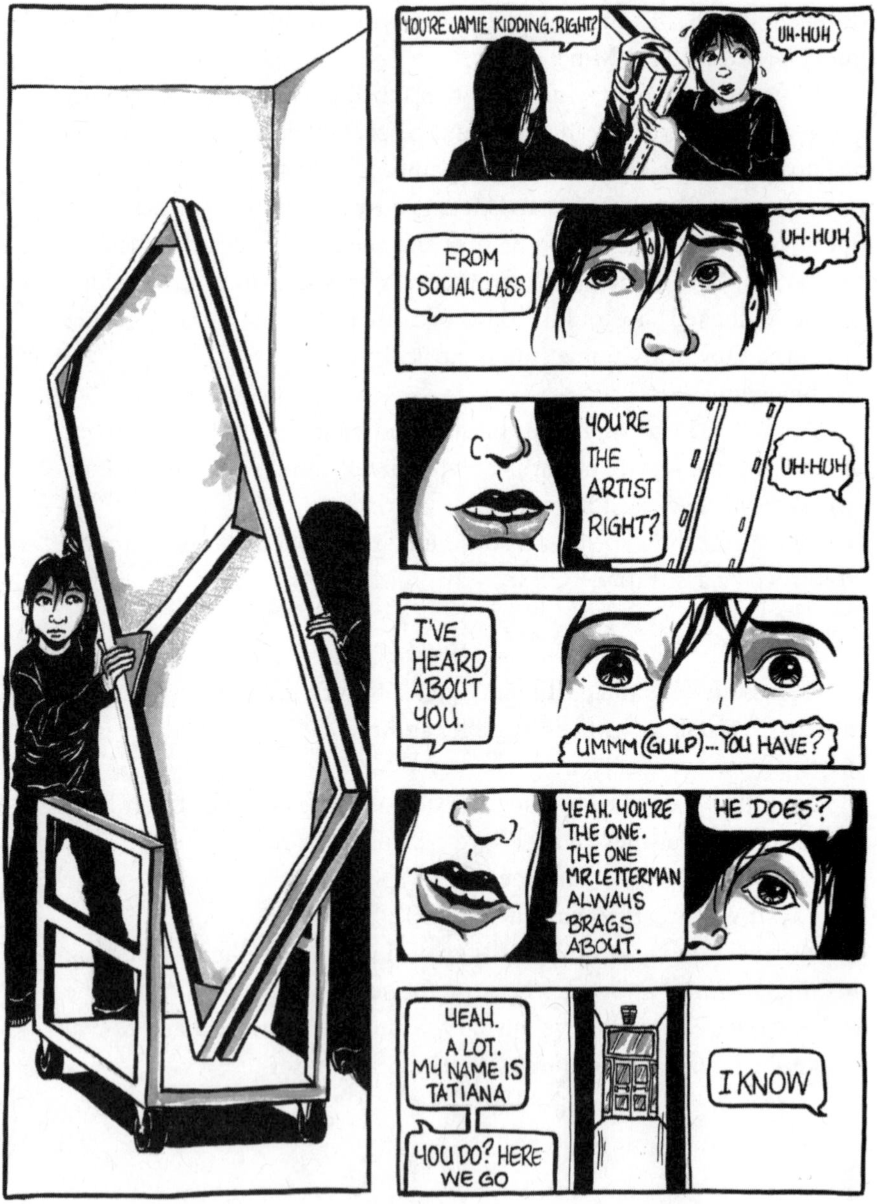
YOU'RE JAMIE KIDDING. RIGHT?
UH-HUH
FROM SOCIAL CLASS
UH-HUH
YOU'RE THE ARTIST RIGHT?
UH-HUH
I'VE HEARD ABOUT YOU.
UMMM (GULP)... YOU HAVE?
YEAH. YOU'RE THE ONE. THE ONE MR. LETTERMAN ALWAYS BRAGS ABOUT.
HE DOES?
YEAH. A LOT. MY NAME IS TATIANA
YOU DO? HERE WE GO
I KNOW

Well, it pretty much went like that. And I pretty much never wanted the elevator rides to end. She asked me about my drawing and what I liked best. No one ever asks me what I like. But she did. And I told her that I love to draw anything, but my specialty is cartooning. We talked a bit about comics vs. cartooning, and she thinks there's a big difference. Just when I thought it couldn't get much better, she told me that she really likes comix, too. Collects them, even.

But then my stomach started rumbling. Despite my wishing otherwise, the intestinal complaints increased. So I began bargaining with my body. "Not now! Please bowels, not now! I'll up my fiber. Increase my roughage. Eat my broccoli. If only you grant me this grace."

But I could tell that my gut stirrings would not be stilled.

It was getting very hard to concentrate on what Tatiana was saying.

Finally, I told her that I'd go up to check for anything remaining in storage, myself. She looked a little hurt. But I had to get to a can. I felt like a heel, but I knew that if I didn't get away from her, I would do something mortifying.

Which, of course, I did anyway, didn't I?

She reluctantly agreed to organize the stuff we'd already brought down, take a stab at sorting through the costumes. I remember the doors of the elevator as they closed, framing her face. I could almost swear she looked disappointed.

And then. Well, I let 'er rip. Had to. The beans. The anxiety of holding it all in. The oncoming purgatious report of my bowels. And as I ascended, my heart sank. Because only then did I remember: no bathroom nearby on the second floor. There was only the storage area at this end of the school. Which stupid bean-counting architect thought that one up? I'm sure he saved the school thousands.

I stood briefly, shifting from foot to foot, considering my options. There was only one. To get back in the sulfurous elevator car and ride downwards to Hades.

Not to mention let a few more baked bean-inspired flatulents fly.

Quite frankly, I don't know when my farts have ever been so putrid. Usually, I'd find humour in the situation. Or at least find a way to somehow entrap and torture my little sister with such offensive odours.

But this was different.

I know it seems funny. But it wasn't. I was in pain. And terror.

Because exactly what I feared came to pass.

No pun intended.

The elevator doors opened. There stood Tatiana. She stepped into the elevator. I could see no other recourse but to bolt.

So I ran. Like the coward I am. I didn't look back. But I heard the elevator doors closing, engulfing Tatiana in my fumes. No doubt she died of asphyxiation.

I'll never see her again.

Even if she lived.

It's enough to make me want to put a gun to my head.

How could I ever face the girl of my dreams again, having doused her with the equivalent of two hydrogen bombs?

I can't even look at myself in the mirror. I'm that embarrassed.

What a complete and utter dufus! As I've said before. But it bears repeating.

The thought of returning to school makes me nauseous. I am dragging my heels this morning. Mom's yelled at me three times about being late.

Think I'll skip school. Run away. Go to live in some monastery where they eat a diet that does not promote flatulence. Except, of course, they'd probably eat beans. And we know that where that path leads is the surest way to hell. For Jamie Kidding anyway.

Aw, screw it! I've got a test this morning. I'll write it. Then tell the drama teacher that's it. I'm through with being artboy for the musical. Then I'll beat it to the park with this book.

I can't bear the thought of running into Tatiana...

Hours later...

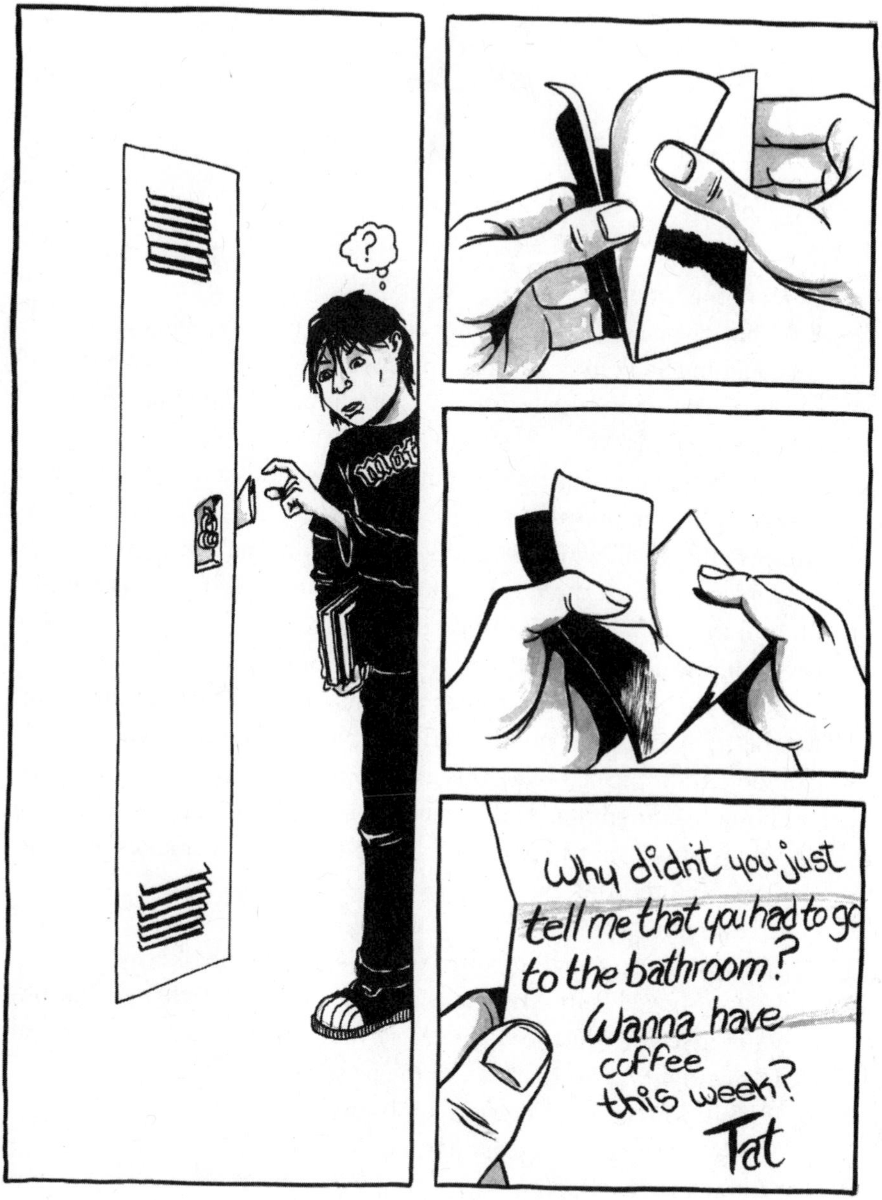
?
Why didn't you just tell me that you had to go to the bathroom?
Wanna have coffee this week?
Tat

"Who's this chick?"

That's when I swallow my hot coffee down the wrong pipe and begin coughing like I'm fit to hack up a lung in front of the only girl who has ever even noticed that I'm alive, on our coffee date that *she* asked *me* on, for gawdsake.

I know my grammar sucks, but that's the kind of moment it was. I wasn't really thinking about perfect parallelism, like Mrs. Sheen always stresses in English, which is hardly one of my best marks, anyways.

So I try to turn the page of my book, which Tatiana has insisted on looking at. Which gives me kind of mixed feelings—somewhere between a warm glow and abject terror. Because no one really looks through my book. I show things to Mom and to Candy. Sometimes Mr. Letterman. But at my discretion. I pick and choose what people can look at. But jeez. Here's this girl flipping along through my treasure book like anything. And I'm letting her. And she comes across the drawings of her that I can't quite complete. And she makes assumptions. And. And. And.

I'm an idiot.

Finally, I stop coughing after she tells me that she knows first aid and asks if I need help. My face is a shade of blushing that she's probably never seen. I must look like a big red pimple. Once she's assured that I'm alright, she turns back to the page.

"Well, who is she?" The girl never gives up.

"Just someone—in a class of mine."

Tatiana keeps flipping.

"Hey! These are my boots! Sick!" Then she turns her perfect eyes onto me. "Why are you drawing my boots?"

"'Cause I think they're interesting."

"Do you have a footsie fetish? I've heard about guys like that."

"N-no."

"Can I have this?"

She wants the picture of her boots. I can't believe it.

"I-I..."

"Of course, I get it. You don't want to tear something out of your book. Maybe you could give me a photocopy."

I nod and try to think of a way to tell her how flattered I am that she wants a drawing of mine. But I just keep my stumbling mouth shut and watch her turn pages.

"Wow! This is a great sketch of Attaman and his goons. Way to go! I loathe that guy."

Who talks like that? Loathe. Smart girls, that's who. Thinking that I'm glad not to be on the receiving end of her loathing, I get up to buy us two more coffees, since Tatiana bought the first round. We're in one of those fancy-ass coffee places where the leather chairs and burnished wood tables and the sagebrush walls come out of designer magazines and the coffee costs a week's wages. I come back to our cosy little table near the fireplace, wondering if I'll ever have a fireplace in my own pad. One day when I'm a famous artist with a loft apartment. I'll have a fireplace then and Tatiana can come over. Hell, maybe she'll move right in. I can imagine us lying together in front of my fireplace. Except maybe it's against fire code to...

"Jamie!"

Tatiana interrupts my thoughts and I spill the sugar I've been pouring in my cup. Millions of granules spread everywhere. Just in time she rescues my book, lifting it off the table and safely away from the crystals.

"Sorry. I-er upset your coffee ministrations."

Who talks like that?

"It's ok. Thanks for sparing my book."

She uses one hand to help me clean up, holds the book safely in the other. I'm blushing again at her attention. Why can't I ever be cool around this girl who talks like an encyclopedia?

When the table is clear, she resumes where she left off, opening to a page where I'd sketched a preliminary strip for the school newspaper.

"I knew it! You, Jamie Kidding, are the comic strip artist."

Tatiana looks right in my eyes. Hers are green. And perfect, did I mention? Mine are nervous and flicking. I probably have a twitch in my cheek muscle, too.

"Umm..."

"Never mind. Your secret's safe with me! I love your work!"

And right then I know that I love this girl. I've always well...had the hots for her. But I can feel I'm on some high precipice (my new word this week) and about to free fall. To hear someone say, "I love your work." Isn't that every artist's dream? Does that make me a real artist? In her eyes? In my own? And then I say the first intelligent thing I've said all afternoon.

"Thanks."

"You're welcome." She flips a lock of that black sheen hair. "Draw me something."

"Huh?"

"Anything." She turns to a new page. Shoves the book over to me. Waits expectantly.

I feel naked.

But I take out my Pilot Hi-Tecpoint V5 black pen and begin.

First I draw Attaman:

FANTASY

Tatiana watches me closely. My hand. My face. I try not to let her affect me. It's hard. But eventually, I get into the spirit of the piece. I offer her the book. She looks at the drawing and groans, rolling her eyes. I take the book back. Turn one page. Then another.

Sometimes I do that. It helps to create a blank slate.
I draw Attaman again:

REALITY

This time, when I turn the book towards her, Tatiana bursts out laughing. It's a great sound. Kind of like pealing bells. I grin and chuckle with her. Wow. When did I last feel so good?

Freefalling...

"Wow! I wish I could show Georgie this."

Splat!

"Georgie?"

"My boyfriend. He's 21. Works at Alternative Video where I do. He's my boss."

Shit. The pealing bells turn to tolling bells. "Oh."

"I know. A video store in this day and age of Netflix and piracy? It's positively inconceivable! But we specialize in undiscovered gems —foreign films, documentaries, stuff that mainly gets screened at independent film festivals. We fill a niche market. Just like an indie record or bookstore. Georgie is a real eclectic expert. He took film studies at university before he decided to take some time off."

She must see how disappointed I suddenly look.

"Hey, it's ok for me to have friends. Georgie wouldn't hurt a fly. And just because he's my boss at the store, doesn't mean he's the boss of *me*."

I shrug and close my book. This was just a coffee. How did I ever allow myself to think otherwise? Who am I Kidding?

We walk out of the snooty coffee place. Our day has turned overcast. She climbs on her bike. I climb on mine. The cool wind is definitely unfriendly. Promising snow and misery. What else do you expect in mid-December?

"Thanks. I had a nice time." She tries to keep her hair from flying up in a gust.

"Me, too." I'm wishing to make a fast getaway. Wishing she'd dump Georgie for me. Wishing I could touch that black hair. Wishing we could ride off into the sunset together.

Then she smiles. When Tatiana smiles, the clouds part. But her smile makes my heart ache.

She rides away. I watch her.

Not for me.

This little refrain plays over and over. In my head, until I want to blow it off.

The next day at school I tried to avoid Tatiana. But she deliberately sought me out at my locker.

"Are you painting for Ms. Sokolotosky after school today?"

"I guess." I closed my locker door and fiddled with the lock.

"Good!" She pushed her midnight hair from her face to look at mine. I couldn't meet her eyes. I knew that would kill me. "You ok?"

I turned to walk down the hall and Tatiana was beside me, her boots in step with my sneakers. She repeated her question, "Jamie, are you ok?"

There was no time to answer because suddenly Attaman and the stooges appeared before us.

"Hey, Kidding! I hear you're painting for the musical. Ms. S. sure has you whipped, Artfag."

"Attaman!" Tatiana speaks up beside me. I'm both thrilled and embarrassed. "Anyone who knows anything, knows Jamie Kidding is not gay. And even if he was, it wouldn't matter, you homophobic loser!"

Despite her courage, Tatiana was really not improving the situation.

"Your little emo-girlfriend fighting your battles for you now, Kidding?"

"She's not my girlfriend, asshole."

Well, that about did it. Suddenly, I was against the lockers. I felt the weight of a Hummer H3 on my chest. My fingers were twitching. If only they had a trigger. But I only had a sketchbook.

"You'd better show me some respect, Kidding." I felt his alpha-male spittle on my face and his knee too near my groin.

"I c-can show you something else."

"What'dya say?"

"Man, he's asking for it, Attaman." One of the bulkboys was hissing in my ear. My head was starting to spin from the force on my ribcage.

"N-no really. I have something to show you."

The pressure eased ever so slightly on my chest. I took a deep breath.

"If you're yanking my chain, Kidding, I'll yank your dick right off." Attaman whispered menacingly.

But he released me. And I seized my advantage. I couldn't run. A crowd had gathered, sensing blood. The goon patrol was strategically planted, ready to rip off my limbs in the narrow hallway. And Attaman was poised for battle, his brute fists clenched.

So I did the only thing I could do. I opened my book to the drawing of Attaman.

Not the one of him as infant. That would have meant certain death.

But the other, flattering sketch: "Fantasy."

Attaman grabbed the book from my hands. I dreaded him turning past the next blank sheet. My safety blanket page. But he just looked at the one picture. Looked at me. Grinned at his buddies.

"Hey! I think ya captured me just right, Artdude."

Artdude. That was new. Less…lethal sounding.

The Attaman attaboys were gathered round now, slapping El Capitan on the back. Others in the gathered throng were craning their necks for a glimpse.

And then Attaman did the unthinkable.

RRRRIIPPP!

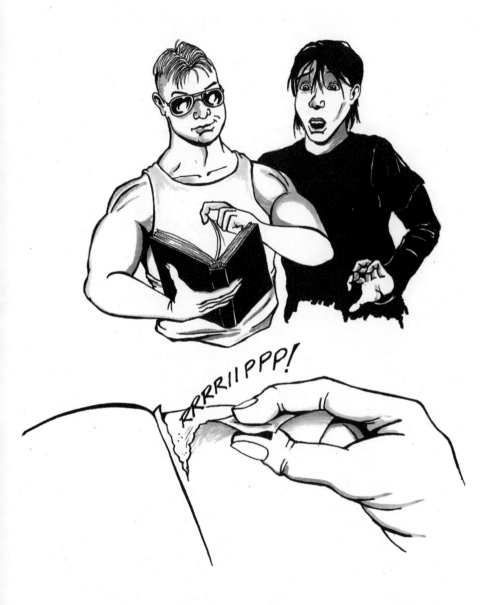

I felt violated—like I might even be sick. But I kept my face absolutely poker straight. He still had my book in his grubby fingers. He could do worse damage. Much worse.

Or he could turn another page and see what I really thought of him. And that would be the end of life as we know it for Jamie Kidding. So I kept my stupid mouth shut.

"I'll be keeping this." Attaman's smirk was crooked and ugly. Proudly, he held the image up for the crowd to see. Laughter rippled through the ranks. A smattering of applause.

"Ok, break it up, whatever it is!" Mr. Causington's voice boomed along the hallway. The principal was making his way towards us so the group immediately dispersed.

Attaman shoved my wounded book into my gut. Then he folded my Fantasy picture into his backpack and took off with his idiot posse down the adjoining hall.

I nearly fell to my knees with grief and relief. Tatiana linked her arm in mine and took me into the stairwell away from the principal and any other gawkers. I lowered myself to the stairs. I was kinda in shock.

"You ok, Jamie? I mean it!"

I couldn't find any words. I was that afraid of crying. Over her. Over my book. Over the danger I'd just averted. I guess I barely nodded.

Sighing, Tatiana sat down beside me. "That was some smart thinking. But it cost you, didn't it?"

I nodded again.

"I'm sorry about your book."

"It's ok," I croaked.

"No. No, it isn't ok. But you'll be."

That was it. I had to leave. I know she probably thinks I'm a rude bastard, but I just couldn't face this girl and my feelings about her and my loathing—yes, that's the word—for Attaman and the seething anger that was roiling up in me. Nothing worse than turning into a bawling baby. Especially in front of the girl I love but will never have.

I gritted my teeth. Stood up. Slammed out of the stairwell exit and into the chill. Didn't stop to do up my coat or watch for traffic. Just blasted home. Up the stairs and into our grotty apartment. Hugh was passed out in his threadbare lazyboy.

Attaman has a piece of my heart stuffed into his backpack. Tatiana has another piece. I wonder how much aortic capacity I have left.

So I did what I always do when I'm feeling particularly f#$ked or f$%ked up. The only thing I can do.

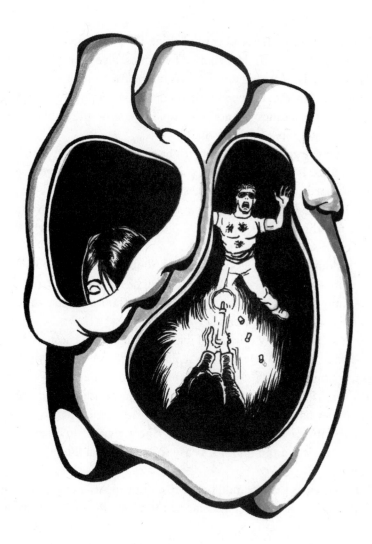

F a la la la la la la la friggin' la.

If I hear one more freakin' carol, I think I'll shoot someone!

Candy dragged me to the hell mall five times. Five times we pushed through the herds. Watched cranky kids in line for Santa and the tired elves slinging cameras. Listened to insipid muzak and overplayed versions of Christmas tunes. Wandered stupidly past bright displays and tinsel and glittery bits of the season.

When you've got limited dough, it's hard to make $$ stretch to buy Christmas gifts. It's hard to look at so much stuff and know you can't have it. It's hard to watch your little sister's face fall. So what else can a guy do? I loaned Candy $10 to help her buy *my* present. GraveRype had paid me, though, so I was ok. I did a poster for their New Year's show at the RockRoooom.

My Kidding sister has good taste. No doubt. She got me a 2-DVD special edition of *The Crow*. And also bought me a poster from the movie. Candy knows I'm a big fan. Especially of James O'Barr, the creator of the original comic series.

The main gift from Molly (and Hugh, though I don't know what *he* contributed) is a new DVD player to replace our dead VCR. May it RIP.

As Christmases go, this one wasn't bad. Nothin' like ten days off of school. Even Molly had a few days' vacation. The house smelled pretty great from her baking, which we all appreciated. Candy plastered the apartment with garlands and shiny shit. She goes a little crazy with the whole decorating thing. But it's easy to get caught up in her Candy Cane spirit.

One bonus was that we didn't have to endure the traditional Boxing Day dinner at Uncle Mac's. This year he took his wife and the terrible

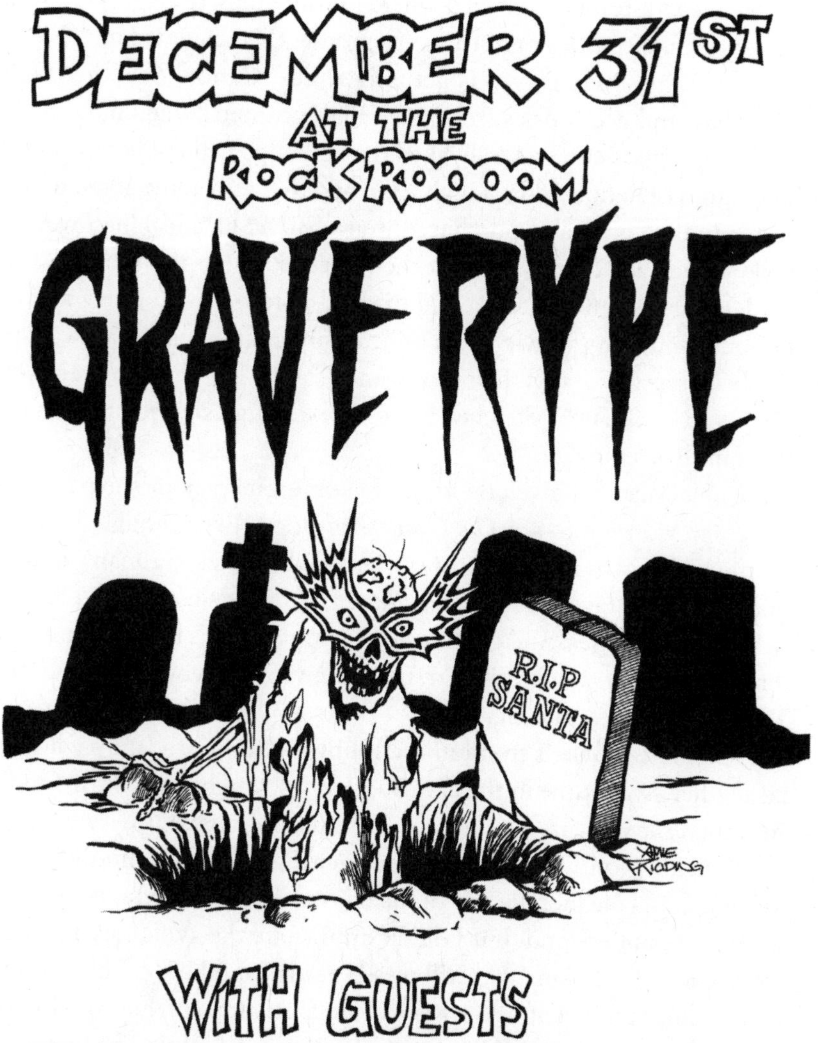
DECEMBER 31ST
AT THE
ROCK ROOOOM
GRAVE RYPE
R.I.P
SANTA
WITH GUESTS
DOORS 8pm TIX $10 ADV $15 AT THE DOOR

twinsome to a resort in Mexico where I'm sure they're all gorging at the all-you-can-eat buffet right this very moment. Feliz Navidad.

And Christmas Day was actually...nice. Candy loved her Hello Kitty bag and accessories from me. Hugh grunted some kinda thanks for his beer glass cooler. Molly liked the new slippers I got her to go with the indigo blue housecoat Hugh gave her. (He tossed me some money, so I actually chose and purchased it at HBC.) She and Hugh were all lovey-dovey. He even helped set the table for Christmas dinner. Molly made a turkey with dressing and mashed potatoes with gravy and her famous pumpkin pie. Me and Candy cleaned up. Then we all watched *A Christmas Carol* together. Molly and Candy, like they do every year, cried over Tiny Tim. I sketched in this book. Hugh snored. It was a perfect family evening.

Uncle Mac had given the sis and I some Cineplex movie passes for Xmas, so we went to see *The Graveyard Book*. Even though it's about a little girl, it was an excellent movie based on Neil Gaiman's book—one of Candy's faves. Gaiman is another of my comic heroes—I love his sick *Sandman* series. And the director, Henry Selick, is the same guy who directed *The Nightmare Before Christmas*. So we couldn't go wrong. The visuals were amazing.

After the movie, I stood in the lobby waiting for Candy who was taking her sweet time in the can. Suddenly, I caught a whiff of vanilla. And then *she* appeared before me: Tatiana Oleshenko.

"Ok. So I know you were upset. I get that. But you could've talked to me. Later, I mean. Like any of the days afterwards. I would've understood. I do understand. But I didn't appreciate the avoidance tactics."

Obviously, Tatiana was still pissed at me for taking off on her after that Attaman incident, the week before Christmas break. I really had tried to keep outta sight. Hers. Anyone's. Jamie Kidding: The Incredible Disappearing Boy strikes again.

"Sorry."

"Fine. Apology accepted. You were justifiably aggrieved. Attaman's a freak of nature."

I nodded. Smiled even.

GAIL SIDONIE SOBAT & SPYDER YARDLEY-JONES 87

Tatiana flashed hers. "What movie did you see?"

"*The Graveyard Book.*"

"That's where I'm headed. Georgie's got our seats, so I'd better motor. See you in the new year!"

"See ya." Georgie. I felt my popcorn coming up in my throat. What a stupid name. What a stupid ass I am for even caring.

Thank gawd for Candy. She relived the entire movie on the way home. Good distraction. Great kid.

I spent a lot of time with her over the holidays. We played board games. Watched bad daytime television. Made a stupid-ass snowman in front of the apartment building. On New Year's Eve, Molly had to work and Hugh had a standing bowling date with his punch buddies. So Candy and me were home alone. I let her beat me at Checkers three times, then I swooped in for a heart-stopping victory. But I let her win Snakes and Ladders. We ate chips and drank pop and watched *The Pink Panther.* Candy fell asleep. Little fart missed the big midnight moment while I was watching *The Crow.* I hauled her off to her bed. She looked pretty sweet snuggled in with her stuffed fuzzy friends.

Not a bad ending to the old year.

Until Hugh the Pugh came home pie-eyed and swinging. Mad about something in his small mean world. He connected once with my arm before I managed to push him into the bedroom where he passed out on the bed.

Now there's a nice purple map of Antarctica on my upper left arm.

Nothing my t-shirt can't hide. Molly won't notice. Hugh won't remember.

Happy friggin' new year.

My amazing life keeps getting better and better. I found out when I returned to school that I flunked my English essay. So then there was this tense after-school meeting between me and Ms. Gable and Mrs. Sheen. Ms. Gable with her eager counsellor toothy smile, saying I can do better. And Mrs. Sheen, English specs slipping down her nose, much less smiley, nodding and clucking her tongue in agreement. Therefore (transitional device), I feel shitty (word choice: miserable) because:

a) Firstly (transition to signal ranking), I don't really like English. Even though I like words, reading long stuff like boring-ass novels (with no pictures) written by aged Canadian women just about drives me flipping crazy;

b) So (link ideas), I find it hard to care whether or not Hagar achieves self-actualization by the end of the novel. Discuss. This has absolutely nothing to do with how and where and why I am. Me. Jamie Kidding. But then, of course, who cares about any of that (rhetorical question)?

c) (Provide evidence for your position.) I suck at prewriting strategies. I suck at outlines (note new attempts at organizing my Jamie thoughts). I suck at the dreaded thesis statement. I suck at writing essays. And I mean really suck. (Use repetition only for emphasis.) I get started and then wander from the point. My topic sentences always bite. I sweat under pressure and suffer chronic brain farts. Then I start doodling in the margins. When I look up, the class is over and so is my time for the in-class essay;

d) (Add further emphasis.) I am trying but nobody—especially my
    English teacher who I can tell remains doubtful that I'm anything
    but lazy—gets this dyslexia thing I fight with;

e) (Use persuasive language.) Mrs. Sheen is about the most bland
    (think: stale white bread—no butter) teacher I have ever met
    and now I have to spend the next five days after school with her
    and her coffee-and-smoker's breath, re-planning and rewriting
    my stupid essay. This will make me: i) nauseous; ii) irritated; iii)
    late for painting the flats for the school musical which brings
    me to the final point of my misery. (Save your most emphatic
    point for last...)

f) In a word: Tatiana.

It's hopeless. I'm hopeless. And every time I see her, which is now
just about every day, my heart behaves stupidly, erratically, irration-
ally. Hopelessly.

On a scale of one to ten, my life is a minus ten.

(Be sure to illustrate your point with evidence from the text.)

What does the Incredible Disappearing Boy do after such an excremental day? He picks up his little sister from dance school. Walks her home through the snowdrifts. And the conversation goes something like this:

"Hi Jamie. Guess what? I get to be the bee in the spring dance show. Isn't that cool? I'm other things, too, in other dances, but I really wanted that part in that dance 'cause I get to dance among all the flowers. And it's kind of an important part 'cause bees are very important, you know. We learned in science that bees are necessary for pollination. The scientific name for the honeybee is *Apis mellifera*. And also we learned that bees are disappearing and scientists don't know why. Except that it might have something to do with insecticides and stuff that are killing all the insects or global warming and that's so sad, you know. So I'm really happy that I get to dance the part of the bee. I love bees. Especially honey bees."

"Uh huh."

"Oh, Mom says that we're going to Uncle Mac's for supper this Sunday."

"Great."

"I wonder if Richard and Victor got DDR for Christmas for their Wii."

"What's DDR?"

"Duh! Dance Dance Revolution. It's this really cool game that you dance to. And I'm pretty sure that Auntie Sue got it for the boys 'cause they're always playing video games and she's worried that they're getting love handles and she told me she'd use it, too, for her own. And also that since I'm a dancer I could come over and play it, too. Sometimes."

"Oh."

"So you'll have to try it, too. And Mom and maybe Hugh the Pugh. And then someday we'll get one."

Right, Candy. But I don't say anything. Allow her some dreams. Just listen to her rambling on and on. But I tune her out after a while. Not because I don't love her, but when she gets overexcited like this, it can wear a guy's ears out. And I have my own stuff to think about.

Like Tatiana. And the musical flats.

There I was painting away. After my essay DT torture. Doing my best imitation of back alley brickwork covered with graffiti (as if buildings today even use bricks, but we're going for a "feel" here or so Ms. Sokolotosky insists). And I signed my tag, just as I've done hundreds, maybe thousands, of times before in real alleys instead of on stretched canvas.

"I've seen that tag before."

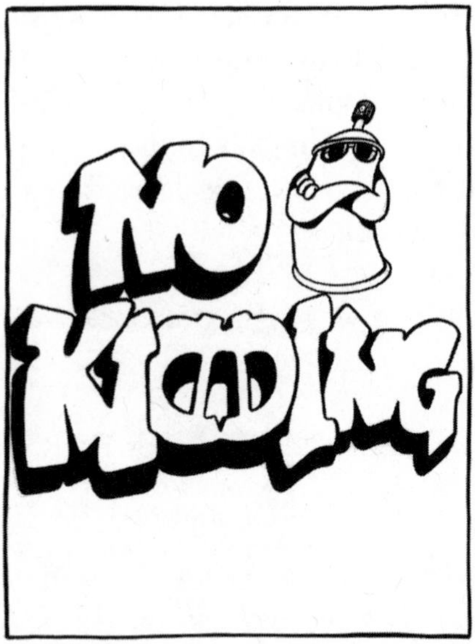
NO
KIDDING

That voice. Sent shivers. I'd been hoping-dreading running into her. Though there's every likelihood, every day, because of the musical, even though I halfways avoid her. Plus I'd already seen her in social class. Social has become both my most awaited and feared class. She sits two rows away and in front of me. I can see the shimmer of her black hair. Can't take my eyes of it usually. She's been turning around to try to catch my attention periodically, but I bury my head in the textbook pages that swim like mush before my eyes. Part of me would like to quit the musical, but of course, another part of me lives for it. For her.

"Yeah, Jamie. No doubt! In the alley behind the place where we had coffee."

Busted.

"That's you, right, Jamie?"

"I guess."

"What else have you done?"

"Those flats over there." I nodded to the corner.

"No! I mean out in the world. The streets. What have you done?"

I wondered to myself what I should tell her. About dumpster diving? Tagging? Spray painting? My graffiti places? My book? My screwed-up family? The gun? And I want to tell this girl everything. I want her to care. I want Tatiana to see me.

Instead I said, "Some stuff. Sometimes."

"I'd like to take a look someday."

But I'm not convinced. I'm wary of this black-haired beauty and her pretend interest. Tatiana, who belongs to some twenty-one-year-old video store manager named Georgie, a guy with an income and who studied film. What's her game, I wonder. Friendship she said. But who ever wanted to be friends with Jamie Kidding? At least since high school started and I changed schools. My other friends went to the other district school and that pretty much ended that. They sorta dropped outta my life. Since then…nada. No amigos.

So why her? Why me? Why now?

I didn't get to ask (insert chickens clucking here) because Ms. Sokolotosky called Tatiana away for pinning and fitting the lead actress costumes. And I turned back to my mock tagging.

"Did you hear me?" I'm brought back to the walk home and my little sister.

"Huh?"

"Why aren't you listening to me? I said 'like Sailor Moon?'"

"Sailor Moon?"

"My birthday present!! I want a comic strip about Caped Crusader Candy Moon!"

"Candy Moon?"

"Yeah, like Sailor Moon. Only it's me! Get it? And I save the planet from the dark forces threatening the bees and the entire world. And you can be my sidekick, ok?"

"Umm…better just stick to your own story. Be the solo heroine."

"Ok. But it's in a week, so you have to get working, 'cause sometimes you leave stuff to the last minute and I want my present on time this year!"

"Fine. Fine. I'll get on it tonight."

So here I am. Slaving over a manga strip about Candy Moon and not having much luck. Given this day, it's no wonder. But I'm trying, for Candy's sake.

I've drawn lots of cute comics for her before.

Candice Kidding has been a featured heroine in Kidding comic adventures since she was a baby. But now she wants manga, which is all reversed and complicated for a Canadian cartoonist. But I'll give it my Jamie best.

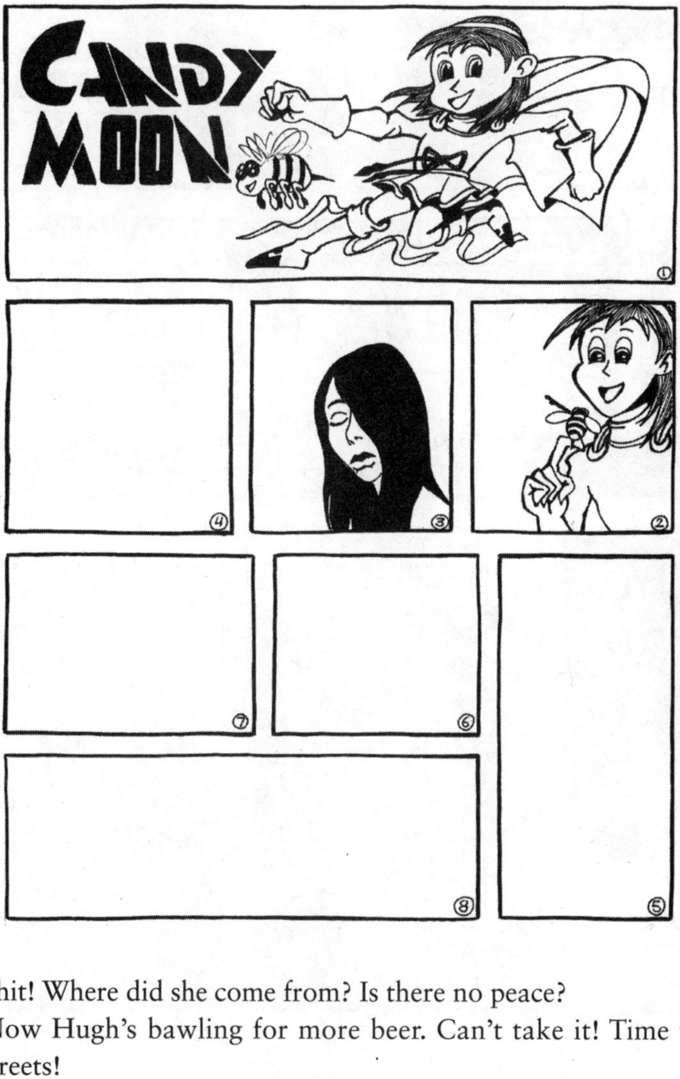
CANDY MOON

Shit! Where did she come from? Is there no peace?

Now Hugh's bawling for more beer. Can't take it! Time to hit the streets!

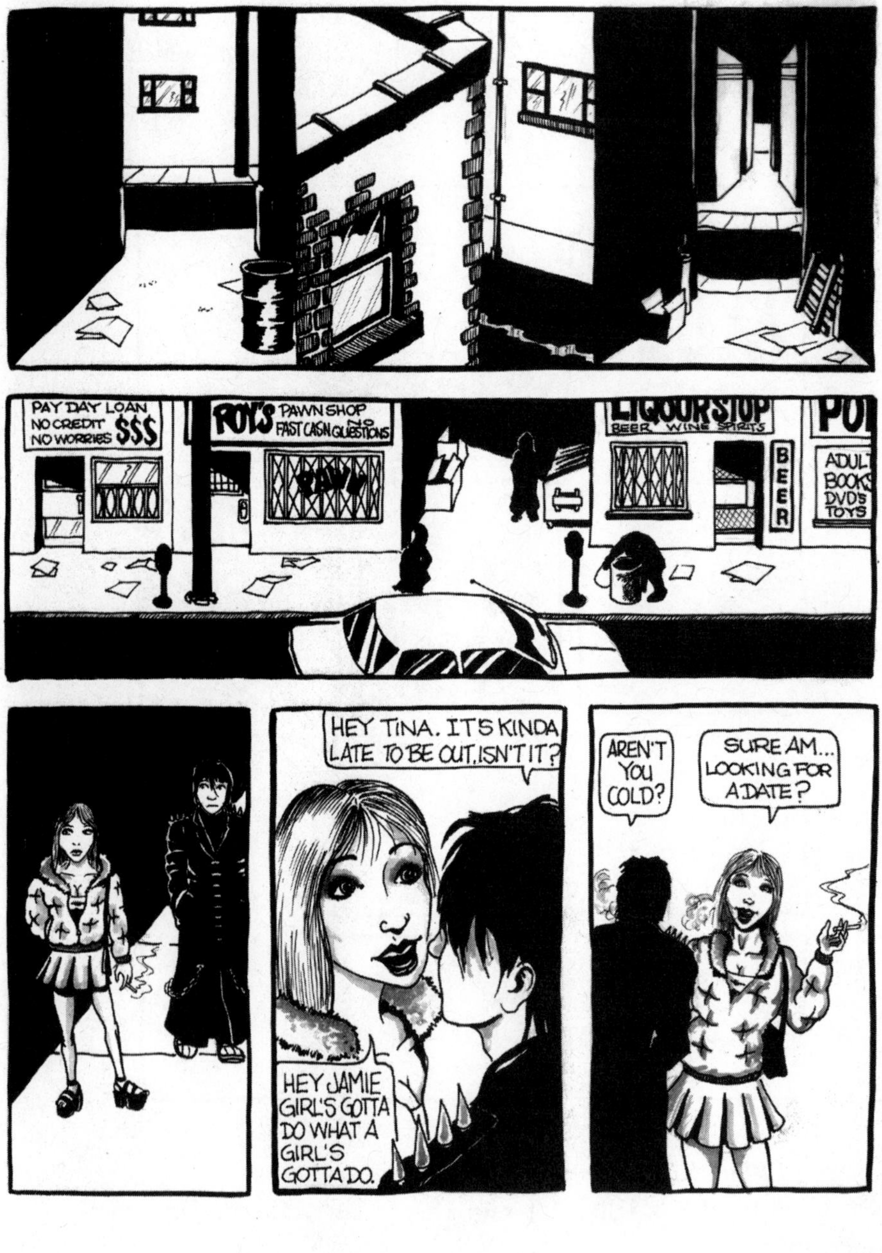
PAY DAY LOAN
NO CREDIT NO WORRIES $$$
ROY'S PAWN SHOP
FAST CASH NO QUESTIONS
PAWN
LIQUOR STOP
BEER WINE SPIRITS
BEER
ADULT BOOKS DVD'S TOYS
HEY TINA. IT'S KINDA LATE TO BE OUT, ISN'T IT?
HEY JAMIE GIRL'S GOTTA DO WHAT A GIRL'S GOTTA DO.
AREN'T YOU COLD?
SURE AM... LOOKING FOR A DATE?

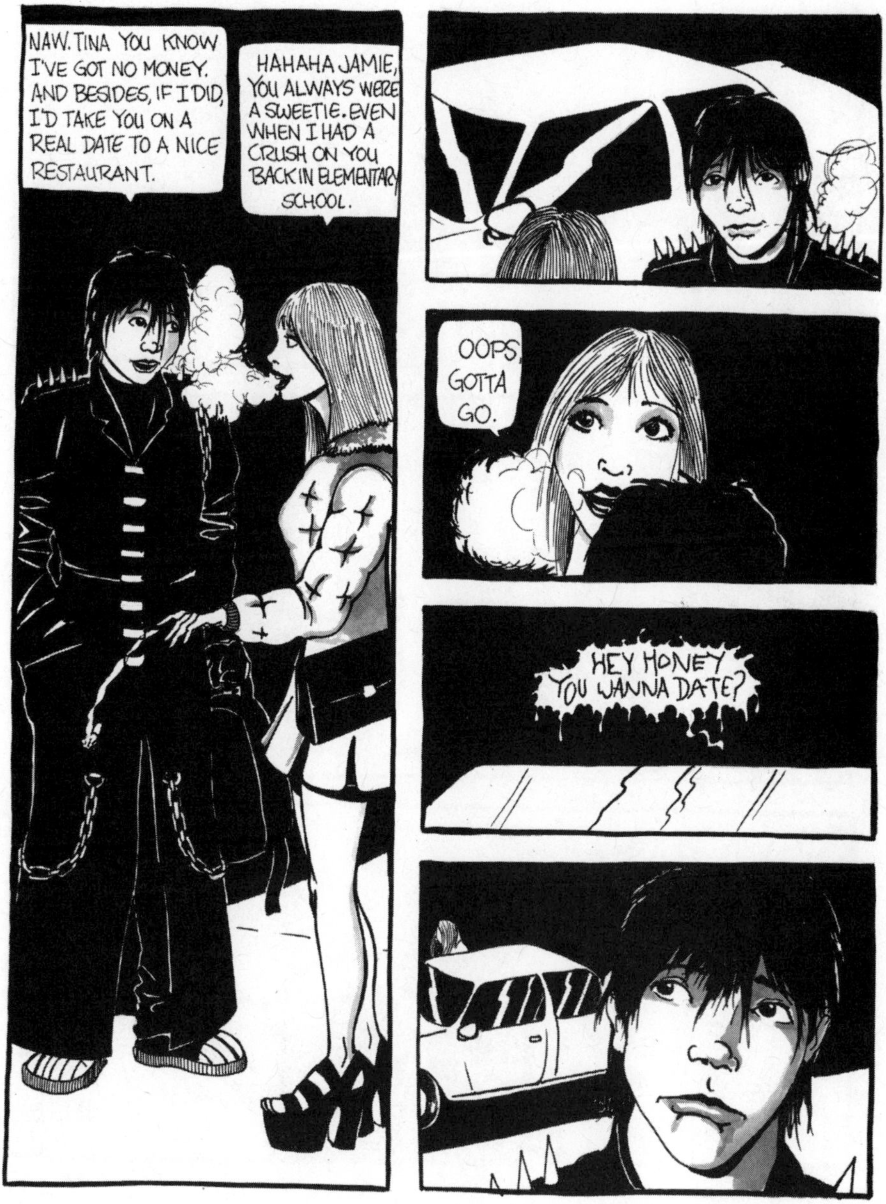
NAW. TINA YOU KNOW I'VE GOT NO MONEY. AND BESIDES, IF I DID, I'D TAKE YOU ON A REAL DATE TO A NICE RESTAURANT.
HAHAHA JAMIE, YOU ALWAYS WERE A SWEETIE. EVEN WHEN I HAD A CRUSH ON YOU BACK IN ELEMENTARY SCHOOL.
OOPS, GOTTA GO.
HEY HONEY YOU WANNA DATE?

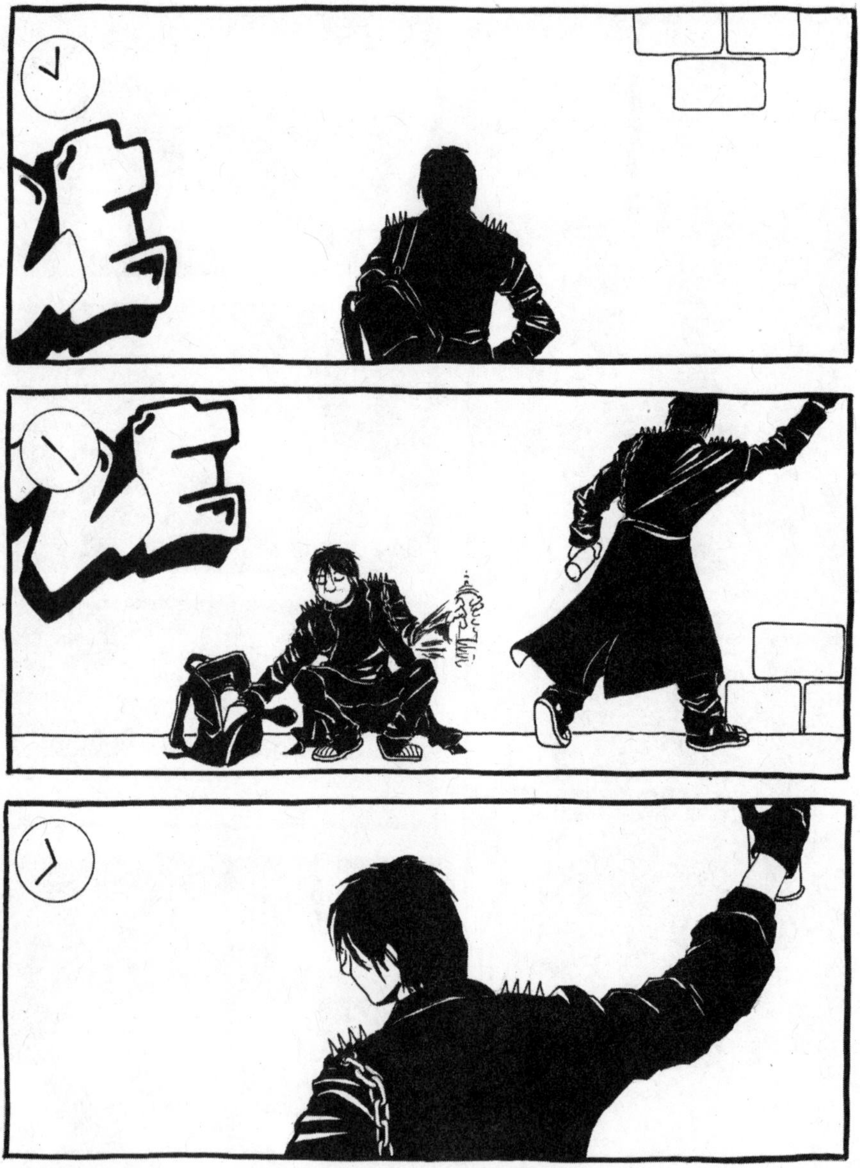

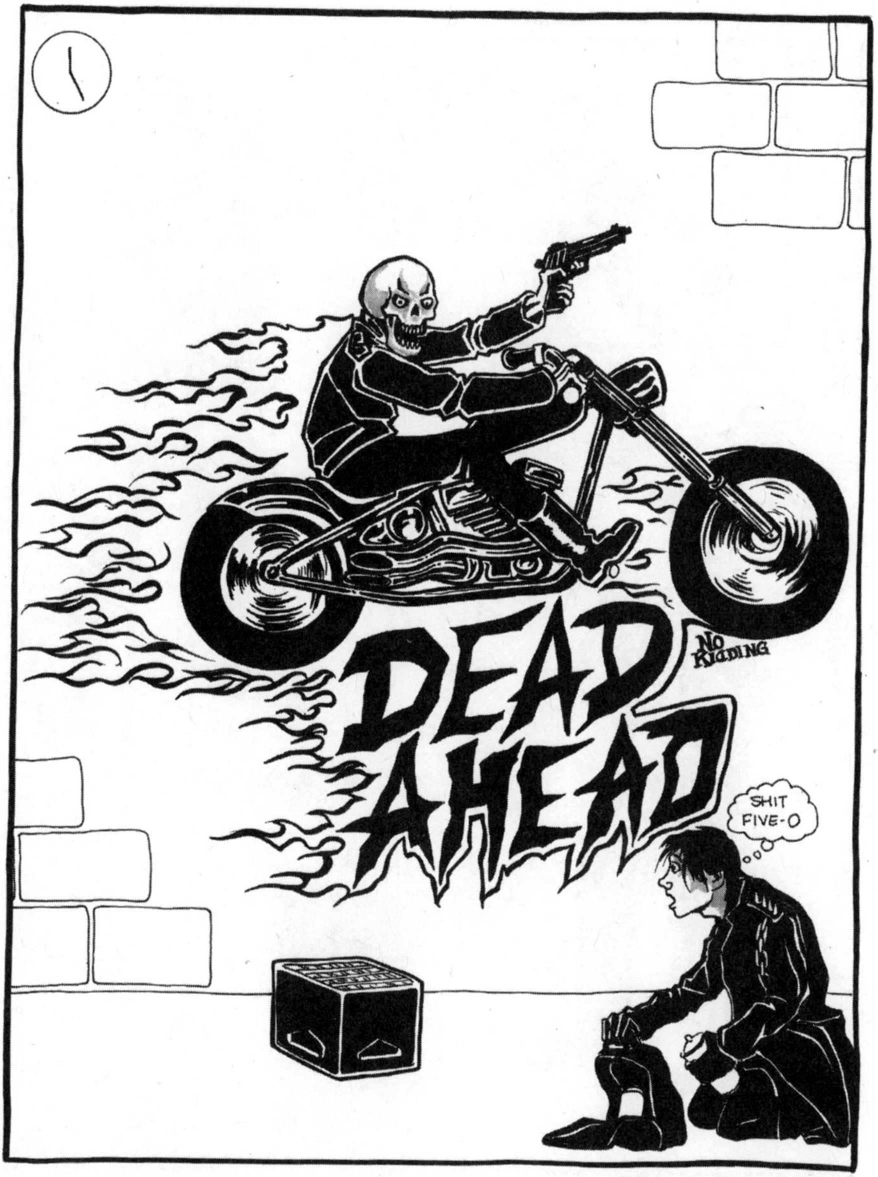
DEAD AHEAD
NO KIDDING
SHIT FIVE-O

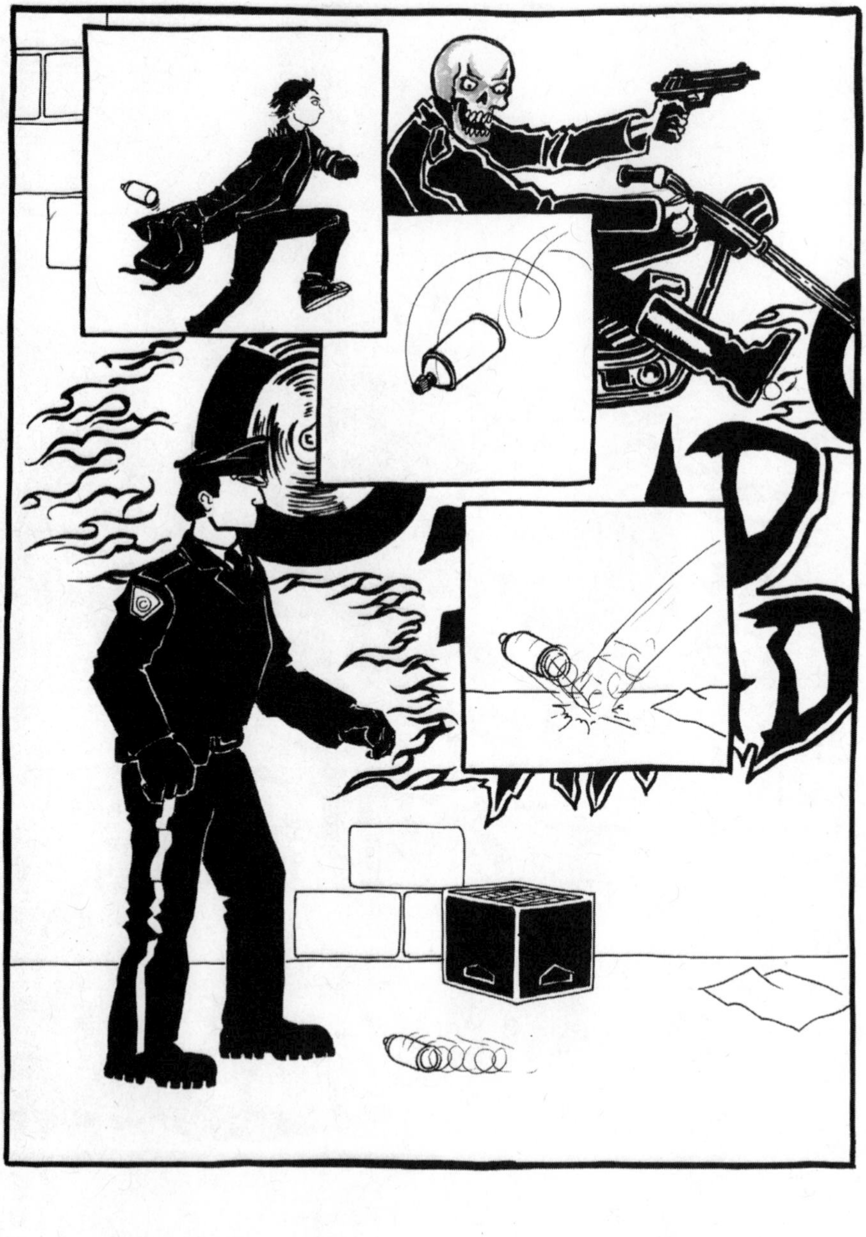

"Bang bang! Yer dead!" Vic and Dick, the little pricks, finger guns afire, slaughtered me for the umpteenth time this Sunday afternoon.

We were playing mobsters and I was the fall guy. What a surprise. At least we were outside in the newly fallen snow, getting some fresh air into the pudgy twosome for a change, instead of shooting at moving targets on a moving screen, endlessly. Candy and Aunt Sue and Molly were downstairs in the basement of my Uncle Mac's bungalow, playing *Dance Dance Revolution*. I could hear them hooting and squealing even out in the backyard. Uncle Mac in his parka was busy with burgers at the BBQ, standing in his huge Sorel boots in several inches of snow on the deck. Hugh, thank gawd, stayed home. He doesn't much like Uncle Mac. The feeling's pretty mutual.

I sat on the deck steps to catch my breath while Vic and Dick attempted to build a snow fort. That's when Uncle Mac decided it was time for his winter lecture. There are about four annually, corresponding with the seasons, though sometimes he throws in an extra one at Christmas or New Year's.

"Thinkin' about cutting that hair?"

"Not really."

"'Cause if people could see your eyes, you might be able to get a job."

I didn't say anything. He knows how my mom feels about me focusing on school, working on my art.

"It's important to see a person's eyes. Best way to make a sale. Look the customer square in the eyes. Gives the impression you're a straightforward kind of guy. Are you, Jamie?"

"Huh?"

"A straight-forward kind of guy?"

I wondered to myself what the hell he was getting at. Am I straight, as in not gay? Am I a straight-laced guy, just like my dear old uncle? Am I straight, as in not strung-out on drugs? Or all three? And what has my hair got to do with anything? Why can't adults talk straight themselves? Why do they muddle everything up? And why don't they listen?

I sure as shit will never tell Uncle Mac anything. He'd be about the last person besides Hugh I'd ever, ever turn to. Uncle Mac is most interested in hearing himself talk. Like most adults. Most people.

But Uncle Mac was waiting for an answer, and I nodded. He had more to tell me, I could see. So I got up and went over to help the hopeless twins erect a stupid fort. Seriously. Those two need to get out more. How hard is it to build a snow fort? But they couldn't manage it. So their big cousin came to save the day. And his reward? They shot him dead a few more thousand times, this time with finger guns and snowball missiles, until Aunt Sue called us in for supper.

Supper was the usual drudgery over at my uncle's. We listened to him bla bla bla about his amazing sales record. To hear him tell it, Uncle Mac should run the dealership if not the whole country someday. I secretly wonder if he's really all that well liked by his co-workers and superiors. His ego is bigger than a Ford one-ton truck. Who could stand that for long?

Apparently, Aunt Sue. She's been with him for fifteen years. No doubt fun-filled. Especially after she bore him the brats. Aunt Sue is nice and meek. I'm sure that suits Uncle Mac just fine. She makes good pie, though. And at least she smiles at me and my mom and Candy. Which is more than I can say for Uncle Mac. He wears a perpetual (new word of the week) scowl.

And I could see he wanted to continue his lecture series with me. But I didn't give him the chance. Didn't meet his eyes. Got up to help Aunt Sue clear the table. Beat it to hang with my little sister and cousins until it was time to go home.

Back to the northeast side. Where we live and he doesn't.

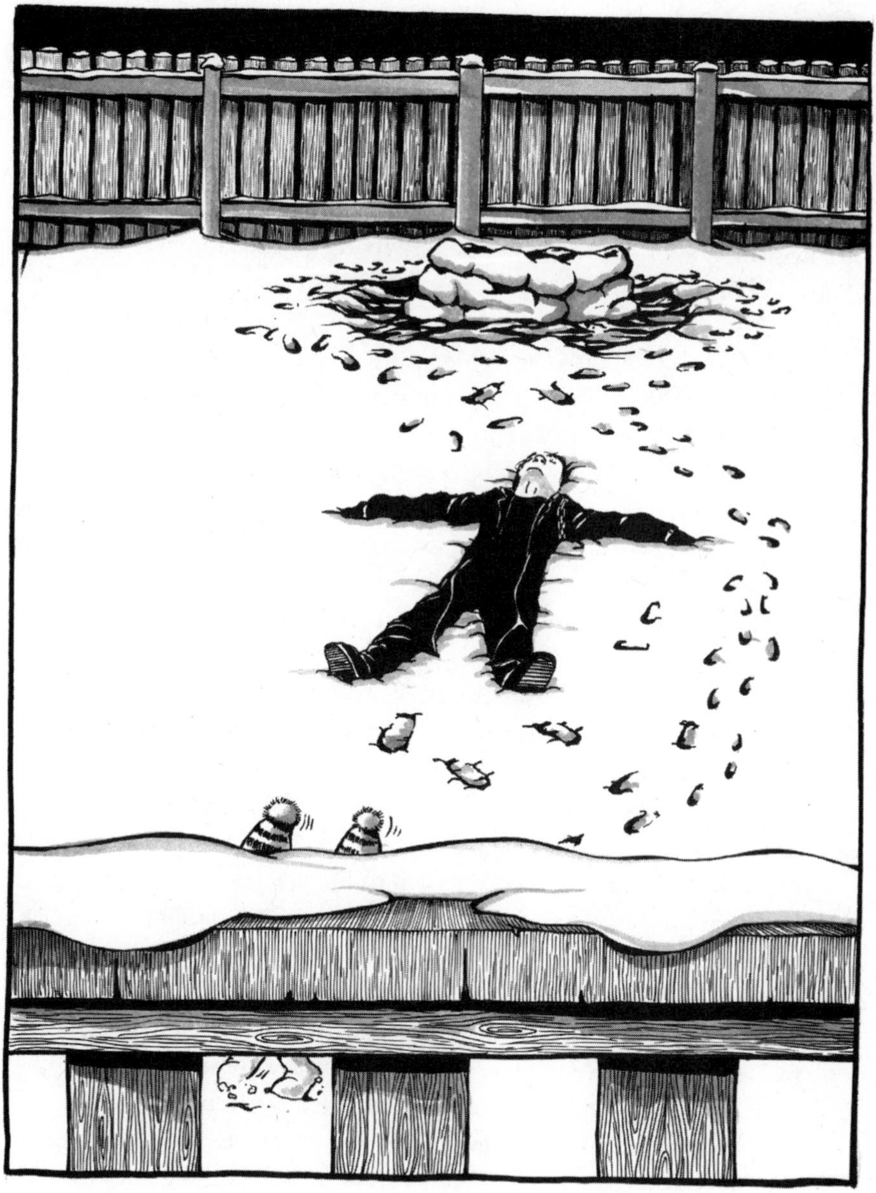

When he closed his SUV door on our backs, I'm sure he returned to his comfortably numb life and forgot all about us, conveniently. Until next time his conscience (read: Aunt Sue) reminds him he has a sister and a family who have a lot less.

We've invited them over to our apartment, but they never come. Never will. Uncle Mac would never venture out this way. Not even for his sister. Not even to tell her how to fix up her life and her kids. Nope, not even to be Lord Smug.

And it's probably better this way, though I sense my mom would really like to talk with Uncle Mac or turn to him when she needed. But there's no talking with – there's only listening to. And she gets plenty of that and more from Hugh.

And so do I.

Like these bruises on my arm.

And the bruise along her jaw that she covered up with makeup so that neither Uncle Mac or Aunt Sue would notice. And they didn't. Mom's a great makeup artist. Aunt Sue is always too preoccupied with the twinbrats and cooking. Uncle Mac's master of being oblivious.

I wish I were a real superhero. I would have been able to do more to help my mom on Friday night...

As it was, I could only come between them. Try to deflect the blows of Hugh, who was on a drunken tirade against my mother, just home from her second job. I managed to ward off most of the blows intended for Molly. But she still took a punch to the jaw.

What kind of a son can't even defend his own mother?

A useless one.

But I've got a plan. Just a little one.

Like my twin cousins, I've been playing a bit of bang bang on my own. I found a place to target shoot yesterday afternoon.

It's an old gravel pit east of the city. I've biked out there before in the summer months. This time, because my ten-speed is parked for the winter, I rode the transit and LRT as far as they'd take me. Then I walked the rest of the way. I didn't mind. I like being on my own. With the gun.

And guess what? Jamie Kidding is not a bad shot. Not bad at all.

M aybe I'm a madman.
Madmen talk like I do. Write stuff like the words in here. Maybe they draw pictures, like mine. Draw up plans. Practice.

I'll bet they feel like there are very few choices in life. That not much makes sense. And that they are alone.

Are all madmen alone? Is that what drives them loopy?

Well, I'm alone. And sure as shit mad. For real. At lots of things. Lots of people.

Things and people I'm pissed at:

- Tina being forced onto the streets
- whichever asshole or addiction or both forced her there
- my stupid after-school English detentions
- Georgie, the video store manager, for snagging the sweetest girl in the world
- my stupid Uncle Mac
- Attaman, for defacing this book
- HP for his cowardly pie-eyed attacks on my mother
- Molly, for not leaving him
- me, for being an ineffectual loser and disappearing boy
- me, for never being enough
- the many and varied injustices of life and this world
- did I mention myself?

I know about the other guys with guns. Marc Lepine. Kimveer Gill. The kid from Taber, Alberta. Michael Slobodian. The school shooters in the States. I know how to look up their stories on the Internet.

But I'm not a woman-hater. A gun worshipper. A death-lover. A psycho cult member.

We do have some things in common.

I am an outsider. I'm different. I don't belong. I do wonder if I'm f#$%ed up enough to walk into school and just mow down a bunch of kids and teachers.

Sometimes I feel that much hate. And it scares me.

I think maybe I'm more of a sniper. An unpaid mercenary whose job it is to rid the planet of all the wastes-of-skin who pass for stepfathers or the steroid jockstraps or the pimped-up pimps on this planet.

Really, would the world be any worse without them?

I think not.

Me and Candy had an argument about it this week. Candy—ever the pacifist—is absolutely against capital punishment. She also doesn't believe revenge ever works. Hates and loathes war and weapons. Has joined the various peace and human rights movements on the Internet. Save the Children. Free the Children. Youth For Peace. The list goes on and on. Silly bleeding heart won't even kill spiders in the apartment. She catches them and puts them outdoors.

"Jamie, you think a bullet is the answer to a bullet? Where does that lead but to more and more bullets? Whoever wins, stupid?"

"I'm just saying, Candy, that the world would be better—safer even—without certain people. There are freaks and foes who need defeating out there."

"Now you're sounding like a bad comic book. Geez Louise, Jamie."

"You know it's true. Tyrants need to be taken down."

"With guns?"

"When necessary."

"And who gets to decide? Who gets to play God? And which God?"

For shite sake, the girl is smart. She gets honours in everything. Wins all the school awards. I know why she's on the school debate team. This week she wants to be a dancer and a lawyer. Little turd'll probably do it, too.

But…although I grasp what she's getting at, I don't see any of those grassroots organizations out there making much difference against the tyrants. I mean there are still gangbangers in turf wars with their AK-7s, drive-by shooters in suburban neighbourhoods and malls, taser guns flattening citizens, car bombs and suicide bombers killing teenagers at nightclubs or theatres or commuters on subways and buses, landmines blowing off limbs, planes flying into buildings, depleted uranium weapons and bullets poisoning Iraq and floating on the winds, more and more multinational plans for bigger better bombs and blinding laser weapons. All this, despite the efforts of the NGOs working for a de-weaponized world.

I may not be smart. But I pay attention. To the news. My social teacher and the current events he always crams down our throats. It pays to pay attention. You never know what could hit you.

Like Hugh's fists. There are still Hugh's fists.

Regardless of Candy's argument, I know that sometimes the hopeless and the helpless need to defend themselves and those they love.

If I had a rocket launcher…

Maybe I am a madman. Like those others. I dunno.

I've finished Candy the Caped Crusader Moon manga comic, just in time for her 13th birthday tomorrow. I think she'll like how I've pictured her. Crusader against injustice, pollution, the killing of bees. Caped Candy fighting the good fight on behalf of all persons battling injustice. No violence – nothing serious anyway. Just a few BOPs and SOCKs. Like the Batman TV series from the 1960s. A finger-wagging victorious heroine. Lessons learned by contrite villains. All restored to proper balance. Every honeybee at its proper pretty flower. Right up her little social justice alley. The story even finishes with a flourish: the dancing heroine!

I bought a card, and I wrapped up the artwork in that sparkly paper girls seem to like.

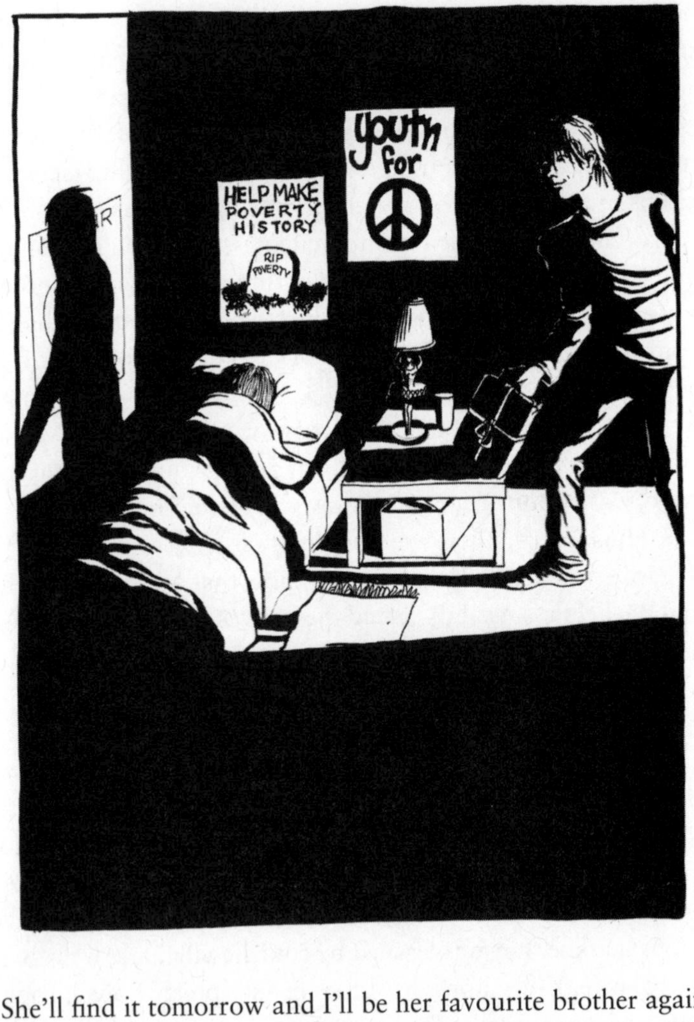
HELP MAKE POVERTY HISTORY
RIP POVERTY
Youth for

She'll find it tomorrow and I'll be her favourite brother again. It's true that Candy has been a little cool since the argument. But this present should do the trick. Win back her admiration. Nothing like a gift-wrapped bribe to convert the little sister.

Happy birthday kiddo. The world is lucky to have you.

I'm especially lucky.

And I swear I'd kill anyone who ever tried to hurt you.

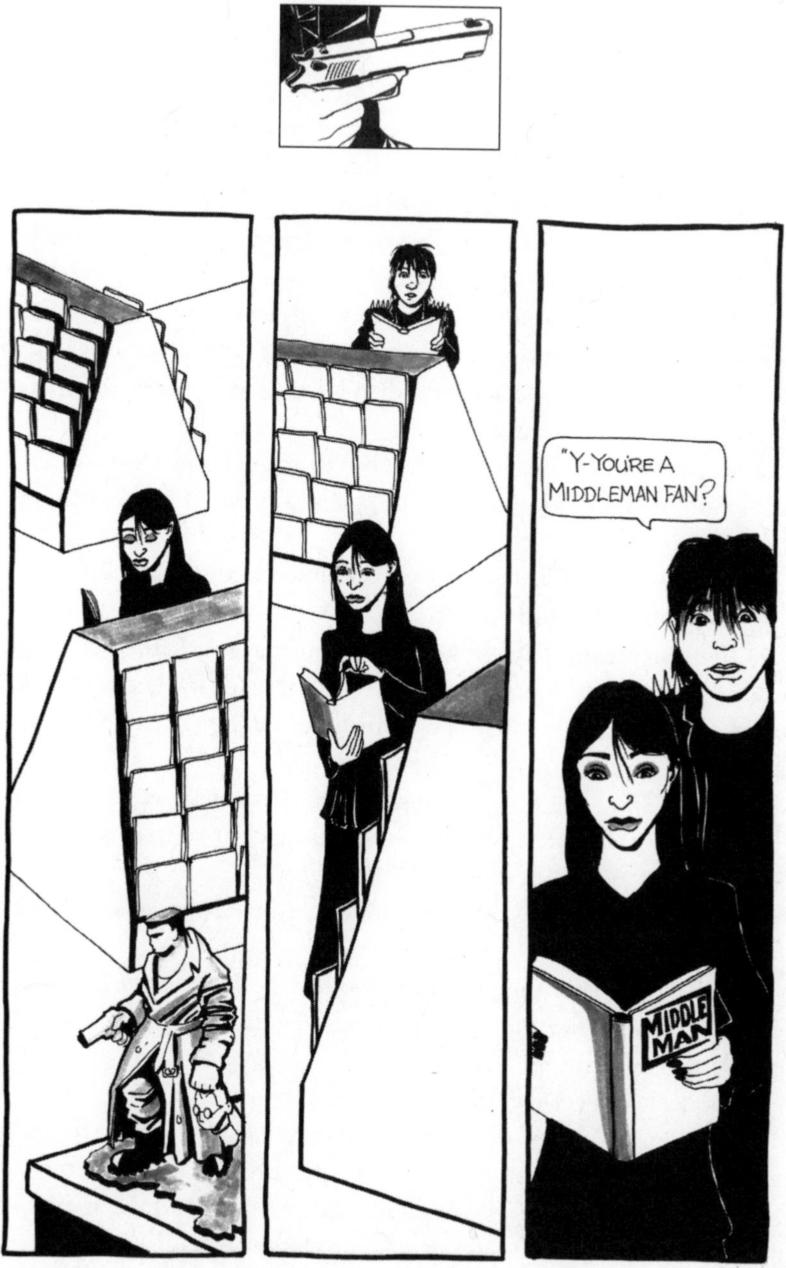
"Y-YOU'RE A MIDDLEMAN FAN?
MIDDLE MAN

"Jamie!"

And then she did the damnedest thing. Tatiana Oleshenko—girl of my dreams—threw her arms around me.

What the eff? I will never understand women.

It was nothing sexy. Just a hug. But she's sexy, so...

Did I mention that it felt fine? Damn fine.

"It's sweet to see you. I thought you were mad at me about something."

"Naw."

"It's like I'd see you in class with your head buried in your social work. Or I'd just miss you at the after school tech for the musical. Once I called your name in the hall, and then you ducked into the can. Playing the avoidance game again?"

It's true. I had been avoiding her. But there at Happy Harbor Comics, off school turf and kinda on mine, I guess I couldn't resist. Talking to her, I mean.

"Sorry. I guess I've been busy. I had a weeklong DT."

"No shit! What did you do?"

"It wasn't really a DT. It was 'extra help.' Because I failed my English essay. But it felt like a prison sentence. And it made me late for working on props and flats. By then you were either already occupied or you'd left for the day."

"Well. Good to know. I thought it was something more."

And it was. I've been laying low, steering clear of Lady Oleshenko. She hurts my eyes. Not to mention my heart.

"C'mon and show me what you're getting. Then let's grab a coffee or something."

So I showed her my purchase. *Johnny the Homicidal Maniac #5*. Turns out she's read the series and gets the dark satire behind Nny's murderous adventures.

She seems to get me, too.

Tat bought *Wet Moon* and *The Middleman* and later, over coffee, we devoured several of each other's pages and yakked about the newest Batman movie and The Middleman TV show and the merits and pitfalls of making movies or shows out of comics.

"I just think that a nod should have been given to Frank Miller for his inspiration. I mean, Jamie, c'mon. So much of the new feel of the last two Batman movies can be attributed to the psychological ambiguity of Bruce Wayne created by Miller in the 1980s when he revamped the series!"

Psychological ambiguity? Who talks like that? I'll be looking that up later! But it sounded complex, like Bruce Wayne himself, so I nodded.

"No doubt, but there's a kind of unspoken code in comics." I took a sip of my Tim Hortons' coffee.

"Like the Comic Code?"

"Naw, I don't mean that. I mean like the storylines, once written, become kind of like public domain. At least for other writers and artists carrying on the tradition of Batman and buddies. Old stories are mined and altered to help shape new plots and characters. At least the Batman films gave credit to Bob Kane, the original artist from the 1930s. After all, Miller retconned Kane's previous ideas. And without a lawsuit. It's just what's done in order for characters to live long and prosper."

Tatiana laughed those pealing bells again. Then she sunk my little ship completely and Spocked me.

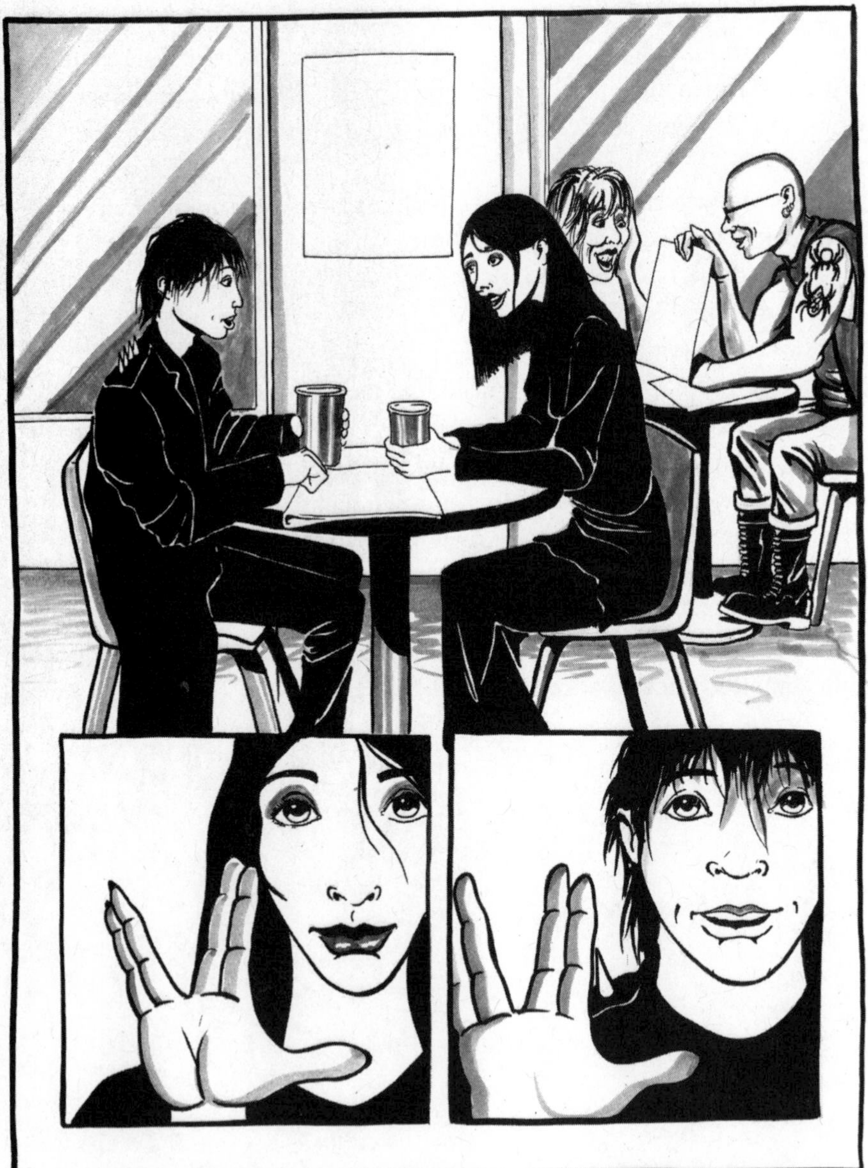

I just sat there like a buffoon staring into her eyes. I could have sworn I wasn't invisible to her then. Finally, Tatiana broke the moment.

"Yeah, Bob Kane, the artist, got a mention in the credits of the Batman movies. But not Bill Finger, the writer."

Since she dabbles—or so she puts it—in writing, no wonder Tatiana sticks up for the writer.

We'd about finished our coffee and inhaled all but one Timbit of our box of twenty. I didn't want the afternoon to end. I didn't want to bring up her boyfriend. I didn't want to hear the name Georgie. I didn't want to let her go.

"Tatiana, I'd really like to read something of yours. I mean…sometime. It doesn't have to be anything private. I'd j-just like to. Is all."

"Ok."

Well, that blew my mind.

"On one condition."

I held my breath.

"You show me yours and I'll show you mine."

If she only knew!

"Take me to see your work. Your pieces. In the streets."

I found myself weakening. Is there no end to the pain I'll put myself through? Why was I buying into the ridiculous idea that this girl is even interested in someone like me?

"Why?" I hadn't meant to ask that out loud.

Tat arched one perfect eyebrow. "Because I like you, Jamie. And I'd like us," she drew her hand through her hair, "to be friends."

Ah, the dreaded f-word. I swirled around in the thought of her and me being friends. Was she merely taking pity on the pathetic? Wasn't her twenty-one-year-old boyfriend paying her enough attention so that she needed to fill some idle hours? Was she playing me for the fool I am? Did she want something from me? Was Jamie Kidding some kind of "save the skinny whales" personal challenge? Does she sense how lonely I am?

"Friends." Again, no intention of saying that aloud.

"It's a simple enough concept, Jamie."

Yeah, but. Nothing is simple about how I feel about you, Tatiana. What am I supposed to do with this ticking bomb in my chest every time you leave me to go back to your real life? Where do I put the ache of not being able to touch you? How do I stopper up my mouth from stupidly blurting out how I feel about you?

If anyone is the aficionado (yes, another new bon mot) at shutting up, shutting down, shutting in, shutting out, it's me, Jamie Kidding. So colour me crazy—I'm already admitting to being a madman—but I'm in on the friends-with-Tatiana thing. Maybe I'll drown. But when the raven-haired mermaid sings, who cares?

"O-ok."

"Then let's go."

"R-right now?"

"No better time."

"It's getting dark."

"Scared of the dark, Jamie?"

I shook my head.

"Besides there's still about an hour before pitch, so let's head'er."

Wow. This girl has a will. What could I do but get up and shuffle after her.

Snow was falling. That light kind of big fluffy snow. The kind that makes a perfect backdrop for a perfect black-haired girl.

"Where to first?" Tatiana's breath fogged the air.

"Well, there's a couple around here."

"Figures."

"Huh?"

"Well, we're right near Happy Harbor. Your home away from home. I bet I know where you're leading me."

Then Tatiana took the lead and brought me over to the dumpster in the alley behind Happy Harbor. It's one I've frequented. Jay sometimes throws out good stuff. I found an only slightly broken Wolverine action figure. It sits on my desk at home.

But she was right. I've also tagged and re-tagged that particular dumpster about ten times.

"'No Kidding.' Great wordplay, Jamie. Love it! Maybe you're a bit of a wordsmith, like me!"

I couldn't look at her. Thank gawd it was getting darker. She'd have seen my pink cheeks.

"There's a few others at the LRT station, if they haven't been painted over."

We trod together, in step, through a carpet of flakes to the nearby station. Felt like I was in a movie. I took her over to the electrical box where I'd sprayed some of my stencils. She really liked the dragon.

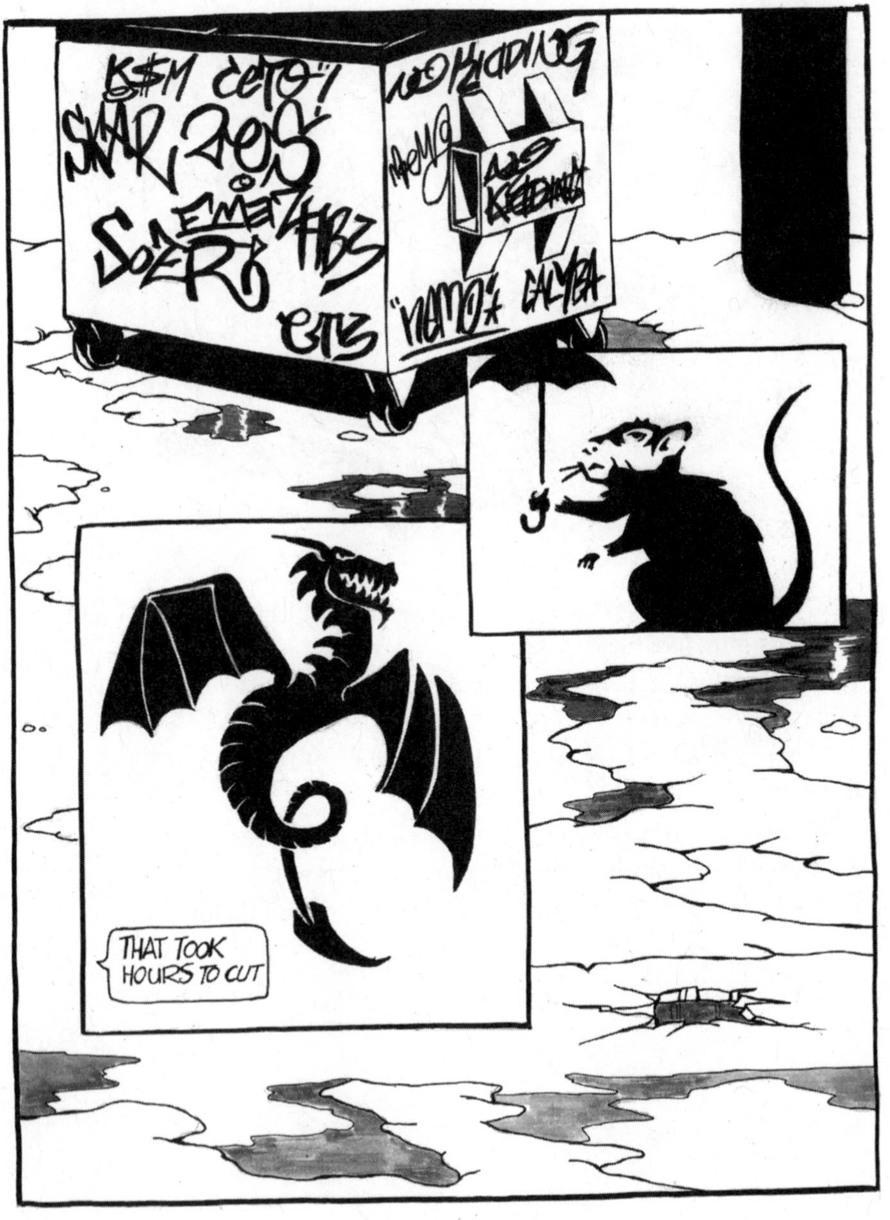
THAT TOOK HOURS TO CUT

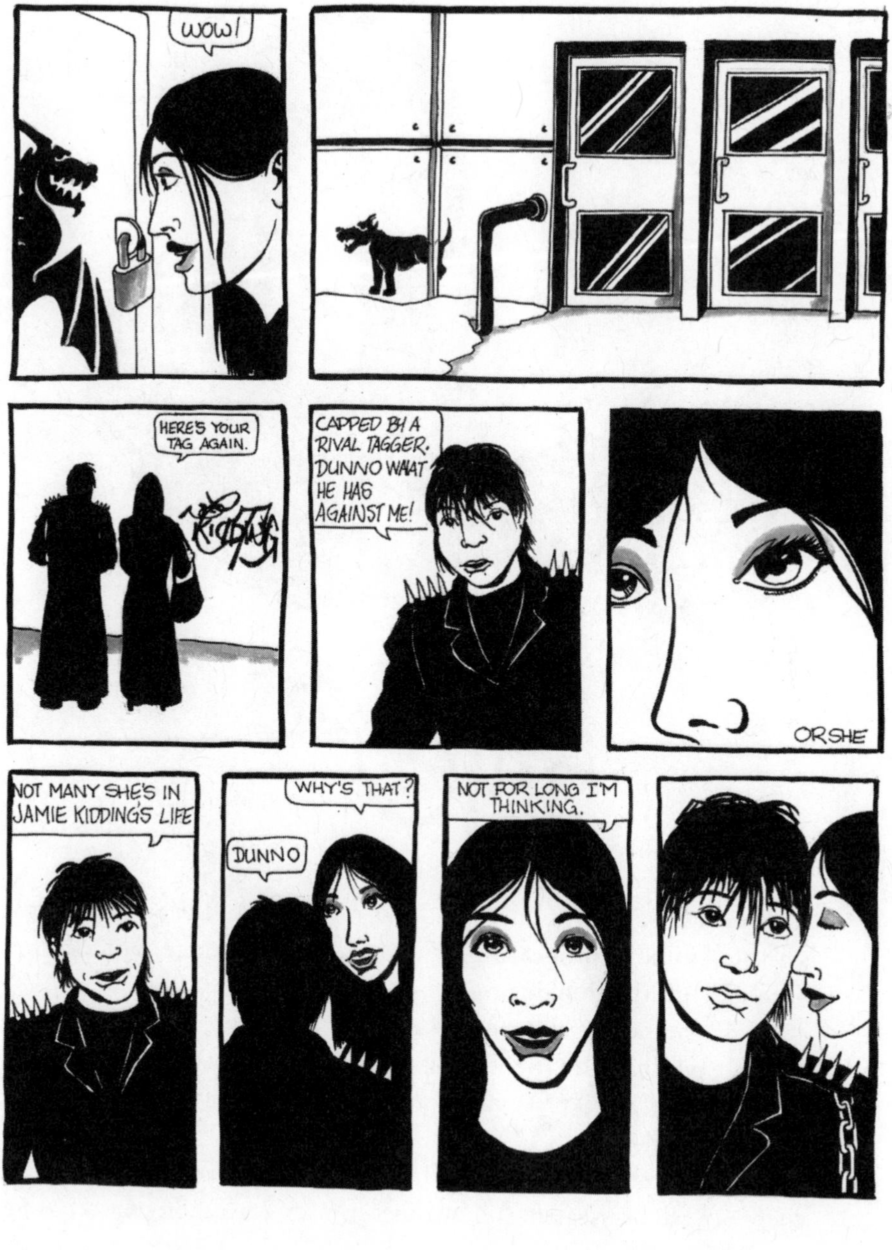
WOW!
HERE'S YOUR TAG AGAIN.
CAPPED BY A RIVAL TAGGER. DUNNO WHAT HE HAS AGAINST ME!
ORSHE
NOT MANY SHE'S IN JAMIE KIDDING'S LIFE
WHY'S THAT?
DUNNO
NOT FOR LONG I'M THINKING.

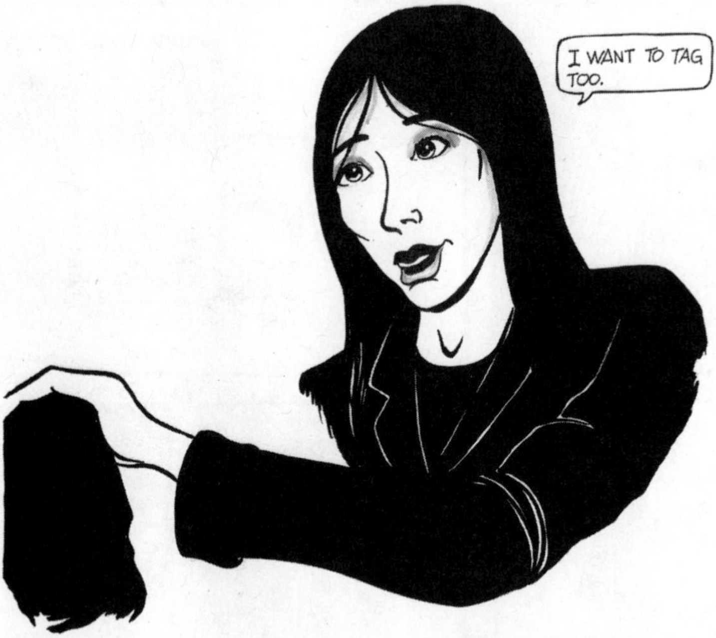
I WANT TO TAG TOO.

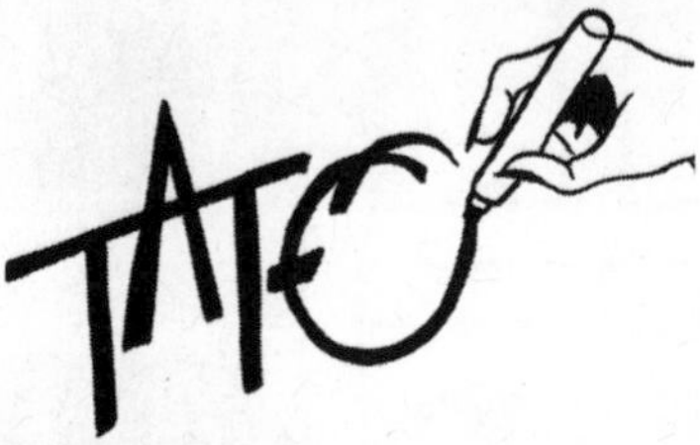
TATO

Speechless, I could only hand her my Sharpie. I tried to will my heart to resume its proper rate. What just happened there? Something? Nothing? Wishful thinking on my part? Or…

"Like 'po-tat-o?'" I hoped I wasn't breathing heavy.

"No, goofball. Tat for Tatiana. Tat-O. 'O' for my last name."

"I like the Tate-O pronunciation better. Think I'll use that." I grinned like a happy idiot.

"You better not!" Tatiana punched my arm. Not hard. But right where my HP bruises are still healing. It hurt. But I didn't let on. And I didn't care either.

There was one other stencil at the station. My newest cut. Created just a week ago. A silhouette of the gun. But it had been capped by some other writer. Actually, I felt a curious sense of relief. I led Tat by without bothering to show her.

"Kind of a date, wasn't it?" Tatiana's teeth glowed under the streetlight of the LRT station.

"A friend date." I didn't trust my voice to say much more.

"Well, let's friend date again soon. I wanna see some of your more major pieces."

"Sure."

"Right...So see you at school, ok Jamie? No more Mr. Avoidance."

"See ya."

Tatiana waved and headed down into the bowels of the LRT.

I suddenly remembered. "Bring your writing next time!" Dunno if she heard.

I couldn't leave without walking by her tag one last time. Just needed to touch...something of her.

Didn't feel much like going to the gravel pit to practice shooting like I'd planned today. Dunno why. Just didn't. So I didn't.

Instead I started cutting a new stencil. Finished her an hour later. A mermaid. She's quite fine, if I do say so myself. And I do.

Decided tonight would be a good one to head out and spray her here and there. Strategically. Maybe even some places Tatiana might pass in her travels.

I checked in on Candy, fast asleep with all of her stuffed animal friends, including her favourite Mr. Bunny, tucked in with her. No room to move with that menagerie. Crazy kid.

Then I snuck past HP Sauce, sauced and snoring in his lazyassboy chair, out of the apartment and out into the winter night. Man, it was cold enough to frost my flakes, if you get my drift.

Just after midnight, I spied Tina shivering on the corner of the strip where the girls work, so I brought her a coffee from the 7-11.

"Gee, thanks Jamie." She offered to pay me, but there was no way.

"It's just a coffee."

"What're you doing out on a school night, young man?"

"I could ask the same of you, Tina."

She laughed and lit up a smoke. Her hand was shaking. "School's out for this chick. Nothin' but streetwise these days. Seriously, though, it's cold enough to freeze the cat. What're you up to?" Tina eyed me sideways.

"I was just out tagging."

"Oh yeah! I forgot that you do that." She took a drag. "You always were a good artist."

I felt a pang as I flashbacked to the little girl in pigtails I used to know as Tina. In elementary school, side-by-side, doing finger painting. Making Plasticine animal sculptures. I even went to a birthday party of hers once. That was a long ways back and many fixes ago, from the look of her now.

"How late do you have to work tonight, Tina?"

"'Til I make enough." Her voice seemed hard.

"In this weather? Who makes those rules?"

Tina laughed then. It wasn't exactly a pretty sound. And then she coughed. She didn't sound healthy. "Tony."

I said nothing. Everyone in our hood knows Tony, at least by rep. Tony the pimp. Drug dealer. Gambler. All around sonofabitch human leech. Rumours are he extorts the small business owners around the neighbourhood, like Mr. Wong who owns the little convenience store. Mr. and Mrs. Bodnaruk who run a little butcher shop. Miss Kim Lee who owns the tiny hair salon where Mom and Candy and me get our haircuts. And he hangs around the schoolyards in this part of town. Always looking for new recruits. Young and vulnerable. Like Tina.

Headlights were heading slowly towards us. I knew what that meant. The other girls stepped from the doorsteps of the closed shops, lousy shelters against the cold. They began to make themselves visible.

Available. Tina stomped out her cigarette and downed the rest of her coffee.

"Gotta beat the competition. Thanks again!" Tina handed me the empty cup. And in impossibly high-heeled boots, she clicked over to the icy curb.

I walked away, feeling empty as that stupid styrofoam.

The freaking cold was affecting the nozzle of my spray can. My mermaids were coming out all drippy and splotchy. Couldn't get Tina out of my worry space. And I was missing Tat—as if I have any right—something awful. I turned the corner to our block.

Nothin' really new on our street, pretty much any night of the week. But cop car lights flashed in front of our apartment block. So I got a little anxious. Hustled closer. And saw the cops bring out a guy, kinda thick around the middle, in cuffs.

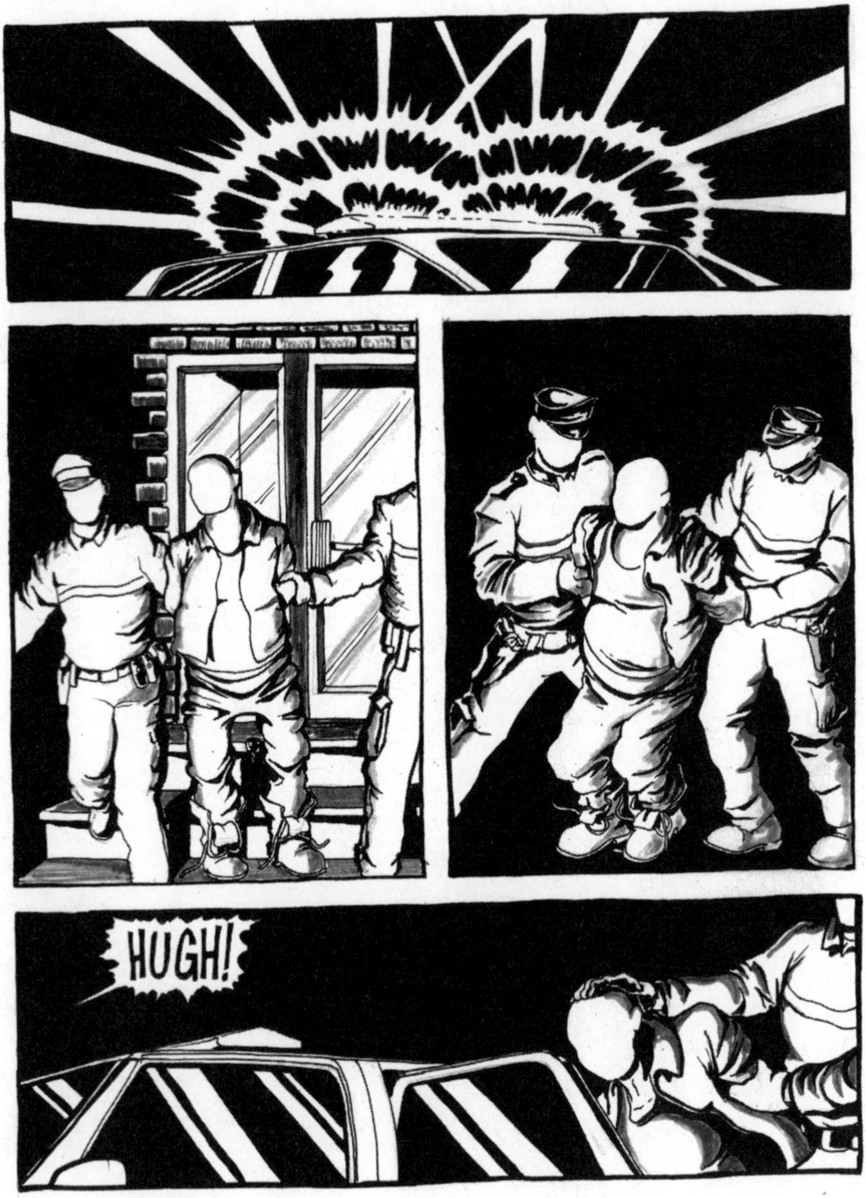
HUGH!

I ran then. Down the half-block remaining and pushed through the gathering crowd. That's when the siren from the ambulance hit me. And some young cop stopped me from entering the building.

A sledgehammer walloped my insides.

My building. My home.

Mom.

Candy.

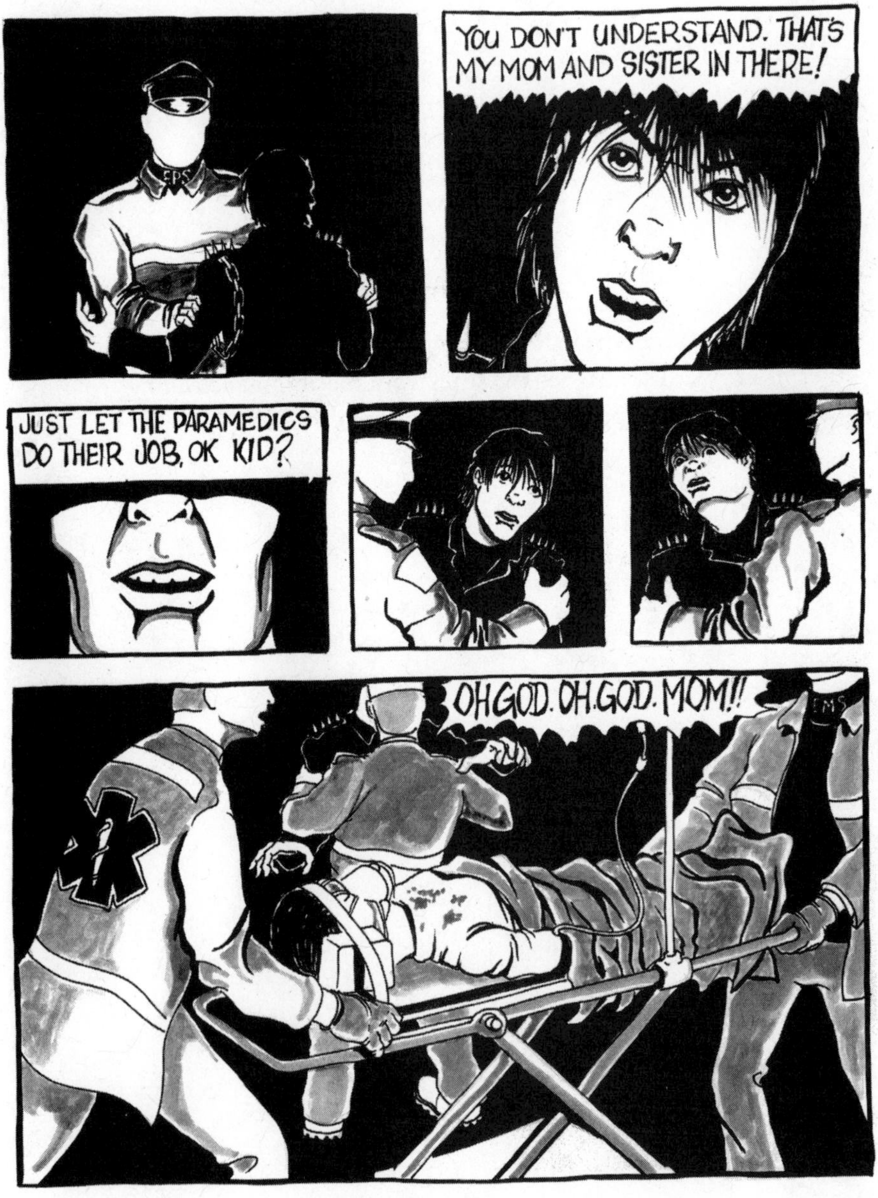
EMS
YOU DON'T UNDERSTAND. THAT'S MY MOM AND SISTER IN THERE!
JUST LET THE PARAMEDICS DO THEIR JOB, OK KID?
OH GOD. OH GOD. MOM!!
EMS

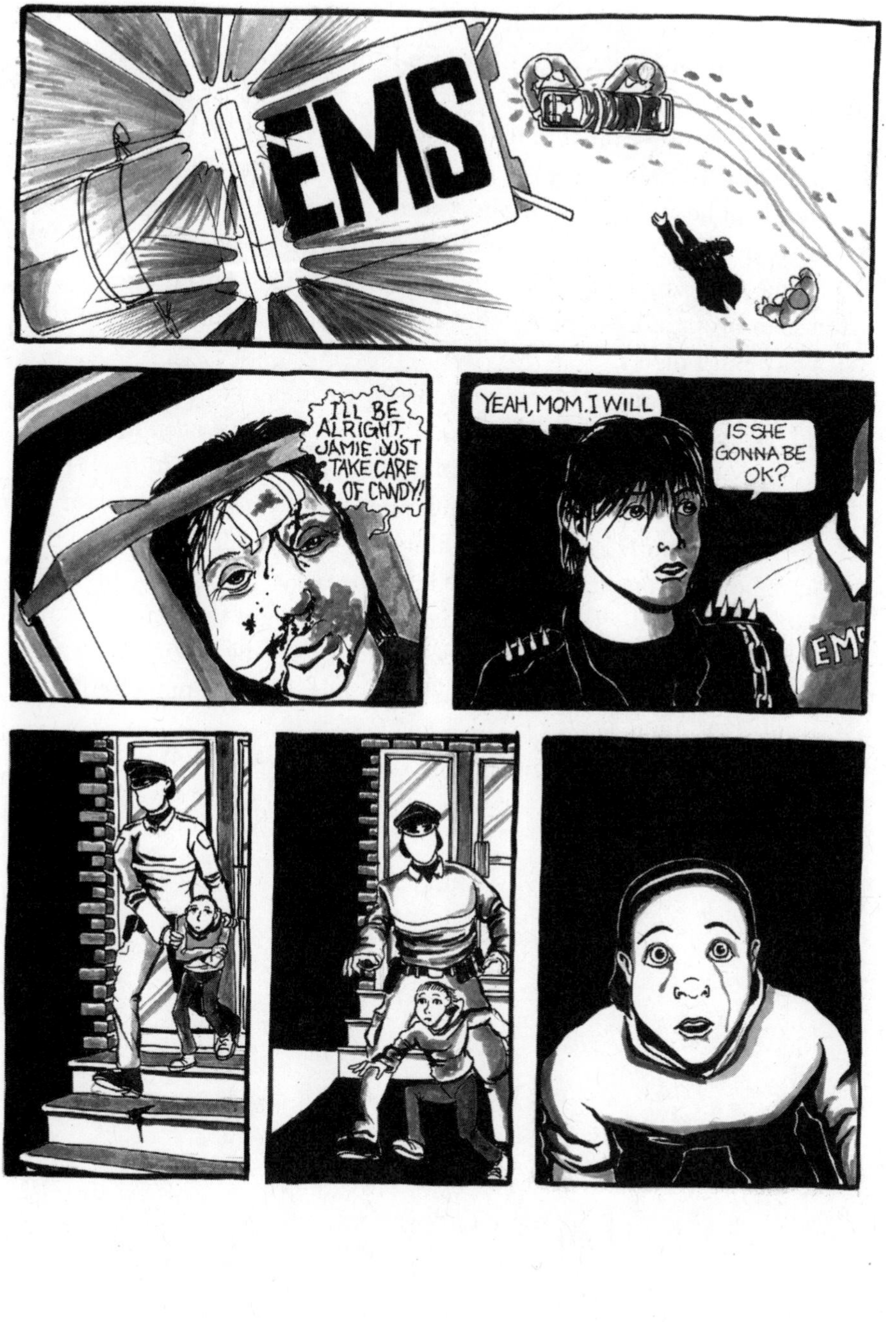
EMS
I'LL BE ALRIGHT, JAMIE. JUST TAKE CARE OF CANDY!
YEAH, MOM. I WILL
IS SHE GONNA BE OK?
EMS

The cops gave us a ride to the hospital. Where we waited hours to hear about Molly. Seems her arm is broken in three places; she has a couple cracked ribs and a concussion. Not to mention a split lip, a gash on her forehead and the usual bruises. New ones to fill in for the old ones still faintly visible. Don't appear to be internal injuries. But they kept her overnight for observation and monitoring, just to be sure. Gave her some heavy-duty pain killers and an anti-swelling cocktail IV. So me and Candy just slumped in the chairs in her hospital room. The nurses brought us some blankets. Candy pretty much fell asleep right away. But I didn't.

This is all my f$%*ing fault. Because if I hadn't been out tagging, I'd have been home where I should've been. I'd have been there when Mom got in from work. I could have stopped the bastard from pummeling her to the point of passing out. Those fists were meant for me, not Molly. I know I'm no boxer; Hugh has a nasty left hook. But I could have been the one. I should have been the one.

I clenched my fists and my jaw tight. So tight they hurt. Because that's what you gotta do in this world. Hit or be hit. Shoot or be shot. Kill or be killed. I aim to protect my family. I got nothin' else. It's up to Jamie Kidding.

I watched my mom twitch and Candy dream, until dawn came up good and grey and ugly.

Social workers pick my bony butt.

First the endless questions. In triplicate. For Molly. Candy. Me.

"How long has Mr. Llewlyn been with the family?

How would you describe his relationship with your mother?

Has he ever been violent before?"

Just look in the file, lady. The history's all there, if you take the time to read it. Courtesy of the police and other social workers just like you. We've been in and out of the women's shelter about four times over the years since I was thirteen. Molly and Candy have seen the counsellors there. Yes, she went back to him. Gawd knows why, but she did. This is the third time she's been to the hospital, but this is the most serious. This is the first time Hugh's been taken away. Before it's been police reports. Trips to Emergency. Some bandages. X-rays. And Demerol. Never this bad a beating. No, Hugh's never hit Candy. At least, not so far. Never mind about me. It's nobody's business.

Then the sizing up of our family.

"Single mother. Two jobs. Two dependents. One female, aged 13. One male, aged 17. Income: $25,000 per year. Common-law spouse. Workers Compensation. Alcohol abuse. Physical, emotional, and psychological abuse."

Then the really personal stuff.

"How are you doing at home?

How are you doing at school?

How would you describe what you're feeling right now?"

Happy as a bunny. What does she freaking think? My mother's lying in a hospital bed and looks like a train wreck, for shit sake! My sister's sucking her thumb again. I'm a bleeping loser. I'd like to knock the social worker woman's stupid clipboard and notes into next Tuesday. And I'd like to put a bullet through Hugh's thick skull. That's how I feel.

Finally, the arrangements.

"We think it's best if you and your sister stay at your uncle's house for a few days. Until things have settled down. To give your mother a chance to heal and think things over. She'll make better progress knowing you're both somewhere safe. Going back to the apartment isn't an option. You're a minor. And there is the matter of the repair to the door before the place is secure again."

What?

Apparently, Hugh ripped the door from one of the hinges. I wonder who's watching over our stuff. (Insert laugh track here.) Like there's anything worth stealing. Still, it's crap to think that someone—neighbours or worse—can just walk in…

And the follow-up.

"We'll check back in a couple of days to see how you and your sister are doing. Someone from Social Services will drive you over to your uncle's place now. Hopefully, you and Candice can both return to school tomorrow and try to normalize. That's the best way."

Normalize? She trying to kid a Kidding?

"In the meantime, there's no need to fear retaliation from your stepfather. He is in lock up at the Remand Centre for now. The police have already pressed charges. And we're…your mother is planning to get a restraining order or Emergency Protection Order, should he make bail."

Good for Molly. Wish they'd lock the prick up in a rat-infested dungeon and throw away the key. I hope Hugh's stinking in his own urine.

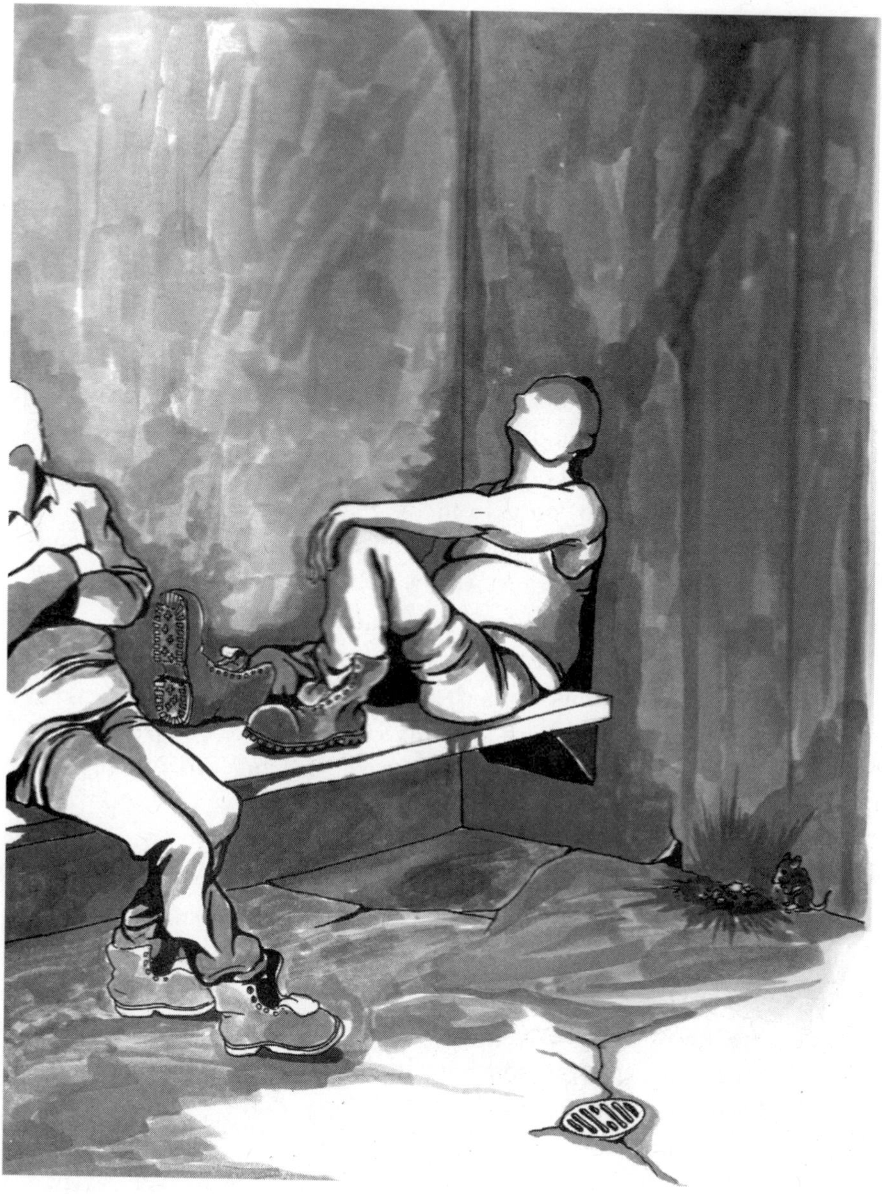

I kissed a groggy Molly goodbye. Took Candy's hand and headed out past the social worker to the waiting car. Pushed my little sister in and got in beside her. It was a stone cold drive to Uncle Mac's. Silent. Grey. Overcast. Perfect.

I kept pulling Candy's thumb from her mouth. But she's stubborn and upset. In the end, I gave up and just put my arm around her shoulders. At least she let me do that much. When we got to the bungalow that looks like all the other boring bungalows on my uncle's boring street, we tumbled out into the midday winter gloom. Candy thanked the driver. I couldn't be bothered.

Aunt Sue came out of the house and caught Candy in a big hug. She smiled past Candy's hood at me. Her words tumbled out, Aunt Sue nervous-style: "How's your poor mom? I've made you some lunch. Your uncle's at work. I'll help you settle in. I've made up the spare room for you, Candy. I hope you don't mind using the couch in the basement, Jamie."

"Don't worry about me, Aunt Sue."

"Come on in." She opened the front door.

"I'm going to go and get a few things for us from home."

"Oh, Jamie. I don't think that's a good idea, do you?"

"We have nothing with us, Aunt Sue. We'll need clothes and stuff." I started backing away from the front steps. "Don't worry. I've got my bus pass. I'll be fine."

"Oh dear. Ok. If you're careful."

"Aunt Sue, Hugh's locked up. There's nothing to worry about."

And before she could argue, I took off. No way in Hell I'm staying at Uncle Mac's. Please. I don't need the aggravation. Or the brats squared. And I sure as shite don't need the daily lectures.

I do know the one thing I need. And I aim to retrieve it.

Hugh's never gonna touch my mom, Candy or me again.

Next time I'll be ready.

No kidding.

First thing I did was shower. Ok. After I rigged a way to close the door and semi-lock it. Then I ate like a whole pot of KD. Drank up the rest of the milk. Straight from the carton. Who's gonna stop me?

Then I checked out our dump of an apartment. Looked like Taz the Tasmanian devil had whipped around and around and right through.

Except that there's no funny cartoon soundtrack to this Looney Tune.

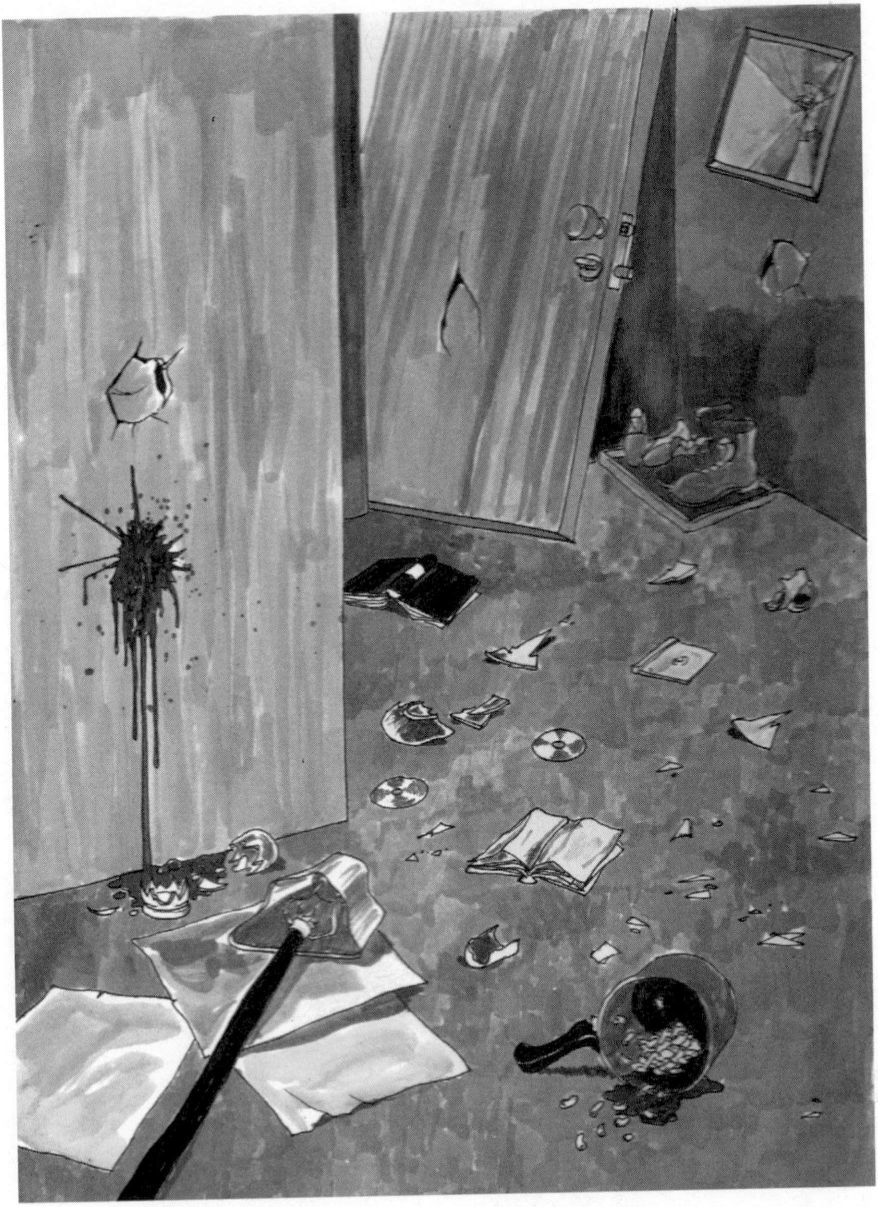

Pretty depressing. I got the broom out and swept up the worst of it. Put stuff back in its place. Tried the lamp which no longer works. Vacuumed up the tiny pieces of sharp shit so small sock feet will go unharmed. Attempted to re-hang my broken picture. My mom loves that one. I gave it to her as a gift. It's not my best work. But she doesn't care.

Don't go there, Jamie. Don't think about Molly. Or do. But only about how you're gonna fix this. Make it right.

I cleaned up the kitchen, too, since no one had bothered with yesterday's dirty dishes. Threw out some green puke liquid vegetables from the fridge. Took out the garbage.

Then I tried to pack a grungy little suitcase for Molly. What does a mom with a broken arm and a concussion need? Where's the Boy Scout's manual for what to pack for your mother whose been beaten up and hospitalized?

Toothbrush. Toothpaste. Hairbrush. Make up bag. It's embarrassing to go through your mother's drawers for your mother's drawers, but I did it. Found her a bra and a nightie, too. Added some pads and tampons. Just in case it's, you know, that time of the month for her.

Geez. This is the kind of stuff you never read about young male heroes doing in comic books.

Then I did it all over again for my sister. What a guy's gotta do!

The two little bags—one grotty and brown, the other one pink with Hello Kitty all over it—sat by the door on its broken hinge. I flopped down on the couch and gave Mrs. McDover, our nosy neighbour and building super, a call about fixing our door. She only asked about 300 stupid snoopy questions and said she'd get a repairman in sometime next week.

Right. And I pee fountains of pure gold.

Next year, is more like. I know the way management works around this slumhole. Slow as constipation.

Finally, it was time to get what I came for.

It was 2:30 pm and full daylight, unlike other retrieval and return times. I had to make sure no one was watching. Especially spy-eye McDover whose kitchen looks right down on the rusty toolshed. But I know my angles and sightlines. I'm an artist, hey? Now also a budding stage flats and props painter. So I managed to keep outta view. Get in. Get out. Gun in knapsack. Bada bing. Bada boom.

School would be just letting out for the day. I made a silent apology to Ms. S. about skipping the musical paint crew this one afternoon. Figured she'd understand, if she knew. But she won't. Not the whole story. At least Molly or Aunt Sue will report today as an excusable absence. No one can call Jamie Kidding a truant. Even with all my learning issues, I never could see the point of goin' AWOL. First off, I'd miss my chance to work alongside Tat. Second, I'd miss art class. Thirdly, I'd get further behind in English and eventually have to face the wrath of Mrs. Sheen. Not to mention that I hate to jerk around my mother. She's got plenty to handle as it is. Doesn't need a delinquent for a son. I'm already enough of a disappointment. And I always try to set a good example for Candy. I'd like her to look up to me. Just a little bit. So Jamie goes to school.

I caught the LRT back to the hospital. Molly was sitting up in bed, alone in her puke puce room. Her face looked like a horror flick. I know that's not a nice thing to write about your own mother. But it's the truth. Her arm in its cast was slung across her chest. She looked so frail in the fading winter light. When she saw that I'd brought her a suitcase, Molly started to tear up.

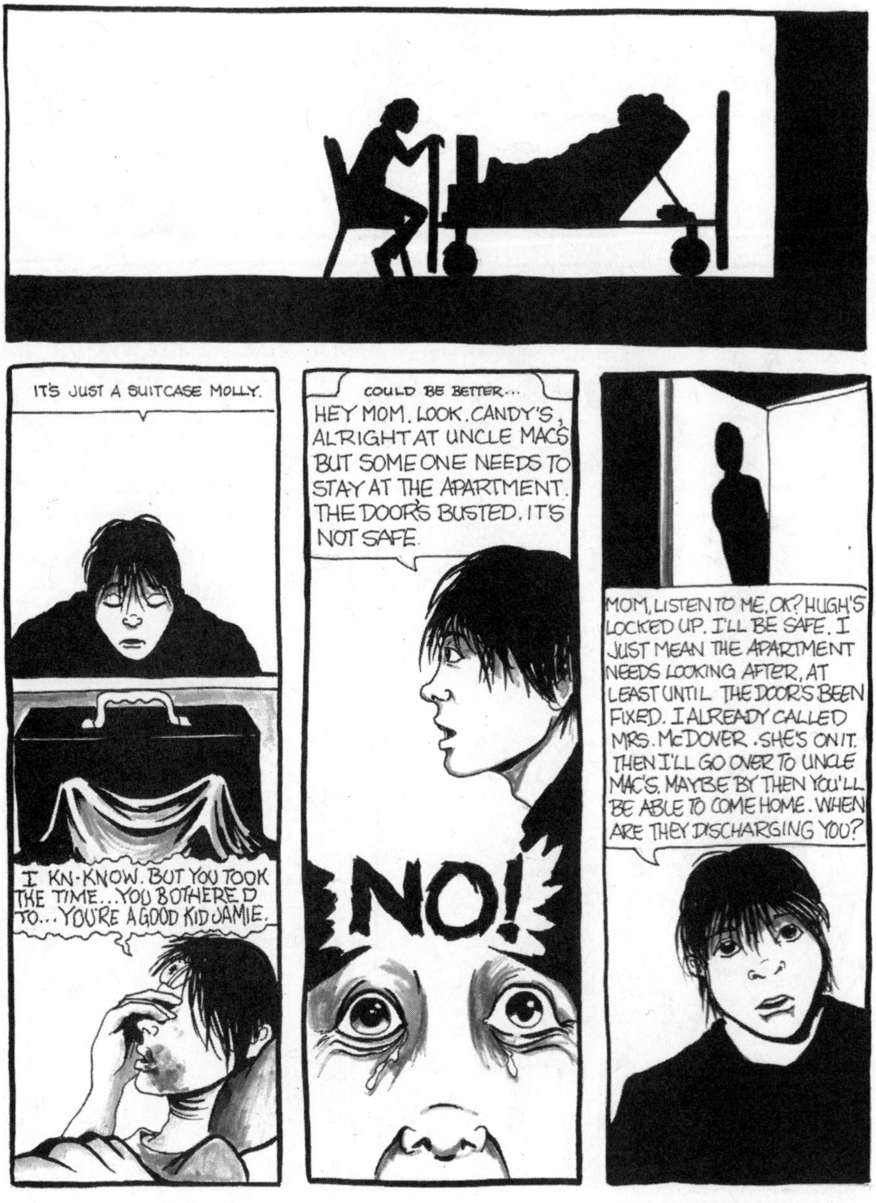
IT'S JUST A SUITCASE MOLLY.
I KN-KNOW. BUT YOU TOOK THE TIME... YOU BOTHERED TO... YOU'RE A GOOD KID JAMIE.
COULD BE BETTER...
HEY MOM. LOOK. CANDY'S, ALRIGHT AT UNCLE MAC'S BUT SOME ONE NEEDS TO STAY AT THE APARTMENT. THE DOOR'S BUSTED. IT'S NOT SAFE.
NO!
MOM, LISTEN TO ME, OK? HUGH'S LOCKED UP. I'LL BE SAFE. I JUST MEAN THE APARTMENT NEEDS LOOKING AFTER, AT LEAST UNTIL THE DOOR'S BEEN FIXED. I ALREADY CALLED MRS. McDOVER. SHE'S ON IT. THEN I'LL GO OVER TO UNCLE MAC'S. MAYBE BY THEN YOU'LL BE ABLE TO COME HOME. WHEN ARE THEY DISCHARGING YOU?

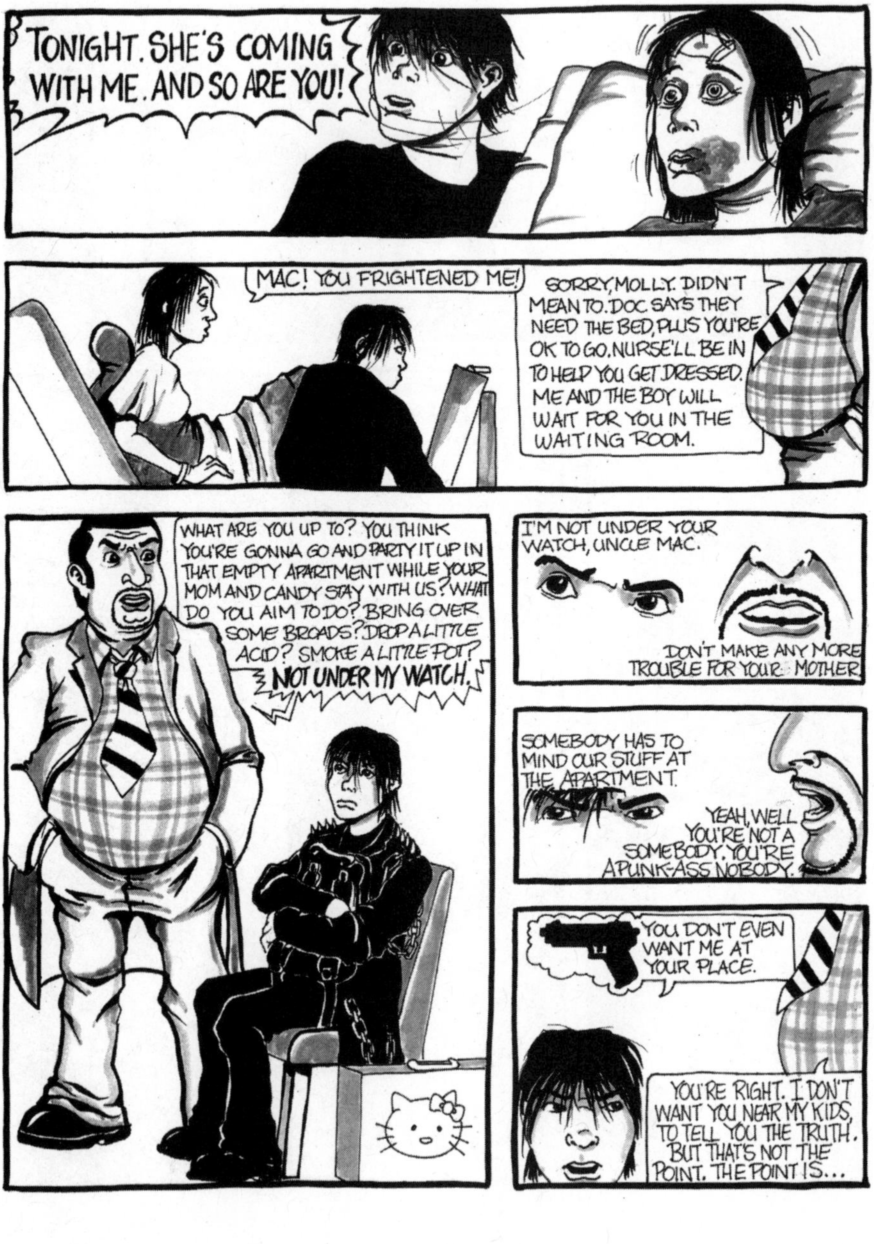
TONIGHT. SHE'S COMING WITH ME. AND SO ARE YOU!
MAC! YOU FRIGHTENED ME!
SORRY, MOLLY. DIDN'T MEAN TO. DOC SAYS THEY NEED THE BED, PLUS YOU'RE OK TO GO. NURSE'LL BE IN TO HELP YOU GET DRESSED. ME AND THE BOY WILL WAIT FOR YOU IN THE WAITING ROOM.
WHAT ARE YOU UP TO? YOU THINK YOU'RE GONNA GO AND PARTY IT UP IN THAT EMPTY APARTMENT WHILE YOUR MOM AND CANDY STAY WITH US? WHAT DO YOU AIM TO DO? BRING OVER SOME BROADS? DROP A LITTLE ACID? SMOKE A LITTLE POT?
NOT UNDER MY WATCH.
I'M NOT UNDER YOUR WATCH, UNCLE MAC.
DON'T MAKE ANY MORE TROUBLE FOR YOUR MOTHER
SOMEBODY HAS TO MIND OUR STUFF AT THE APARTMENT.
YEAH, WELL YOU'RE NOT A SOMEBODY. YOU'RE A PUNK-ASS NOBODY.
YOU DON'T EVEN WANT ME AT YOUR PLACE.
YOU'RE RIGHT. I DON'T WANT YOU NEAR MY KIDS, TO TELL YOU THE TRUTH. BUT THAT'S NOT THE POINT. THE POINT IS...

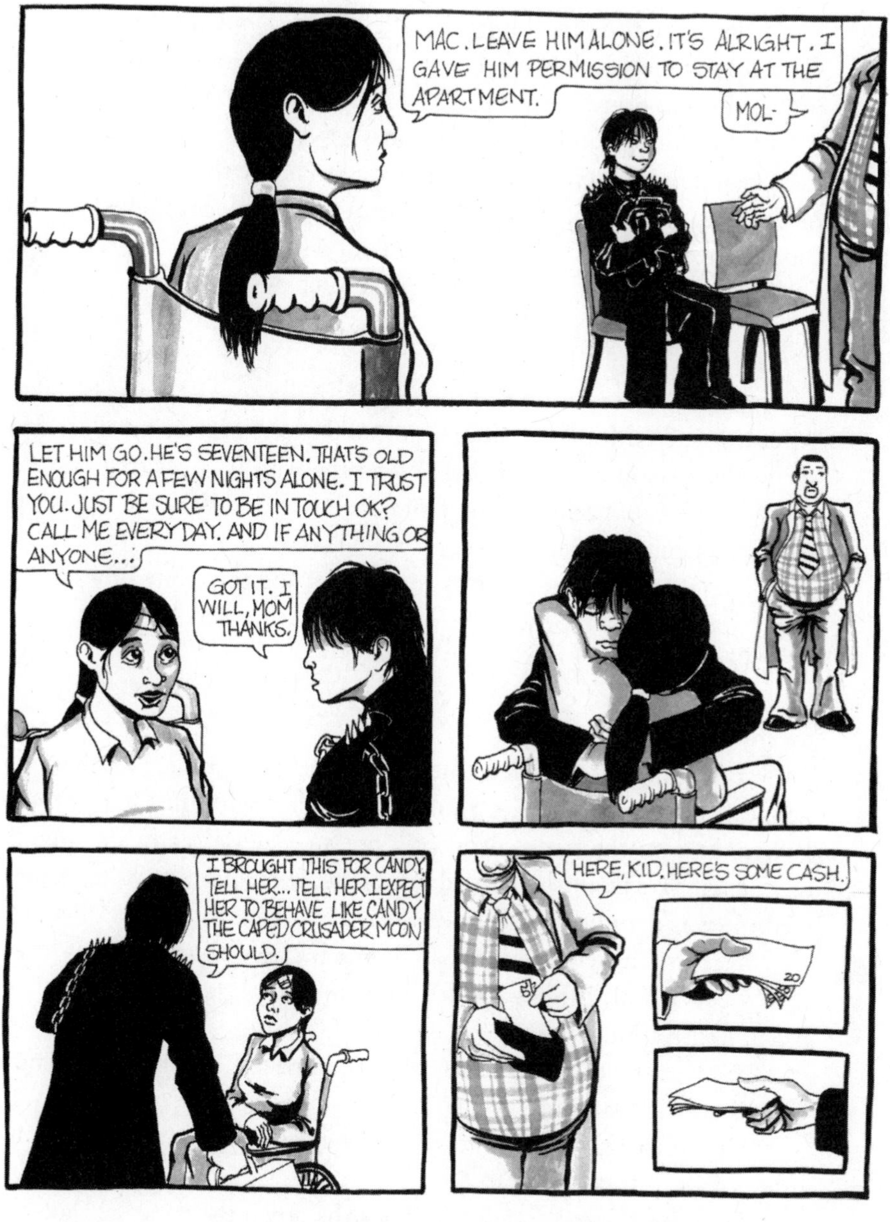
MAC. LEAVE HIM ALONE. IT'S ALRIGHT. I GAVE HIM PERMISSION TO STAY AT THE APARTMENT.
MOL-
LET HIM GO. HE'S SEVENTEEN. THAT'S OLD ENOUGH FOR A FEW NIGHTS ALONE. I TRUST YOU. JUST BE SURE TO BE IN TOUCH OK? CALL ME EVERYDAY. AND IF ANYTHING OR ANYONE...
GOT IT. I WILL, MOM THANKS.
I BROUGHT THIS FOR CANDY. TELL HER... TELL HER I EXPECT HER TO BEHAVE LIKE CANDY THE CAPED CRUSADER MOON SHOULD.
HERE, KID. HERE'S SOME CASH.
20

I hate that I took that dough. Uncle Mac was only putting on a big show for my mother. But what was I gonna do? There's almost no food in the fridge at home.

Face it. Jamie Kidding has no spine.

I beat it outta there before Mom had the chance to change her mind or before Uncle Mac changed it for her. I'm sure he harangued her all the way over to his bogus bungalow. Poor Molly.

Why are the men in my mother's life such assholes?

My foolhardy feet found their way eventually to Alternative Video. After I'd walked for three hours, the sudden warmth of the cluttered shop was welcome. One of the TVs on the wall was playing *Harold and Maude*. Tatiana looked up from the cases of DVDs she was sorting at the front counter.

"Jamie! Hey! Where were you today?" She took one look at my face. "Something happened."

"Yeah."

Then she yelled out to the empty store, "Hey, Georgie! I'm goin' for my break."

From a door at the back emerged a short little dude. Nothing like I expected. Shorter than Tat. Squat. Tight t-shirt with the Quaker Oats guy smiling on the front. A bit of a pot stomach already starting. A few piercings. Tiny little pretend mustache. Dirty blond hair in spikes. Georgie was definitely underwhelming. Meh. Tatiana deserves better.

"You just started your shift an hour ago." Even his voice was meh.

"Georgie, this is my good friend from school. Jamie. The one I've been talking about."

Tat's been talking about me? Her 'good friend'? To her boyfriend? What's up with that?

"Hey." Georgie nodded at me, but was otherwise uninterested. In either of us.

"Jamie and I need to talk. We'll just be down the street at Dadeo."

"Fine. Fine. Take your thirty minutes."

We left through the glass door and trudged along the sidewalks. The trampled snow was dirty and ugly under the streetlights. Tat tried to look at me but I kept my focus on my feet.

"Here we are." Tat pushed open the door and I found myself transported. We sat down in a booth. Red pleather seats. I looked around at the chrome fixtures. Vinyl albums and album covers all over the walls. Little Richard. Elvis. Some chick named Patti Page, and some very white guy, Bobby Darin. It could have been 1955. There was an old jukebox on the wall of our booth.

"This is Dadeo?"

"Kind of like stepping back into a rerun of *Happy Days*, isn't it?" Tatiana slipped a quarter into the machine. Selected E-21. "Walk Away, Renee" by a 1966 band called The Left Banke. Whoever they were. The sad strains of strings began, followed by a sad singer. Sad song.

A gum-smacking waitress right out of the movies brought us two menus. The badge on her striped pink shirt read 'Flo.' "Hi honey. New friend? Just coffee? Or you want eats?"

"We'll take a look." Tatiana waited until we were alone. Then she interrupted the flute solo. "Flo's not bad." She shrugged and smiled. "It's a job."

I thought of my own mom. One of her waitress uniforms has 'Molly' on the left side of the chest. I wondered if customers at House of Pancakes ever gave her a second thought. Tatiana interrupted mine.

"You must be hungry."

I nodded numbly.

"You look a little pale, Jamie. Worn out."

"Yeah. I didn't sleep last night."

"What? Wait. First things first. You need to eat. The Po Boys are great."

I ordered a Po Boy, sweet potato fries to share with Tat, and a Coke. She ordered a coffee. Chose another song, "California Dreamin'." At least I'd heard of that one.

"Spill it."

"What?"

"You know you want to tell me. Or you wouldn't have braved the elements to come over here. So tell."

I wanted to tell her. Everything. I really did. But we only had thirty minutes. And a sappy 50s/60s soundtrack. And she had a boyfriend waiting next door. And the clock was ticking. I felt like a vice was gripping my innards. If only I could release it. I tried. I did try to tell her. But all I could manage was the bare minimum.

"My stepfather got drunk and beat up my mom and she had to go to the hospital last night."

Her hand with a third shiny quarter stopped mid-air.

"Oh my god, Jamie. Is she alright? Are you alright?"

"She's ok. Or she will be."

"What about you?"

I shrugged. "My stepfather is in lock up. Probably still sleeping it off."

"Did he hit you?"

"No." At least, not this time. But I didn't tell Tatiana about any of that.

"Holy shit. That really sucks. You must be so upset. What can I do to help you? Jamie?"

I couldn't answer. What was I gonna say? I was very afraid of what my voice might do. Not to mention my eyes. So I just concentrated on my fists on the table. And then the girl pulled another classic Tatiana move.

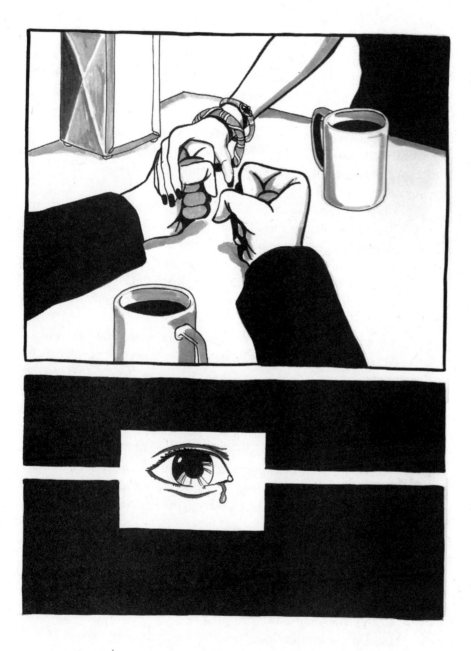

Then she had to get back. And I had to go.

Before the entrance to Alternative Video she gave me one of her amazing hugs. "Hey, Jamie. She pushed something into my hand. This is my cell number. Call me, if ever. If you ever. You know. Need to. Want to."

Wow. I know it's dumb. But we've known each other for months. She'd never given me her number. I'd never asked. Not after learning about Georgie. Now here she was, handing me this gift. Well, that's how it felt, anyways.

I looked at the number—587-614-2876—and burned it into my mind's eye. She already knew I didn't have and couldn't afford my own cell phone. And she was that decent not to rub it in. Then I put the little precious slip in my inside pocket, right next to my heart. I know. I know. Heavy on the fromage. But that's what I did.

"There's something for you out back, Tat. Check it out, if you have a moment before you go home."

She grinned. She knew. Tatiana is just that cool. That beautiful.

My mermaid. I am afraid I'll drown. But for now I'm still managing to tread water.

The apartment was pretty lonely. Sad looking, despite my earlier cleaning frenzy. If I ever make a mint from my art (insert fake applause here), I'm gonna buy Molly some new furniture. Thrift-shop chic is romantic bullshit for rich kids who can afford better. Molly deserves a decent couch and flat screen TV. Some matching chairs. A dishwasher. One day.

Instead, I phoned to reassure her I was safe and sound. Promised to get my ass over to Uncle Mac's early in the morning and take Candy to school.

Though I was exhausted, I just couldn't get sleepy. So I flipped aimlessly through the channels on the TV Hugh had neglected to break. What a surprise. And what another surprise: reality shows with almost every click.

Reality bites. Trust me.

I surfed a little more. Info-mercials for crapola no one needs. Re-runs of *Royal Canadian Air Farce*. A thrill-a-minute documentary about ice fishing. *Pretty Woman* on the old movies station. Hurrah! Julia Roberts turns into Cinderella.

57 channels and nothin' on. No shit, Sherlock.

So I decided to dart out and see one more person before hitting the sack. It was getting late, and a nasty wind was whining around our streets. But there she was like a bad habit. Tina: Our Lady of the Strip.

I handed her another steaming offering from the 7-11.

"Mmmm. Hot chocolate this time. Nice." She smiled at me, but her pupils were pinpricks.

"Yeah. I'm a guy likes to change it up."

She chuckled and sipped. Her eyes closed dreamily.

"Tina?"

She opened her baby blues again.

"I just want you to know something, ok?"

"What's that, Jamie?"

I unzipped my knapsack. Showed her what was inside. Just a quick glance. But it was enough. She sobered from her stupor.

"Where'd you get that, Jamie?"

"Doesn't matter. What does is that I've got your back. Ok?"

"Don't go fooling with stuff you don't know about, Jamie. I mean it!"

"I do, too, Tina. I got your back."

"I think you should just gimme that gun, Jamie..." She made a sloppy grab for my pack, but I easily sidestepped her. Not before seeing her left arm emerge from beneath the fake fur sleeve of her winter coat.

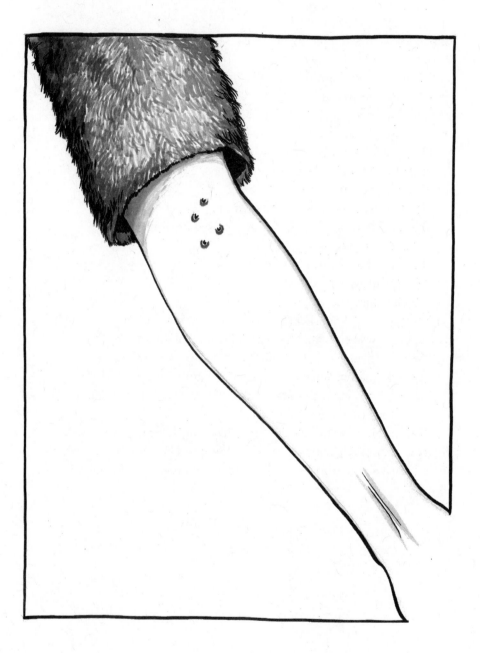

Just what I'd figured. Tina's a heroin whore.

"I don't think so." I backed away from her. "But remember what I said."

I left her and trudged back home, thinking how life is so not like a Julia Roberts movie.

Candy was curiously quiet. Fidgety. Jumpy. At least there was no thumb sucking. But she didn't say a word on the bus all the way to our stop. We walked four blocks from there to East Hill Junior High. But she kept dragging her feet. Driving me crazy. I tried to get her to look at me. Made stupid faces. Farting noises. Usually that stuff cracks her up. Not this morning, though.

"Wuzzup, Candy Cane?"

"Don't call me that!"

"Why not? I've called you that millions of times. We all do. Mom. Hu…"

Me and my big mouth.

"Well, I want you to stop."

"Ok. Ok. Geez. Dunno what I did to deserve the grumpy guts treatment."

She stopped dead in her snowy tracks. "What did you do, Jamie? You weren't there, that's what!"

"Huh?" But I knew what she meant. Guilt flooded through me.

"I needed you. Mom needed you. Where were you that night?" Candy began to blubber. Which she does quite effectively. And loud.

"Hey, Candy." I scrambled to find a Kleenex, but I never have those on me at the best of times. "Shit. I'm sorry."

"Don't swear!" And her tears doubled. Turned to sobs. I collected my sister into my arms.

"Sorry. Sorry. Listen. I know I wasn't there Sunday night when Hugh… I had to get out. Sometimes I feel so suffocated. You know?" She just kept shuddering into my shoulder. "Look. I won't let him hurt you. I'll be there for you…" I scrambled to find the right words.

"Hey, I know. You can hang with me, ok? Come after school and help me paint flats for the musical. Then we can go over to the apartment and chill out for an hour or so. Just you and me. Maybe on the way we'll grab a donut. What do ya say?"

Candy nodded and pulled away from me, trails of snot connecting my shoulder to her nose, like some glistening umbilical cord. She found a tissue in her pocket. Several snotty minutes passed.

"I look gross now, don't I?"

She did, but I said the smart sibling thing. "No, you look fine. By the time you get to school, no one will ever know. Take some deep breaths. That always helps."

So she did. And I stood there, moronic loser of a big brother. Then she gave me a big Candy hug. As if I deserved it. We walked the rest of the way to her school. I promised to walk her over to my high school across the field just after dismissal time. She was smiling when she went through the doors.

But I felt like puking. I almost did. Somehow I made it to the doors of East Hill Senior High with my Cornflakes intact.

Guess who greeted me in the foyer?

"Art fag! I been lookin' for you. Seen you with that kid across the field. That your new girl?"

"Piss off, Attaman." I clenched my teeth and felt for my pack.

"What happened to the other be-atch? This new one's a little young, ain't she? But maybe cradle robbing's the only way you can get some. Ha ha ha!"

I had my pack in front of me now. "Shut up about my sister, Attaman, if you know what's good for you. I wouldn't push it..."

Before my next breath, Blade had my face against the glass partition, my backpack contents digging daggers into my gut, my arm twisted almost to the breaking point behind my back.

"What's that, numb nuts? You got somethin' to say to me? No, I don't think so. *I* got somethin' to tell *you*. I'm on to your little cartoon caper, asswipe. And that's exactly what you're gonna be: *my asswipe!* If you ever draw me and my buddies in any stupid lame or insulting way ever again, bitch."

Then the creep took my head in his meaty hand.

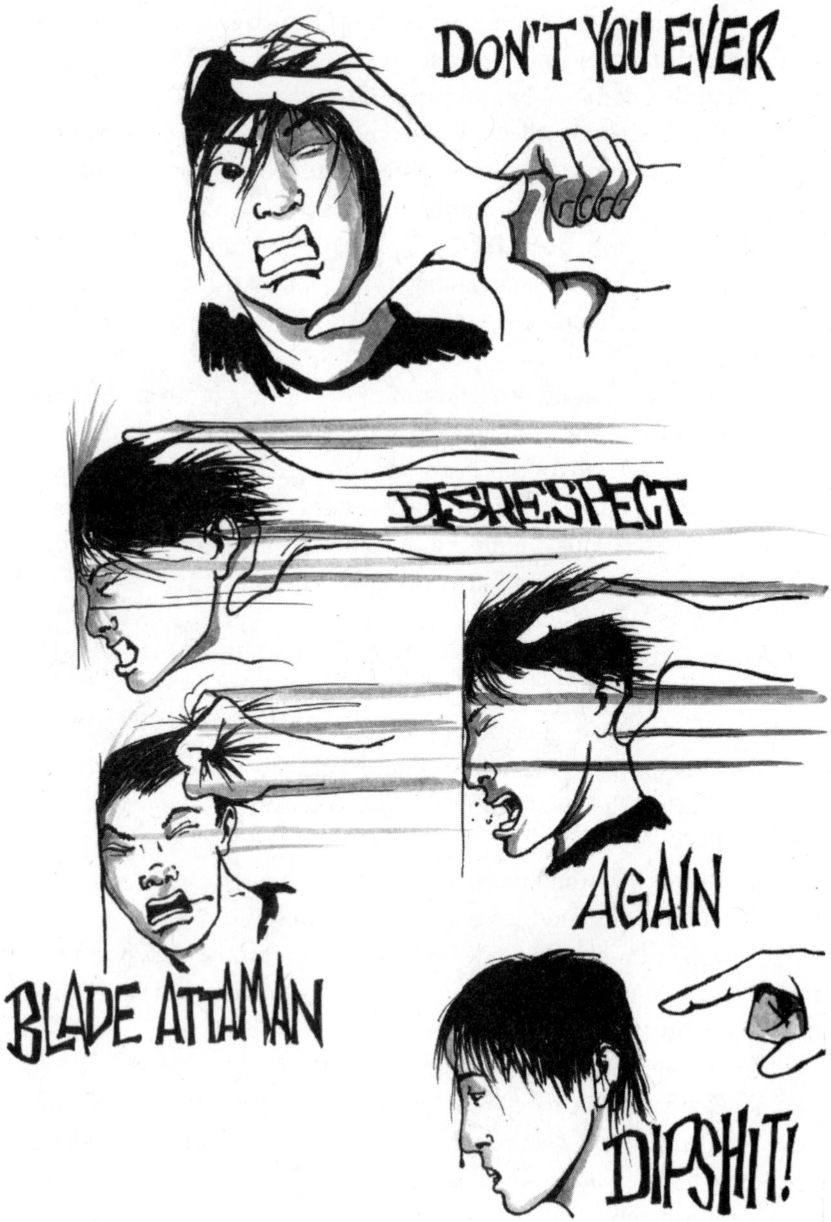
DON'T YOU EVER
DISRESPECT
BLADE ATTAMAN
AGAIN
DIPSHIT!

From somewhere in a galaxy far, far away, I heard, "What's going on down there?!"

I kinda slumped to the floor in a daze. Blade was outta there in a flash, like the slippery eel he is. Next thing I knew, Mr. Letterman was bending over me.

"Jamie!"

"I-I'm alright." The first class warning bell pierced my now pounding head. The halls were swarming and my vision swimming.

He helped me to my feet and we threaded our way to the nurse's office. Mr. Letterman wouldn't hear any argument. I sat with an iced gel pack against the goose egg forming on my forehead. My art teacher sat with me. I'd gone from near-puking to total humiliation. And it was only 8:45 am.

"If that was Attaman, he'll be suspended."

I groaned. That's all I need. Blade Attaman wandering the streets, with a vendetta and a knife. "Mr. Letterman, that'll only make it worse."

He sighed. "What do you want me to do, Jamie?"

"Nothing."

"If I do nothing... if we continue to do nothing, Mr. Attaman and friends will continue to get away with harassing and bullying, in addition to their other illicit and crude behaviour."

I shrugged.

"I'm sorry you're afraid, Jamie. If you're going to be an artist and a cartoonist, you're going to come up against thugs and bullies again and again. Whether they be newspaper editors, the general public, or the art censors, sometime, someday you'll meet the goon squad again. Will you run? Clam up? Or take a stand for what you believe is right and just?"

Oh, I aim to do that, Mr. Letterman, believe me. But I just said nothing. He left me alone as the nurse returned to check on my arm. I told her it was fine now. But my splitting headache felt like 7.5 on the Richter scale. When I asked her for some aspirin, she threatened to call my mom. That's the last thing I need. Or Molly needs. Finally, I convinced her that I don't have an ASA allergy, and I didn't require parental permission to have a couple of mild painkillers.

I put the ice pack back on my forehead and lay down on the cot in the infirmary. Mr. Letterman came in with a Coke for me.

"About *The Adventures of the Incredible Disappearing Boy...*"

"Yeah. I guess I pushed it a little far."

"I'll say, Jamie. If you're going to have an Attaman lookalike in your comic strip, maybe don't depict him with a urine cake collection as a hobby."

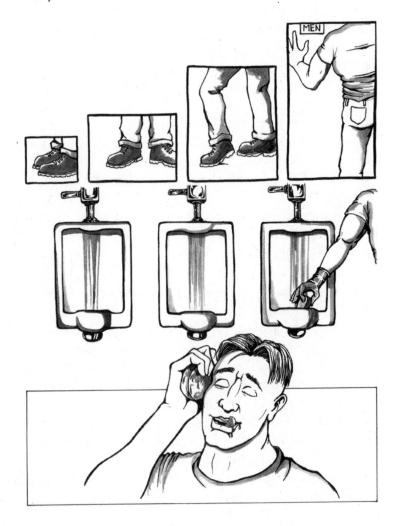

More like a piss puck fetish, I'd say. But I didn't correct Mr. Letterman. He had a valid point. I should have been more careful. Less deliberate in my characterization.

"Are you the Incredible Disappearing Boy, Jamie?"

"Naw. He's just a character."

"Hmmm. Because you don't have to disappear or be invisible. There are other ways of making a mark than by subversive cartoons in the school newspaper."

"Yeah."

"There's a summer art camp, for young artists such as yourself. For example."

Mr. Letterman's a good guy. Hell, he probably even saved my skin or at least my skull, this morning. But he doesn't get it. "Thanks, Mr. Letterman. But my family... I just don't have the money for somethin' like that."

He was decent enough not to push it. Or to embarrass me further. Instead he left me alone. I dozed off and on through the first two periods. By lunch I was feeling better and headed to the drama room to explain yesterday's absence to Ms. Sokolotosky.

She had that pity expression teachers get for certain pathetic students. You know the look. Apparently, the whole school knows. Well, my teachers do, anyway. I guess Molly called and explained about our little family feud to the counsellor, Ms. Gable. Yay. Could the day get any better?

Well, yes it could! Seems I'm behind in my schoolwork. There's an English essay AND a social essay due next week. The good news just doesn't quit.

I worked in the library, trying to take a stab at my essays. A few minutes before the end of afternoon classes, a monotone voice over the intercom summoned Jamie Kidding to Ms. Gable's office. (Insert Happy Face icon here. Not.)

"How're you feeling?" The traditional counsellor question.

"Fine."

"Really? After what happened at home? What happened today? Mr. Letterman filled me in. But he only told me. Not the VP."

"I'm coping."

"Wanna talk about anything?"

"Not really." I like Ms. Gable. I do. She's been good to me. But she's still a perfect stranger. Even if she smiles at me a lot. Why is it that school counsellors want to know about feelings? Especially mine. Doesn't she have enough to worry about what with student grade point averages and career options and university entrance requirements and high school cheerleaders with relationship breakups or eating disorders?

"Maybe later," I offered, hoping she'd take the bait. Let me off the hook for now.

It worked. "My office door is always open." That smile again. "Mr. Letterman always speaks so highly of you, Jamie. He wants you... we all want you to succeed. I know this is a tough time for your family. Your mom, well, she tells me she's got someone to talk to. But she's worried about you."

Great. My mother is discussing my personal life with my school counsellor. "She doesn't need to worry. No one does. I'm fine."

Gable gave me one of those long teacher gazes. Searching. Like maybe she'd find diamonds if only she looked long enough. But we all know by now that Jamie Kidding is no diamond. Not even in the rough. Yet another disappointed adult in my life.

Screw it! I was mad suddenly. Tired and fed up with the unwanted, unnecessary attention of the last two days. Where were all these well-meaning social working psycho-babblers before our family imploded? Who'd be there next Tuesday? Or the week after that? Underneath it all, who really gave a flying fornication about yet another single mom with two kids in Northeast Edmonton?

"I need to pick up my sister across the field at the junior high."

I know I sounded abrupt. Rude. But I thought I might punch something if I stayed in that office any longer.

Ms. Gable's voice was mild. "You can go, Jamie. No one's holding you prisoner. Not on this side of the desk, at least."

I got up and slouched towards the door.

"I didn't tell your mom about the incident with Robert Attaman."

Robert? Blade has a real name?

"Not yet, anyway. And if you like, I can get you an extension for those two essays due next week."

I felt my resentment drain out of me. Ms. Gable isn't the enemy. She's just a nice lady trying to do her job. Trying to be nice to me. At least I could be civil.

"Thanks," I muttered.

I felt shame colouring my face as I left her office.

"Your sister's pretty cute." Tatiana smiled over at Candy painting a basic grey wash across a canvas flat. "Must run in the family."

What do you even say to something like that? Was she flirting with me? I kept my head down and focused on the detailing I was trying to finish with my paintbrush. We could hear strains of the rehearsal backstage where we painted and Tatiana pinned, in the work area.

"Hopelessly devoted to you."

How corny. And exactly how I felt. Feel. About Tat.

Being there with Candy and Tatiana was the very best thing about my day.

"Kinda catchy after the 300th time, isn't it?" Tat bobbed her head as she pinned up the skirt of one of the Pink Ladies.

"I totally love this song!" chirruped Candy. "It's like my favourite and so romantic. I love Sandra Dee!"

"Of course, you do. Who doesn't?" And Tatania winked at me.

I really thought I'd melt into the floor, right there and then. I covered my crimson face and the bump on my forehead with my hair. My gawd. It's ridiculous. Jamie Kidding's life is a cross between a made-for-TV movie and a stupid high school musical.

"You know, Candy, I need a little help with one of Sandy's costumes. Would you like to try it on? Just to help me with the fitting?"

"Omigod! Can I?" And an ecstatic Candy ran to the dressing room, flouncy costume in hand.

"I thought that costume was already fitted last week." I couldn't help grinning at Tat.

"Sure was."

We laughed then. And there's seriously nothing like sharing a laugh with the girl that you love. Seriously.

I watched as Tat pretended to check over the fit and worked her magic on Candy within mere minutes. I could tell my sis pretty much adored her.

So what are you gonna do when the woman of your dreams charms your sister and winks at you? Invite her for donuts, what else?

Timmy Ho's was packed, but it was warm and dry after our snow-blown walk to get there. Candy had a hot chocolate and a Boston Cream; me and Tat each had a large double double and a French Cruller.

It was easy to be together. Who knew it could be so good? Why do good times never last?

Candy and I said goodbye to Tat, then fought the wind and snow on the walk to our apartment. As we got closer, my kid sister seemed real anxious. "How do you know Hugh isn't there, Jamie?"

"Because I know, Candy. He's locked up."

We stomped the snow off our boots and mounted the stairs to our apartment floor. Candy lagged behind again.

I unlocked the door. She hesitated in the hall.

"Look. I'll go in and check all the rooms, ok?"

She nodded. And I spent the next few minutes checking for bogey-men. Well, one bogey in particular.

"All clear! You can come in, Candy."

She took a look at the damage and heaved a great big sigh. "That's where Mom's head hit... That's when I dialed 911."

We stared at the broken drywall. "Good move on your part." The apartment was still. No noise but the whirring of the electric clock and the fridge humming from the kitchen.

"We haven't got too long to hang out here. If you want anything, Kidding Sister, you'd better grab it so I can get you back to Uncle Mac's in time for supper."

Candy disappeared down the hall to her room.

I unzipped my backpack. There it was. The HK45. Today I'd found it on Google Images during my research on gun control laws in Canada.

And today I also learned on the Internet just what such a piece costs. $1,233.84 CAD. I thought about what a sum like that could do for our family. And I thought about what a gun like that could do for our family. The choice was pretty clear.

If Hugh showed up at the apartment, I'd be ready.

I pulled out my book and started to draw.

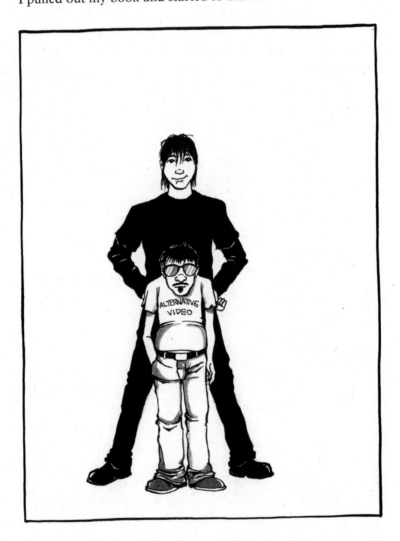

"Whatcha drawing?" Candy appeared at my right shoulder. Mr. Bunny was tucked under her arm.

"Tatania's boyfriend. And me."

"She has a boyfriend??? He's kind of a dweeb. I thought she was your girlfriend!"

"Yeah, well. She's not. We're just friends."

"But you'd like to be more than friends."

"Well, yeah, but that's not..."

"What is THAT??!!"

To my horror, she'd looked down at my backpack. The same one I'd stupidly forgotten to zip up. The same one with the HK45 gleaming up at us in the light of the kitchen. Stupid. Stupid. Stupid.

"Geez Louise, Jamie! WHAT ARE YOU DOING??? WHERE DID YOU GET THAT GUN??!!!!"

"Calm down, Candy. I found it, ok? In a dumpster. I've kept it hidden until... until Hugh..."

"ARE YOU OUT OF YOUR FREAKING MIND?"

"Listen, Candy." I closed my book and put it in the backpack which I zipped up firmly. "Hugh is NOT going to hurt this family again."

"I'm telling Mom."

I grabbed her by her shoulders and shook her. "No you're not."

"You're hurting me, Jamie."

And then I saw what I was doing. Released her immediately.

"You're just like him."

"No, Candy. I swear. I'm not. I'm sorry I was rough. I'm- I'm not gonna let him near you or Mom again."

She turned away from me.

"Candy. Please. Please understand. Please DON'T tell Mom or anyone about the gun. Promise me this one thing. I need you to promise me."

I guess she understood something from the note in my voice. She faced me. "I HATE this, Jamie."

"I know. But who else is gonna keep us safe? Can you name one person? And don't say Uncle Mac. But I'll take care of you. And Mom. Just promise to keep my secret."

Sighing, she did. But she wasn't happy about it. At all. I made her hold out her hands to show no crossed fingers. I've been caught by her tricks before.

Candy cares about me, her screw-up brother. And she knows what I feel about her. We're a team. And I intend not to let her down.

"Take me back to Uncle Mac's, ok? I don't wanna be here anymore."

Like a repeat of this morning, we waited in silence another fifteen minutes at the bus stop, then rode, without speaking, across the city to Uncle Mac's. It took us an hour because of the snowstorm and the traffic.

Mom was sure glad to see our faces at the door. Her own was pretty rough, stitched up like Frankenstein and her right eye swollen shut. She looked like some kind of humanoid alien. The swelling of her mouth made her words sound like she was talking through a pillow.

"Stay for supper, Jamie. Afterwards the three of us need to chat. In private."

So I did. Aunt Sue's meatloaf was pretty good. Uncle Mac was mostly bearable, except when I pushed the hair from my forehead without thinking. Then he interrogated me about the bump. I explained it away as a basketball mishap in gym class. That seemed to satisfy him. Candy wouldn't look at me. The twins took most of the attention away from the rest of us, so that was a relief, at least.

After supper Mom trotted us down to the basement rec room. We sat together in a little triangle.

"I want you kids to know that we're going back to the apartment. We're going home. Tomorrow or the next day. I've told Uncle Mac, and he has offered to pay to change the locks and fix the door."

"There's a big hole in the drywall," Candy blurted.

"That, too."

"What about Hugh? When does he get out?" I couldn't look my mother in the eye, fearing what she'd say.

"He's probably already out. The police can't hold him indefinitely while we... while we get our lives back together."

I shuddered. Please Molly. Don't take him back. From the paleness of her face, I could see Candy felt the same.

"I'm sorry, Candy and Jamie, that I went back to Hugh all those other times. I'm deeply ashamed. Embarrassed. It's just that I couldn't imagine a life without him, you know?"

We nodded. But we didn't know. Not really. Going back to get beat up again just never made any sense to me.

"I've felt so out of control. Like a great big nothing. I felt I couldn't do anything on my own. I was in a trap. I needed Hugh. God. We needed his cheque, small as it was from Workers' Comp. And I believed there was nothing better out there for me. As my mother used to say, 'you made your bed, now sleep in it.' But this time..."

I dared to look into my mother's open eye. Even though it was bloodshot and teary, I could tell she meant what she said.

Molly took a deep breath. She reminded me of Candy. Hell, she reminded me of me. "This time will be different. I've agreed to an Emergency Protection Order. I'll go to court and testify, if I have to. But Hugh's not coming back. We can do this on our own. The three of us."

"Just us three?" Candy was truly amazed. So was I, to tell you the truth. "But what about if Hugh tries to come home?"

"Honey, that's why we're talking. There's a chance that he will, though he's been ordered not to. We have to take precautions. The EPO is one. Changing the locks is another. I've already got a little money stashed away. We'll each keep an emergency bag packed. And we have to be alert. If we see Hugh or hear from him, we call the police immediately. Jamie, I'm going to rely on you to get Candy to and from school safely and to be the sitter when I'm on evening shift. No more ducking out at night."

"Mom, I'm sorry..."

"Son, it wasn't your fault what happened. I'm beginning to see that it wasn't mine, either. But you can't blame yourself. Neither of you must blame yourselves."

Candy started to sniffle. Molly, too. I could tell I wasn't far behind. Tried to keep my fool's face from contorting.

"Mom, I'll be there for Candy. For you. I promise." I cast Candy a meaningful look. She kept her mouth shut. "And I'll get a job."

"No, Jamie. School and your artwork have to come first…"

"Even if it's once a week when you're not working, it'll help."

She sighed. Blew her nose. "Let's take it a step at a time, ok? Tomorrow the social worker is going take me to the apartment. I'll box up all of Hugh's things. Then I'm going over to both restaurants to check in with Lou and Charlie. Hopefully, they'll understand that I need these few days off from work. Especially when they see how my face would scare away the customers." Molly tried to laugh, but I could tell the effort hurt her.

"Uncle Mac… Uncle Mac has been great. He's given me some money to tide us over."

"Do you think he'd buy us a new TV?" Candy's eyes were wide with hope.

Molly smiled, despite her fat lip. "Don't push it, honey. And Jamie. Just try to be nice to him, ok?"

"Ok."

We talked a little longer, and there were more tears, but not the bad kind. Aunt Sue brought us some tea. And she asked me to stay the night. Given the weather conditions, my uncle's generosity and Aunt Sue's nervous but kind eyes, how could I refuse?

Molly and Candy decided to turn in early, so I did, too. I slept the sleep of the dead on my Uncle's pull-out couch, my backpack right beside me. Just in case.

I woke before dawn to find I'd wet the freaking bed.

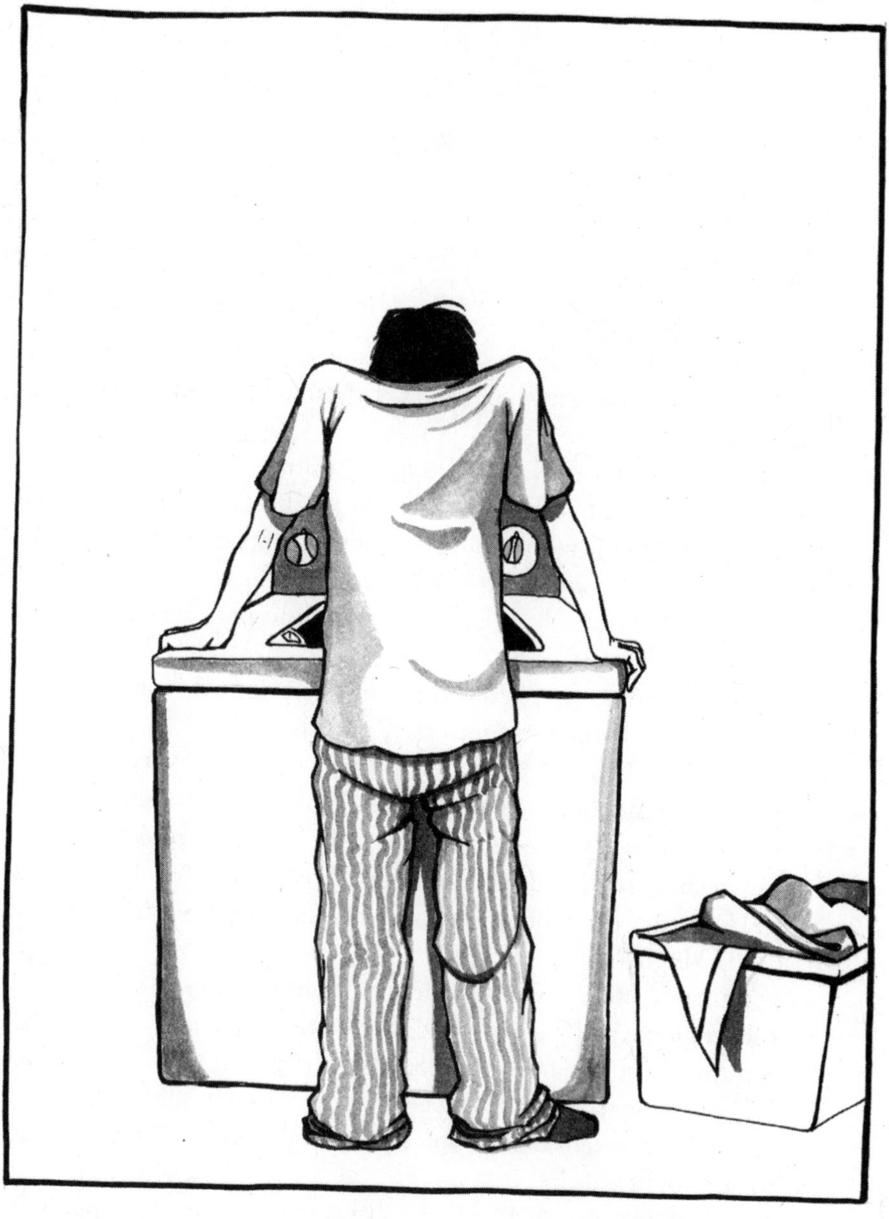

Painting is excellent therapy.

No shit. Millions of bucks could be saved if people in analysis just picked up a paintbrush and got off the couch.

Ok. I'm not saying my mom and Candy aren't being helped by talking to their counsellor.

But talking isn't for Jamie Kidding. Painting works just fine. I've repainted the entire living room. After the workman came in and fixed the door and the hole in the wall, I took the job of priming then refreshing the walls with a nice buttercream colour and white trim, picked out by Molly and Candy at Canadian Tire, and paid for, courtesy of Uncle Mac.

He still hasn't set foot in our apartment. But he made good on funding the repairs and the locksmith to change the locks.

No sign of Hugh the Pugh. Not a word. Not a peep.

Molly and the social worker got rid of his few boxes of clothes and dusty trophies and assorted crap. Me and the workman took HP's ugly, beat-up recliner out beside the dumpster. Somebody's already hauled it away. Hope they get a lot of use out of the thing. We're glad to be free of it. And Hugh.

A bunch of other stuff ended up in the garbage, too. Molly donned her rubber gloves and put her foot down. Out with the junk of our lives! Broken toys. Old magazines. Clothes and shoes that we've outgrown. The great purge of the twenty-first century. Followed by the scrub down. The whole place smells of Pine-Sol. Everything looks fresh. Late-winter cleaning, Candy calls it.

I say, good riddance. Our home seems lighter. Hard to explain. It just does.

Candice the smartass bounded into the living room with a helpful suggestion. I just gave her the wind-up digitus impudicus (love those Latin guys!).

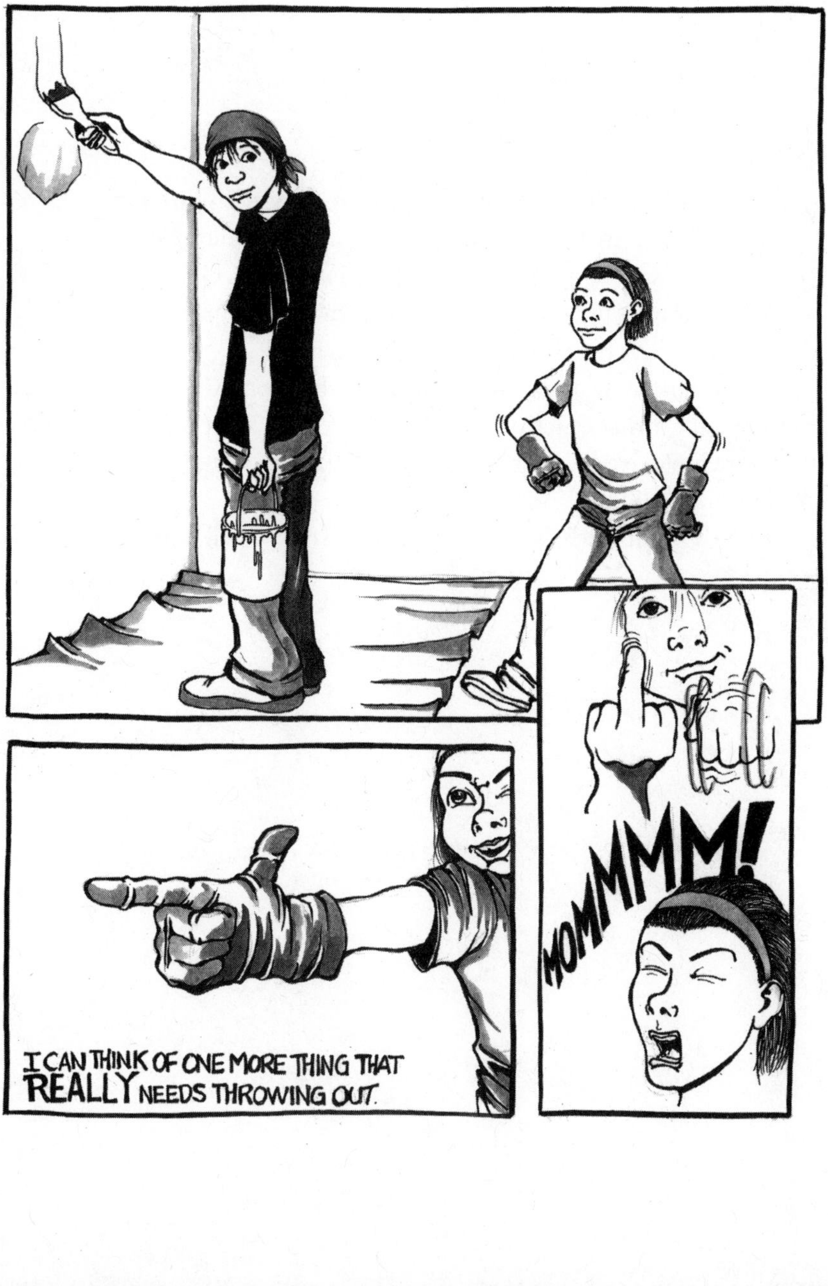
I CAN THINK OF ONE MORE THING THAT REALLY NEEDS THROWING OUT.
MOMMMMM!

Got in trouble for that one. But I split my gut laughing.

Secretly, Candy loved it, though she ratted me out. I know because she's used the same gesture on me several times since. Gotta love that kid.

I may double my bottle bobbing efforts in the spring to finance the repainting of her bedroom. Pink. What else?

But I look forward to the work. The whole painting-cleaning thing has brought a real quiet to the apartment. I think none of us realized how much we needed that. We've been walking on eggshells for years. And now... peace.

So last night I finally worked up the nerve to call Tatiana.

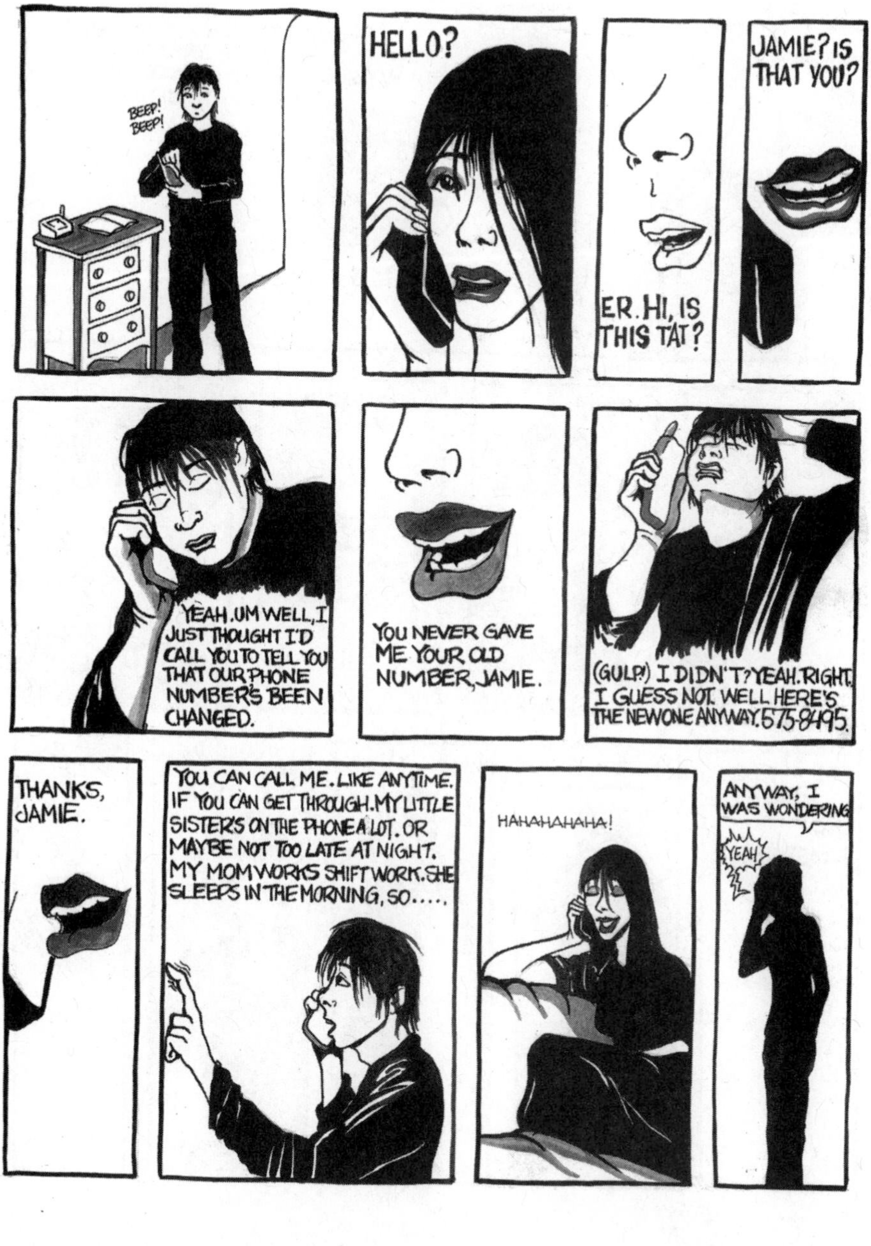
BEEP! BEEP!
HELLO?
ER. HI, IS THIS TAT?
JAMIE? IS THAT YOU?
YEAH. UM WELL, I JUST THOUGHT I'D CALL YOU TO TELL YOU THAT OUR PHONE NUMBER'S BEEN CHANGED.
YOU NEVER GAVE ME YOUR OLD NUMBER, JAMIE.
(GULP!) I DIDN'T? YEAH. RIGHT. I GUESS NOT. WELL HERE'S THE NEW ONE ANYWAY. 575-8495.
THANKS, JAMIE.
YOU CAN CALL ME. LIKE ANYTIME. IF YOU CAN GET THROUGH. MY LITTLE SISTER'S ON THE PHONE A LOT. OR MAYBE NOT TOO LATE AT NIGHT. MY MOM WORKS SHIFT WORK. SHE SLEEPS IN THE MORNING, SO.....
HAHAHAHAHA!
ANYWAY, I WAS WONDERING
YEAH

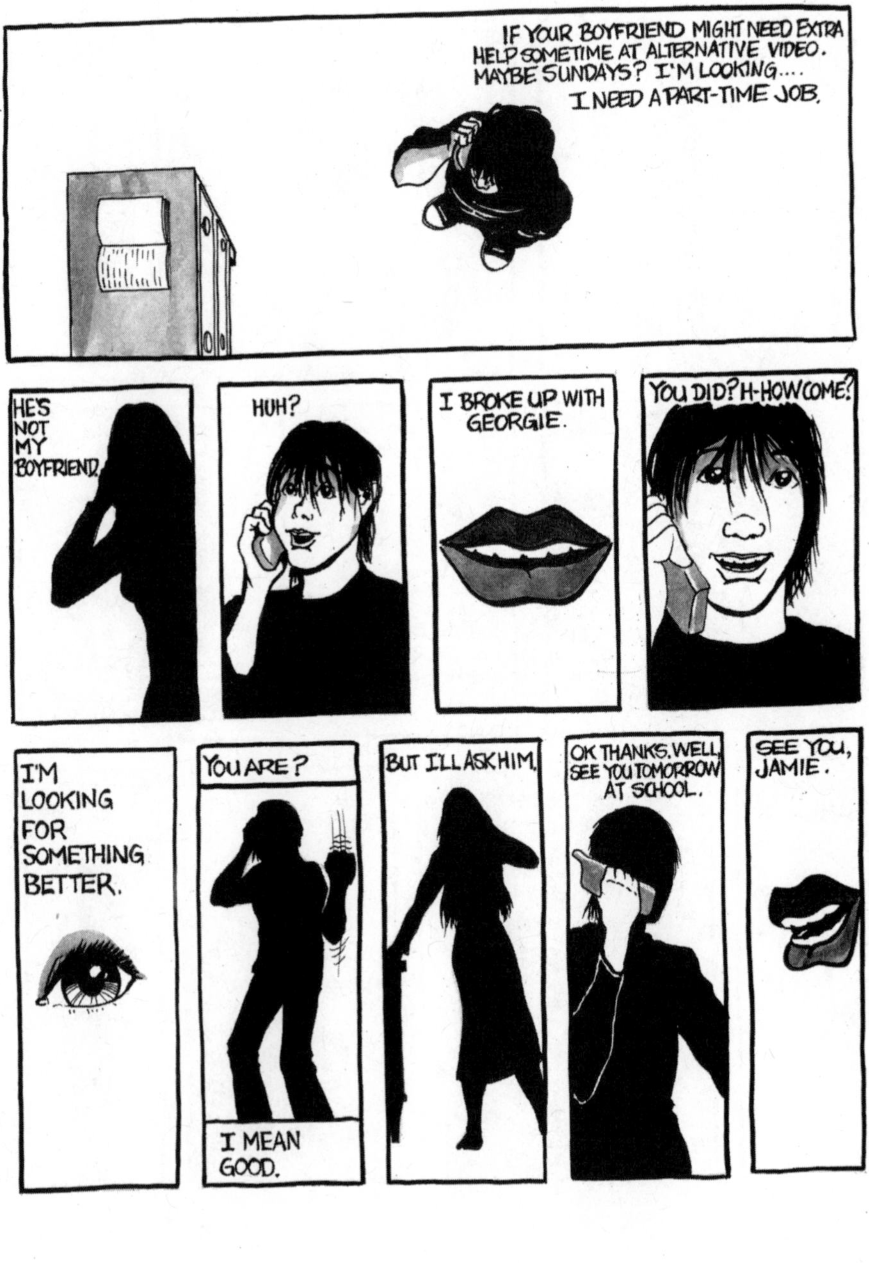
IF YOUR BOYFRIEND MIGHT NEED EXTRA HELP SOMETIME AT ALTERNATIVE VIDEO. MAYBE SUNDAYS? I'M LOOKING....
I NEED A PART-TIME JOB.
HE'S NOT MY BOYFRIEND.
HUH?
I BROKE UP WITH GEORGIE.
YOU DID? H-HOW COME?
I'M LOOKING FOR SOMETHING BETTER.
YOU ARE?
I MEAN GOOD.
BUT I'LL ASK HIM.
OK THANKS. WELL SEE YOU TOMORROW AT SCHOOL.
SEE YOU, JAMIE.

I spent the next fifteen minutes hyperventilating.

What a complete ignoramus I am with women!

I still don't know what to make of the whole conversation. If you can call it that.

Am I the "something better" that Tatiana's looking for?

If so, the poor girl is deluded.

But still... I'd like to be.

Right. And tomorrow a cute little leprechaun will drop by with a fricking pot of gold and some Lucky Charms. Just for Jamie Kidding.

Where's the sign that says "kick me"? I know there has to be one. Might be invisible. But it's there.

First thing. I get to school today after dropping off Candy and what do I find? Someone has buggered my combination lock. Poured some kind of sticky sports drink all over it and through the slots of my locker door. Had to have happened hours earlier. Everything was nicely dried and stuck and stiff. The custodian tried to open the lock but ended up cutting it off. My binders and textbooks are a greenish tacky mess. A sickening sweet smell greets me every time I open #414.

Thanks Attaman. Or one of your stupid steroid stooges.

I'm just grateful that the HK45 was safe in my backpack. It could've been damaged or worse. I take the gun everywhere now. Never let that pack out of my sight or out of quick grab range.

Next thing happened at lunch time. I slid on a French fry in the cafeteria and well... total humiliation.

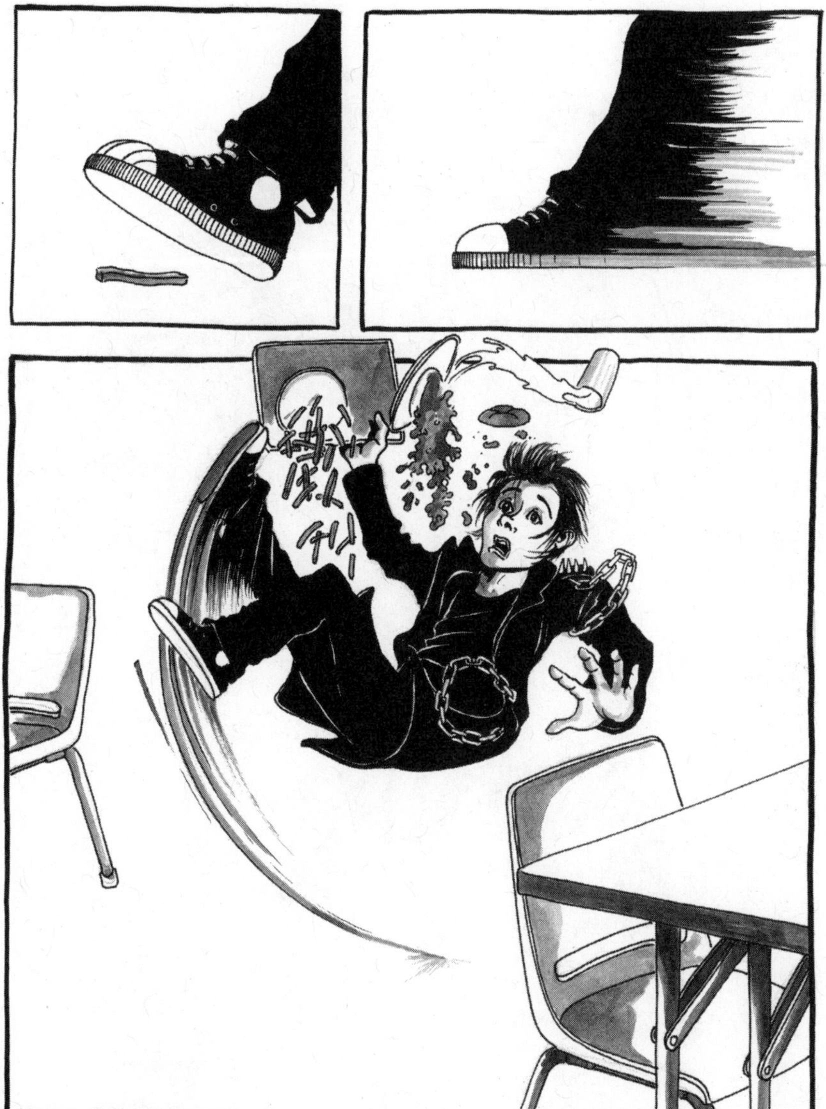

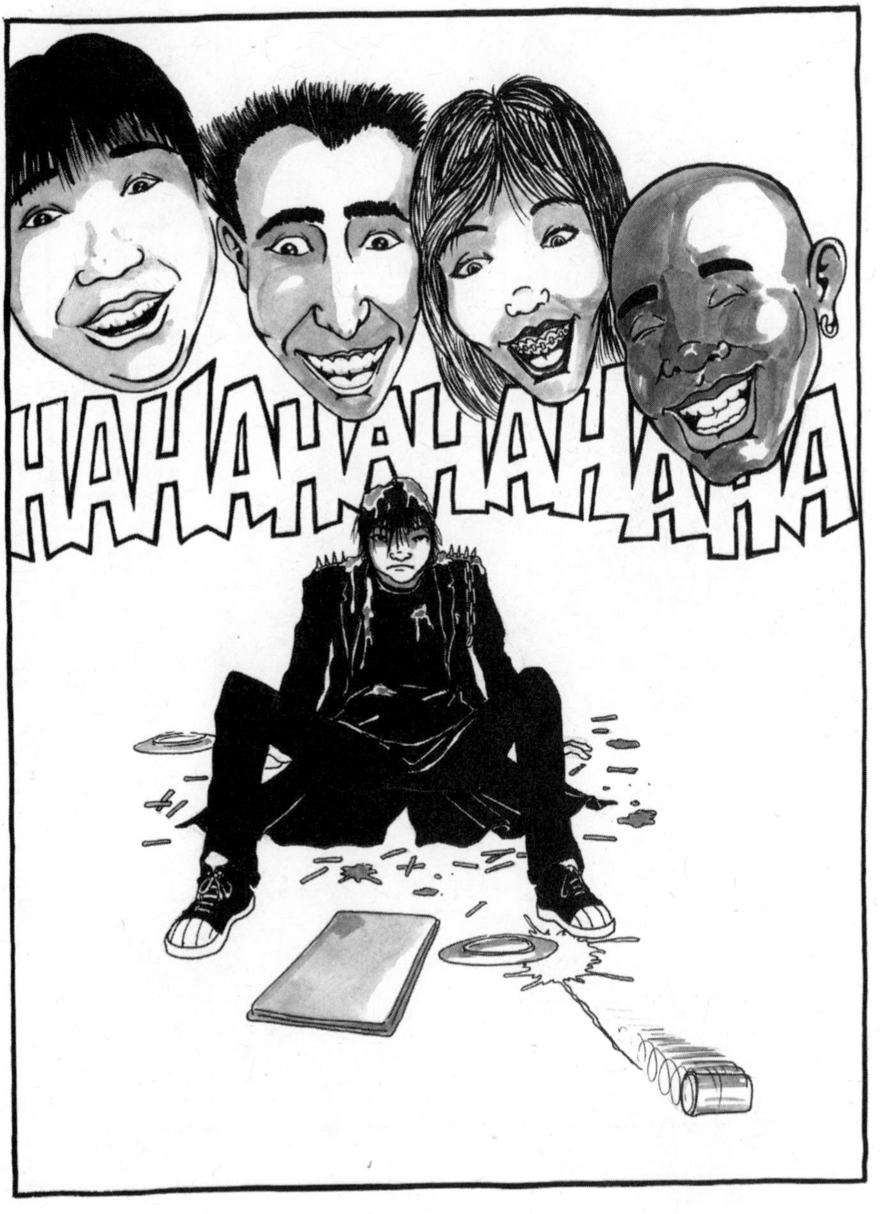
HAHAHAHAHAHAHA

Took me twenty minutes to clean up my hair. And now I have to pay to get my coat dry cleaned. And man, that's expensive! Plus, I went without my midday meal. Not good for a skinny Kidding. I'd only had enough money for one sloppy joe. Lunch was supposed to be a treat from Molly. I don't get paid from Alternative Video for another week and a half. Back to bag lunches tomorrow. They're safer.

No lunch meant a grumbling Kidding stomach throughout my afternoon art class. How embarrassing. I kept pretending that it wasn't me. But everyone could tell it was.

Finally, Mr. Letterman tossed me an apple from the still life we were meant to be drawing. I ate it, but my cheeks were the same colour as the fruit.

Work on the musical tech crew was pretty boring because Tatiana has been home with the flu. This started on Sunday, my first day at the video store. I trotted in, anticipating my inaugural shift with Tat, just as she ran out, white-faced and homeward hellbound. I haven't seen her since. Georgie showed me the ropes about cleaning the DVDs and re-boxing, working the cash, restocking the shelves. He has the personality of a three-toed sloth. But he's pretty harmless and seems alright with me around. Long as I do my work and stay my full shift.

Somehow the geek-savant seems completely unmoved by the fact that Tatiana has broken up with him.

What's up with that? Oblivious video nerd.

But by far the worst part of my day happened late tonight. I'd gone to get a few groceries for Molly at the Mini-Mart. I heard the pounding music—the Be-Atch Boys, who wouldn't recognize their gangsta beat?—from the car before it slowed down to a jaguar's purr beside me...

Black Mercedes SUV. Black tinted windows. Vanity plate: MeMoFo.

Who else but Tony the pimp?

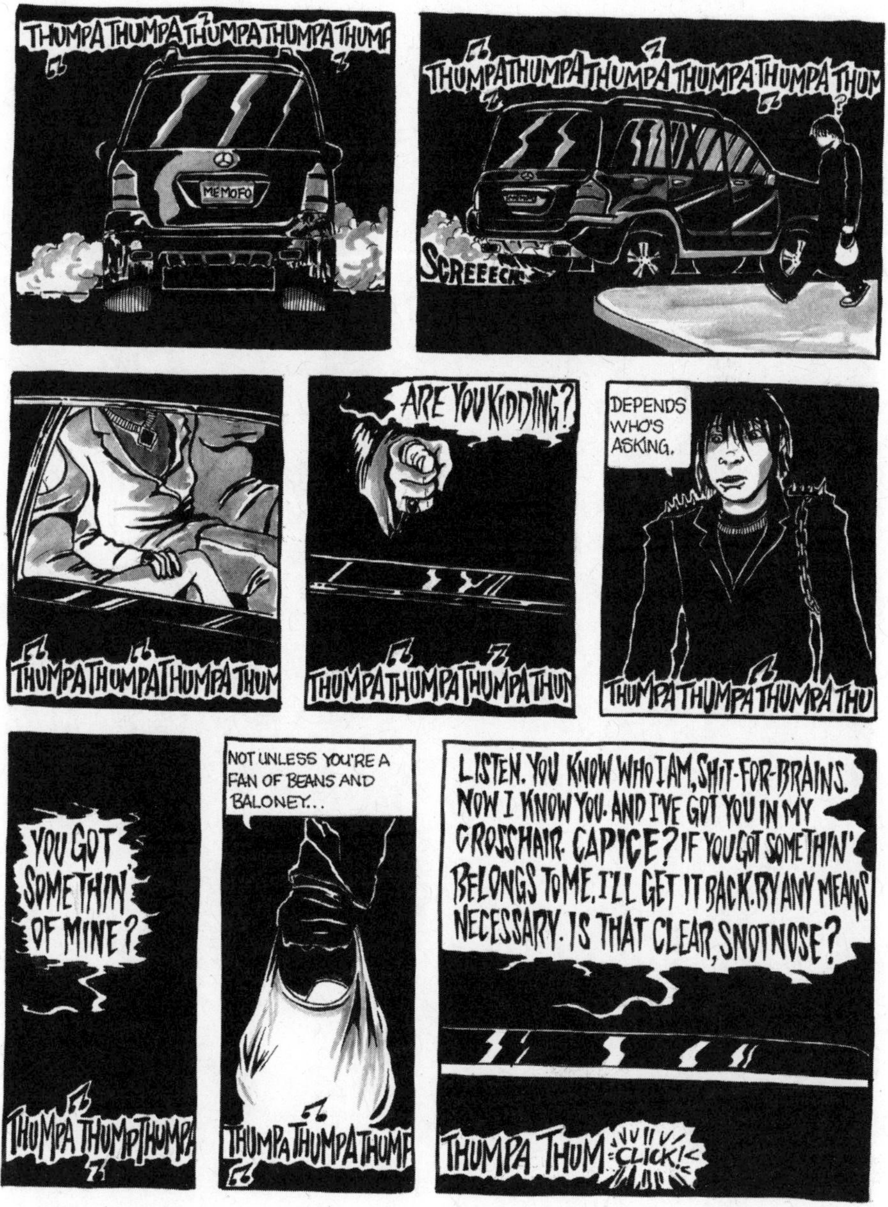
THUMPA THUMPA THUMPA THUMPA THUMP
MEMOFO
THUMPA THUMPA THUMPA THUMPA THUMPA THUM
SCREEECH
THUMPA THUMPA THUMPA THUM
ARE YOU KIDDING?
THUMPA THUMPA THUMPA THUM
DEPENDS WHO'S ASKING.
THUMPA THUMPA THUMPA THU
YOU GOT SOMETHIN' OF MINE?
THUMPA THUMP THUMPA
NOT UNLESS YOU'RE A FAN OF BEANS AND BALONEY...
THUMPA THUMPA THUMP
LISTEN. YOU KNOW WHO I AM, SHIT-FOR-BRAINS. NOW I KNOW YOU. AND I'VE GOT YOU IN MY CROSSHAIR. CAPICE? IF YOU GOT SOMETHIN' BELONGS TO ME, I'LL GET IT BACK. BY ANY MEANS NECESSARY. IS THAT CLEAR, SNOTNOSE?
THUMPA THUM
CLICK!

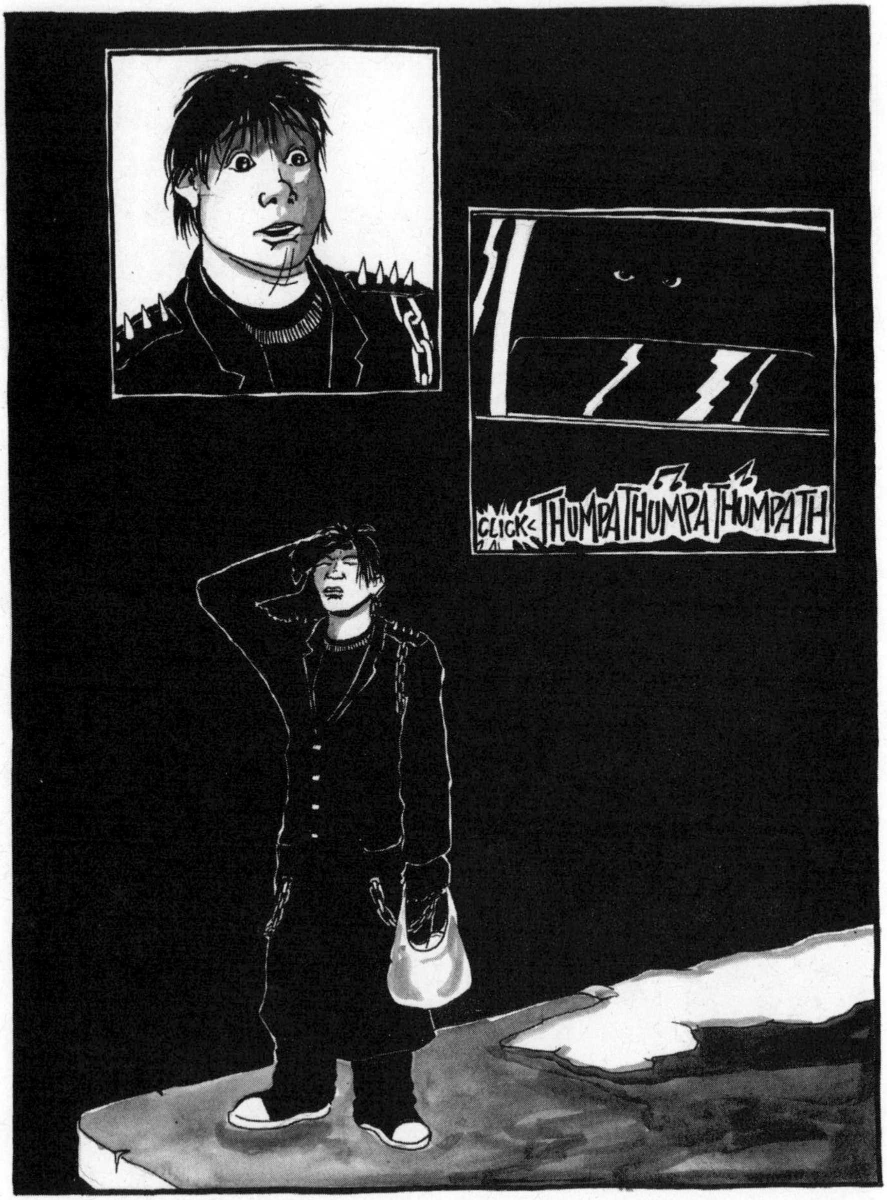
CLICK
THUMPATHUMPATHUMPATH

I vomited a little in my mouth.

My balls completely retreated up into my throat until the Mercedes disappeared around a corner, and I remembered how to walk. I took my numb legs home and shivered under my bedcovers most of the night.

There's no doubt in my mind now that the gun belongs to Tony. It was dumped or stashed for pick up later. But a dumpster diving dipshit found it first and kept it.

And he's not giving it back.

Have to kill me first.

Jamie Kidding needs the gun more than some gangsta pimp artist who's probably got ten times that many weapons in his arsenal. It just means that I was stupid to show Tina.

What did I expect? Tina's totally Tony's. She's his girl. His property. He owns her. His slave. Especially because he's got her hooked up on H. And a good little slave is gonna tell all. For better treatment. For a lighter beating. For a little bit of love. And for more junk.

By sharing my little secret with a junkie I've endangered my life. Maybe my family's. What an imbecile!

Kee-rist!

I sat up in bed.

Tony could've easily popped me there and then. Ripped the back-pack off my shoulders, found the gun and ended my short *happy* life.

I'm sure the police would then spend about ten minutes on the case, despite Molly's pleas for justice. Just another dead deadbeat Northeast kid.

I gotta play this smart. No more sharing with boyhood crushes turned street tarts. Keep a low profile, Kidding. You of all people, Incredible Disappearing Boy, know how to do that.

Or you *will* disappear. No Kidding. For good.

Tatiana Oleshenko was kissing me. Deeply. Madly. I wanted to pinch myself to see if it was really true. But she kept distracting me with those red Russian-Canadian lips and what and where her hands were travelling down and down my...

"Jamie! Get up!"

And with a thwonk my little Kidding sister landed on my bed and knocked me back to waking life.

Sometimes a little sister should just not come into her brother's bedroom. Especially when he is having the best dream ever. And especially when... if you know what I mean. I had to roll over on my stomach quickly. Will the embarrassment that is my life never end?

But Dandy Candy was far too excited to notice anything tent-like about my bedcovers.

"It's Saturday and the day of my spring dance concert! C'mon! Mom's made blueberry pancakes and then we have to *go!!!*"

"Get off my bed!" My breath in my pillow really stank.

"Fine, sour puss! But don't ruin my perfect day by being late."

"I'm up! I'm up! Get outta here so I can get dressed."

She slammed the door and went whining off to Molly about my laziness and general ineptitude. Good word. Fits like a glove.

Found it when I went thesaurus hunting for Attaman adjectives for this week's school newspaper comic. Discovered an even better phrase for Attaman, though, straight from the English bard himself:

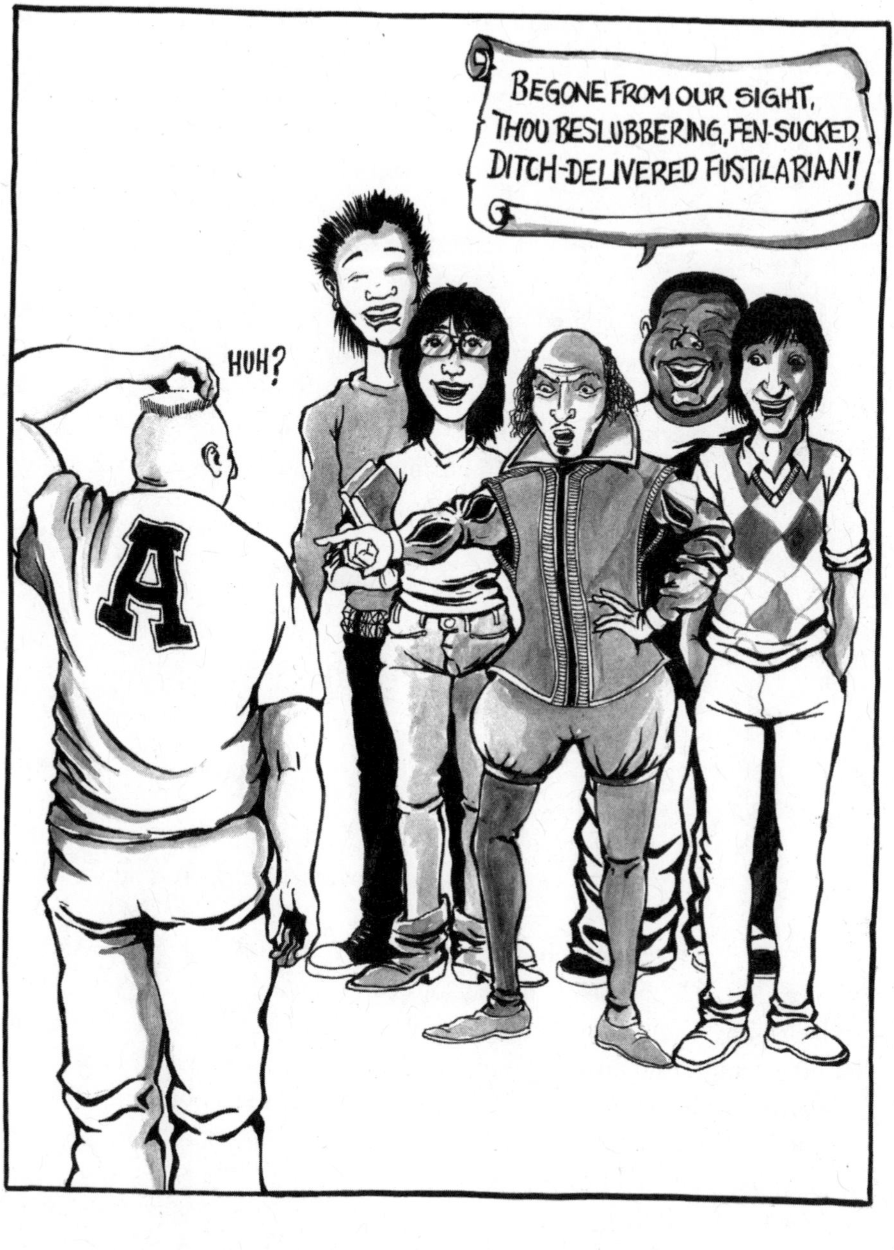
HUH?
BEGONE FROM OUR SIGHT, THOU BESLUBBERING, FEN-SUCKED, DITCH-DELIVERED FUSTILARIAN!

Molly managed to calm the bumblebee dancer down long enough to eat and then sent her to get her dance stuff together. As I stuffed my mouth with blueberry pancakes loaded with butter and syrup, she brought out my black coat, covered in dry cleaning plastic and good as new. My mom knows the way to a son's heart. She'd taken the coat to the cleaner's next door to Lou's restaurant. Paid for the cleaning from her tips, which are never that great, so she must've saved up. Gotta love that woman!

I was pretty excited and nervous about the spring dance concert myself. Tatiana was invited. On account of Candy. I'd called the girl of my dreams, just to check on how she was feeling after the flu took her out for a week. Candy flopped on the couch next to me. Which made any kind of intimacy pretty much impossible. Not that I'm much good with the intimacy thing. Or telephone conversations.

"Ask her to come!"

I put my hand over the receiver. "Shut up!"

"I know you're talking to your girlfriend."

"She's NOT my girlfriend."

"Ok. I know you're talking to Tatiana."

"How do you know?"

"For Pete's sake! Just look at your face? It's as red as a beet! Who else would you be talking to?"

"Keep your voice down!"

"Only if you ask her to come to my dance recital this Saturday."

"No way!"

From the phone, I heard, "I'd love to come. Tell Candy, yes. And tell Jamie, too." And then that delicious Tatiana laughter. And my ears were burning. And Candy grabbed the phone away from me and gave her all the details. And now it was Saturday and I was a wreck. But happy, too. Grinning like a dope on the three-bus ride where I stood next to Molly and Candy as we travelled to the MacEwan University auditorium where the recital would be held. I was loaded with my backpack, Candy's costumes, her make-up and hair products bag, her other bag with shoes and tights and whatever else little dancer chicks need. But I didn't mind a bit.

And I didn't mind when we stepped off the bus into the slush in front of the MacEwan theatre and there was a raven-haired beauty smiling at all of us.

I introduced Tatiana to my mother. It didn't go too bad. Molly was super polite without being über interested. Thank gawd. Then Candy was pulling us by the hand inside the building and got caught up in the whirlwind of pre-show preparation. The Kidding sister and Molly went off down the backstage hall to the dressing rooms.

"Break a leg!" Tatiana shouted.

She and I headed to our seats.

Looking at her, I remembered my morning dream. I begged my body to behave. In the dark. Sitting next to her. It didn't. But Tatiana, watching the dancers, didn't notice. When Candy pranced on and bumbled like the bee she'd always dreamed of being, Tatiana grabbed my hand in excitement and pride that matched my own.

I thought I'd die of happiness.

Again, heavy on the cheddar. I know.

But my heart was getting jiggy in my chest. And it all felt great.

Afterwards we went for Chinese food at Charlie's. Since she works there, Molly gets a deal and invited Tat along, too. We sat around the table and mostly listened to Candy chatter about the performance and ask us how great we thought it was.

"You were my favourite." Tatiana pointed her chopsticks at our beaming bee.

Everyone smiled, especially Molly. Even though she still has some jaw issues from the beating. The bruising and swelling are almost completely gone.

Molly was also pretty cool when I told her I'd be home a little later. No embarrassing questions. She and Candy waved to us from the bus window.

I wanted to show Tatiana my Grim Reaper piece and led her through the streets to the alley. I made her back her way in and I covered her eyes. Then...the reveal. The girl actually gasped when she saw it.

"This is sick, Jamie!"

I felt my heart shooting around in my chest again. This girl could kill a guy. Seriously.

"I'm not kidding! No pun intended." She chuckled and then traced the motorbike with her gloved hand. "Do you have photographs of this? You should! You should make a portfolio of your street art. Put it up on a website. I could- I could help you with that."

I couldn't meet her eyes. "Um. We don't. We don't have a computer at home, Tat. And the only camera we have is Candy's little cheapo. But thanks for the offer. Really. I mean it."

Tatiana didn't miss a beat. "No problem! We'll do it in school! I'll talk to my design teacher, Mr. Kraft, and you talk to Mr. Letterman. We can borrow the school camera. Use the design studio. Build a website in the computer lab. And at the same time create a portfolio—in print, on USB and in the cloud—for you!"

It was hard not to get caught up in her enthusiasm. "O-ok."

"Great! And we'll probably get extra credits in CT or something! That'll be the icing on the cake!" She'd grabbed my arm in her excitement. I could feel the warmth of her hand through my coat.

"Jamie! I'm so into this! Let's start this week, ok? The first sunny day."

I nodded and she hugged me. And then...

Jamie Kidding was speechless. So he just handed Tatiana Oleshenko the envelope he'd brought for her. In it was a drawing that the young artist had slaved over for a week. A kind of glad-you're-feeling-better-and-by-the-way-do-you-know-that-I-love-you-but-I'll-never-tell-you present.

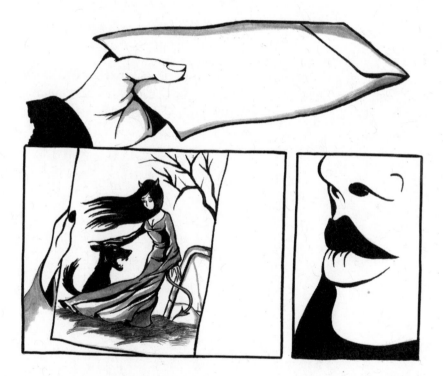

I sorta floated home. Got off the bus stop nearest our place. Didn't even care when I stepped into a puddle of cold ice melt. Probably looked like one of those mental case homeless dudes, grinning and whistling down the sidewalk. Wondering if sometimes dreams come true…

Then the black SUV drove by.

I think I made it into the shadows without anyone seeing me.

But I can't be sure.

I swear I almost shat my pants. Who can blame me?

Midnight, my shift ended at Alternative Video. I rode the LRT home to our station. Usually, it's a quiet ride. Only one or two night commuters. Tonight I was alone in car B-102. From the Belvedere station I can hop on another bus or hoof it home. But tonight I almost didn't make it.

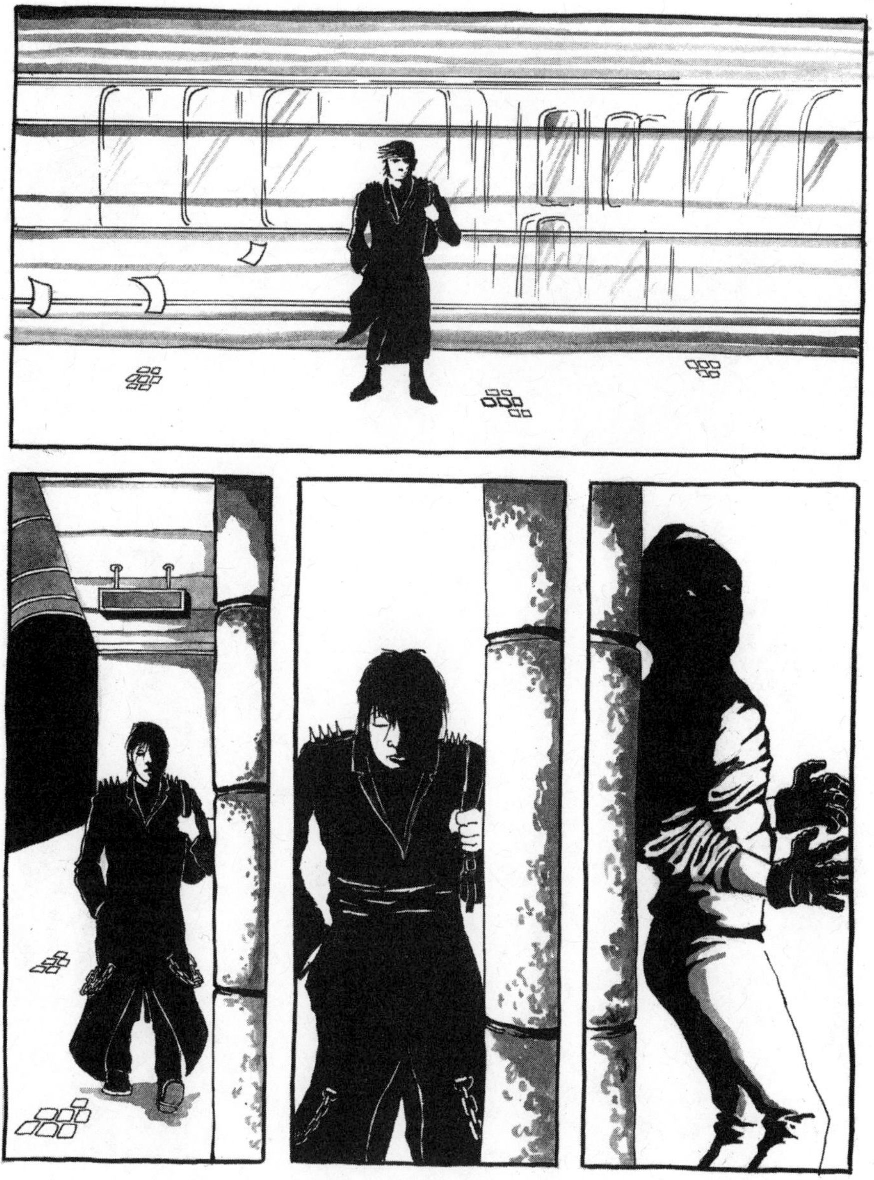

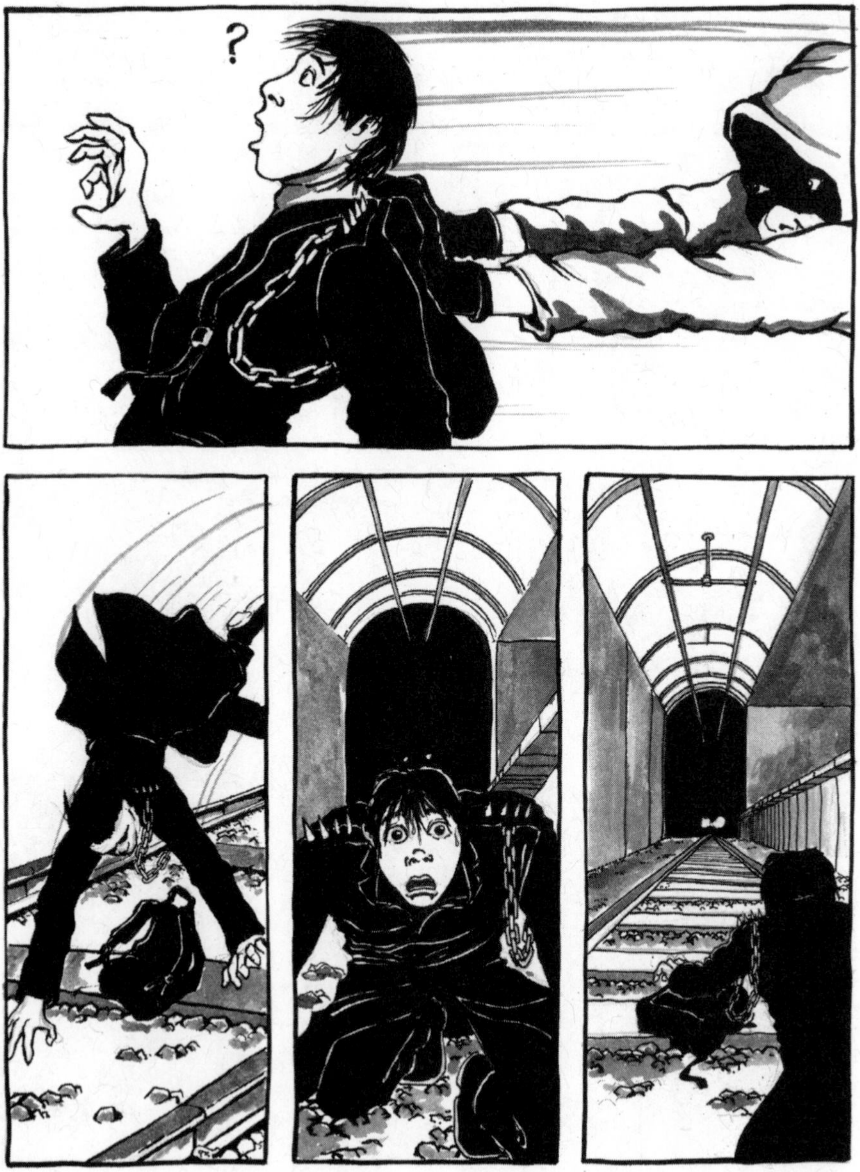
?

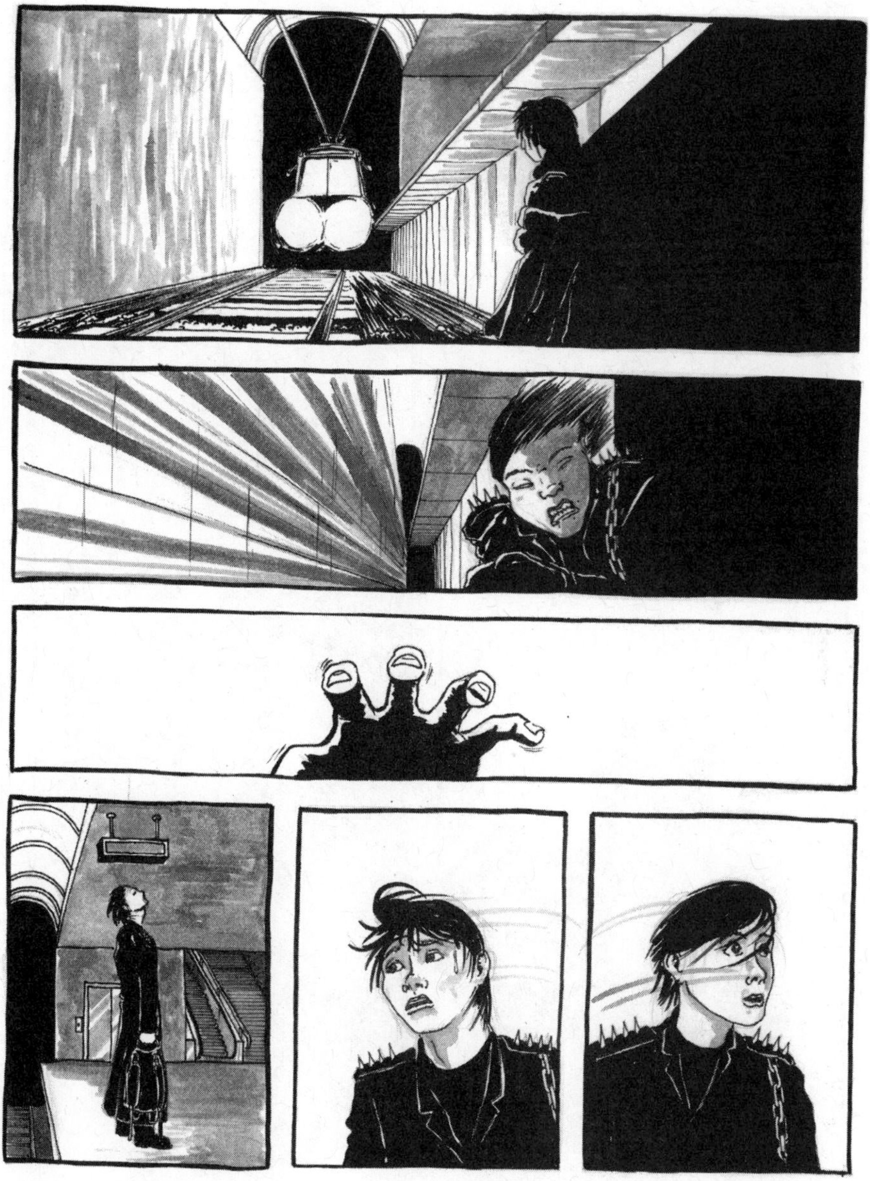

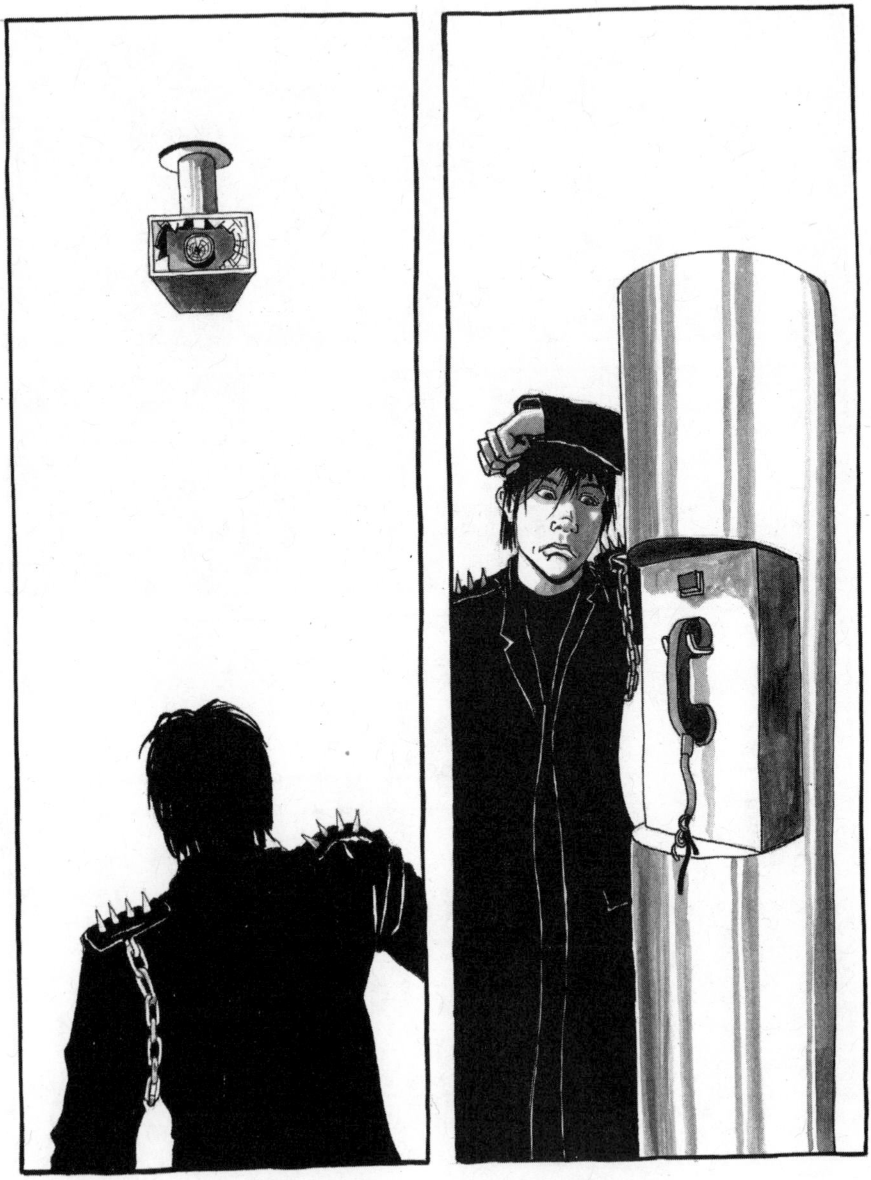

I banged my knee in the fall, but otherwise I was unhurt. Except for the near-stroke and the sudden stopping of my pulse from pure terror. I limped home. Kept looking over my shoulder. Wiping my eyes. Staying in the shadows.

I passed Tina's corner. The other girls were out, but no sign of Tina. Not that I had any interest in talking to her. Or anyone. Instead, I kept kinda praying I'd make it safely to our apartment. Man, I was that freaked. I ran up those stairs fast as my foolish feet would let me. Unlocked the door and bolted it from within. Nearly sobbed with relief.

I was home much later than usual. Tried not to wake Mom or Candy. Took a hot shower to try to stop my shaking.

Because I can't shake the feeling that whoever did this had it in for *me*. That whoever did this knew me and knew my Sunday route. Was waiting for me behind that pillar. Wanted Jamie Kidding dead.

What the hell for?

Who the hell?

I listed the likely suspects.

Hugh. But we haven't seen hide nor hair of him since his arrest. And why would he want me bloodied and mangled? Unless he blames me for Molly kicking his sorry ass out. Or unless he was just d & u. Drunk and ugly.

Blade Attaman. Or one of his muscle monkeys. Would they try to kill me? Over a stupid comic series? Doesn't Blade prefer knives when he wants to spill someone's guts?

And then, of course, I couldn't ignore the scariest possibility of all: Tony. I'm packing his heat. He's gotta grudge. And a killer rep.

But why wouldn't he just gun me down? Why go to the trouble of a sneak attack? From behind?

Unless. Unless I wasn't meant to be killed. Just warned.

Well, consider me warned.

Armed.

And dangerous.

Whoever the pushy asshole is, I've got an HK45 fits in the palm of my hand with a grip like it was custom made for me. Think I'll take to carrying it in the breast of my coat from now on, whenever I'm alone. Someone surprises me like that again, I'll be ready. And willing.

I barely slept last night. Night sweats. Nightmares. Night terrors. Shadowy figures in mad pursuit. I kept tossing. Waking. Drifting. Twitching.

Like a finger on a trigger.

Tina's missing.

It's been over a week since I saw her last. I first noticed her gone from her "post" that fateful Sunday when I nearly bit it. Or got bitten.

I asked a couple of the other girls. They just laughed and offered me sex. I don't have that kinda dough. Or that kinda desire. I just feel sorry and sad. For them. For Tina.

And now I'm freaked out for her. Where is she? What has that prick pimp done to her?

I'm considering going to the police. But I doubt they'd take me seriously. Who cares about a missing hooker? Still, I might drop in to see Officer Jack, the police liaison guy at our school. Just for some advice. Maybe. If Tina doesn't turn up in a day or two.

I shudder to think what that might mean...

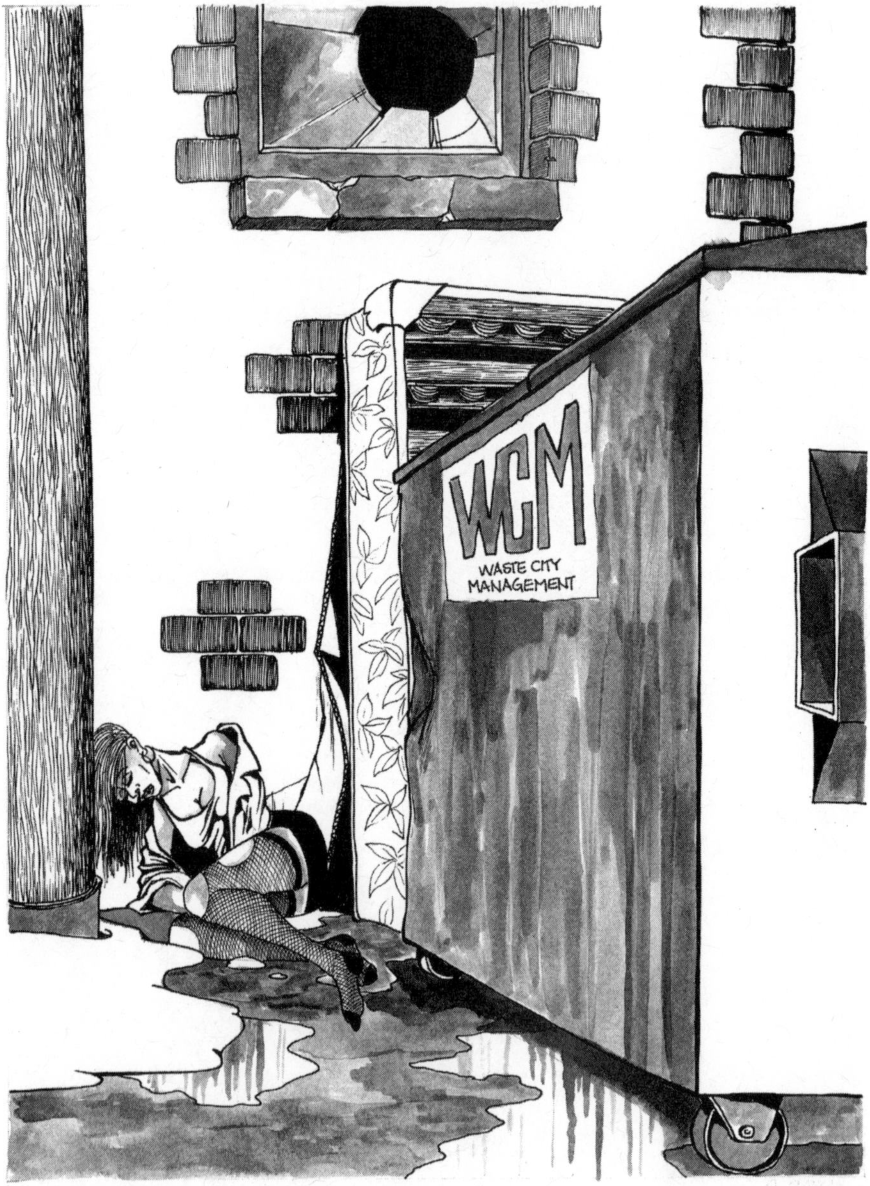
WCM
WASTE CITY
MANAGEMENT

Shit. She's only seventeen.

Just like me.

I'm pretty jumpy these days. Ask Candy. I nearly bit her head off the other afternoon. She leapt out from behind her school building, as I was coming to get her for the walk home.

"For Chrissake, Candy! Don't flipping DO that!"

"Lighten up, Jamie. I'm just playing. What's got into you? Lose your sense of humour somewhere?"

"I-I just got things on my mind."

"Like that gun."

"Huh?"

"Ever since that gun. You're not the same Jamie."

"What're you talking about? You're imagining things."

"*You're* like a loaded gun."

"That's crazy."

"Yes, it is."

I apologized for barking at her. But the walk home was pretty chilly.

This afternoon Tatiana and I finally got permission to begin our photography shoot of my street art. At first the school administration wasn't too keen on supporting the idea of the artist as vandal. We assured them that the pieces we'd photograph were on abandoned buildings or places where graffiti is permitted in public spaces.

It's a load of crap, of course. But Tatiana knows how to make creative arguments. Stretch the truth.

I don't go downtown to vandalize shiny new buildings. Mostly I stay in my own ugly neighbourhood which, to be honest, could use a little colour. Alleys and backways and dumpsters are my specialty. I'm not interested in messing up some shop owner's small business.

I am interested in saying something. So someone will look. Listen. I have a story to tell. And I tell my story best with pictures.

So we got access to the school camera and we spent the remaining daylight digitally. Shooting that is. It was a riot!

First, there's nothing compares to a beautiful girl admiring your art-work. What a rush! And Tatiana absolutely loves my mermaid stencils —my tribute to her, and I think she knows it.

Second, it was sweet to work the camera and try out my hand at framing and composition. One day maybe I'll buy my own fabulous Nikon. Yeah, it'll fit in nicely with my loft apartment with the fireplace.

Finally, it was a scream to take pictures of each other. How could we resist? We got some hilarious shots next to statues in the park. And I caught a great moment with Tatiana on a swing. We snapped photos, pretending to be famous models. We posed. We vogued. We laughed ourselves silly.

It's been a long time since I did that. Maybe not even since I was a really little Kidding. My dad used to have that effect on me, joking around or throwing me up or tussling in the fall leaves.

For a few hours, with Tatiana, I felt like a kid again. Is that how other seventeen-year-olds feel?

Tomorrow we download the photos and start building a portfolio and a webpage. Wednesday through Friday are also the tech rehearsals for the musical. Saturday is a full day for the dress rehearsal. Sunday night I work at Alternative Video. So this week I'll spend most of my waking hours with Tatiana Oleshenko.

I'm down with that!

But it's hard to get to sleep. I feel jumpy. Excited about time with Tat. Distracted by other stuff in my life. Like Tina. Like who's out there wanting to hurt me.

The banging started around 11:30. I must've fallen asleep after all. But I couldn't have slept for long. Molly was still at the restaurant. I grabbed my pack and headed for the door. Squinted through the peephole.

It was Hugh the Pugh. Wasted. Weaving in the hallway.

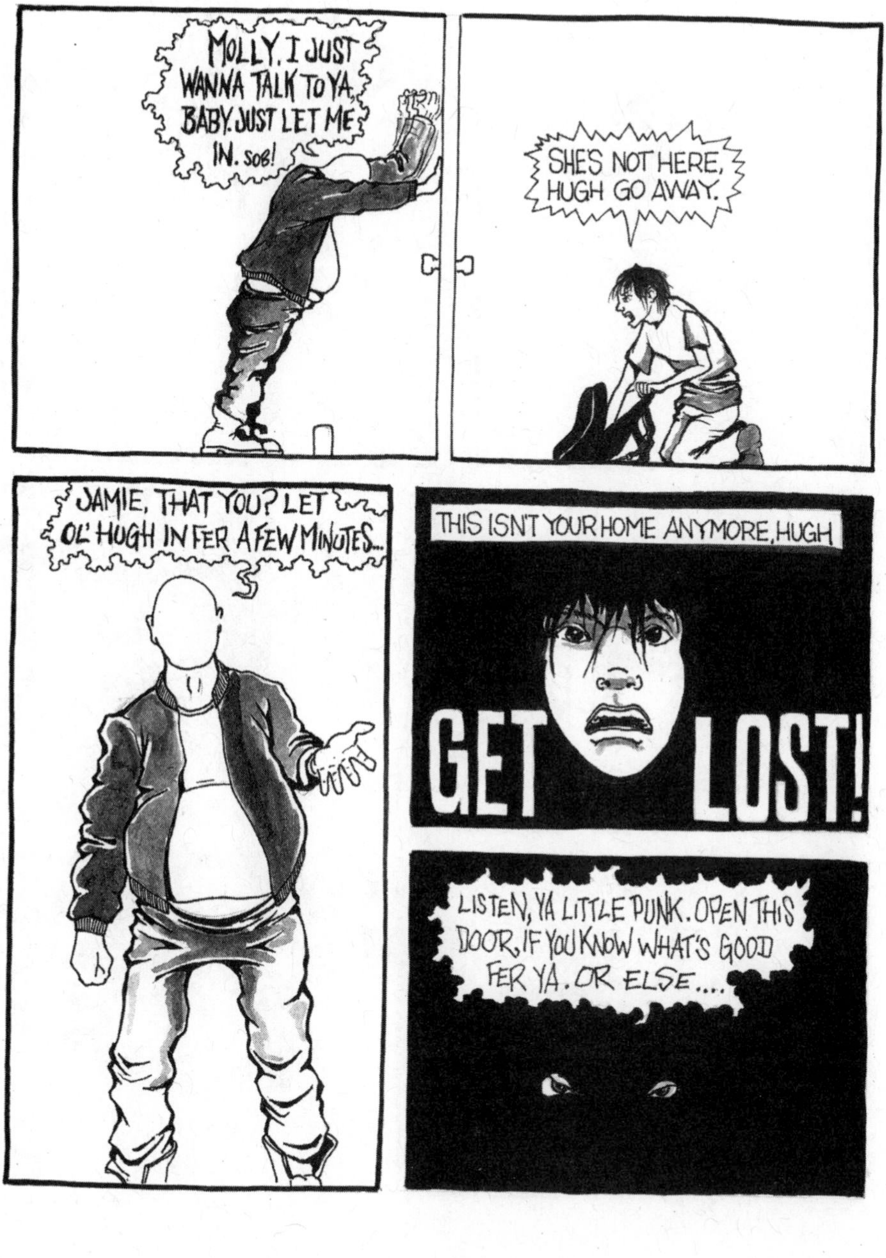
MOLLY, I JUST WANNA TALK TO YA, BABY. JUST LET ME IN. SOB!
SHE'S NOT HERE, HUGH GO AWAY.
JAMIE, THAT YOU? LET OL' HUGH IN FER A FEW MINUTES...
THIS ISN'T YOUR HOME ANYMORE, HUGH
GET LOST!
LISTEN, YA LITTLE PUNK. OPEN THIS DOOR, IF YOU KNOW WHAT'S GOOD FER YA. OR ELSE....

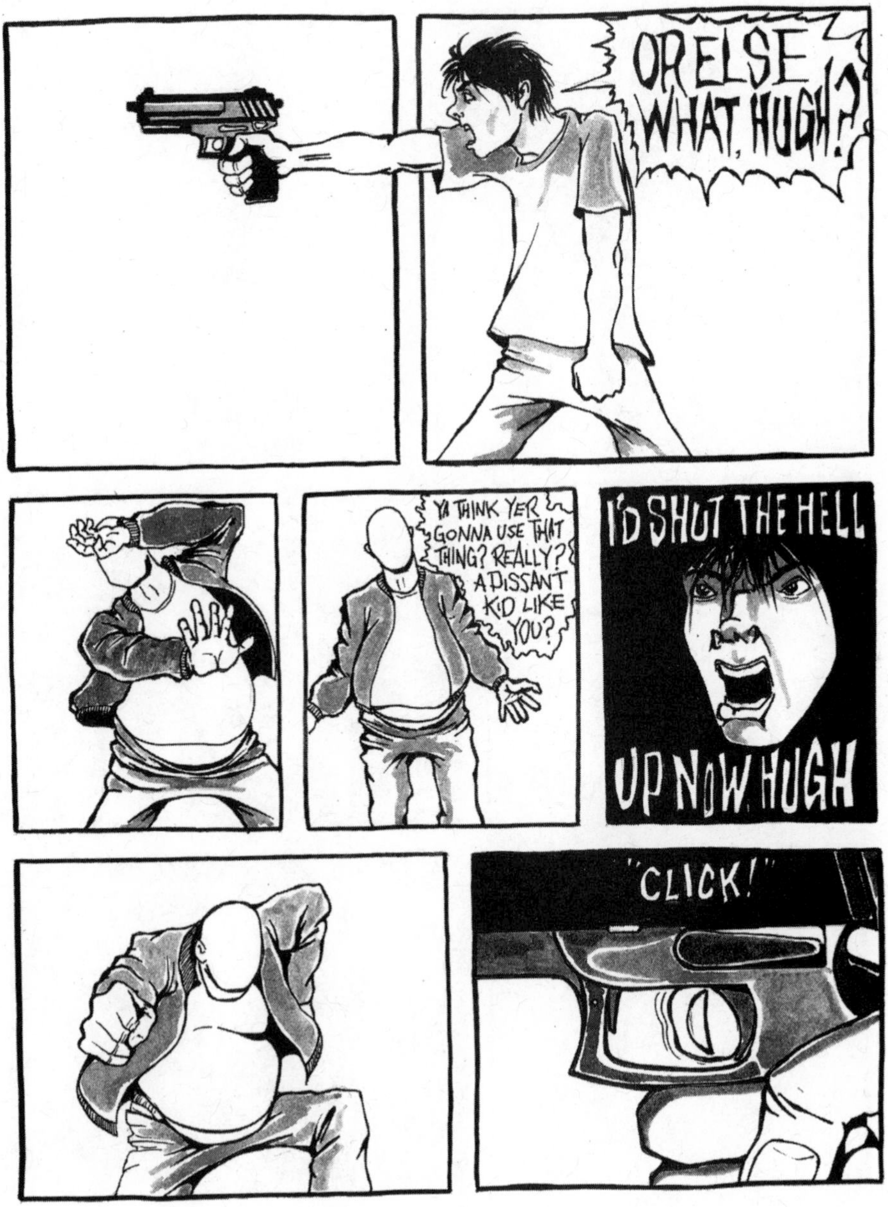
OR ELSE WHAT, HUGH!?
YA THINK YER GONNA USE THAT THING? REALLY? A DISSANT KID LIKE YOU?
I'D SHUT THE HELL UP NOW, HUGH
"CLICK!"

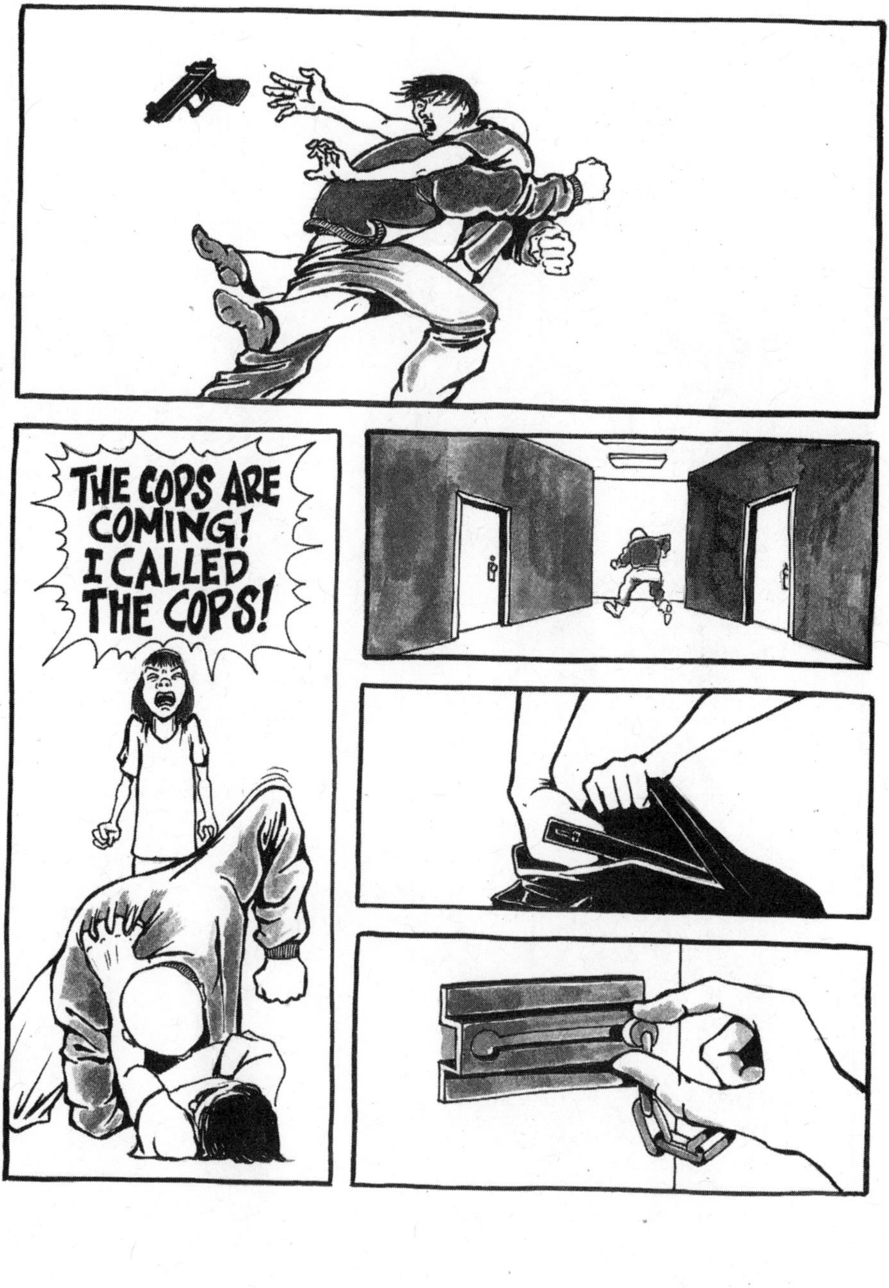
THE COPS ARE COMING! I CALLED THE COPS!

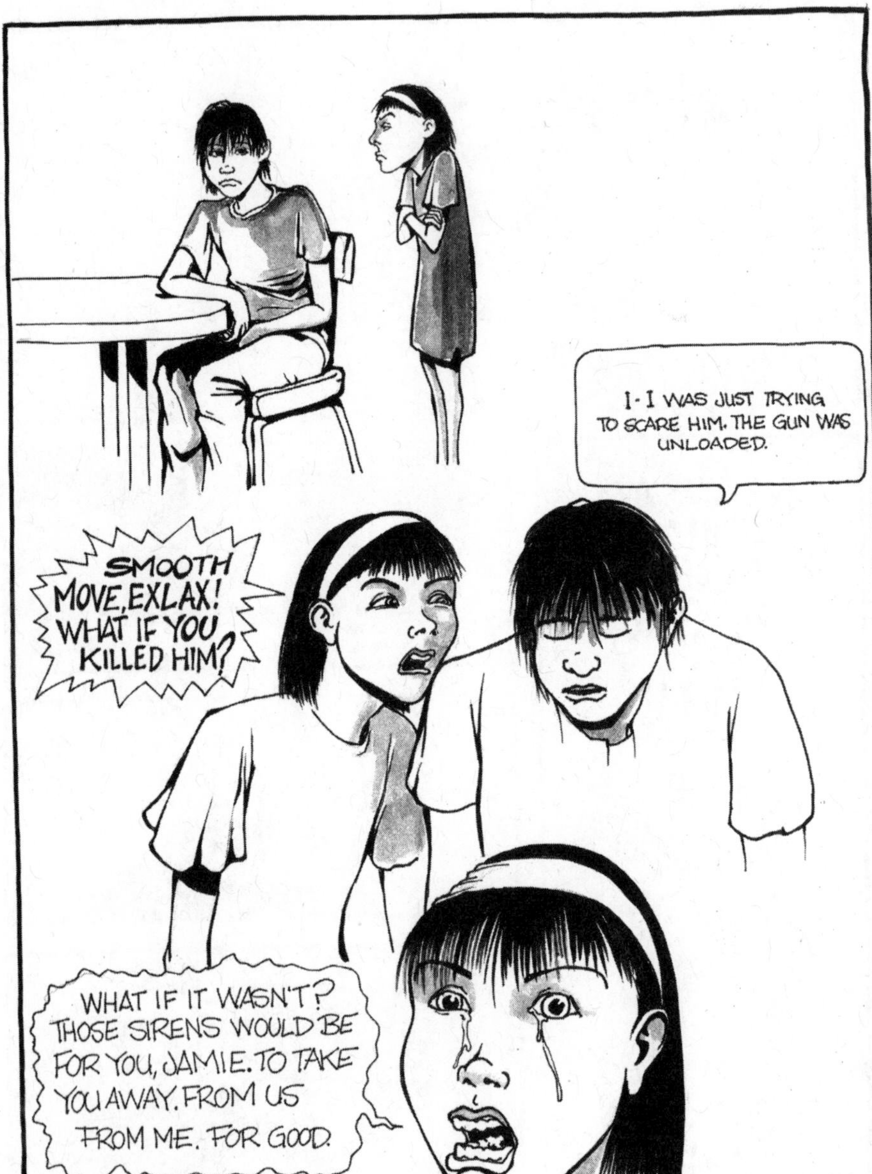
I-I WAS JUST TRYING TO SCARE HIM. THE GUN WAS UNLOADED.
SMOOTH MOVE, EXLAX! WHAT IF YOU KILLED HIM?
WHAT IF IT WASN'T? THOSE SIRENS WOULD BE FOR YOU, JAMIE. TO TAKE YOU AWAY. FROM US FROM ME. FOR GOOD.

She stormed away into her bedroom and slammed the door. Left me to deal with the police. Fill out the report. Explain the whole incident—minus the part about the gun—to a worried and tearful Molly when she arrived home twenty minutes later.

My Kidding sister hates that I have this gun. But she doesn't understand that it's for her protection, too. You can't explain anything to a stubborn thirteen-year-old.

But she's right about one important thing. I would've shot Hugh. In self-defense. If I'd had the sense to load the gun after my last shooting practice. If I wasn't such a numbnut numbskull, tonight there'd be one less piss tank pugilist on this planet.

There's always next time. My gun is loaded.

Guess it really must be spring. Though you'd never know it from the chill in the air. I can't stand this teeter-totter weather. One day is sunny and mild. The next, the sky is threatening to storm. Most of the snow has melted or dirtied into that pile of grey sludge that holds on almost to June. This city is looking pretty ugly.

Except for one thing named Tatiana. And she pretty much sees something beautiful everywhere.

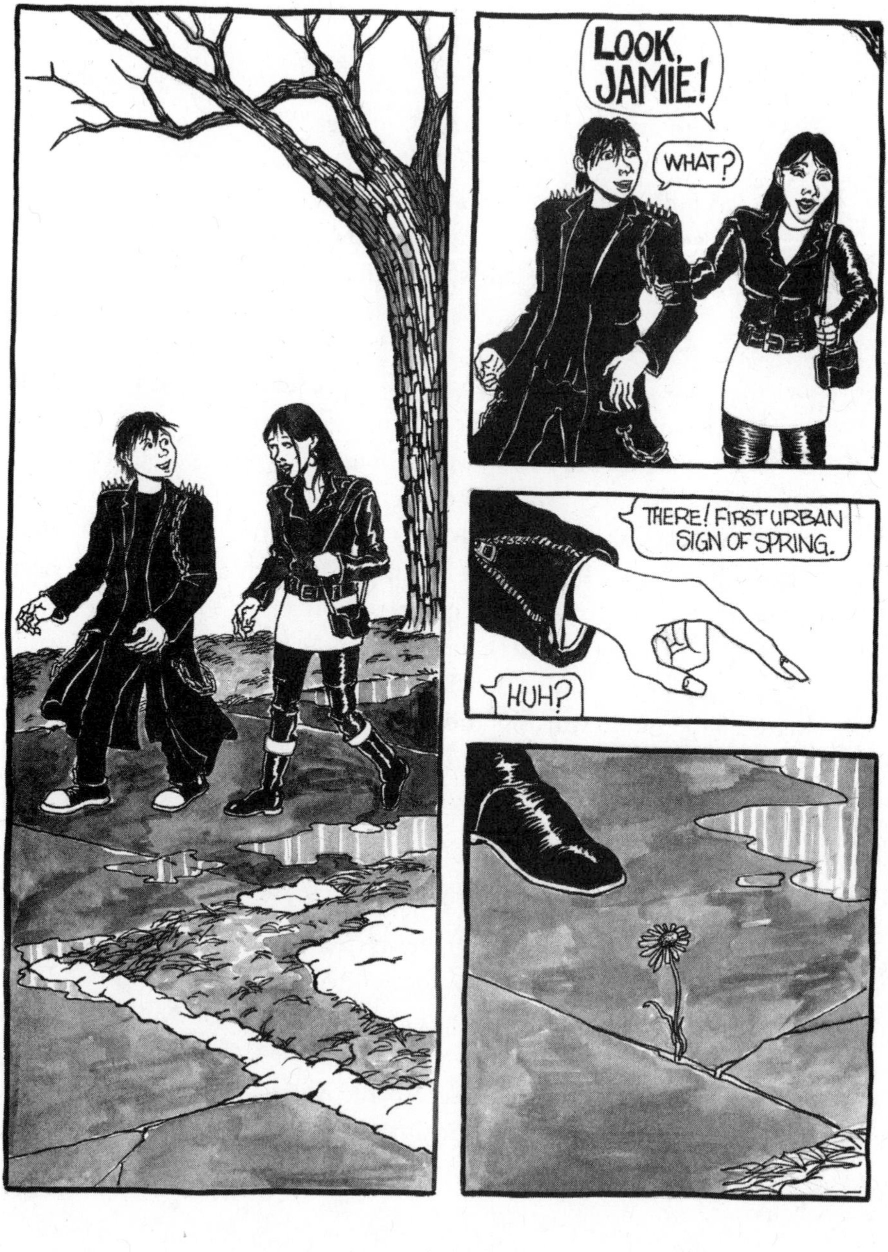
LOOK, JAMIE!
WHAT?
THERE! FIRST URBAN SIGN OF SPRING.
HUH?

Unbelievable. I'll bet this nutso girl likes dandelions, too. I bent to pick it for her. But she said no. Let life be.

So I did.

I have to admit that the school musical is going great guns. The actors are impressive. Ms. Sokolotosky got most of the squeaks and squawks calmed down in the singers, too. The leads have the best vocals. So it's all working. And the tech crew is top notch!

Can't help but feel I made some kinda contribution. Tat insists that the tech people are the magic behind the scenes. It's true. Her costumes are really cool. Lighting and sound are super slick. And the sets are... well... professional looking. That's what Mr. Letterman, Ms. S., Tatiana and the rest of the tech team are saying, anyways.

Their attention could make a guy blush. If a guy were prone to blushing.

We all were given two comp tickets to the play to share with friends and family, so Candy and Molly are coming to tomorrow night's opening. I'll admit that I'm excited for them to see my work. All our hard work. I know that Candy will love the show.

But I also have to admit that my favourite part of the musical is being backstage, in the dark, with Tatiana Oleshenko. We pretty much know all the stupid words to the stupid lyrics, so we fart around mouthing words behind the set. At Saturday's dress, Tatiana grabbed me and started waltzing in the backstage shadows during the love duet. She was just joking around. But I swear you could've seen my heart thumping like a mad beast under my t-shirt.

Grace under pressure, that's me, Jamie Kidding.

Today in the computer lab we started designing my webpage together. I'm learning tons about design techniques, software and applications. It's the coolest thing. I never knew school could be so fun. Outside of art class, I mean.

I even looked up from the screen and caught Tatiana staring at me. I mean really staring. It was unnerving and exciting at the same time.

I dunno what's going on most of the time with that girl. But I can't help but feel...

Shut up, Jamie. Don't jinx a good thing. Just shut up.

Ok.

I would. Except I can't deny what happened this evening during the preview show. She grabbed me during the love waltz again.

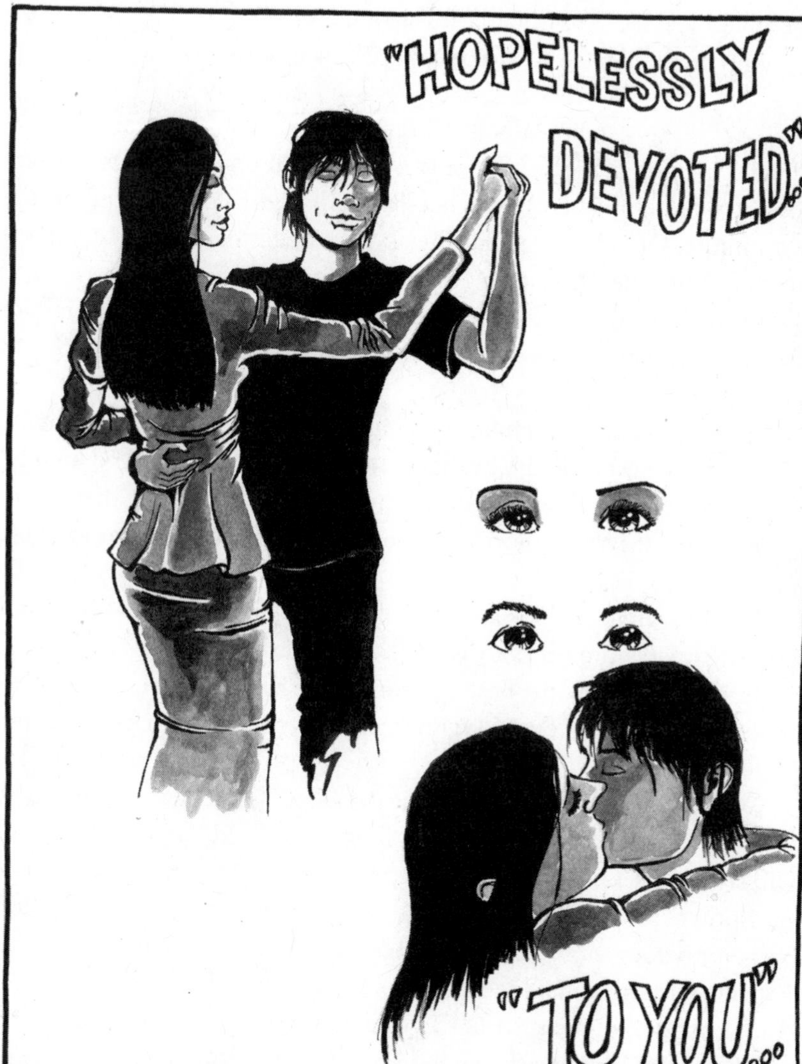
"HOPELESSLY
DEVOTED"...
"TO YOU"...

So that has to mean *something*, doesn't it?

Well, it did to me.

It means that Jamie Kidding has leapt into the deep end. A perfect swan dive. (Applause here.) I hope that I can keep swimming. Most of the time I feel like I'm floundering around Tat-O.

Maybe she'll have to give me mouth-to-mouth.

Phew! Opening night went almost without a hitch. There was one late sound cue. A ripped costume that Tat managed to pin together at the last minute. One damaged flat that I duct taped together during intermission. But otherwise, darn groovy, as Tatiana likes to say.

I could hardly wait for the love duet. I thought all day about taking the lead this time. In the dance. And in the kissing department.

So I did.

I took Tatiana Oleshenko in my arms to dance. And I kissed her.

Then the best thing EVER happened. We kept kissing. And kissing. We broke apart to do our backstage duties, of course. But then every spare moment, every opportunity, one of us grabbed the other and just well...kissed.

She is an amazing kisser. And I am addicted to vanilla, that beautiful scent she wears. And her body is well... like a little bit of heaven on earth.

It was absolutely the best night of Jamie Kidding's life.

Except for. Only one thing marred my otherwise perfect evening. Blade Attaman.

Why the hell he was at the musical, I can't figure. But after the bows when the house lights came up and most of the audience had filed out, who should I see? Talking to my little sister?

I practically leapt off the stage. But Attaman darted out the side exit. Not before shooting me a sniggering look. I'd have loved to wipe that smirk off his rancid face.

"What did he say to you?" I grabbed Candy by the shoulders.

"Nothing! He just asked me if I was Candice Kidding and your sister. He said he was a friend of yours and did I like the show?"

"Candy," I forced myself to keep my voice calm and ease my grip. "You gotta know that Blade Attaman is *NOT* a good guy. He is a mean bastard, who is definitely *NOT* my friend."

"What's he done to you?"

"Nothing. He's just been a jerk off."

"Right." She sounded suspicious.

"Don't *EVER* talk to him again, ok? Just walk away, if he approaches you. Promise me!"

"Ok. Ok. Geez. You sure have a lotta secrets lately, Jamie."

"Secrets?" Molly had returned from powdering her nose or whatever else it is women do in the can.

"Yeah, Jamie has quite a few."

"Really," Molly eyeballed me.

"Here comes one now." Candy's voice and smile were all sarcasm. "Jamie's girlfriend. Hi Tatiana!" she cooed.

Molly just chuckled at me.

But I was seeing red. I'm sure my mom and sis thought it was about Tatiana. Candy's little disclosure. I didn't care about that. Right now all I could think about was Blade Attaman coming anywhere near my sister. And what I would do about it. I was finding it hard to breathe so I excused myself and went outside.

Tatiana followed me.

"What's up? You ok?"

"No. Yes. I dunno. Attaman was talking to Candy."

Tatiana felt as I did. "That's not good."

"No. It's definitely a bad thing."

"But no harm was done, right?"

"No. Not yet. I warned Candy about him."

"She's a smart kid, Jamie. Candy will keep her guard. Her distance."

"Yeah."

"Listen, I have to get home, but... I made you something."

"You did?"

"I mean I-I..."

Tatiana Oleshenko, woman of cool, was stuttering. Shy. I couldn't believe it.

"Well, you gave me something you drew, Jamie. So I felt... I wanted to give you something I wrote."

She pushed a folded paper into my hands. And then she kissed me. And bolted.

What a frigging rollercoaster of a day.

I didn't open it right away. Something about her words made me want to wait. Until now. In the safety and relative privacy of my room. So here goes:

this

this warm soft evening
almost as soft as your fingers
i spy a defiant daisy
white and yellow against all odds
pushing through a pavement crack
and i think
how very like that daisy
this tender tenacious love

by Tatiana Oleshenko

I have to look up the word 'tenacious.' But I know what the rest means. I know what Tatiana Oleshenko means. To me.

Being dyslexic sucks, did I mention? I got on the wrong bus twice today. Meant to go out tagging this morning in my usual hood and then near Happy Harbor. Got on the number 6 bus instead of the number 9. I ended up in China Town. Which is nice and all. But not where I intended to be. Later, my brain managed to mangle number 68 with 98, which I figured out just a block into the ride, but I was still late for work at the video store.

Sometimes stocking shelves at Alternative Video is murder. Especially when I have to re-shelve films with Ns or Ms, Vs or Ws in the titles. It helps if I read them aloud, so Tatiana and I devised a system where I read out the name of the movie and she double checked to make sure I'd got the right alphabet letter and shelf as I restocked. Now I can manage alone with the same technique. It's made a big difference and I don't make nearly as many stupid mistakes.

But I'm on my own with the buses, unless Candy's with me. I have to concentrate really hard on the number before I can be sure. If I'm daydreaming or distracted, that's how I make transit bloops. So embarrassing when I have to ask the bus driver to let me off. I can feel all the passengers' eyes boring into my back. That's why I like to take my bike, rather than the public transit.

But there's still no chance of that right now, given the recent dump of spring snow.

The musical is over, so no more after school tech duties or painting of sets. I kinda miss it. Ms. Sokolotosky threw a big pizza party for the cast and crew in the drama room. We watched the video of the show together. It was pretty cool to see, I have to admit. After the very final performance, the tech crew members were all invited onto the stage with the cast. I looked as dweeb-like as can be expected. Tatiana, of course, was beautiful. Ms. Sokolotosky made a big deal about all of us and our contributions. It felt good to be thanked. She's a cool teacher.

So is Mr. Letterman who is keen about my building a portfolio and is a cheerleader for Tat's and my work on the website. He's been searching the Net for the best art programs in the city and possible art scholarships I might be eligible for next year. It blows me away. That he cares. Wow.

Who'd ever believe that Jamie Kidding might actually start to like school. WTF?

Tatiana is also responsible for my new Facebook platform, as she calls it. We use the school computers, even though there's a firewall up. Tat the Hack knows a few tricks. And she insists that it's important for me to have a profile and fan page. She picked one of my art pieces—a close-up of a demon I drew—for my profile photo. It's amazing, but I actually have a few Facebook friends. Fans even, who liked my work on the musical sets. Go figure.

And go figure again. I practically have the poem Tatiana gave me memorized, I've read it so often. Especially on my dark days. Which I have many of. We were walking together at night, after our shift at the video store, when I first brought the subject up, the Sunday just after the musical closed.

"Um. I read your poem."

Tatiana couldn't or wouldn't look at me. "Oh yeah?"

"Yeah. It's really good."

"It's derivative." Big Tat-O word again.

"Don't sell yourself short. I mean, Tat. I've never had a poem from a girl before. I've never had a girl write me anything before. You gotta believe. It means a lot. You know?"

"You like it?"

"Hell, yeah!"

Then she smiled. And I grinned. And she went to kiss me, but her bus was coming, and we kinda smashed teeth. But no harm done. There's been more attempts since. Many. I'm getting better and better at this snogging thing.

Neither of us like PDA much. But we know some quiet corners of the school. And in the computer lab at lunch, we're pretty much left to ourselves. Sometimes she holds my hand. I have to say. It all feels amazing. Like I'm spinning. Floating. Falling.

I guess I have. Fallen.

Who'd have thought she'd ever pick me? The Incredible Disappearing Boy. Holy reversal of loser trend, Batman!

One day I'd like to take Tatiana Oleshenko out for dinner. I've never done that. Gone to a real fancy restaurant. I'd probably use the wrong fork or something. Typical dyslexic. But I don't care. One day I will.

I'm putting the finishing touches on GraveRype's May Day! May Day! concert. Think I'll save the money for a change. For me and Tat and that dinner out.

Given the excremental year I've had, is it really so bad to be you know...

Jamie Kidding. Big Spender. Latin Lover. Fool Fallen.

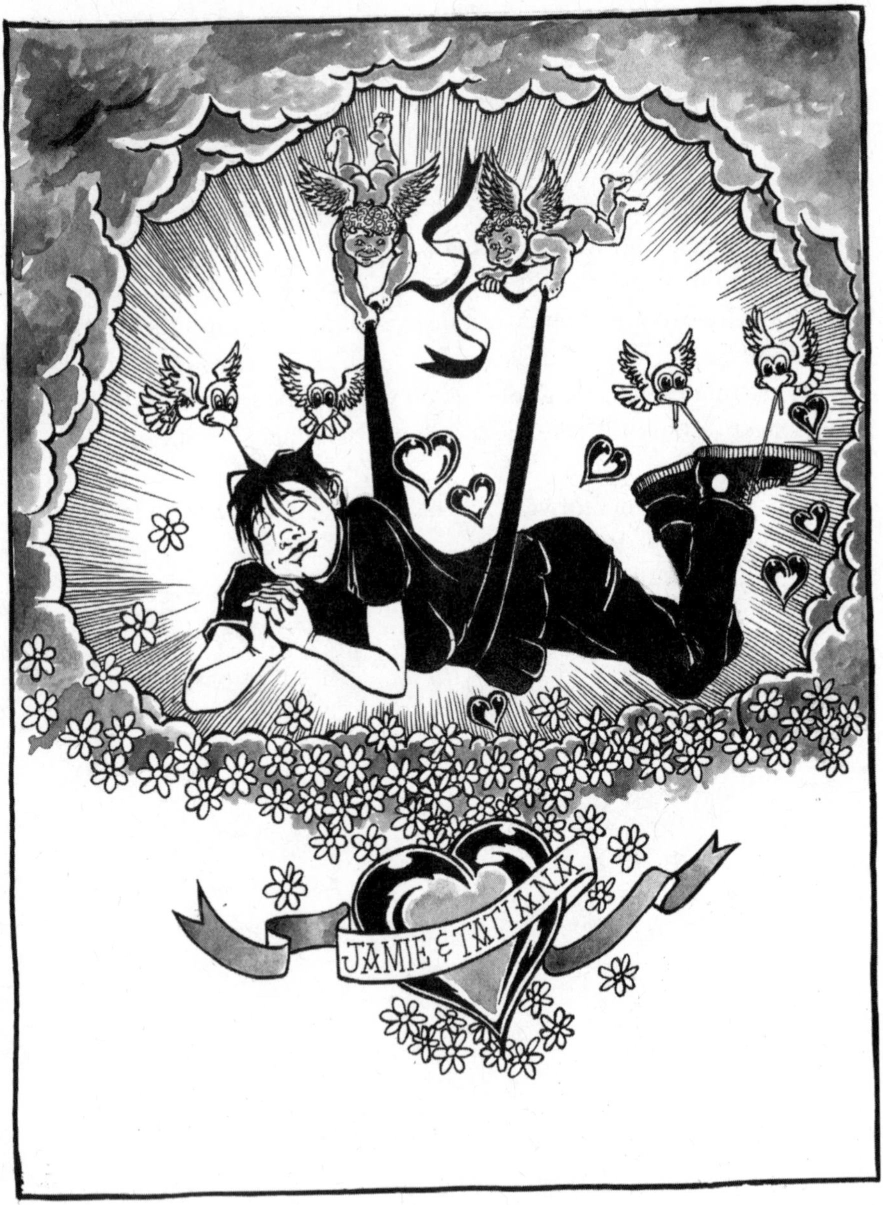
JAMIE & TATIANA

Still sometimes it feels like I'm slipping into a black hole. It's like Eliot what's-his-face said in his poem that we're dissecting to death in English right now: "April *is* the cruellest month."

First, I had a fight with Molly. She wants us to move on account of the little visit Hugh paid us last month.

"But Mom, we just fixed the place up. I painted my ass off."

"Jamie, I know you worked hard to clean up the apartment. We all did. But I thought you hated this place. You've called it a dump enough times. And frankly, I thought you'd be more supportive of me. Of my decision to turn my life—all of our lives—around."

"I am." She was being harsh.

"The housing co-op in the river valley is our chance to do that. If I get accepted to college in the fall, we'd be much closer to the downtown campus so that it won't take me hours to commute."

"Candy and I will have to change schools."

"So that's what this is about? You! And your inconvenience!"

"I said, me and *Candy.*"

"But you meant *you*, Jamie. I'm trying to fix our lives. Get us out of this neighbourhood of druggies and street girls. All bad examples, for you and for your sister. But you can't see that, can you, Jamie?"

"The neighbourhood isn't all bad. There's good people here."

"Of course, there are. I'm not calling down the good folks who live here. But you know yourself about the crime and the creeps who hang around. And you also know that as long as Hugh knows our address, he'll keep coming by, trying to bully his way back into our lives."

Yeah, well, I've gotta plan for Hugh. But I kept my mouth shut.

"Look. Uncle Mac is being real supportive. He thinks this is a good idea."

"Uncle Mac? When did he start to care?"

"Jamie, that's not fair!"

But I didn't stay to listen any longer. I took my pack and split. So yeah, maybe Uncle Mac has noticed his sister's shit-for-life. But he could give a rat's ass about me. Nobody really gives a damn that I've found the first happiness for the first time in my crumby Kidding life and NOW I have to change schools.

Second thing is that Tina is still missing. I try to remind myself that it's none of my business. That she's a big girl. But I know better. Who's gonna care if I don't? Who's even looking for her? How does a seventeen-year-old fight back on a bad date?

I'll bet that prickbrain Tony knows where she is.

I even considered approaching him with an offer to trade the gun for information on her whereabouts. I thought about it. Briefly. Very briefly. Until I remembered that if I admit to actually having his property, he could just waste me on the spot and take it back. Then there'd be one dead Kidding and still no Tina. What good would that do?

Besides I'm not ready to drop my weapon.

Jamie's gotta few scores to settle. (Soundtrack of cheesy 70s cop show here.)

Especially because I spied the pimped up car of the pimp in question patrolling the schoolyard around our schools. Mine and Candy's. Looking for new girls. Vulnerable and lost. The ones who come from broken families or who already have broken lives. That's what Tony does—he preys on the weak and the lonely. Those standing alone in the schoolyard. Away from the others. The shy ones walking home solo.

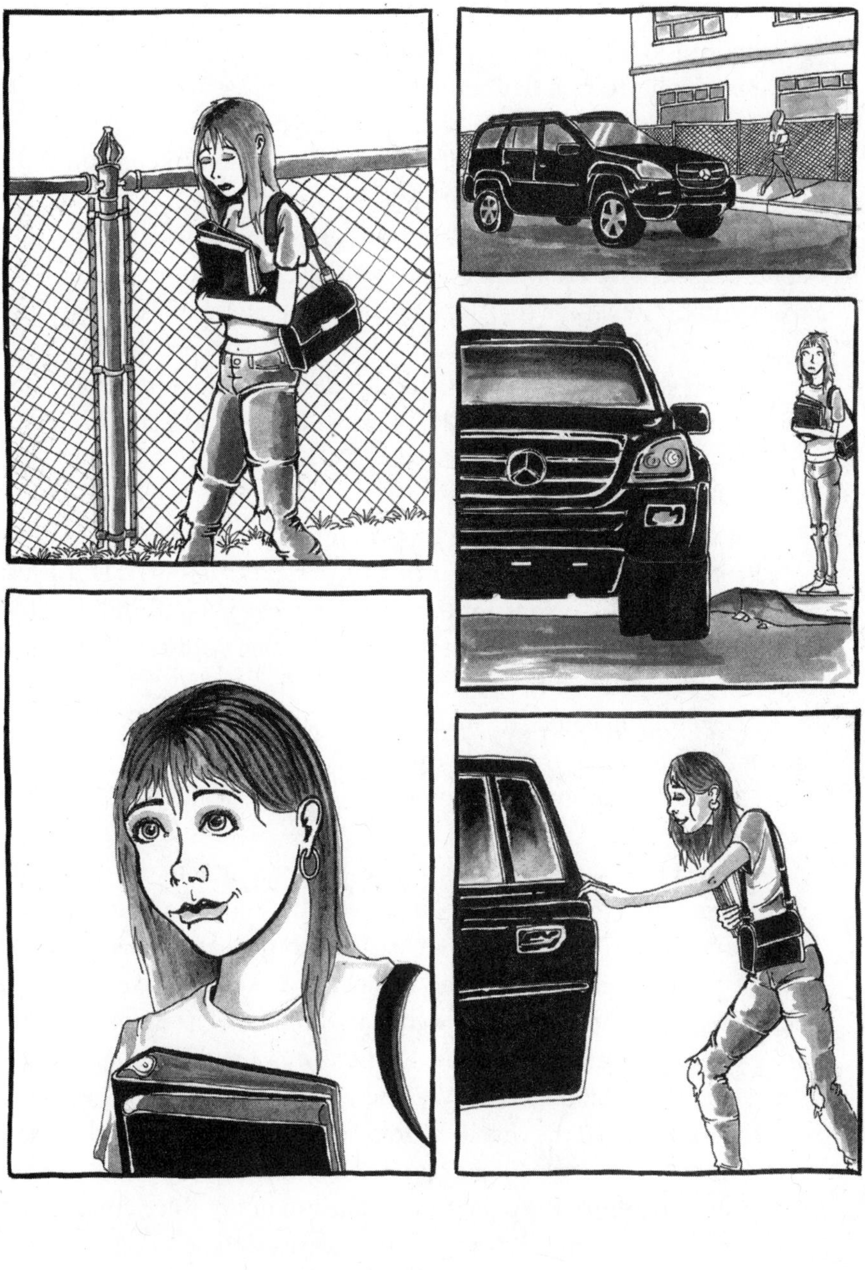

It drives me crazy that Tony and guys like him are recruiting in our neighbourhood. That another young mixed up kid is about to fall into his trap. About to ruin her body. About to ruin her life.

Maybe Molly's right. We gotta get outta here.

But not before Jamie Kidding does a little damage control. If the fricking snow would let up. It's April, did I mention? And blizzarding.

But they never close our city schools because of inclement weather conditions. There could be a nuclear holocaust and we'd still have to attend classes. Not that I mind too much these days. Because of you-know-who.

I swear she's the only one with the lifeline that's keeping me from being sucked into the black hole vortex. I told Tat about my mom wanting to move.

"It's not a bad idea, Jamie."

"Excuse me?"

"Well, your mom's got a good plan for a new start, seems to me."

I kinda slumped in my seat in front of the computer. Did I just dream the romance events of the past few weeks? No, I did not. But was Tatiana so casual about us that she'd be fine with me attending a school halfway across the city?

"Besides, you could still make the trek out here, if you want to stay at East Hill for your grade 12 year…with me."

Great. An hour and a half-plus commute every morning. Every afternoon. I sighed.

Tatiana lives with her father in the district a little to the north and west. He's a firefighter and makes a good living. She has about a twenty-minute bus ride. But she could have easily gone to another school, the King Edward Fine Arts Academy, for instance. And I'd have never met her. Instead she chose East Hill Secondary because of its drama and creative writing programs. Tat feels that here, in a smaller school, she has some chance of standing out. Winning a scholarship. Making a mark.

For Tatiana and the chance of some sort of grade 12 year that matters, I'll stay. Commute. I'll make it work. I figure Molly will agree, if I state my case calmly. Keep the snotty tone out of my voice. Agree to do my share, keep up my grades, and take care of Candy.

I feel bad about our fight this morning. Maybe I'll draw Molly a funny picture. Her son in a dunce cap. That should clear the air.

I smiled at Tat and nodded. Then Tatiana Oleshenko put her head on my shoulder and I forgot who and where I was. Until the bell rang.

We split up for afternoon classes. I went to my locker to get my books.

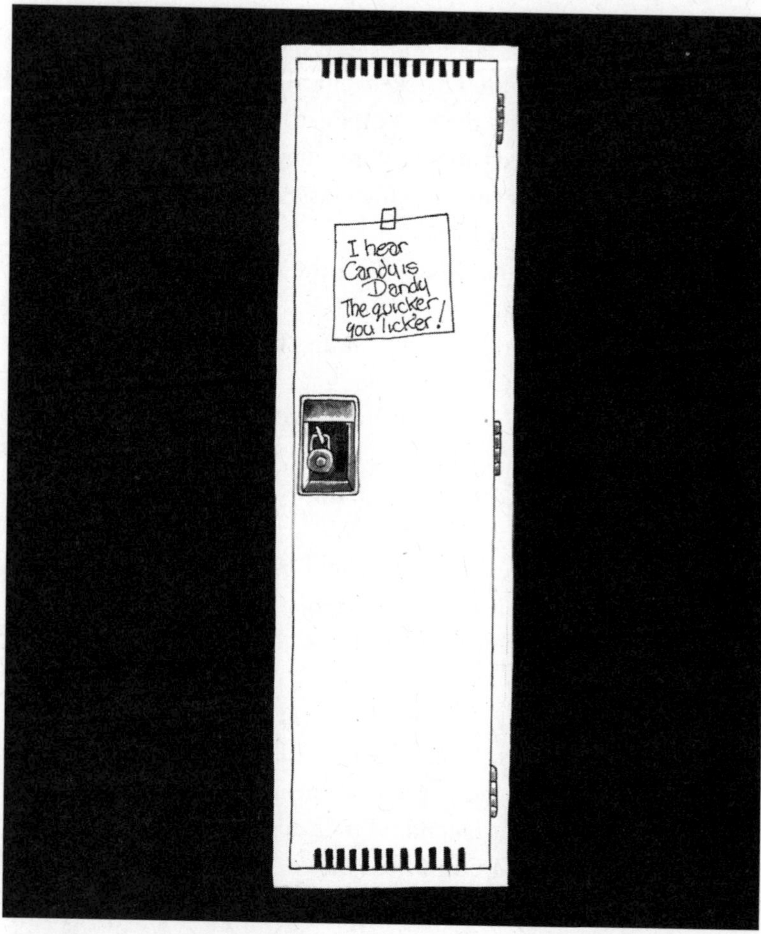
I hear
Candy is
Dandy
The quicker
you licker!

ATTAMANASSHOLE!!!

I feel myself being sucked into the vortex of that black hole again. So be it. Blade Attaman's coming with me.

I went out looking for him. Checked out all the Attaman haunts. His drug dealing post behind the school. East Hill's smoking aka smoke-up pit. The nearby billiards and bowling alley where Blade and his stud crew spend most of their time cutting classes.

No sign of the Prince of Pricks.

I walked Candy home. Molly had the day off, so we had a rare supper together. But I wasn't hungry. My only appetite is for revenge.

"Hugh came by the restaurant last night. Drunk."

I froze. So did Candy seated beside me.

"I handled it, ok." I could tell that Molly was trying to keep her voice casual. "Lois called the police while I spoke to Hugh outside." My mom took a sip of her lukewarm suppertime coffee. "He wasn't abusive at first. Just crying. I felt sorry for him."

"You did?" I could feel my macaroni forming a lump in my throat.

Molly looked from me to Candy. "Don't worry. I told you both that I won't take him back. I meant what I said. I won't. I'm moving on. So I told him that, too."

"Then what?" My fist tightened around my fork.

"Then... well, you can guess. He started his usual. Cussing me out. The world. I could see where it was all headed, so I turned back into the restaurant. Lou came outside. Hugh took a swing. Hit the brick wall and hurt his hand. Lou pushed him off down the sidewalk. The last I saw of Hugh, he was stumbling his way onto a downtown bus. The cops came fifteen minutes later."

"Figures."

"I made out a report. They'll pay a visit to the YMCA where Hugh's staying. Chat with him about violating his restraining order."

"Will they arrest him?" Candy's voice had risen two pitches.

"No, honey. They'll probably just fine him. But he'll get the message. And we'll be alright. I know it."

"That's why we're moving, right?" Candy was blinking back tears.

"Yes, sweetie. A new neighbourhood. A new life."

I groaned.

"Something wrong, Jamie?"

I shook my head and took another bite of mac and cheese.

"I wish you'd talk to me. I'm here to listen."

I shrugged my shoulders.

"Or if you'd rather, there's always the psychologist ready to work with you whenever…"

"Nothing's wrong. I'm just a little stressed out."

Candy cast me a glance. In that look, I saw that she wanted to add her two cents. I glared at her. She managed—barely, I could tell—to keep her Kidding sister mouth shut.

"School? The move? Hugh?"

"Yeah. And stuff."

"How are you and Tatiana?"

"Fine, Mom. I'm going to see her at the video store, right after the dishes." I got up and started clearing the table.

Candy came up to me at the sink, tea towel in hand. She spoke in a hush. "You should tell Mom, Jamie."

My hands clutched a glass under the soapy water. "You should mind your own business," I hissed back.

"Then I'm going to tell her, Jamie."

"No. You're. Not!" I felt the glass snap in my hand. Pulled it and my bleeding finger from the sink. "You're not, Candy. I can't… I won't let you."

"You're scaring me, Jamie!"

I realized that I was holding the sharp broken edge of the glass in her direction. But I swear I didn't mean it as a threat. Did I?

I reached into the cupboard under the sink and threw away the broken drinking glass. Rinsed off the blood from the small cut to my index finger. "Just a little while longer, ok Candy? Keep my secret."

"I don't know…"

"I need to hang onto… you know…*it* for a few days more."

"Why, Jamie? *It's* not good for you. You're so… so sad. And… mad. All because of *it*. I think, anyways."

"I'm just working somethin' out. I'll be ok. I need the… you know. *It*."

"I need *you*, Jamie."

What do you say to that? I kinda felt the world blurring. So I just hugged her. Grabbed my coat and vamoosed. Left Candy with the tea towel, still drying the dishes. She's always such a slowpoke. Daydreamy kiddo.

That's why someone like Attaman with his perverted mouth and his sick thoughts and his fat fists and his garbage drug-dealing career needs to be taken out. He ruins young lives and he filths up the world with his presence.

So I intended to find him.

I looked at the numbers I'd scrawled with a Sharpie on my palm. I'd found them in the phone book. An address not far from where we live. I looked up to make sure they matched. This was it. Attaman's place. A small, run-down little white house. A duplicate of the others on the street. I rang the front doorbell. Felt the gun against my chest.

A very small woman answered the door. She was dressed in a shabby bathrobe that she kept closed at the throat with her left hand. Her hair was in rollers under a scarf, and she had a nose piece attached to an oxygen tank on wheels.

"Mrs. Attaman?"

"Yes?"

"Is Bla—er—is Robert home?"

"No, I'm sorry. Robbie's gone out."

"Oh. Ok. Sorry to bother you."

"Are you a friend of his? Can I tell him you came by?"

"Er—that's ok. I'll find him. Maybe he's playing pool."

I beat it off the steps of the house. So Attaman had a mother. An ailing mother. He wasn't some alien life form hatched from an egg cluster.

He had been born in the usual human way. Someone cared about him. Someone who called him Robbie.

I didn't really know what to do with all of that. So I trailed through the dark over to Alternative Video. Stood in front of the window. Inside, I could see the wall of TVs playing scenes from various movies: a multi-car chase and huge explosion, a jarring scene of bombs decimating the jungle, a blazing gun battle between crazed drug lords, a gun-toting hostage taker with screaming victims, two starships locked in a violent laser beam confrontation, a fist fight between two steely-eyed cowboys, several hard-bodied foes locked in a lethal Marshall Arts combat. As though she was the cure to all of this and the sick-to-my-gut feeling, Tatiana walked in front of the screens.

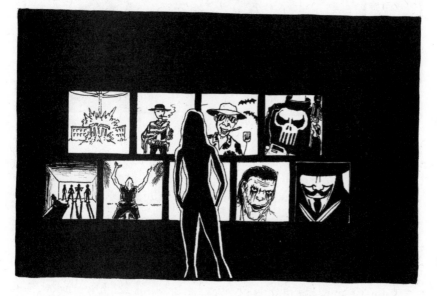

I just watched her. Kind of like a peeping Tom, I know. But I'm glad I did.

Because the next minute Georgie followed. She turned to face him and they were having some kind of conversation. Which ended with her leaping to hug him. It wasn't just a friendly hug, either.

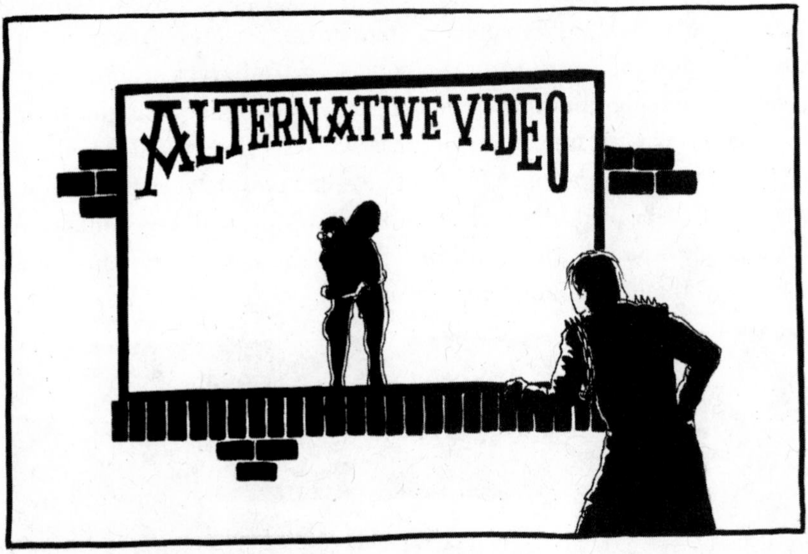
ALTERNATIVE VIDEO

Tatiana Oleshenko is playing me.

What a fucking fool loser, I am.

I felt the gun against my heart. Felt like I'd been shot. Felt like I needed to get the hell out of there. Felt like killing... Killing someone. Killing myself.

I went out tagging with a vengeance. Bombing my way through the city. Capping others' tags. I was that completely pissed off. Hours passed. I didn't let myself think about the time ticking by.

I don't remember finding my way back to our neighbourhood. But I did, somehow. I was in that much shock and awe. Who knew that a heart could ache like this? Break like this.

The garish lights from the 7-11 beckoned me in from the night chill. I wandered in and bought a coffee. That's when I saw her picture on the front page of the daily newspaper:

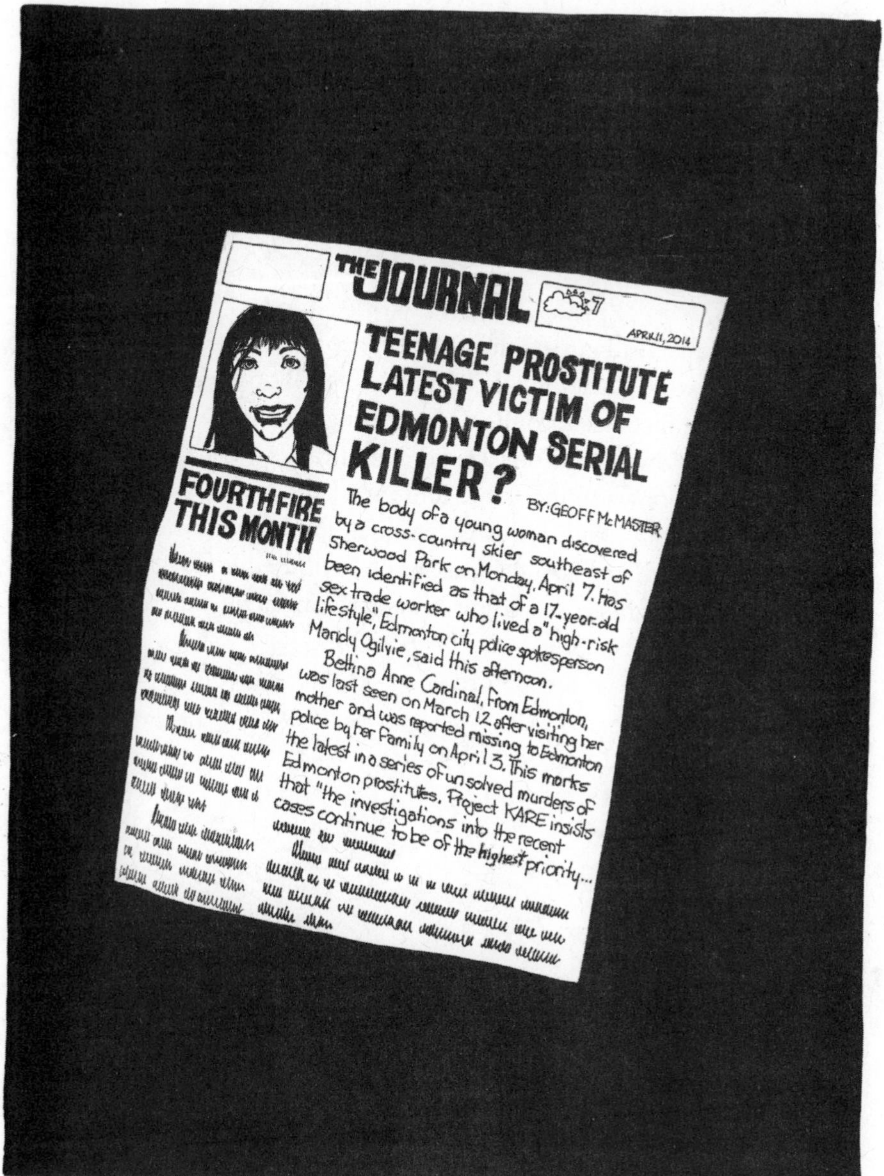
THE JOURNAL
7
APRIL11, 2014
TEENAGE PROSTITUTE LATEST VICTIM OF EDMONTON SERIAL KILLER?
BY: GEOFF McMASTER
The body of a young woman discovered by a cross-country skier southeast of Sherwood Park on Monday, April 7, has been identified as that of a 17-year-old sex trade worker who lived a "high-risk lifestyle", Edmonton city police spokesperson Mandy Ogilvie, said this afternoon.
Bettina Anne Cardinal, from Edmonton, was last seen on March 12 after visiting her mother and was reported missing to Edmonton police by her family on April 3. This marks the latest in a series of unsolved murders of Edmonton prostitutes. Project KARE insists that "the investigations into the recent cases continue to be of the highest priority...
FOURTH FIRE THIS MONTH

I couldn't read any further. I left my coffee on the counter and ran out of the store. Into the alley. Upchucked all of what was left of my macaroni and cheese into the dirty melting snow.

That fucking pimp Tony. He got her into this doomed life in the first place. Sure. Some john took her and raped and beat her. Killed her and left her. If I could find that waste-of-life, I'd kill him, too. But the pattern began with Tony. And I was sure I could find him...

First things first. I found my way to the all-night café. Ordered cup after cup of coffee. Pulled out this book.

Make a plan, Jamie. Before you excecute. Draw it out. That's how you work best.

So I did. And I have. And I will.

Here goes everything...

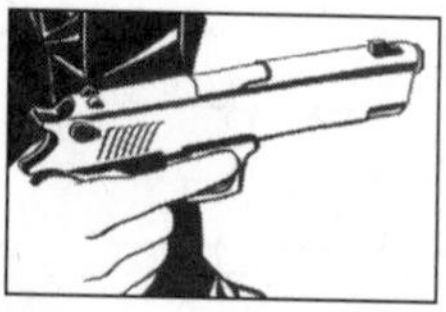

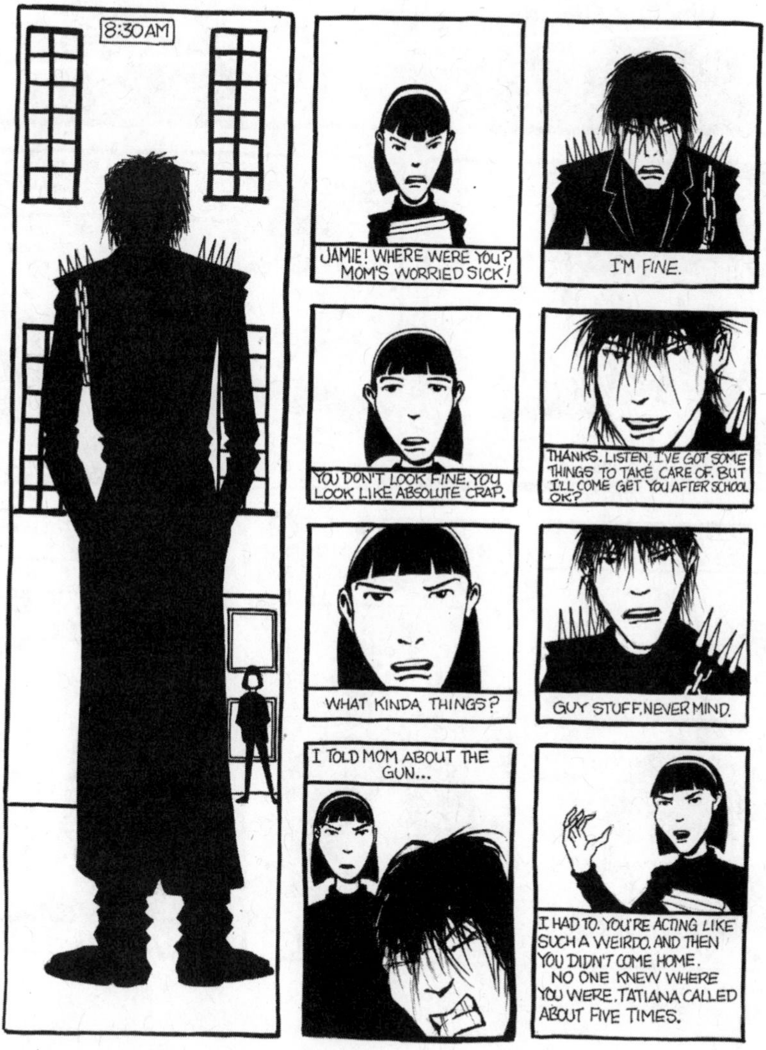
8:30 AM
JAMIE! WHERE WERE YOU? MOM'S WORRIED SICK!
I'M FINE.
YOU DON'T LOOK FINE. YOU LOOK LIKE ABSOLUTE CRAP.
THANKS. LISTEN, I'VE GOT SOME THINGS TO TAKE CARE OF. BUT I'LL COME GET YOU AFTER SCHOOL OK?
WHAT KINDA THINGS?
GUY STUFF. NEVER MIND.
I TOLD MOM ABOUT THE GUN...
I HAD TO. YOU'RE ACTING LIKE SUCH A WEIRDO. AND THEN YOU DIDN'T COME HOME. NO ONE KNEW WHERE YOU WERE. TATIANA CALLED ABOUT FIVE TIMES.

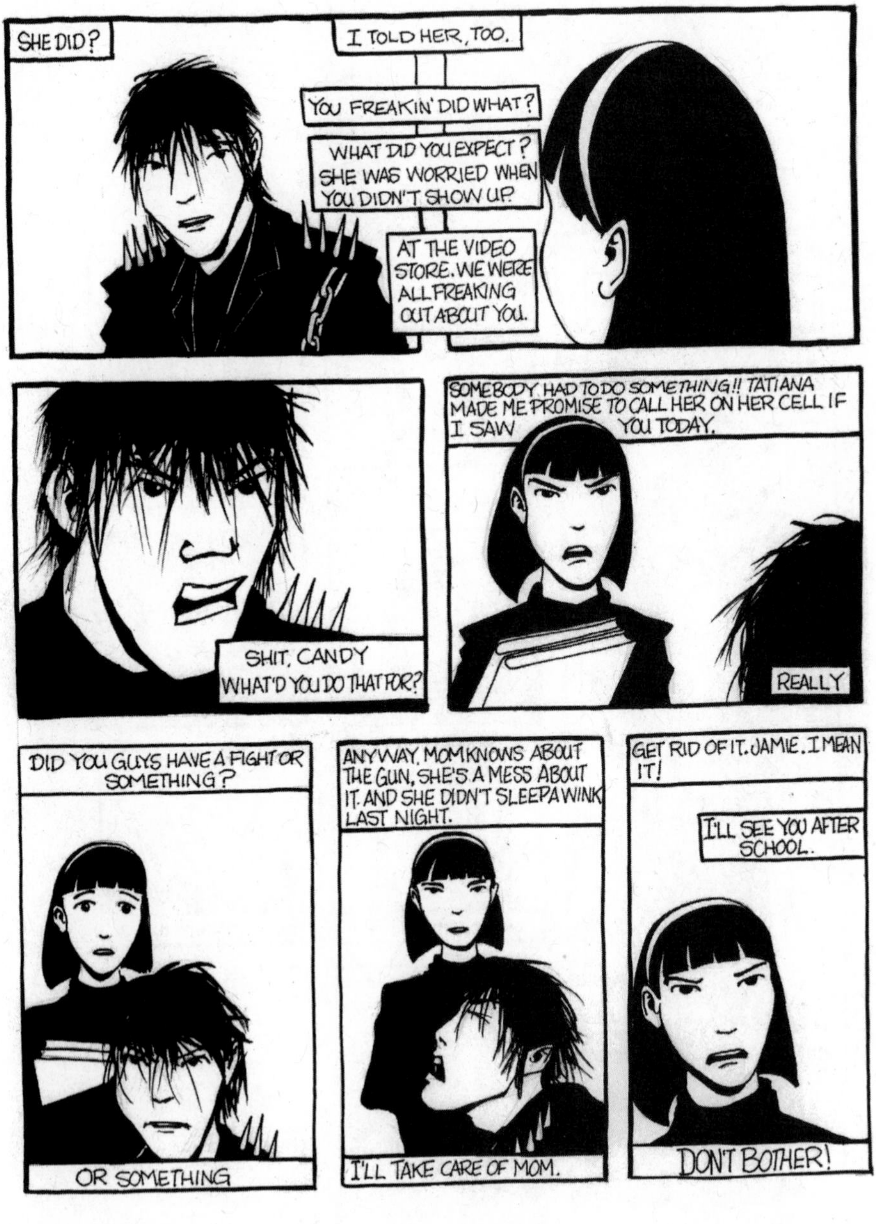
SHE DID?
I TOLD HER, TOO.
YOU FREAKIN' DID WHAT?
WHAT DID YOU EXPECT? SHE WAS WORRIED WHEN YOU DIDN'T SHOW UP.
AT THE VIDEO STORE. WE WERE ALL FREAKING OUT ABOUT YOU.
SHIT, CANDY WHAT'D YOU DO THAT FOR?
SOMEBODY HAD TO DO SOMETHING!! TATIANA MADE ME PROMISE TO CALL HER ON HER CELL IF I SAW YOU TODAY.
REALLY
DID YOU GUYS HAVE A FIGHT OR SOMETHING?
OR SOMETHING
ANYWAY, MOM KNOWS ABOUT THE GUN, SHE'S A MESS ABOUT IT. AND SHE DIDN'T SLEEP A WINK LAST NIGHT.
I'LL TAKE CARE OF MOM.
GET RID OF IT, JAMIE. I MEAN IT!
I'LL SEE YOU AFTER SCHOOL.
DON'T BOTHER!

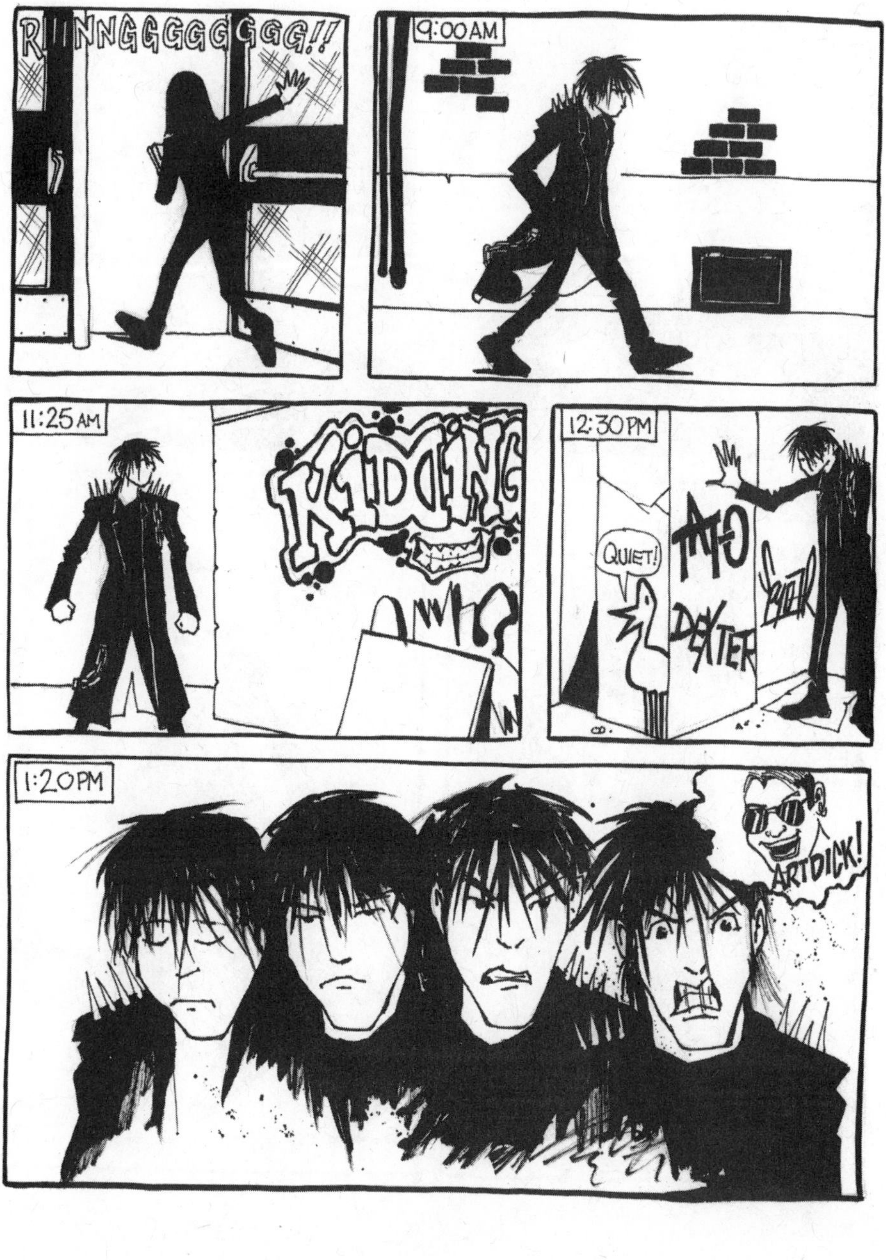
RINNGGGGGGGG!!
9:00AM
11:25 AM
KIDDING
12:30 PM
QUIET!
DEXTER
1:20PM
ARTDICK!

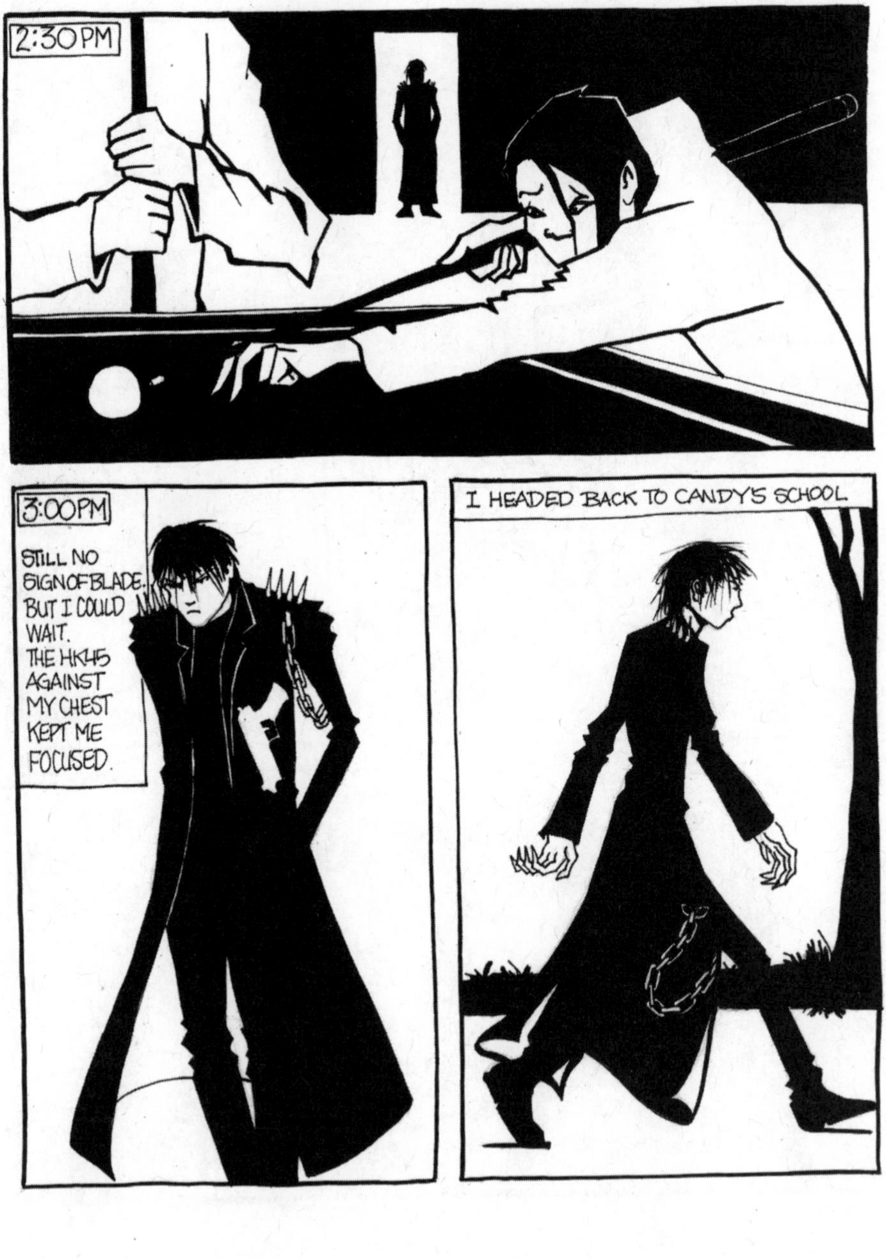
2:30 PM
3:00 PM
STILL NO SIGN OF BLADE. BUT I COULD WAIT. THE HK45 AGAINST MY CHEST KEPT ME FOCUSED.
I HEADED BACK TO CANDY'S SCHOOL

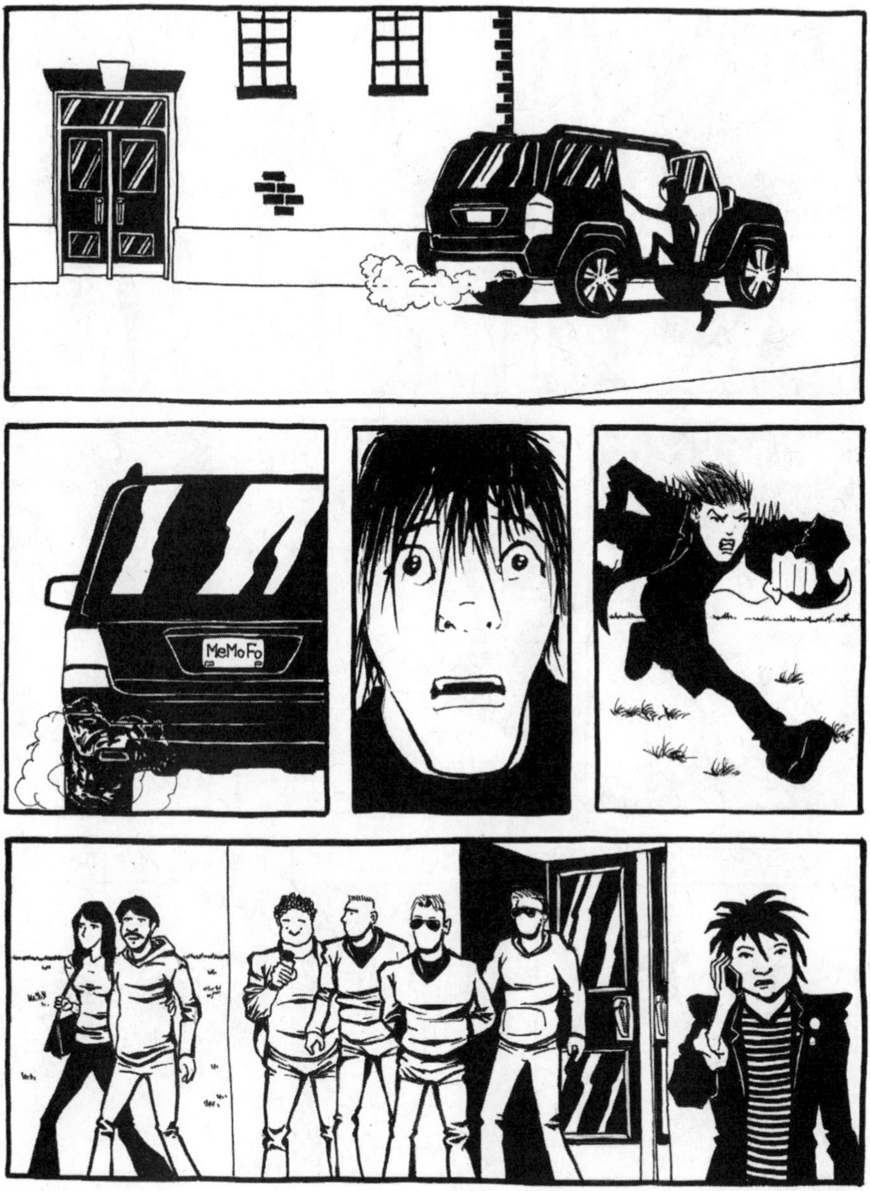
MeMo Fo

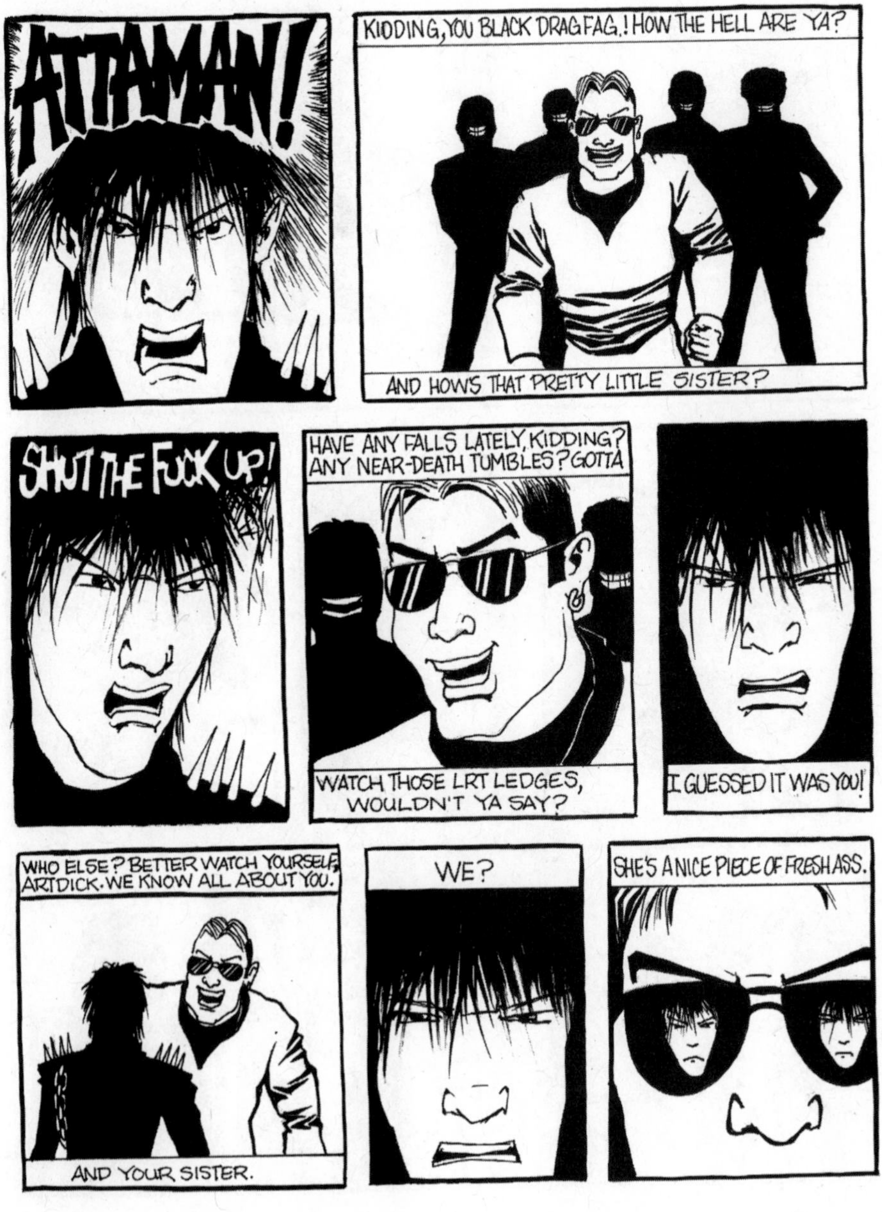
ATTAMAN!
KIDDING, YOU BLACK DRAG FAG.! HOW THE HELL ARE YA?
AND HOW'S THAT PRETTY LITTLE SISTER?
SHUT THE FUCK UP!
HAVE ANY FALLS LATELY, KIDDING? ANY NEAR-DEATH TUMBLES? GOTTA
WATCH THOSE LRT LEDGES, WOULDN'T YA SAY?
I GUESSED IT WAS YOU!
WHO ELSE? BETTER WATCH YOURSELF, ARTDICK. WE KNOW ALL ABOUT YOU.
AND YOUR SISTER.
WE?
SHE'S A NICE PIECE OF FRESH ASS.

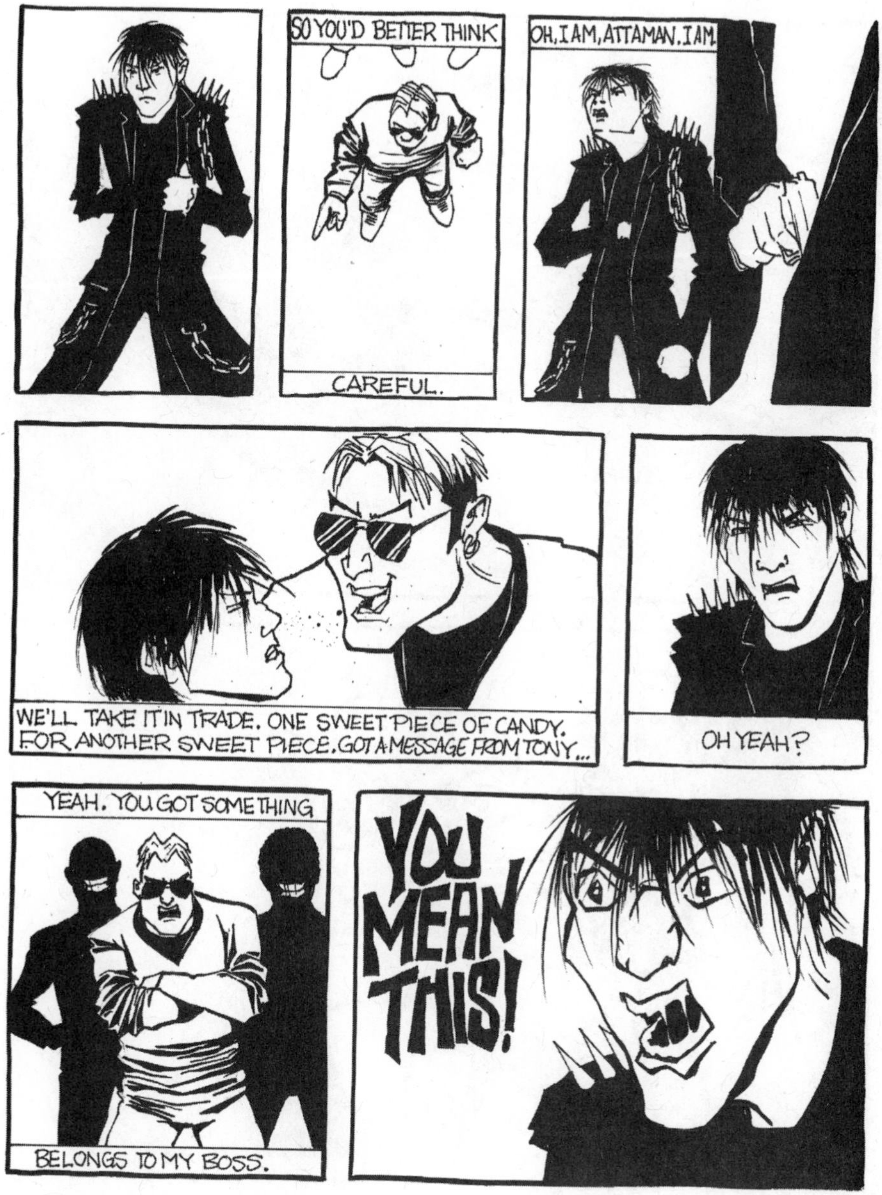
SO YOU'D BETTER THINK
CAREFUL.
OH, I AM, ATTAMAN, I AM.
WE'LL TAKE IT IN TRADE. ONE SWEET PIECE OF CANDY. FOR ANOTHER SWEET PIECE. GOT A MESSAGE FROM TONY...
OH YEAH?
YEAH. YOU GOT SOMETHING
BELONGS TO MY BOSS.
YOU MEAN THIS!

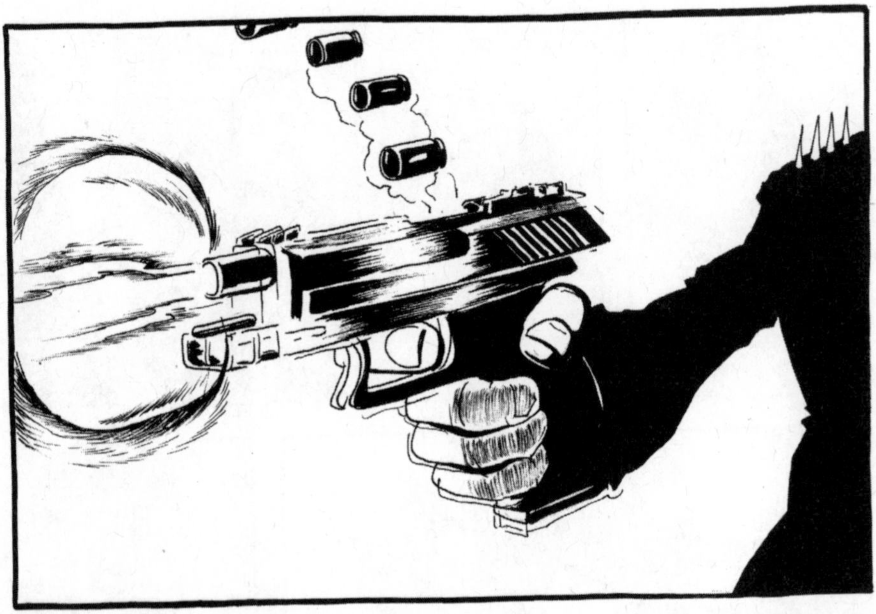

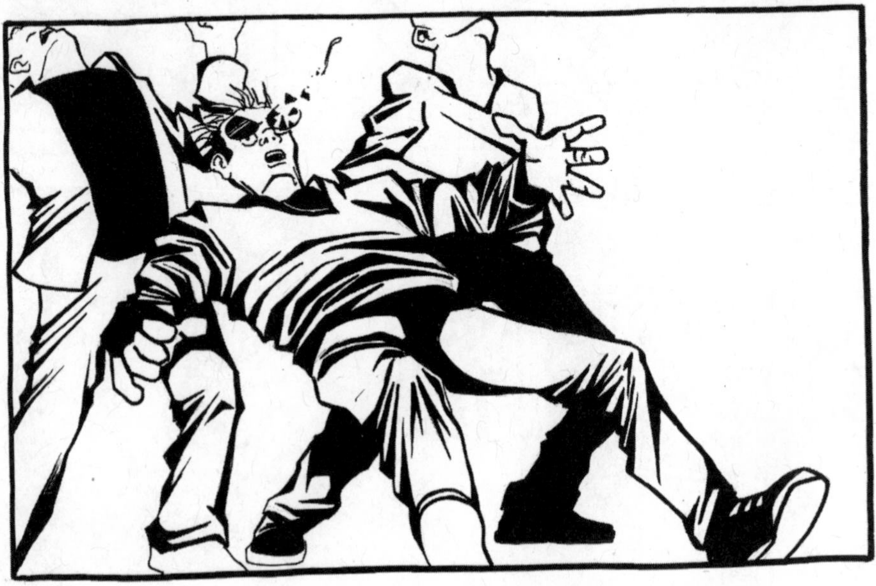

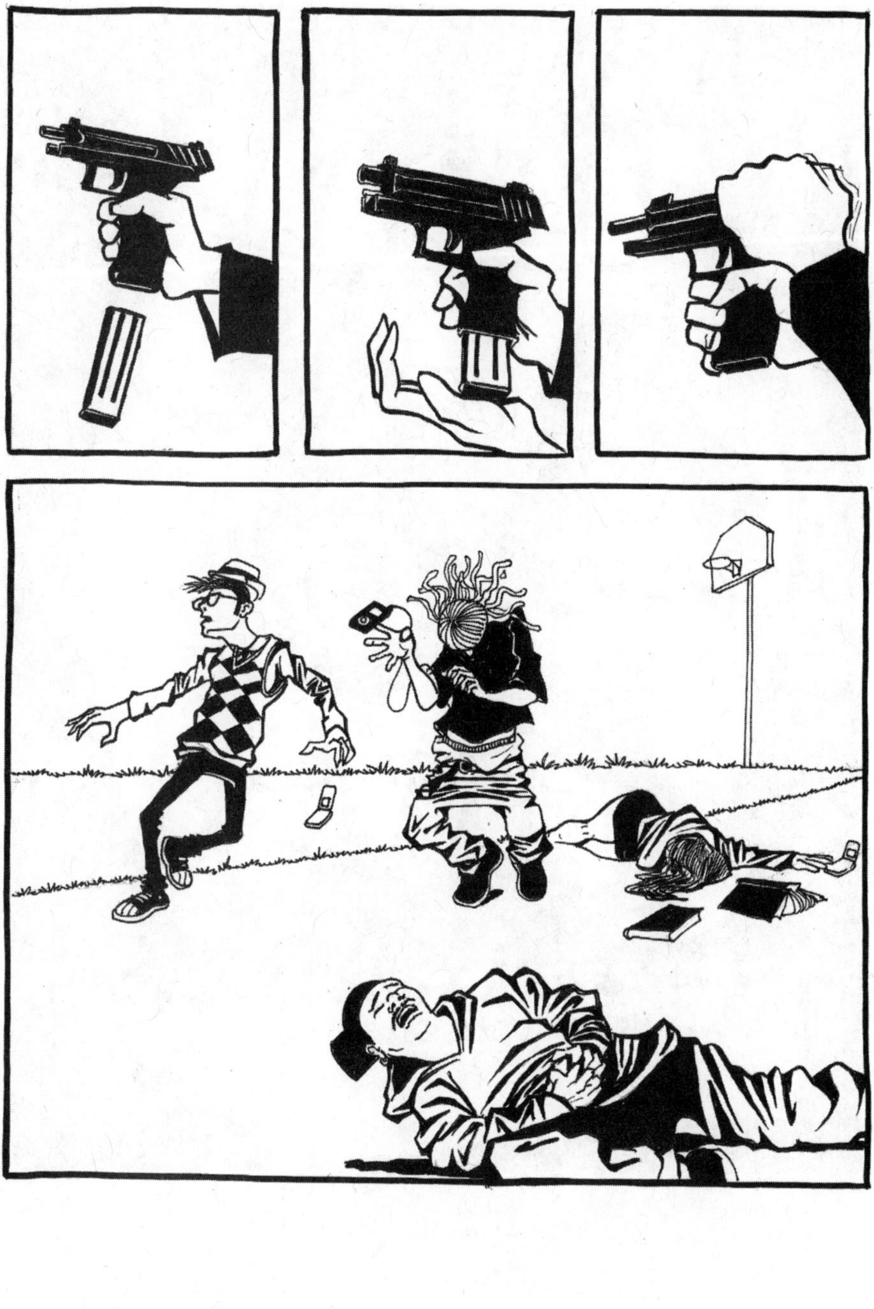

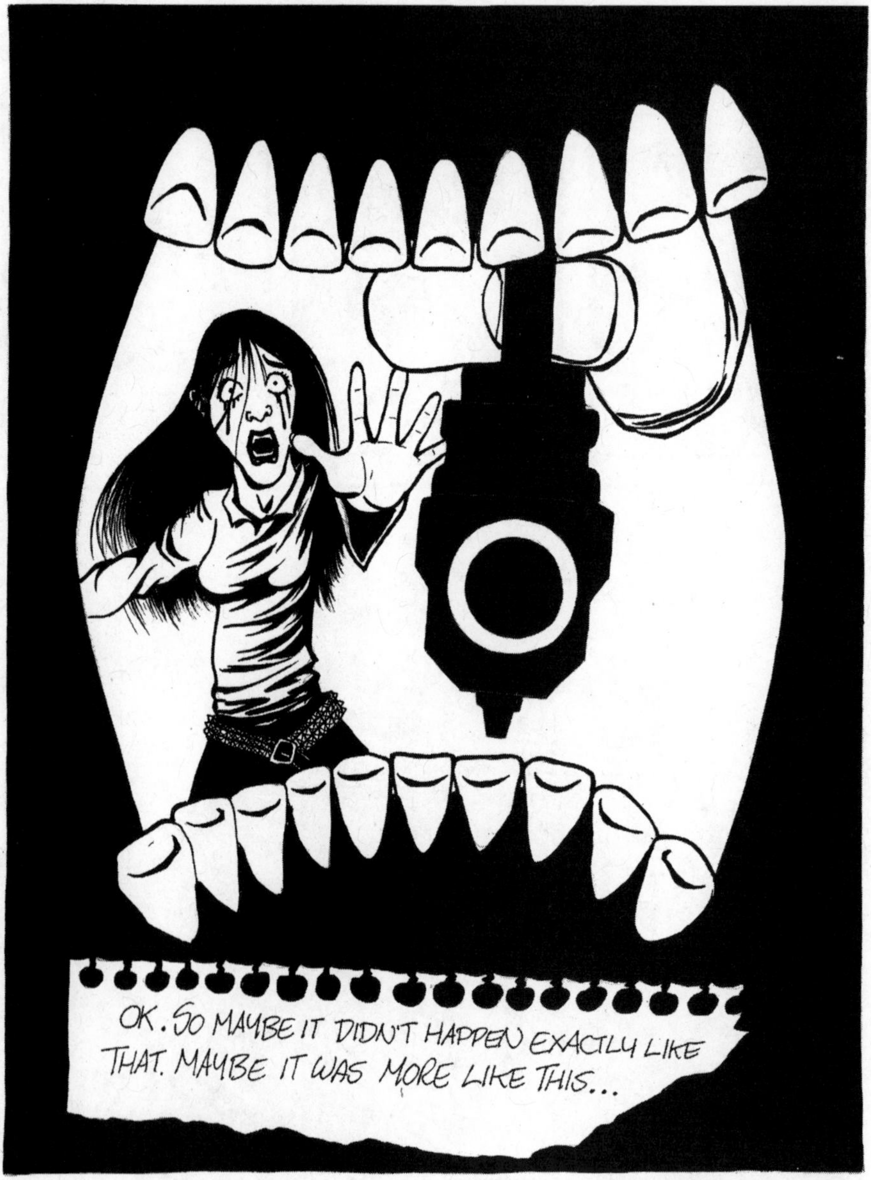
OK. SO MAYBE IT DIDN'T HAPPEN EXACTLY LIKE THAT. MAYBE IT WAS MORE LIKE THIS...

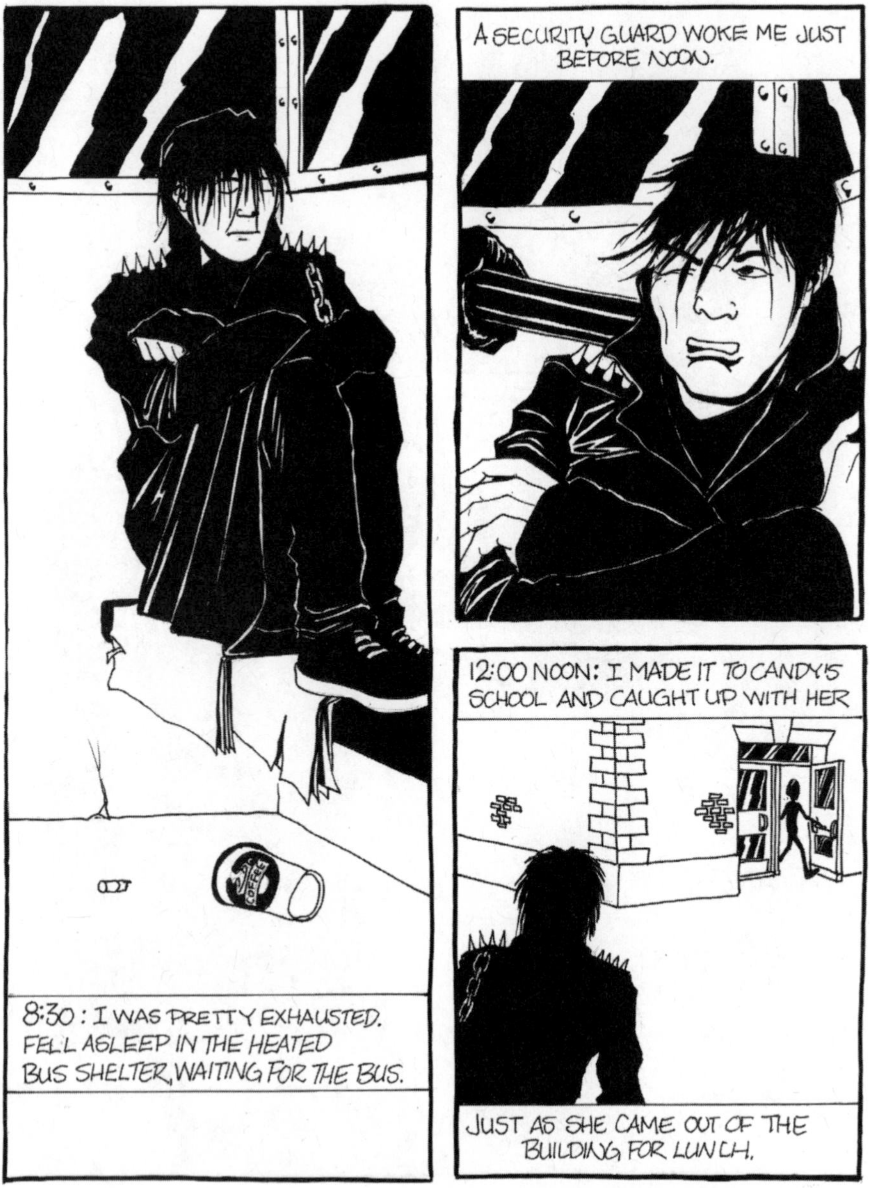
8:30 : I WAS PRETTY EXHAUSTED. FELL ASLEEP IN THE HEATED BUS SHELTER, WAITING FOR THE BUS.
A SECURITY GUARD WOKE ME JUST BEFORE NOON.
12:00 NOON: I MADE IT TO CANDY'S SCHOOL AND CAUGHT UP WITH HER
JUST AS SHE CAME OUT OF THE BUILDING FOR LUNCH.

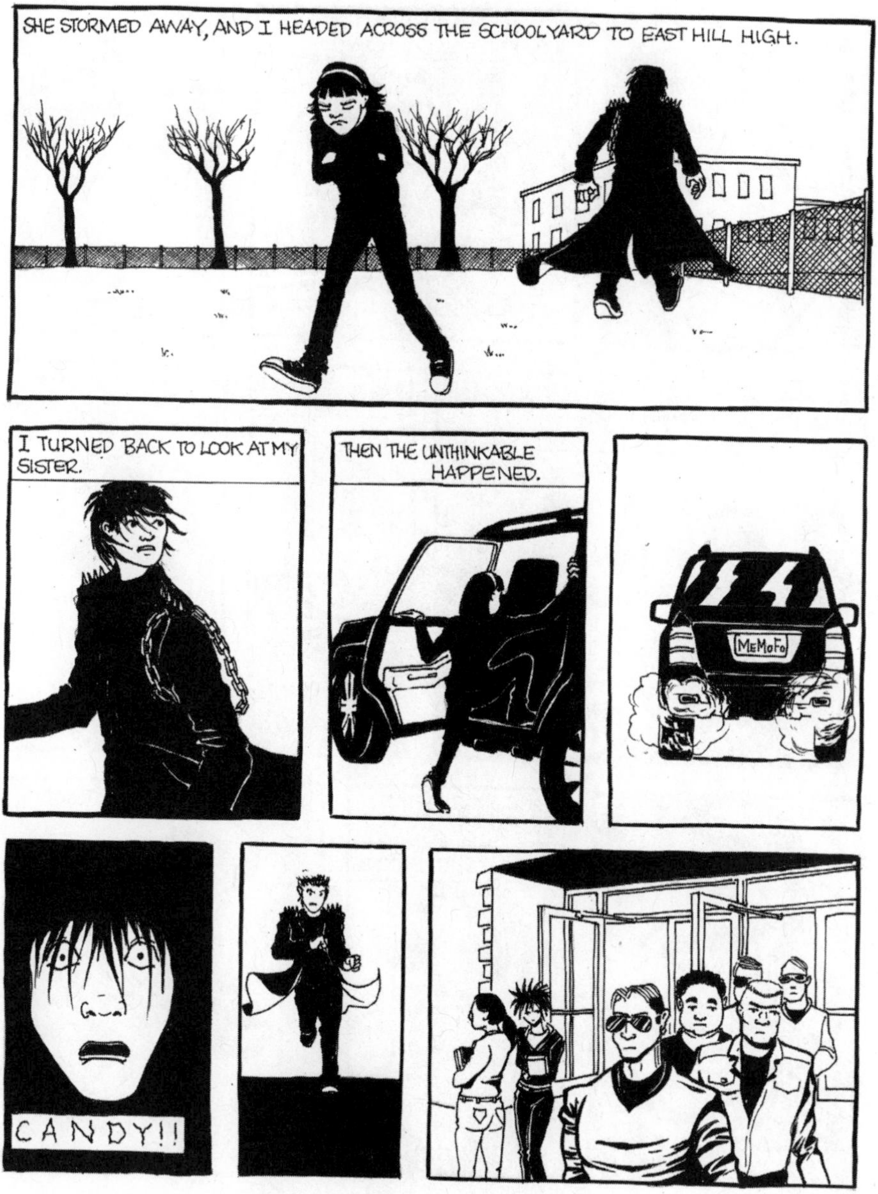
SHE STORMED AWAY, AND I HEADED ACROSS THE SCHOOLYARD TO EAST HILL HIGH.
I TURNED BACK TO LOOK AT MY SISTER.
THEN THE UNTHINKABLE HAPPENED.
MEMOFO
CANDY!!

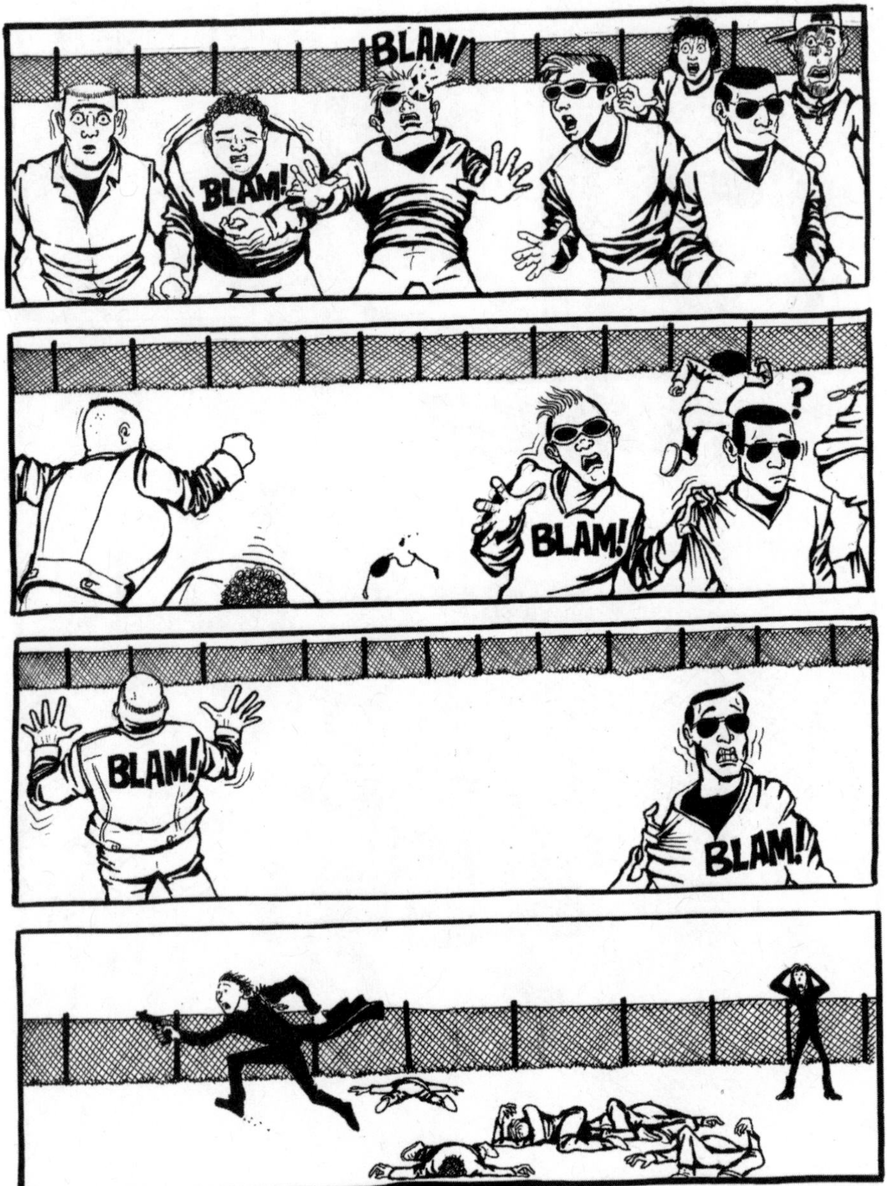
BLAM!
BLAM!
BLAM!
?
BLAM!
BLAM!

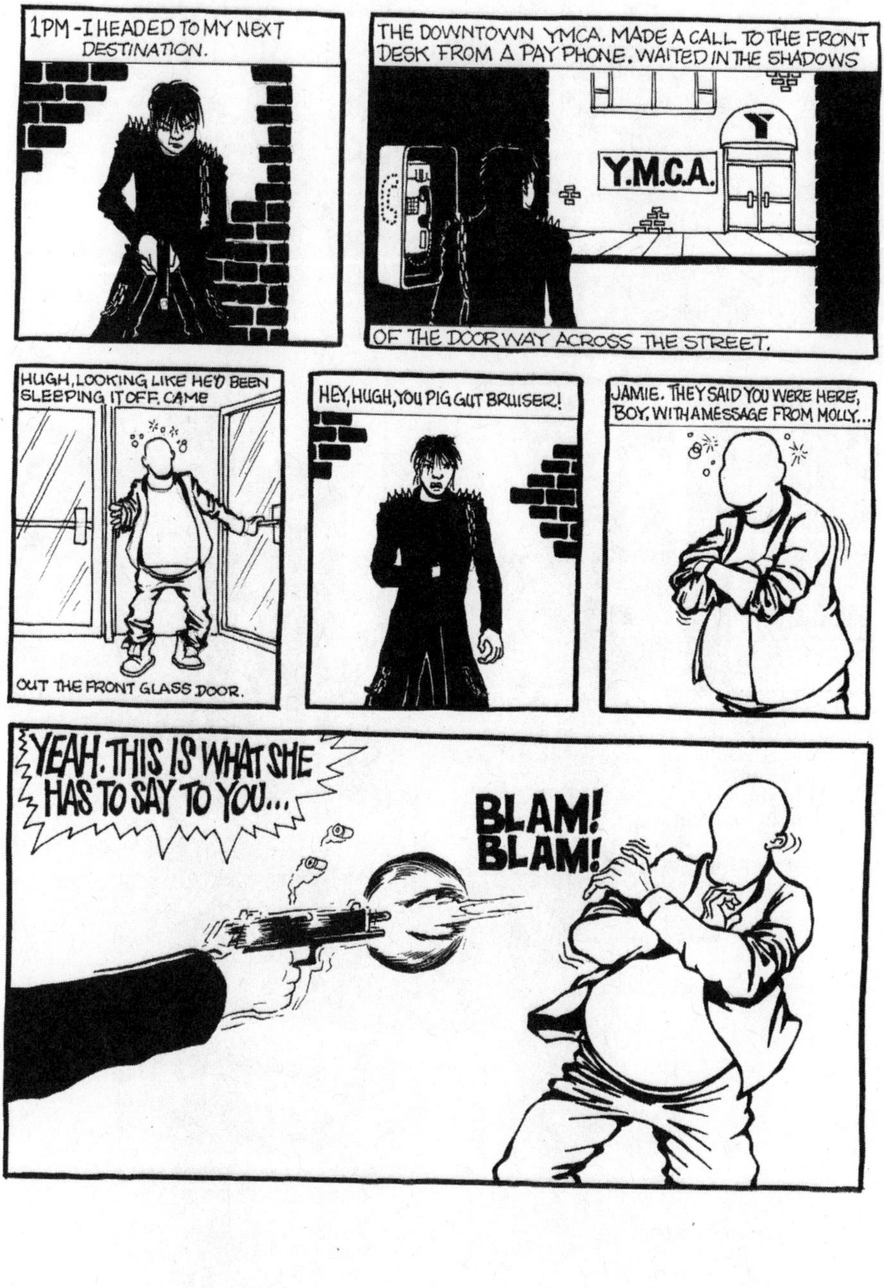
1PM - I HEADED TO MY NEXT DESTINATION.
THE DOWNTOWN YMCA. MADE A CALL TO THE FRONT DESK FROM A PAY PHONE. WAITED IN THE SHADOWS
Y.M.C.A.
OF THE DOORWAY ACROSS THE STREET.
HUGH, LOOKING LIKE HE'D BEEN SLEEPING IT OFF, CAME
OUT THE FRONT GLASS DOOR.
HEY, HUGH, YOU PIG GUT BRUISER!
JAMIE. THEY SAID YOU WERE HERE, BOY, WITH A MESSAGE FROM MOLLY...
YEAH. THIS IS WHAT SHE HAS TO SAY TO YOU...
BLAM! BLAM!

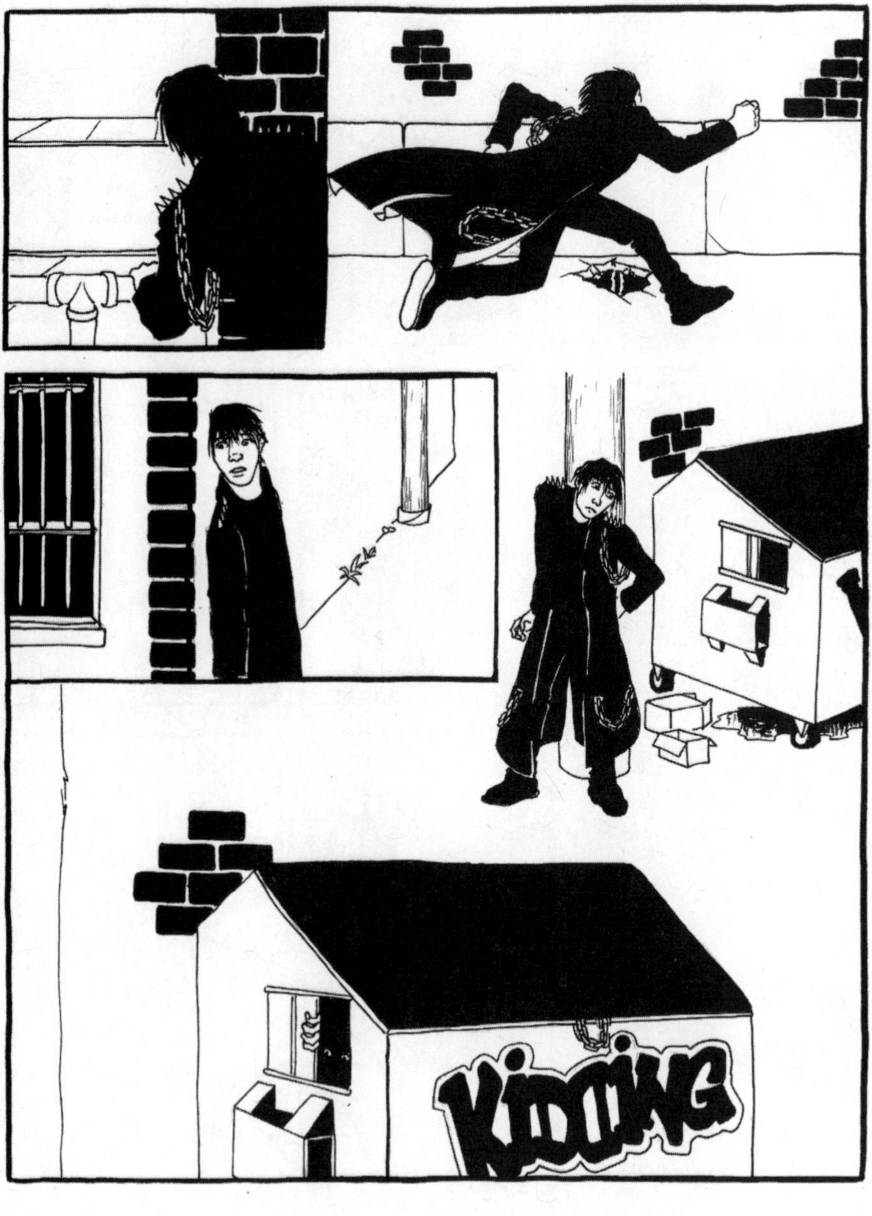
KIDDING

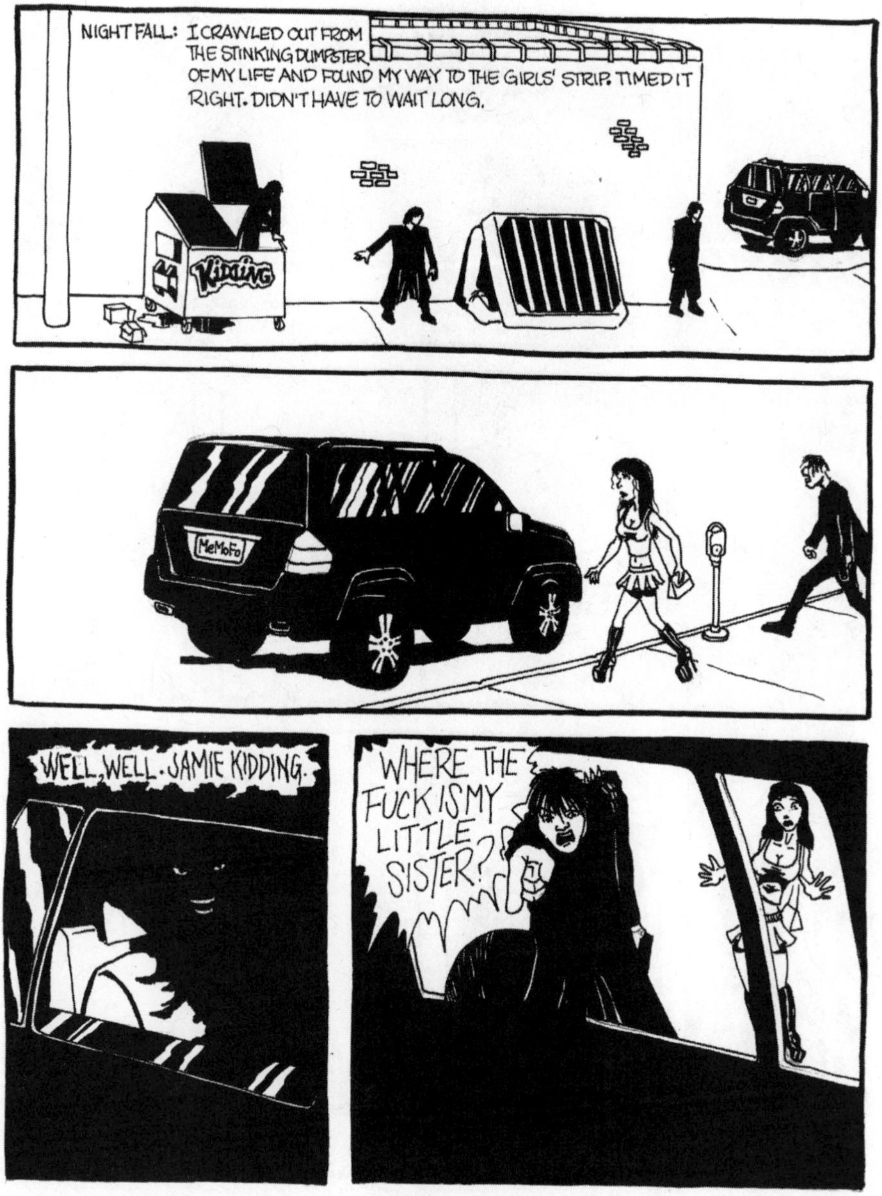
NIGHT FALL: I CRAWLED OUT FROM THE STINKING DUMPSTER OF MY LIFE AND FOUND MY WAY TO THE GIRLS' STRIP. TIMED IT RIGHT. DIDN'T HAVE TO WAIT LONG.
KIDDING
MeMoFo
WELL, WELL. JAMIE KIDDING.
WHERE THE FUCK IS MY LITTLE SISTER?

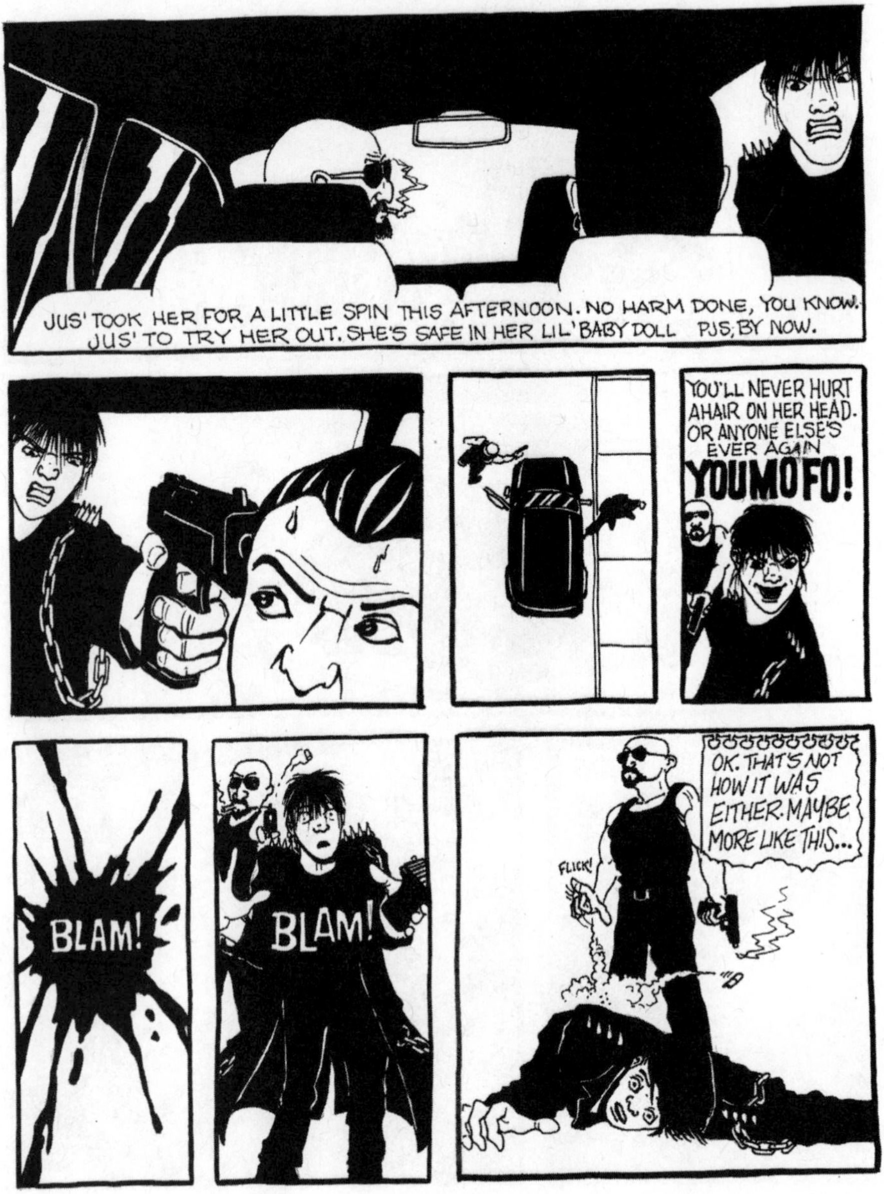
JUS' TOOK HER FOR A LITTLE SPIN THIS AFTERNOON. NO HARM DONE, YOU KNOW. JUS' TO TRY HER OUT. SHE'S SAFE IN HER LIL' BABY DOLL PJS, BY NOW.
YOU'LL NEVER HURT A HAIR ON HER HEAD. OR ANYONE ELSE'S EVER AGAIN
YOU MOFO!
BLAM!
BLAM!
OK. THAT'S NOT HOW IT WAS EITHER. MAYBE MORE LIKE THIS...
FLICK!

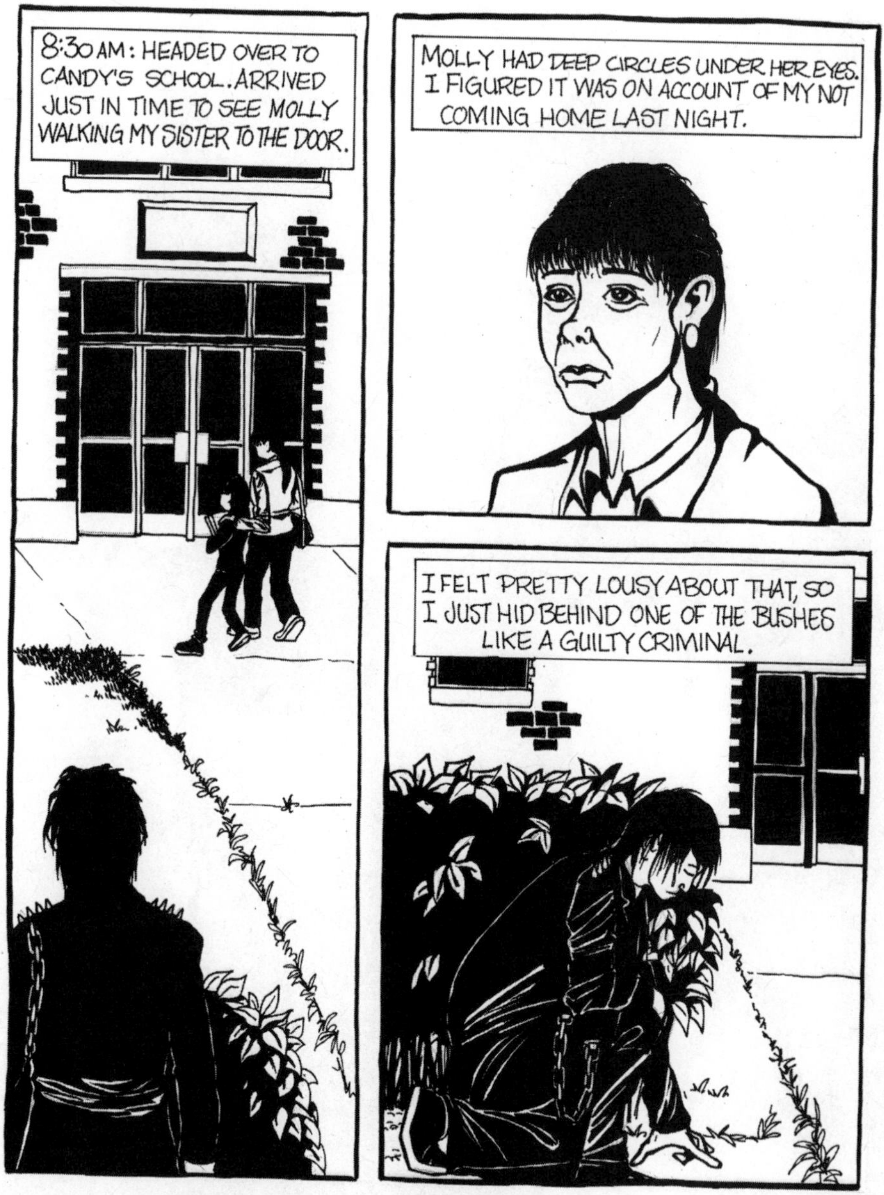
8:30 AM: HEADED OVER TO CANDY'S SCHOOL. ARRIVED JUST IN TIME TO SEE MOLLY WALKING MY SISTER TO THE DOOR.
MOLLY HAD DEEP CIRCLES UNDER HER EYES. I FIGURED IT WAS ON ACCOUNT OF MY NOT COMING HOME LAST NIGHT.
I FELT PRETTY LOUSY ABOUT THAT, SO I JUST HID BEHIND ONE OF THE BUSHES LIKE A GUILTY CRIMINAL.

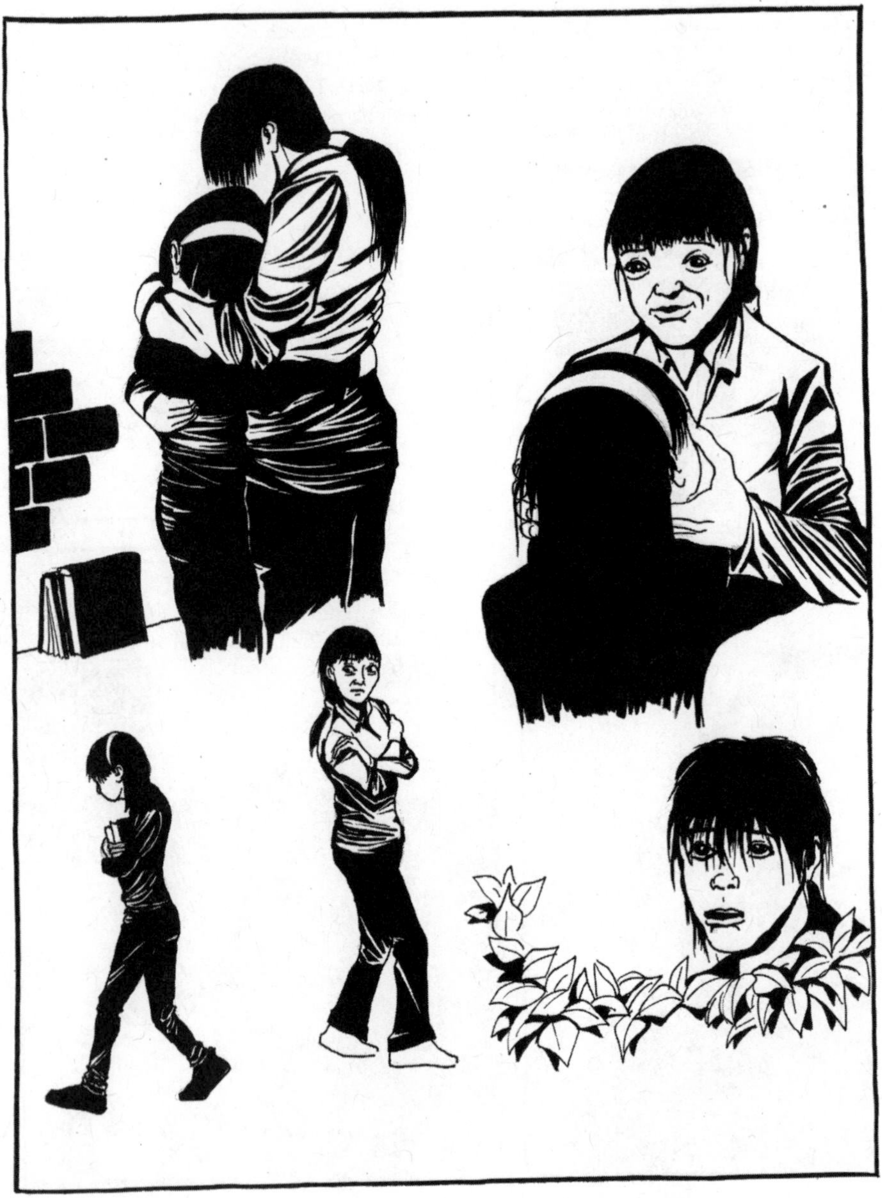

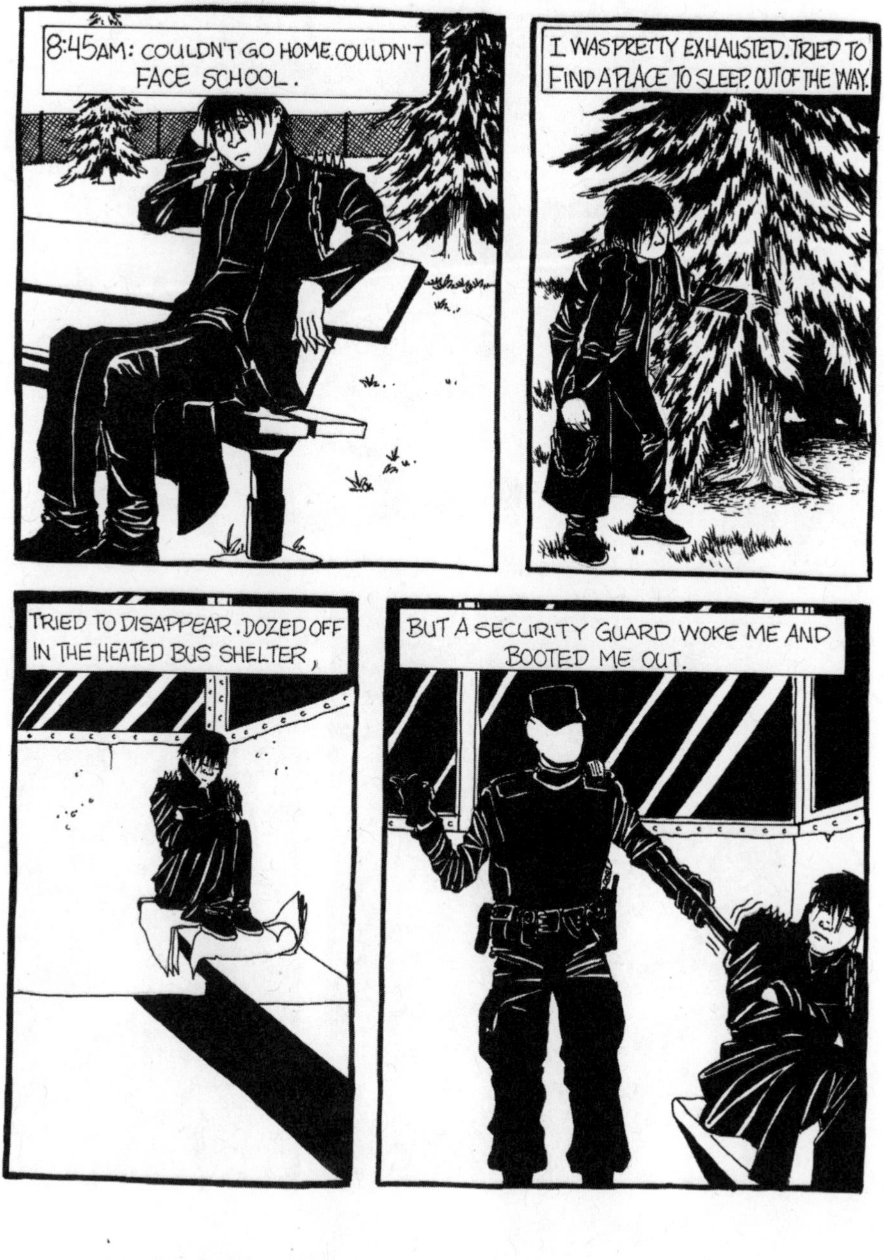
8:45AM: COULDN'T GO HOME. COULDN'T FACE SCHOOL.
I WAS PRETTY EXHAUSTED. TRIED TO FIND A PLACE TO SLEEP. OUT OF THE WAY.
TRIED TO DISAPPEAR. DOZED OFF IN THE HEATED BUS SHELTER,
BUT A SECURITY GUARD WOKE ME AND BOOTED ME OUT.

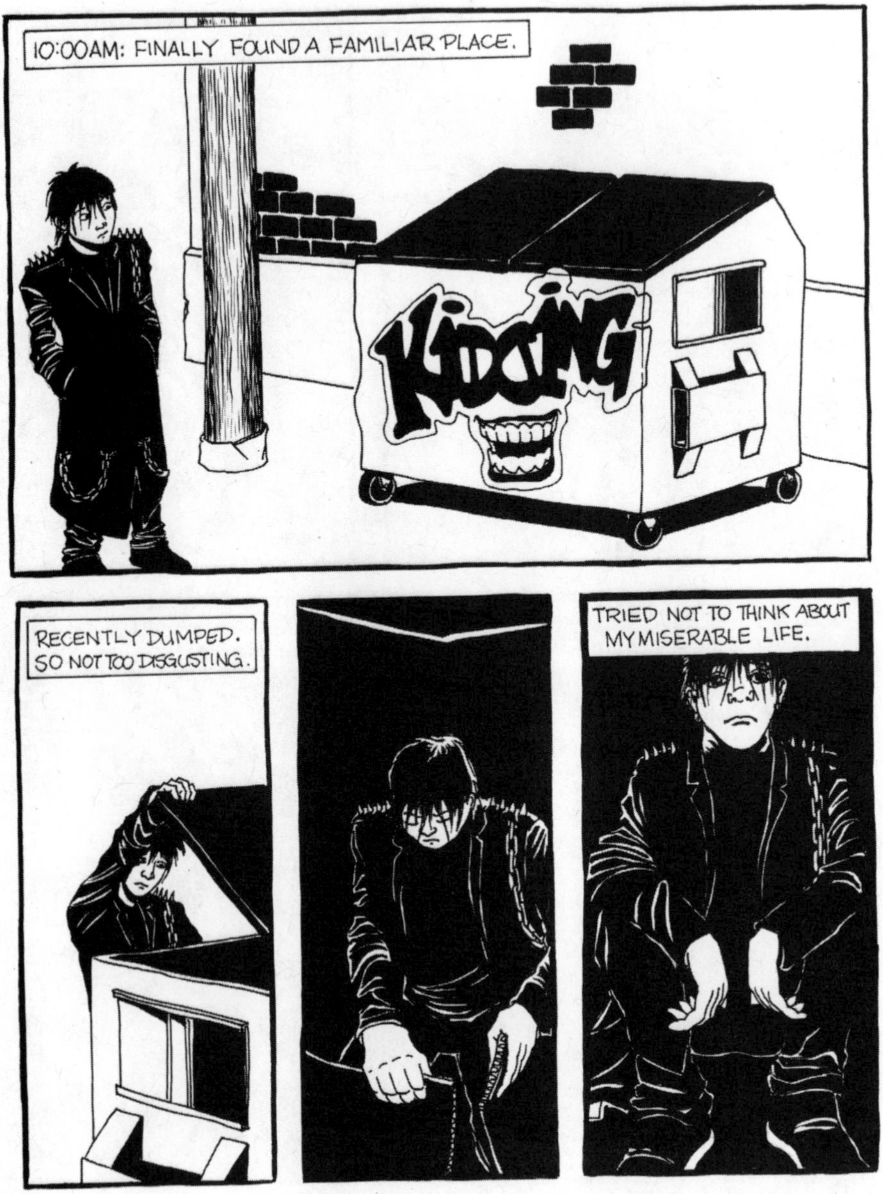
10:00AM: FINALLY FOUND A FAMILIAR PLACE.
KIDDING
RECENTLY DUMPED. SO NOT TOO DISGUSTING.
TRIED NOT TO THINK ABOUT MY MISERABLE LIFE.

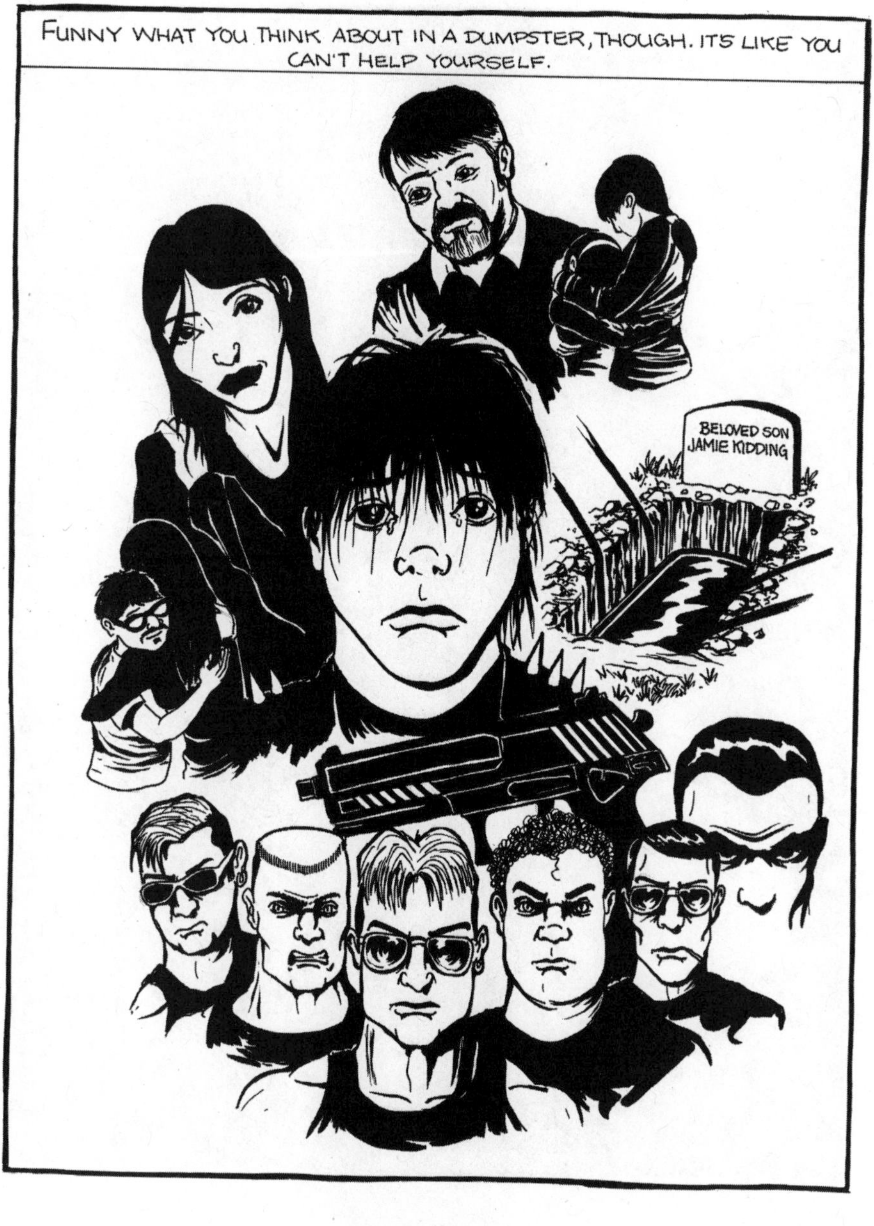
FUNNY WHAT YOU THINK ABOUT IN A DUMPSTER, THOUGH. IT'S LIKE YOU CAN'T HELP YOURSELF.
BELOVED SON JAMIE KIDDING

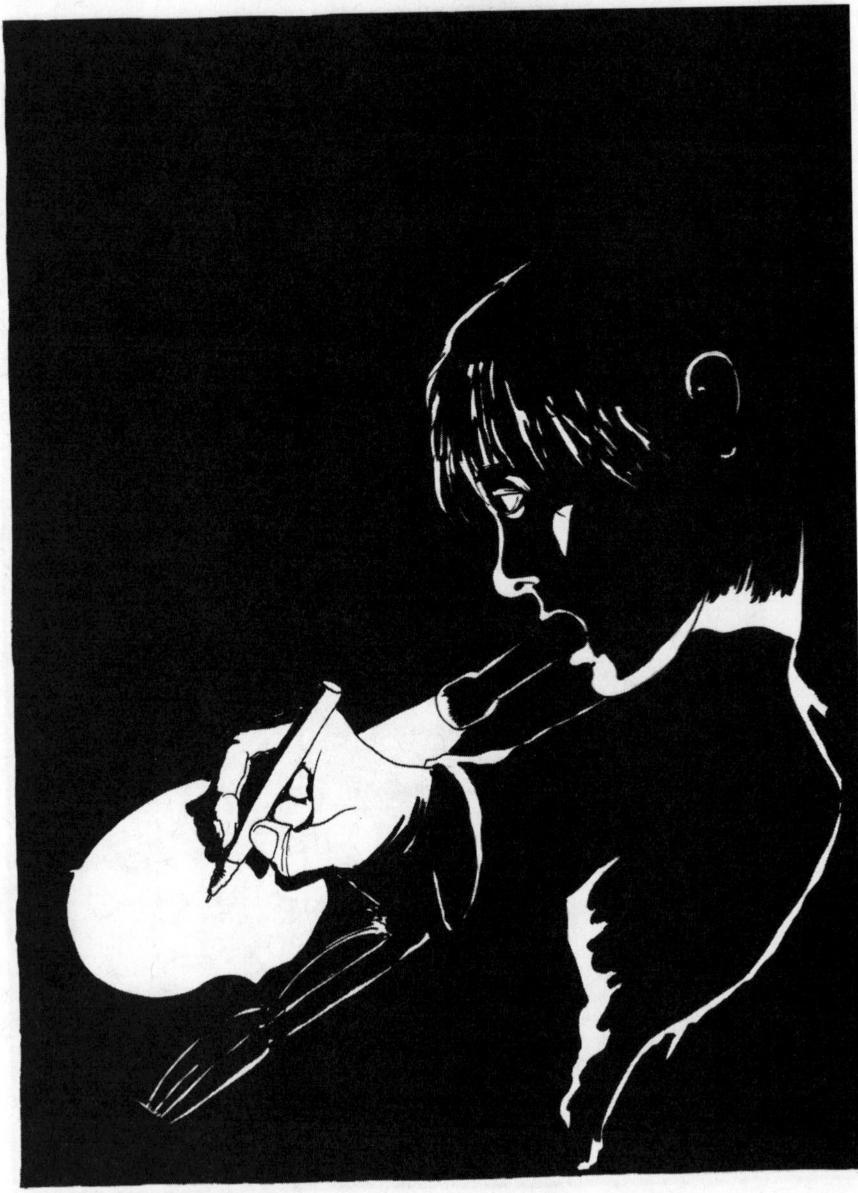

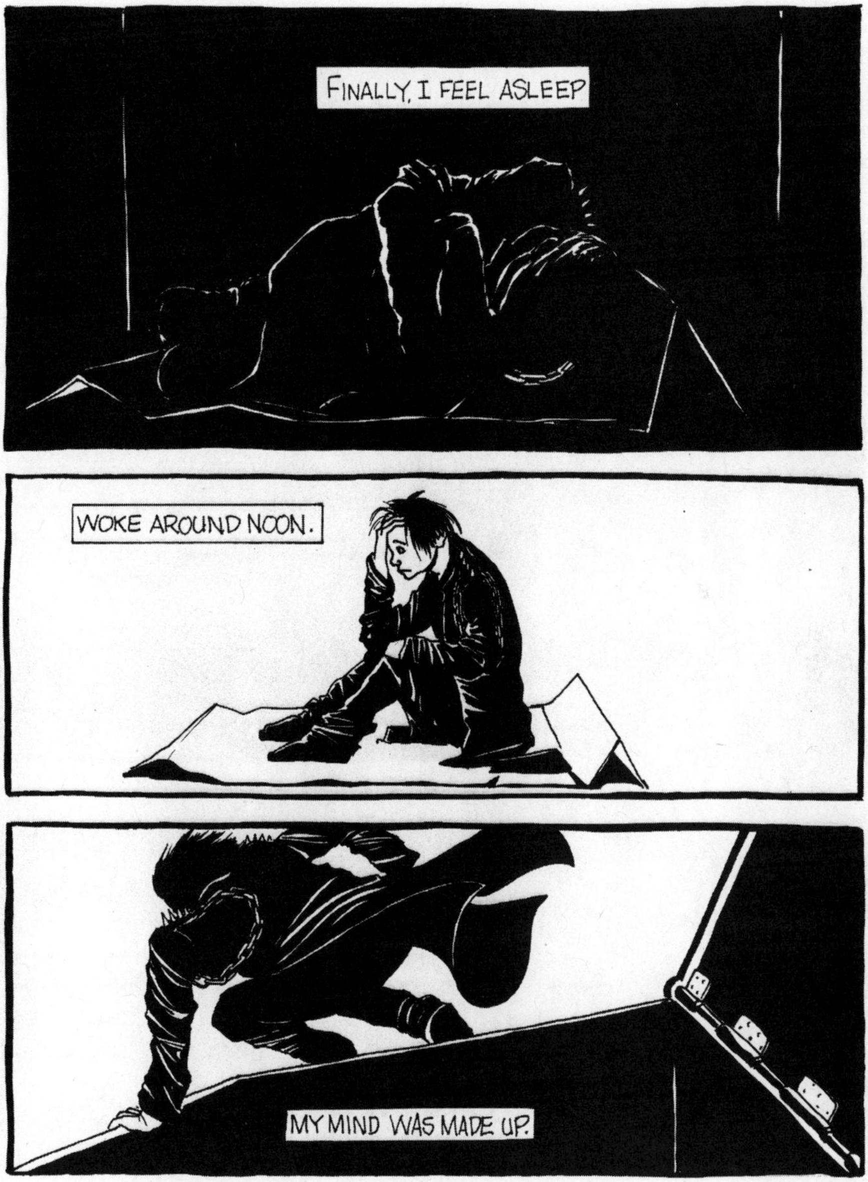
FINALLY, I FEEL ASLEEP
WOKE AROUND NOON.
MY MIND WAS MADE UP.

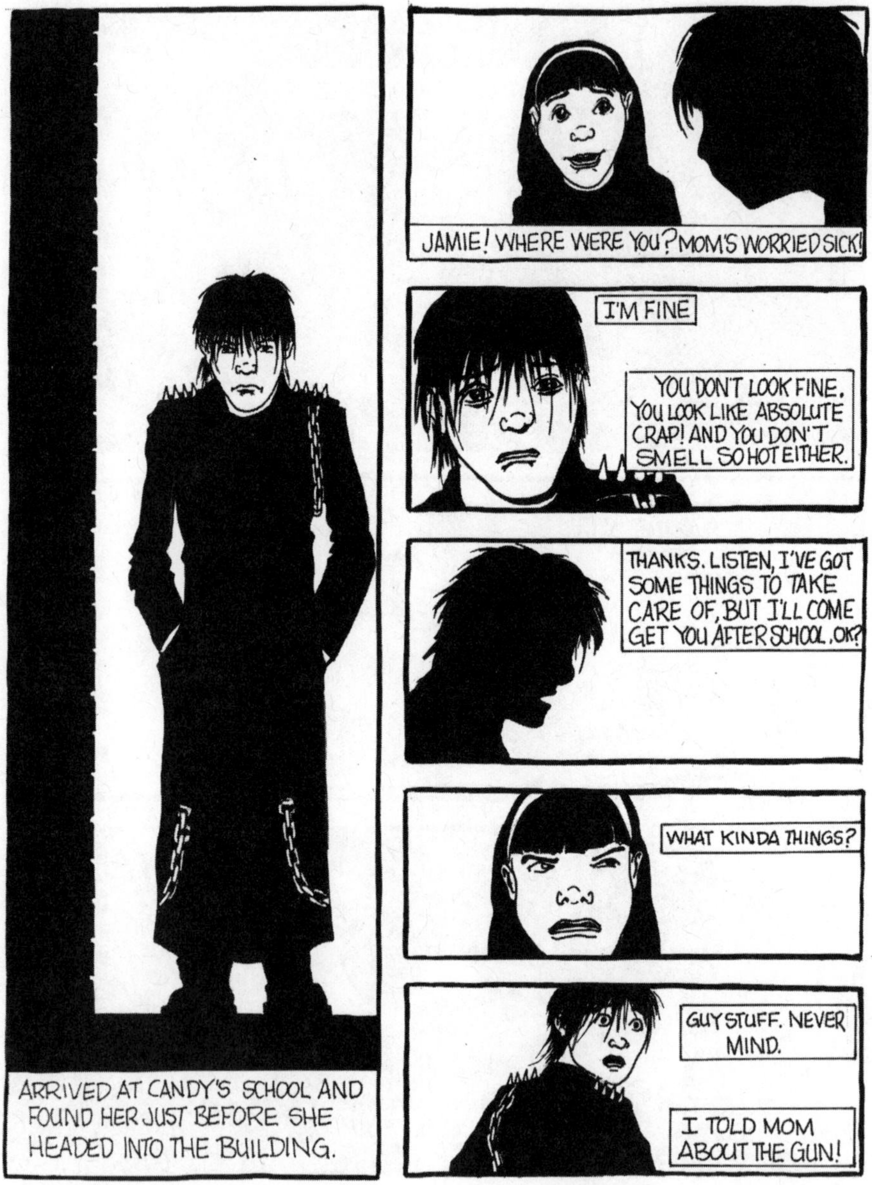
ARRIVED AT CANDY'S SCHOOL AND FOUND HER JUST BEFORE SHE HEADED INTO THE BUILDING.
JAMIE! WHERE WERE YOU? MOM'S WORRIED SICK!
I'M FINE
YOU DON'T LOOK FINE. YOU LOOK LIKE ABSOLUTE CRAP! AND YOU DON'T SMELL SO HOT EITHER.
THANKS. LISTEN, I'VE GOT SOME THINGS TO TAKE CARE OF, BUT I'LL COME GET YOU AFTER SCHOOL, OK?
WHAT KINDA THINGS?
GUY STUFF. NEVER MIND.
I TOLD MOM ABOUT THE GUN!

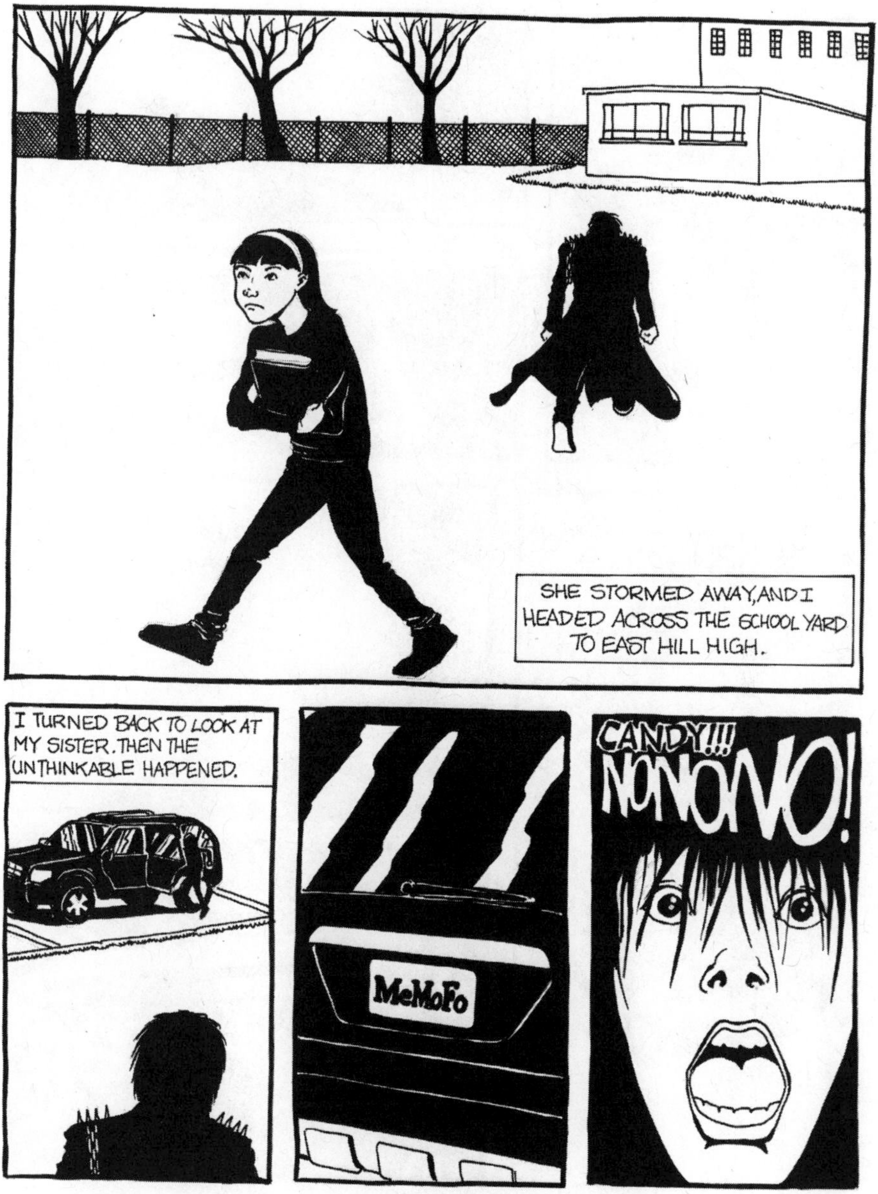
SHE STORMED AWAY, AND I HEADED ACROSS THE SCHOOL YARD TO EAST HILL HIGH.
I TURNED BACK TO LOOK AT MY SISTER. THEN THE UNTHINKABLE HAPPENED.
MeMoFo
CANDY!!!
NONONO!

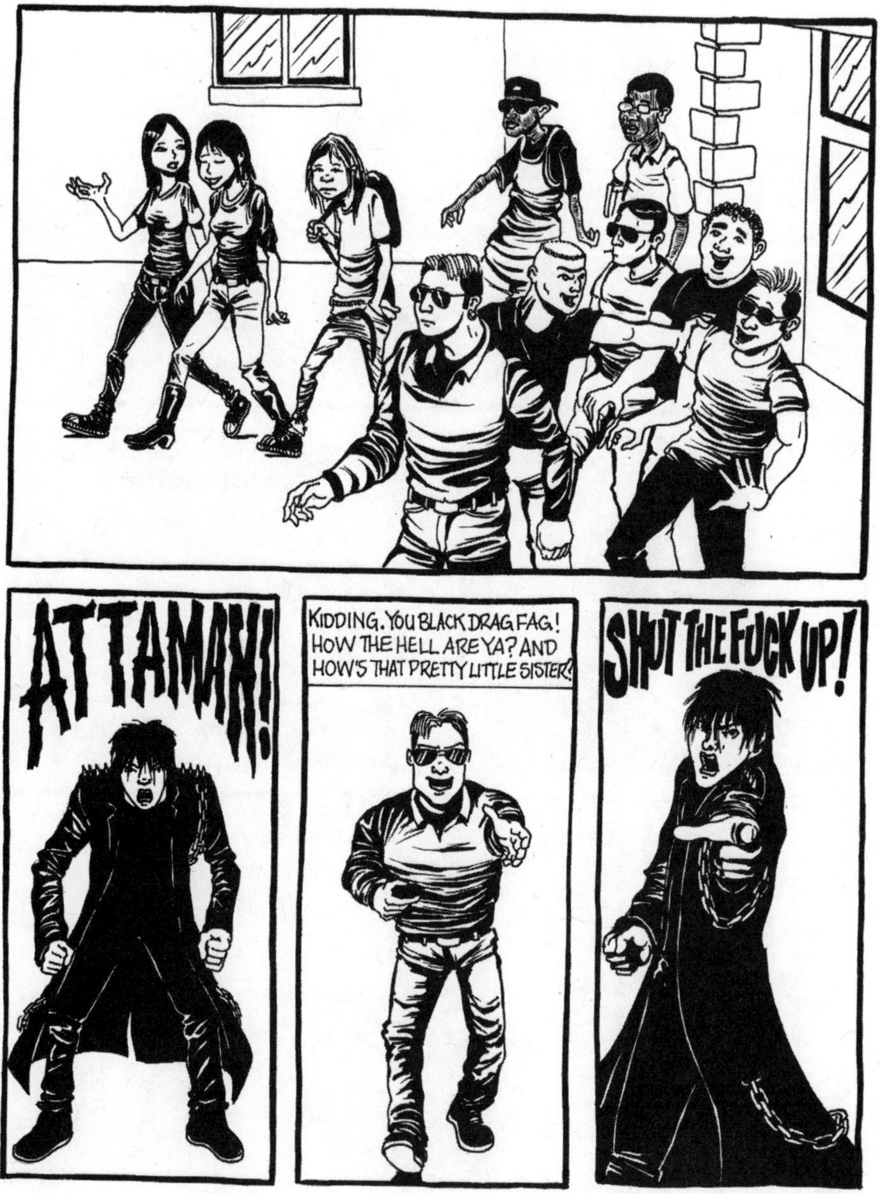
ATTAMAN!
KIDDING. YOU BLACK DRAG FAG! HOW THE HELL ARE YA? AND HOW'S THAT PRETTY LITTLE SISTER?
SHUT THE FUCK UP!

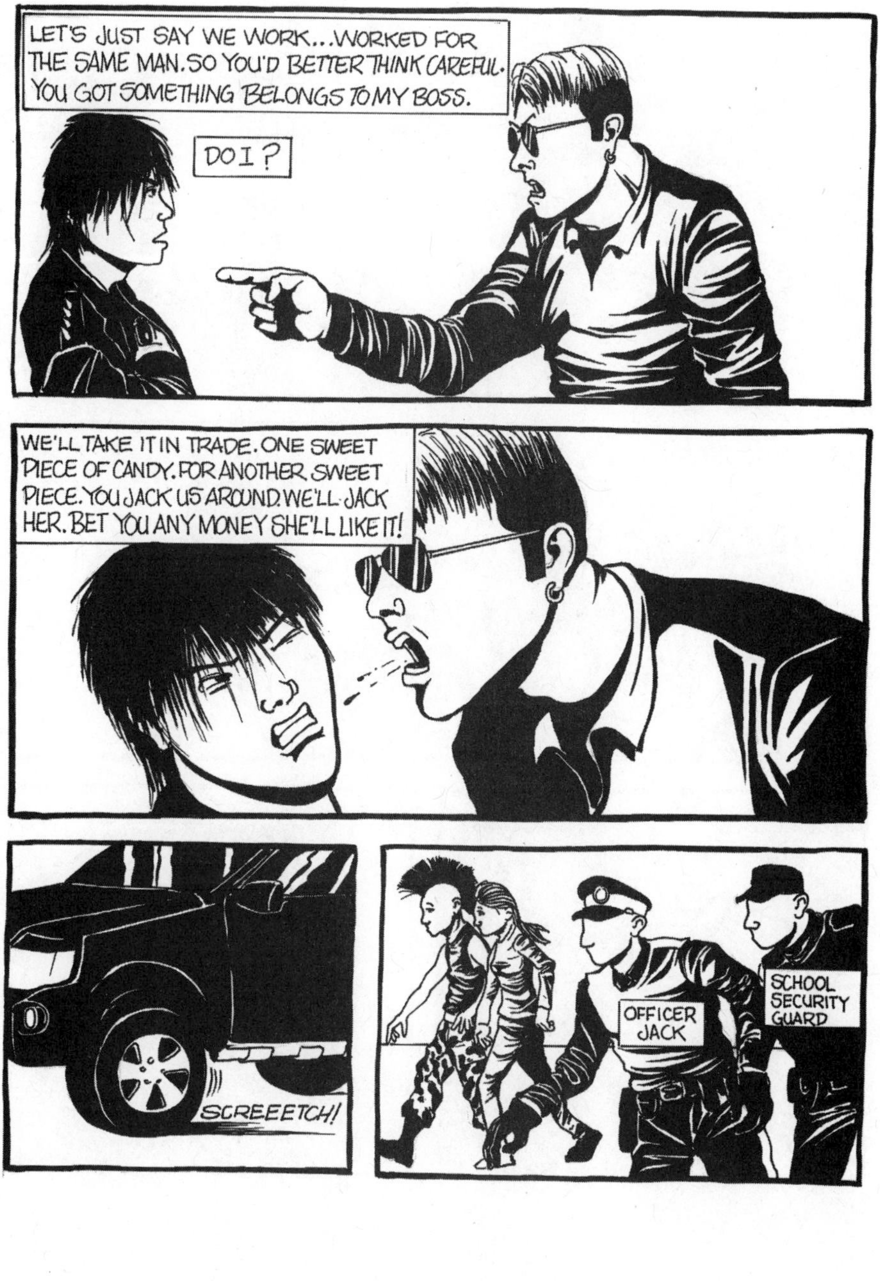
LET'S JUST SAY WE WORK...WORKED FOR THE SAME MAN. SO YOU'D BETTER THINK CAREFUL. YOU GOT SOMETHING BELONGS TO MY BOSS.
DO I?
WE'LL TAKE IT IN TRADE. ONE SWEET PIECE OF CANDY. FOR ANOTHER SWEET PIECE. YOU JACK US AROUND. WE'LL JACK HER. BET YOU ANY MONEY SHE'LL LIKE IT!
SCREEETCH!
OFFICER JACK
SCHOOL SECURITY GUARD

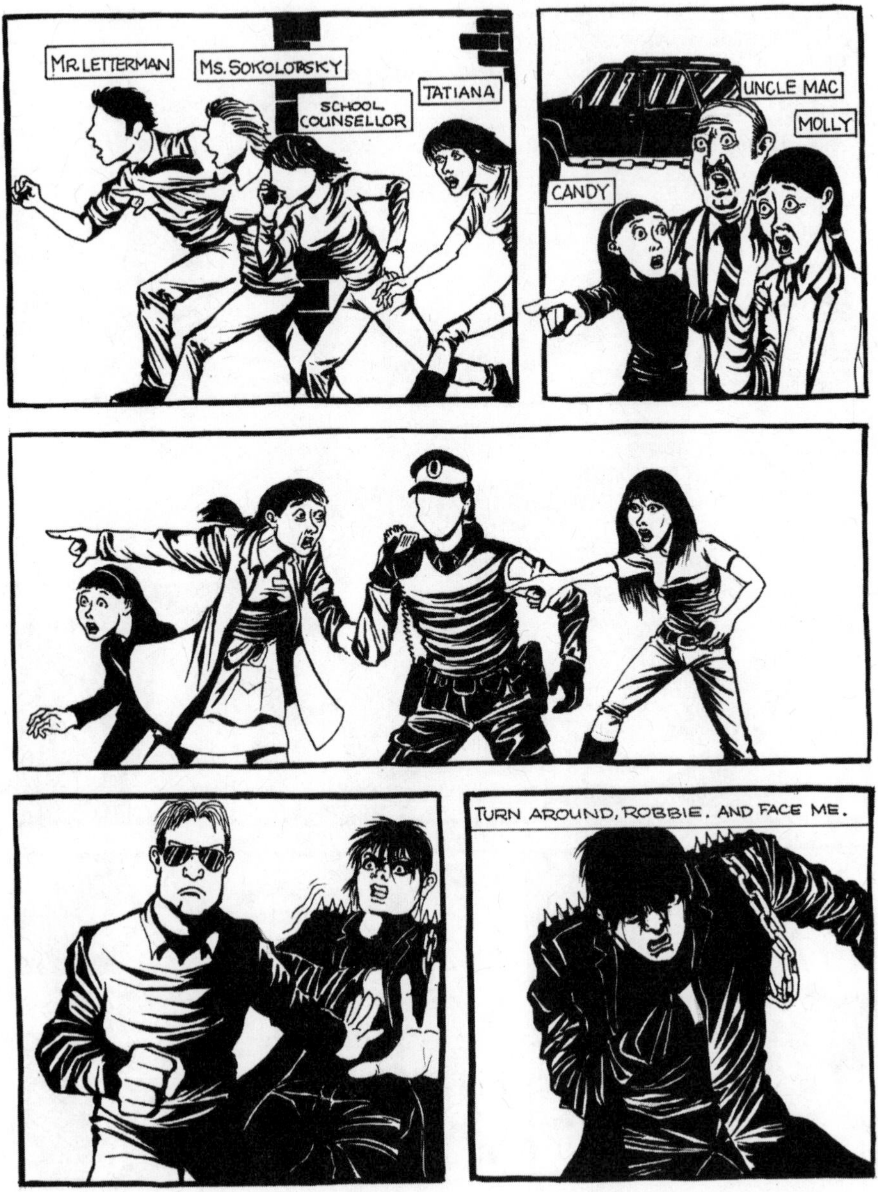
MR. LETTERMAN
MS. SOKOLOBSKY
SCHOOL COUNSELLOR
TATIANA
UNCLE MAC
MOLLY
CANDY
TURN AROUND, ROBBIE. AND FACE ME.

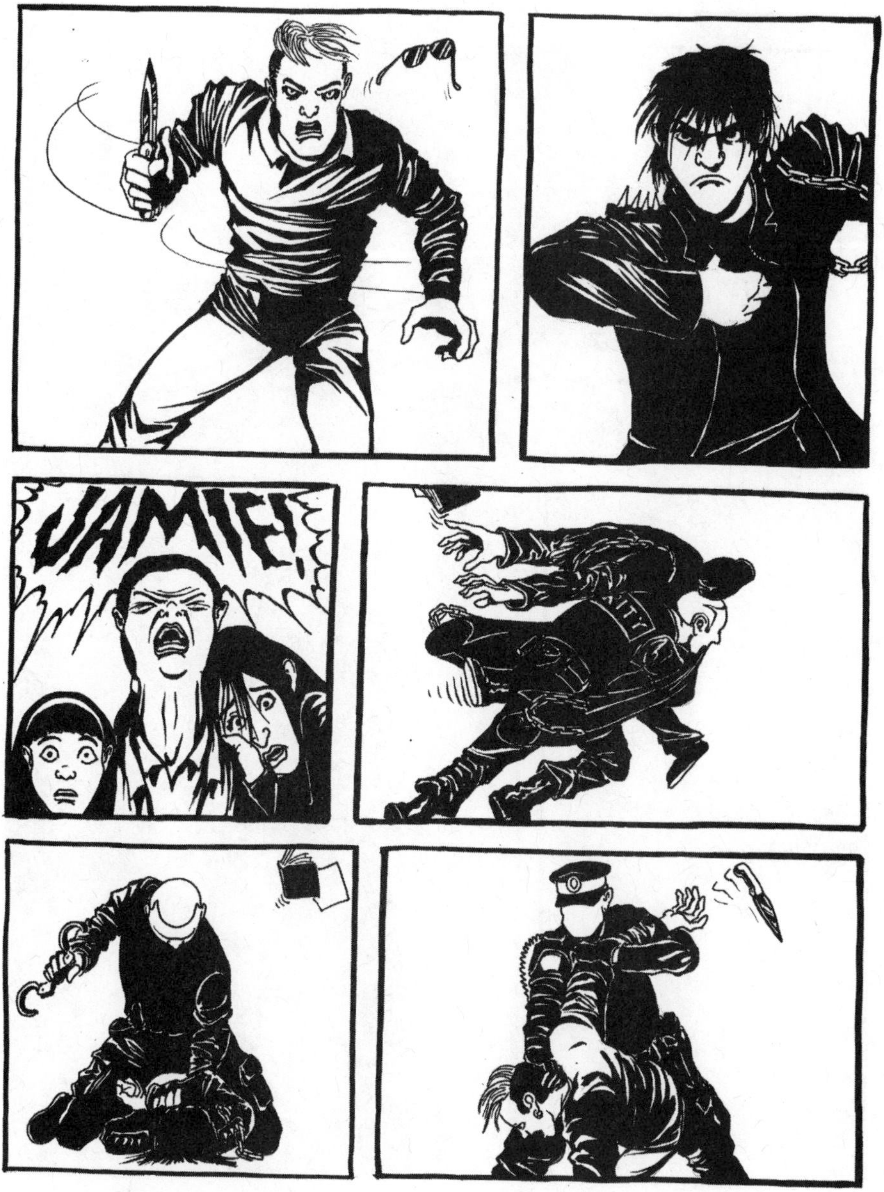
JAMIE!

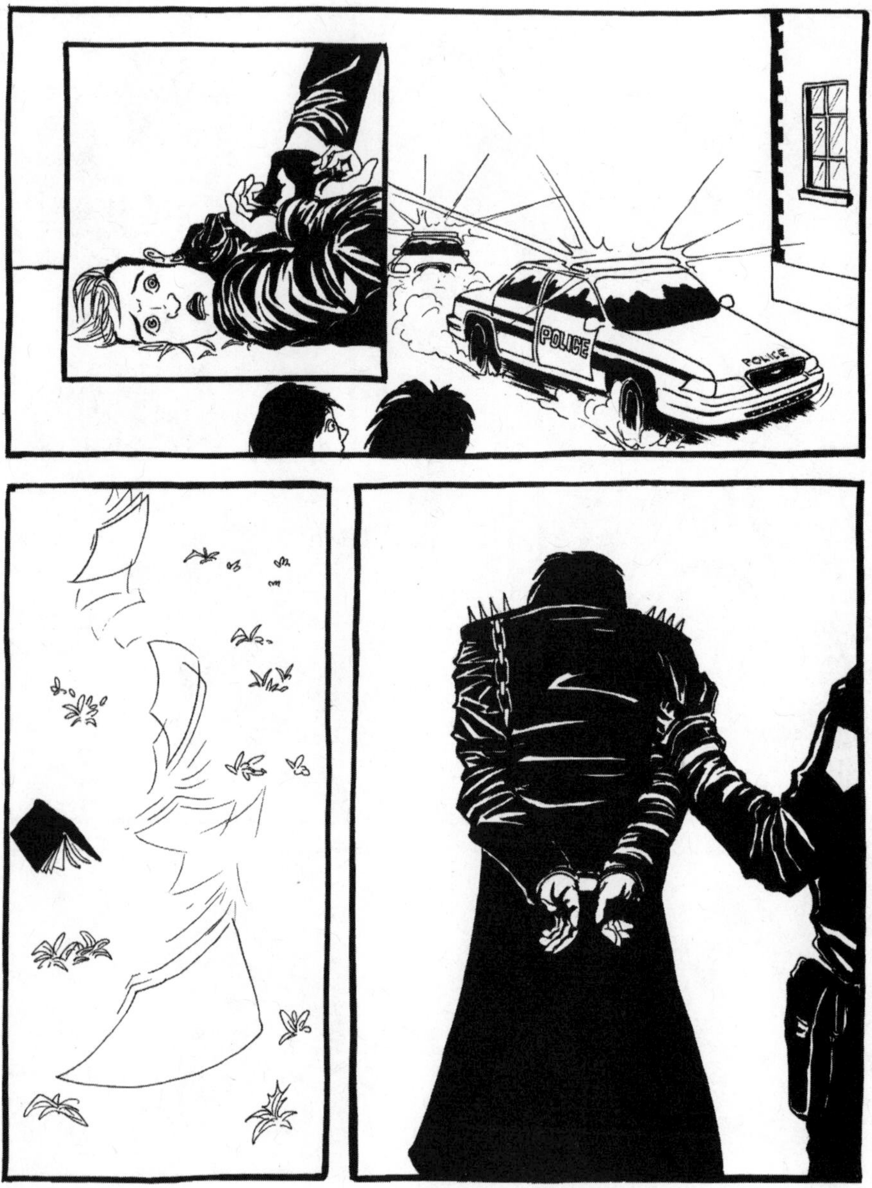
POLICE
POLICE

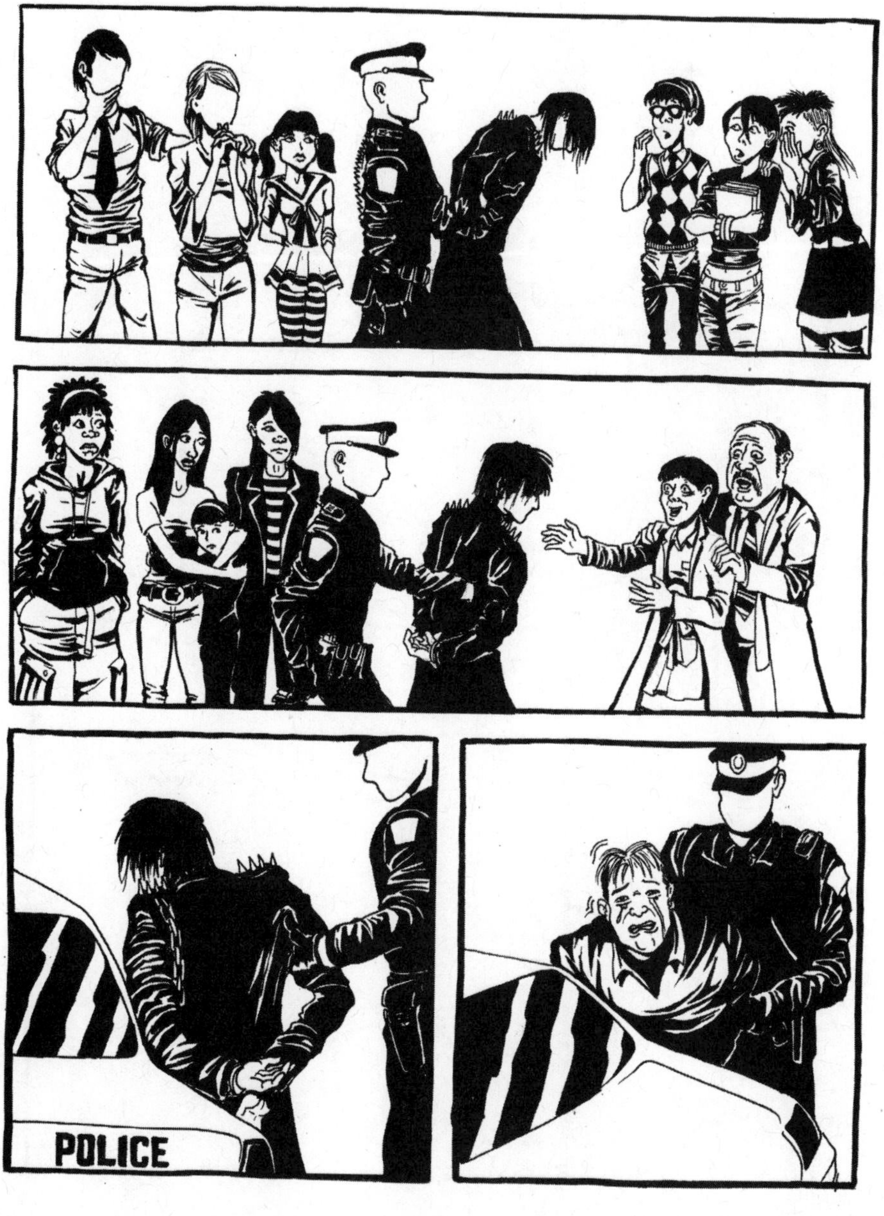
POLICE

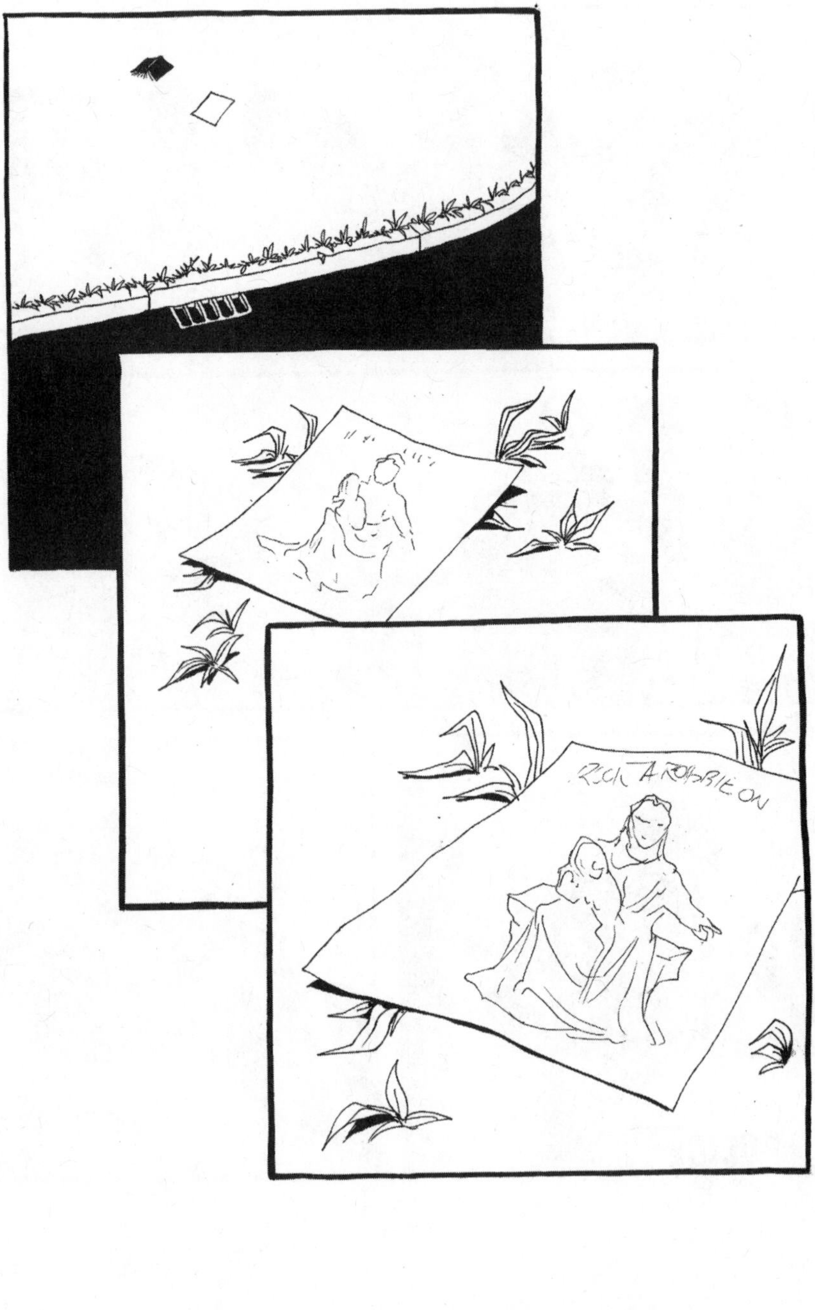

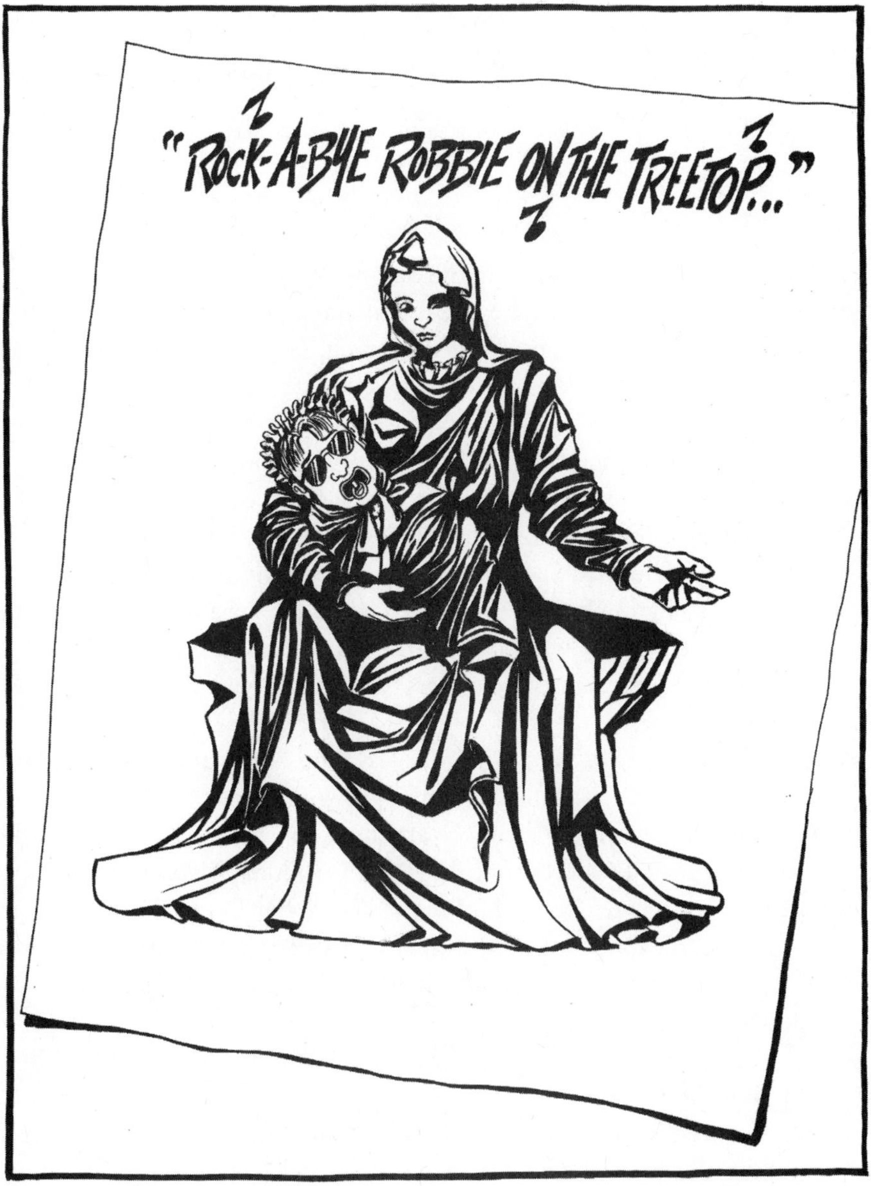
"ROCK-A-BYE ROBBIE ON THE TREETOP..."

The police found the gun in the dumpster where I'd left it.

Maybe all that stuff at East Hill High happened. Maybe not. Memory is a tricky thing. Especially under stress. So is eyesight. Under stress. And when you're dyslexic.

I spent a lot of time telling my side of things to the police. How I found the gun. Wanted to use it. Planned to use it. Finally put it back where it belonged. The cops have it now. No other prints on it but mine. Figures. I told them whose gun it was. They seemed mildly interested. Gave me a stern legal lecture about the perils of vigilante-ism. Then let me go.

Not so happy Robert (Blade) Attaman. He's charged with carrying a concealed weapon with the intent to harm. He's already on probation, and because he's eighteen, he'll probably see some jail time.

Single tear.

So that's one less arsewipe, one less semi-automatic weapon on the shat-butt streets of one Canadian city. Big deal.

How many thousands more are there out there? Who knows?

But I guess I do know one thing: Jamie Kidding is no killer. Could've been. And that really freakin' scares me. What I'm capable of. What any of us is capable of, I guess, with a loaded gun in our hands. And the wrong life. No friends. Bullies—at home or at school. Black as doom days.

I had my finger on the trigger. Jamie Kidding, *almost* a killer.

But I'm not.

So much for my bad-ass, short-lived rep. Good riddance. What a weight off my shoulders. I didn't even realize.

It was harder, in a way, to explain the whole thing to Molly. Mom. She cried and cried. Candy, too. Me, too, if I'm telling the truth.

Turns out Uncle Mac was picking up Candy that afternoon, as a favour, to take her to the dentist. Molly had managed to get the time off work at the last minute to accompany them, and that's why she was in my uncle's vehicle, too. Uncle Mac sped over to the high school as soon as Candy spied me from the moving SUV. He called the East Hill school office on his cell to give a heads-up about my possible deadly intentions. That's why the security guard and Officer Jack were alerted. But no one had time to issue a lockdown for the school because the bell rang, letting loose all the East Hill students.

There could've been massive chaos, death, and casualties.

Or there could've been just one. Me. Slashed to bits by Blade's blade.

Instead I got a paper cut. That's about all. What a joke.

Jamie Kidding. Saved by the bell.

I still don't know how Tatiana found her way into the mix. Dumb luck, I guess.

And I realize now just what a dumb Kidding ass I am. I let my imagination and jealousy get away from me about Tatiana Oleshenko. Turns out it was just a friendly, if excited, hug with Georgie that fateful night. Guess he found out that he'd been accepted to the Vancouver Film School. That's his big dream. So understandably Tatiana was thrilled for him.

And I'm a putz for thinking otherwise about her motives.

"This isn't going to work if you don't trust me, Jamie!"

"I know. I know. And I do. I trust you, Tat. I was j-just… outta my head that night."

"No kidding."

Ha ha.

I apologized. She forgave me. Kissed it all better, even. More than a few times. She's that kind of great girl. And I'm very lucky to have her in my life. Don't I know it.

And don't I know how lucky I am to have Molly for a mom. She forgives me, too. And a Candice Kidding to bug me and bring me around to finally using my faulty brain.

I owe her $50 for using the f-bomb. But we're going for double or nothing. One more year. I'll see how I do.

Because Keath says that it's better to swear and yell—out loud at inanimate objects or in my art book—than to resort to... well, what I was about to do. Keath Francis Conrad. My counsellor. Oh yes. I have one now. I had to give in. Pressure from absolutely everywhere. Everyone. The cops who hauled my ass in that day. My teachers. The school counsellor. Officer Jack. Candy. Molly.

Sheesh.

So I surrendered. Told the guy in our first meeting that I wasn't sure I could respect a psychologist with KFC for initials. He laughed. In fact, he laughs a lot. For a counsellor, throw-back hippy dude. Keath finds me hilarious but takes me serious, too. Listens. To me, Jamie Kidding. Right now we're talking about my dad in our sessions. Quite a bit.

Wish I could say everything ends HEA. But it didn't. It doesn't.

Tony the pimp's still making the rounds back in our old hood. Guess some things never change. Never will.

Tina's still dead.

And there are so many more just like her out there. Disposable people. Easy targets.

I went to her funeral and thought long and hard about that. How very close Jamie Kidding himself came to disposing of people, taking a life or lives. Easy targets: school kids, teachers—basically innocent human beings. Maybe even taking my own.

They haven't found Tina's killer yet. I hope they do. Her picture at the front of the church reminded me. How fragile we are.

And how strong. For example, look at Molly go! Interior design school in the fall. I'm so flipping proud of my own kick-ass mother! Uncle Mac even bought her a computer. We don't have Internet in the house yet, but maybe someday soon.

I like the new place, really. It's old and got some character. Creaky wooden floors and plaster walls and old dormer windows. We're painting again, a room at a time. Candy's bedroom first. Go figure.

Hugh hasn't shown his ugly face anywhere near here. We're all grateful and relieved. Maybe that part of our lives is really over and done. (Insert thunderous applause here.)

The river valley is drop dead beautiful. And we actually have nice neighbours. They brought over a freaking pie the day we moved in to the co-op. Who does that? Well, the Fitzgeralds do.

Candy will attend the smallish nearby school this fall. It's got a gifted program. They don't know what they're in for! She's settled right in to our new digs. Even started a dog walking service and is making not bad money. Little fancy pants. Gotta love that kid! Well, I do anyways.

As for me, my portfolio's looking pretty sweet, I have to say. As is my new fledging website. My Facebook fan page. And another exciting development: I get to go to the summer art camp in August, after all. East Hill High School has given me a partial scholarship to attend. How sick is that?

I'm working several part-time summer jobs to make up the difference. Washing cars at the Ford dealership where Uncle Mac works. We don't say much to each other. I do my job. He does his. We function.

At Alternative Video we have a new manager, Zandra. She's copasetic, to use Tatiana's favourite new word. I've upped my hours to several nights a week. More time with Tat.

Best new employment opportunity: I teach kids how to cartoon once a week at Happy Harbor. Jay caught me tagging the dumpster—what else?—behind his store. Said there was money in tagging, if I took it inside. So I did. Little farts are pretty good, too. I have a group of five who show up faithfully every Saturday morning. And on top of it, in the fall, Jay's commissioned a graffiti piece for the side wall of the building. From me, Jamie Kidding. Can my studio loft be far away?

That about wraps up this book. I've bought a new one with fresh clean pages just waiting for my pen and pencil. My fingers are itching to open it and begin.

Tatiana dreams of us writing a graphic novel together. She writes the words. I do the illustrations. A million dollar book contract. Animated movie to follow. Tim Burton as director! Holy radical concept, Batman!

But after the fact, can I really recreate what happened? At best I'm representing the truth. As Jamie Kidding sees it.

So I'm not telling this story.

Besides, who'd read it anyway?

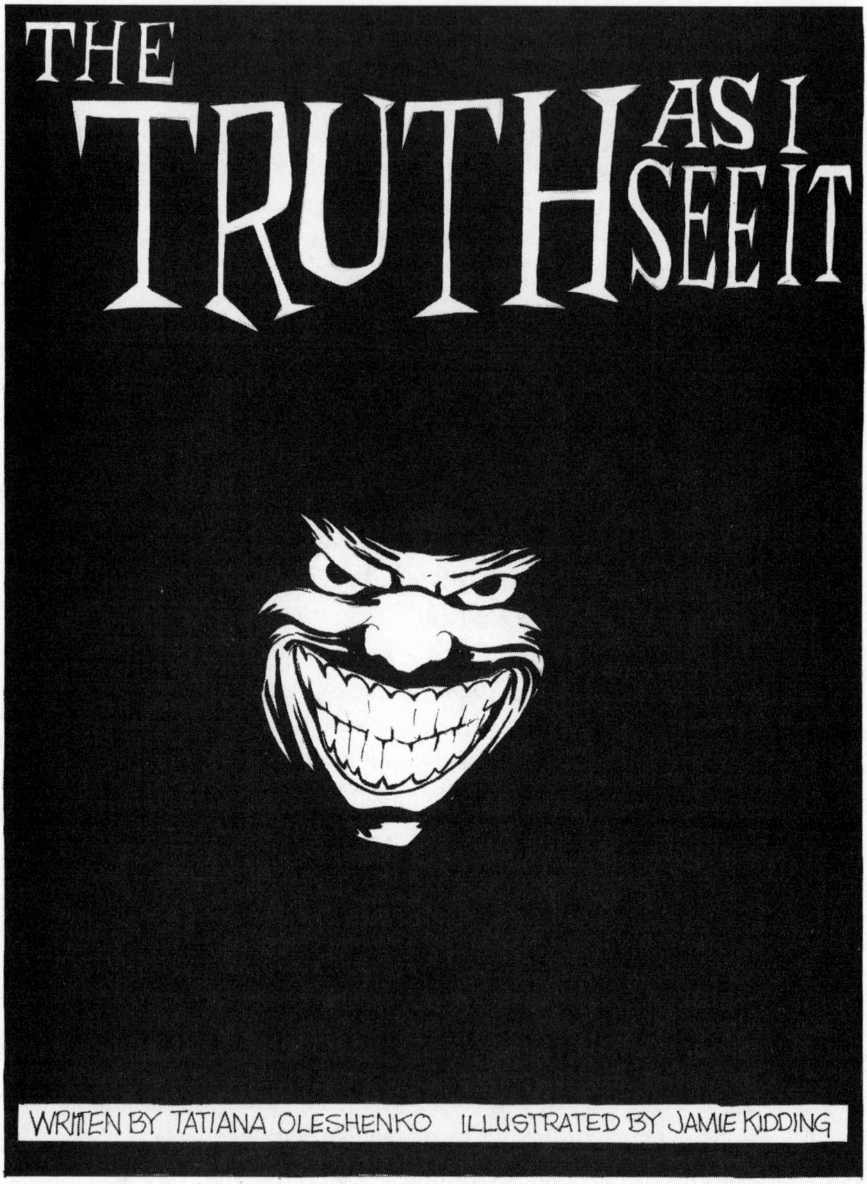
THE TRUTH AS I SEE IT
WRITTEN BY TATIANA OLESHENKO ILLUSTRATED BY JAMIE KIDDING

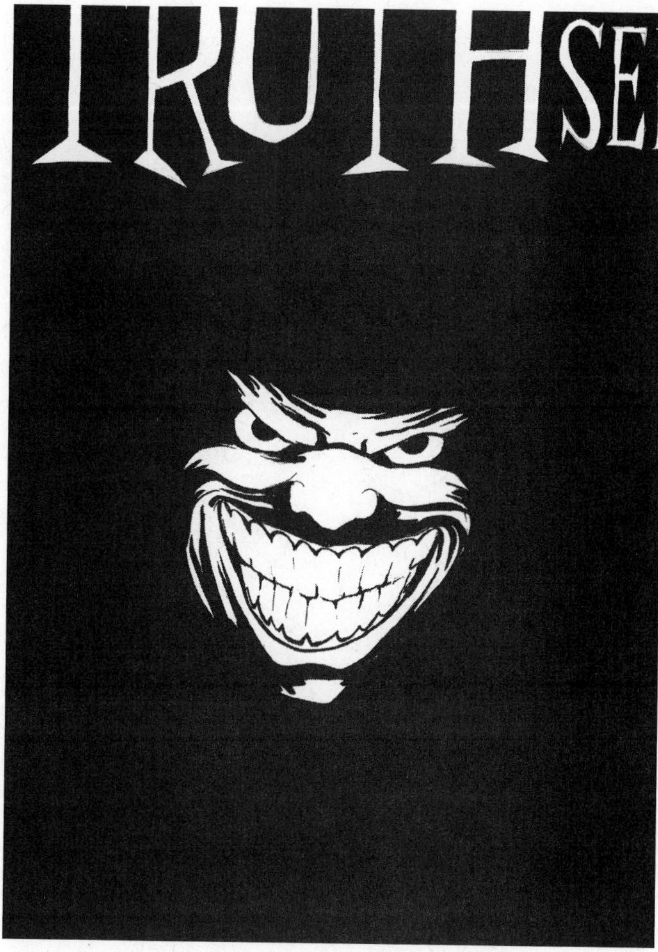
TRUTHSE

Thank you to Paul Yardley-Jones—you make pretty "drawrings" and I know the secret of your marshmallow heart; to my cabal of reader supporters who never desert me, even in my bleakest hours: Jeannie Sobat, Carolyn Pogue, Mark Haroun, Thomas Trofimuk, and of course, Geoff "Tisman" McMaster, who wields a mighty editorial pen. Special thanks to Crown Prosecutor Ronnie Pedersen, for his legal advice and for always being older than I ever will be; to Heather... wherever you are; to Gregg and Great Plains for believing in this novel and to Terry Corrigan for the great design work; to the character models, Noel and Maica. And finally, to the amazing librarians and booksellers who promote my books and to my readers and fans who buy and read them—Je t'adore.
—GAIL SIDONIE SOBAT

Quotation, page 5: Walt Whitman "O Me! O Life!" from *Leaves of Grass* 1892

Great thanks to: Gail S. Sobat for asking me to illustrate her first graphic novel and being a great friend; my brother and sisters, who without knowing it, in their own way helped me out; Terry Robinson and her family for being close and dear friends. And to all my friends who have followed and supported my art over the many years, I thank you all.

—SPYDER YARDLEY-JONES